The Possessions of a Lady

BY THE SAME AUTHOR

Firefly Gadroon
Gold from Gemini
The Gondola Scam
The Great California Game
Jade Woman
The Judas Pair
Lovejoy at Large
Moonspender
Pearlhanger
The Sleepers of Erin
The Tartan Ringers
The Vatican Rip
The Very Last Gambado
The Lies of Fair Ladies
The Grail Tree
Spend Game
Paid and Loving Eyes
The Sin Within Her Smile
The Grace in Older Women

THE POSSESSIONS OF A LADY

Jonathan Gash

C

CENTURY

First published in 1996

1 3 5 7 9 10 8 6 4 2

The right of Jonathan Gash to be identified as the
author of this work has been asserted by him in accordance
with the Copyright, Designs and Patents Act, 1988.

First published in the United Kingdom in 1996 by
Century,
Random House UK Limited
20 Vauxhall Bridge Road, London, SW1V 2SA

Random House Australia (Pty) Limited
20 Alfred Street, Milsons Point, Sydney,
New South Wales 2061, Australia

Random House New Zealand Limited
18 Poland Road, Glenfield
Auckland 10, New Zealand

Random House South Africa (Pty) Limited
PO Box 337, Bergvlei, South Africa

Random House UK Limited Reg No 954009

A CIP catalogue record for this book
is available from the British Library

Papers used by Random House UK Limited
are natural, recyclable products made from wood grown in
sustainable forests. The manufacturing processes conform to
the environmental regulations of the country of origin.

ISBN 0 71 2677267

Typeset by Deltatype Ltd, Ellesmere Port, Wirral
Printed and bound in Great Britain by
Mackays of Chatham plc, Chatham, Kent

Dedications

To Ts'ai Chen, the Chinese God of lucky guesses
made when buying, this story is humbly dedicated.
Lovejoy

For

Old neighbours of York St, Bolton, Lancashire.

Thanks
Susan

I

LIFE IS WOMEN and antiques, nothing else. Antiques are found
everywhere, but women are the only supply of women. It's
where problems begin. One problem is fashion.

Fashion is embarrassing. I'd never been to a fashion show before.
Women find them thrilling. When you're a duckegg like me, you
have to laugh at yourself to stay sane. You occasionally have the
luxury of having a laugh at others. A dangerous game, though it
seems worth it at first. Later, horror comes a-hunting, and all smiles
vanish.

Getting things wrong's my way of life, me being the best antique
dealer in the known world. I'm also the only honest one. Women'll
tell you different. See who you believe, them or me.

I didn't know I would face ruin at such a glitzy gathering. Thekla
was all excited, said it would be the most wonderful afternoon on
earth. It was nearly that all right, no thanks to a load of under-
nourished birds parading in daft rags. That's what a fashion show is.
End of message, start of trouble.

'Stay still, Lovejoy. For heaven's *sake*!' She was tying her husband's
bow-tie on me.

'I feel a right prat.'

'You're making a silly fuss about nothing, Lovejoy,' Thekla kept
saying, dolling me up.

'Thekla, love.' I wobbled giddily. 'I'm ill ... '

'Stop making it up,' she scolded, enjoying herself. She looked
superb, having started getting ready at dawn, though her clothes
today were really strange. 'You've had a dozen illnesses since we got
out of bed. Worse than a child.'

'There's an antiques auction, Thekla.' That brainwave also bit the
dust.

'No, Lovejoy. And just stop *that*.' She shoved my hands off her and stepped away to admire her handiwork.

'I've buyers coming,' I invented, desperate. If the other dealers saw me at a mannequin parade I'd be finished.

She went all sarcastic. 'From Christies? Sotheby's, hmmm?' She combed my hair, tutting when it didn't stay down. 'Millionaires beating a path to penniless Lovejoy's cold cottage in East Anglia?'

A motor honked in the lane. It was now or never. I collapsed, groaning. She stood there in glacial rage.

'My old wound, love,' I gasped. 'My malaria.'

'Lovejoy. I phone Ricard if you're not in that car in two minutes.'

Which made me surrender. Her husband's an innocent killer – innocent according to law, but a murderer to the truthful. Being a pushover's hard enough without collecting more trouble.

'Coming, love.' I forced a smile. 'I'm quite looking forward to it, actually. Will they have those new velveteen Florentine panel-striped gaberdines?'

'I haven't heard of those, Lovejoy!'

We left arm in arm, Thekla really interested. I hadn't either, having made it up.

'No, dwoorlink? That designer, Galberti Rappada of Manchester. I was at school with him.'

'I'd no idea, Lovejoy!' she cried, the cottage door banging on loose hinges. 'See? You *love* it!'

We drove in her long saloon. Thekla's from Aldeburgh, so can mill around our old town almost with impunity. Thekla Paumann's wealth is independent of her husband's criminally weighty wallet.

She insisted on arriving at the Moot Hall's front entrance, all lights and commissionaires, crowds ogling as though we were up for Oscars. Thekla stood smiling in queenly condescension while I tried to eel in without being noticed. Done up as I was like a tuppenny rabbit it was impossible. Oddly leapt out of the throng, grabbed my arm.

'Lovejoy? That you?' He stared in disbelief.

'Hello, Oddly.' I was shamefaced.

'Never seen you spruced, Lovejoy. You nicking antiques inside?'

'No.' I coughed, red. 'With, er, a lady.'

His brow cleared. 'Oh, you're after grumble. Thought you'd gone strange. Here, that mazarine's gone.'

'Gone? It can't have.' I was aghast. It was happening again.

All around people were surging, arriving motors revving. Thekla

2

was furious at the world's attention being deflected away from her gorgeous apparel. She eyed Oddly. He eyed her. He looked off-the-road, blue ex-R.A.F. greatcoat heavily patched, wellingtons from some mucky farmyard, about as elegant as — usually, but not today — me.

'Lovejoy!' she spat, smiling ice. 'Inside!'

'In a sec, love. Oddly's got vital … '

She whisked me up the steps and into the perfumed parlour with a grip like a haulier's clamp. I tried to scramble back for Oddly's news but she held me until we were circulating and smiling and being given that acidy wine that gives you indigestion.

People called Thekla 'dahling' and me 'daaahhhling'. They were mostly women, cooing with more eyebrow play than a Victorian melodrama. They had a way of looking meaningfully over the rim of a glass that made my spine funny. The blokes were very, very quaint. I prefered Oddly's brand of oddity. He earned his nickname by blowing bubbles in soapy water dripped into his ear. I really envy him. I tried it, but it hurts. He does it for charity, quid a time, in the Donkey and Buskin pub.

'Who's *this* feral theriac, Thekkie?' warbled a bird in a tuxedo and no skirt that I could see.

'He *found* me, lovvie!' Thekla trilled, causing laughter from trendy folk of uncertain gender.

It was all strange. I heard sly whispers. 'Have you *seen* those crashy stilletos, lovvie? In ultraish garishimmo fustian? *I would kill for one!*' Flapping hands, exotic wrists.

Two women, shackled together at the ankles, paused. One asked me, 'Am I being unreasonable? Syndronised hair slides should be shot. Yes?'

'Er,' I said brightly.

'He *loves* syndronised,' her chainee pouted.

'You fascist *pig*.' They hobbled off.

A bloke in three cloaks swept up. He wore Turkish chainmail, posed dramatically.

'Tell me, liebkin,' he snarled. 'Tetrafluoro-ethylene-coated cotton's utterly pass-*say*, *non è vero*? Yea or absolo *nein*?' He waited, mailed foot tapping.

A passing mauve geranium in mountaineering gear with taup bells on his yard-long fingernails paused to help out.

'What *if* Teflon makes material waterproof and wear-lasty? Who *does* crave twice-wearability?' They tripped away together.

3

A lady almost poked my eye out with a mile-long fag holder, genuine ivory to show she wasn't hoodwinked.

'Daaaahhhling,' she cooed. 'Penny for 'em?'

Where I come from you have to be truthful when asked that. 'Somebody nicked my mazarine.'

'Nicked … ?' She rotated slightly, stared. Her voice sank to a whisper. 'You look positively *murderous*, daaaahhhling.' And there in the press of a perfumed throng she moaned, kneading my arm. '*Sweet*heart! What's a mazarine?'

You've to pity ignorance. 'Think of a beautiful silver dish, fenestrated like a flat sieve, inside a silver fish container. Made by the greatest silversmiths the world's ever known. A mazarine.'

'What's so special, Lovejoy?' She was honestly asking. I didn't throttle her, a miracle of restraint.

'I divvied it – felt its vibrations – as a genuine antique,' I said, rage thickening my throat. 'I pretended it was a cheap fake, yet still some dealer bought it.'

My mind flickered, went blank.

The best I can hope for in life is to get only one thing wrong at a time, but I usually do it in clusters. It all comes down to understanding. The more you think you understand, the less you actually do. I suppose the end comes when you've lived through umpteen monarchs and know ten gross of nowt. It's scary.

My other flaw is to be terrified of authorities, of violence, wrongful arrest – or rightful, come to that – accidents, or getting caught with a sumo wrestler's missus. Oh, and mystery. Umberto Eco claims that all stories are detective stories, so we ought to like mystery. But when it barges in and upsets my world then I truly hate it. Mystery ought to keep out and let me get on.

Here in this fashion turmoil I was doubly baffled, trebly worried, fourbly alarmed. The silver mazarine was my best attempt to collar the enemy, and I'd failed. The fashioneers brought me back.

'Naheen, dear. Where *ever* did old Thekla buy him?' This from the arm-kneading fagholder, gazing into me. She wore a dress made solely of, I swear, green and purple planks. They clattered as she moved.

'More to the point, Dovie, *how much*?' said a blonde in a chequered kaftan, a steel helmet.

They trilled laughs. Three were gathered about me, with smiles that didn't mean it.

'He's bursting with questions,' Dovie said, clacking her planks. 'Ask away, Lovejoy daaahhhhling.'

'Ta.' I asked the third lady, a petite dark-haired lass, 'Why are you the only one with proper clothes on?' I'd wondered if she was rich and the others'd had to raid their attic rag bags. She wore a smart violet suit, blouse frothy at her throat.

The world collapsed in a rollicking heap, shrieking. Folk rolled in the aisles, splitting their sides. It was all guffaws, uncontrolled laughter, everybody falling about and dropping drinks. I was mystified. What had I said? I'd only tried to make conversation.

Except three weren't laughing. Me, nonplussed. Thekla, white with anger, inevitably at me. And the quiet lass, also white with anger, i.a.m.

'Faye's the reporter, Lovejoy!' Thekla's voice was almost too tight to make it. 'We're the fashioneers!'

She was beside herself with fury. Wouldn't speak to me again for a week, with luck.

The pandemonium slowly abated, people telling each other of my gaffe, loudly reminding red-faced me that I was an idiot and they weren't. But why were they dressed in junky tatters and this bird not? It seemed worth asking.

'Why're they all dressed in junky tatters?'

'Lovejoy!' Thekla spat. 'I'll talk to you later!'

Dovie clattered off sounding like a two-stroke outboard, with Naheen, recounting the story to gusts of hilarity. I was being punished, left alone and palely loitering. I stood like a lemon. Thekla and her fashion-daft mates had wafted, sanity taken wing.

Faye hadn't. She wasn't mad at me any longer. Why not? My mind gave up.

'Proper clothes?' she said. 'Proper clothes?'

Best stay mum, my brain warned. I blurted, 'Well, you're the only one doesn't look a pillock.'

'Wrong, Lovejoy.' She had a dry voice, now quite smiley. 'I'm off-the-peg. They are the height of fashion.'

Well, if she said so. Doubtfully I gazed about. There were now some two hundred, hallooing extravagantly, all admiring all. I'd not a hope in hell of reaching the buffet. I was starving.

'Then why do you look bonny and them duckeggs?' I was puzzled. 'If that's their best, I'd give up.'

'Forgive me, Lovejoy, but what are you doing here?'

'God knows. I should be hunting.'

'Hunting?' Startled.

'Not foxes and that. Just some dealer.'

Her hand crept to her throat. 'Not *hunt*, though? You sounded, well, menacing.' She laughed nervously.

'Course not, love,' I said, all innocent. 'I only meant look for, see how they were doing it.' And why, I added silently.

'What've they done?'

'Brought me to ruin.'

'You sound melodramatic, Lovejoy.' She looked at the throng, came back. 'These folk use those expressions and sound harmless. You ... don't.'

'Thekla's funding me. Hence ... ' Hence I'm looking stupid among tinsel mongers.

'What will you do when you catch them?'

A hesitation I hoped she didn't catch. 'I'll ask them how they outguess me in antiques. Nobody does that.'

A gong went, almost jarring the teeth from my head. Everybody squealed and rushed.

'Look, Lovejoy,' Faye said quickly. 'Can I see you after the fashion parade? Please? Phone.'

She gave me a business card. Fashioneers hurtled past. Some saw Faye's card and called suggestive comments. I went red.

Thekla caught me near the exit, angrily swept me to where total glamour ruled. That's what it said on the posters.

6

FASHION'S NOT ONLY embarrassing. It's a joke, very expensive. It's the physical equivalent of party politics, simple to the point of imbecility but barmy. It works like this. You take any material – plastic, metal, wood, glass even, silk, cotton – colour it, dress some skeletal subnourished bird in it, then make her prance/strut/gallop along a ramp, to inappropriate music.

Purpose? None. Embarrassment factor? Up through the stratosphere. I know. I've been and seen. Worst truth: fashion is hype, no more, no less. You want proof? Joseph Briggs.

Cut to smoky old Accrington's industrial heyday. Stout-hearted Joe noticed some brightly coloured glass things, chucked out, rejected, sheer dross. Not even worth barrowing to the junk shop, those hacky lampshades, vases, floral glassware. That vibrancy, those brilliant Art Nouveau colours of the 1890s and after, were frankly out of fashion. Who wanted such 'ugly' objects? Nobody.

But Joseph was resolute. Against all opinion he thought, 'But it's beautiful!' So Joe salvaged every single piece he could lay hands on. The moral? Decades later, half of Joseph Briggs' rescued glass pieces are now in the museum at Accrington. He donated them. People come from the world over to admire the amazing collection of Tiffany glass, for that's what the pieces were. Every so often, one of Louis Comfort Tiffany's specials – like the thick, bulbous, almost shapeless vases of so-called 'lava' glass – turns up on some road show, amid delirious excitement. Without Old Joe, we'd never have known. So light a candle for him, who stood firm against the tide of fashion, and virtually saved an art form.

See? Fashion's as near to zero performance as mankind gets. It's almost always wrong.

The show began with spotlights, and the inevitable *Thus Spake Zarathustra*, strobes to set off your epilepsy. You're supposed to go all agog. Then some announcement about somebody who'd studied a million years to achieve What You Are About To See, and out come the models wearing gunge. They all had ironing-board figures, coat-hanger shoulders, spindle legs. I felt sympathy, recognising starvation when I see it.

Thekla seemed some sort of supremo, giving out orders, beckoning Faye and saying to bring the photographers and quick about it. She pretended to be bored, disagreeing harshly and getting an astonishing amount of compliance. Astonishing because it's my experience that women don't agree much among themselves. I sat trying not to meet the models' eyes, but they swaggered ever nearer doing their insolent saunter. They'd evidently heard of my gaffe. I sat wondering what fashion's for. I mean, anyone ever see a woman on the bus dressed in a black net bolero, cavalier thigh boots and ostrich feathers? No, so why bother?

There also were bloke models, admiring themselves in the wall mirrors, swinging their jackets. They didn't look thin, but I wondered how they felt. I mean, how did it compare to a real job?

We had to clap every apparition. I dutifully applauded, but was shamed. I once knew this lass who cooked. Well, that's not quite true because she was a gourmet, a nosh supremo, the world authority (she said) on pickles. No, honest. She wrote about meat, fish, sauces – God, did she write about sauces – in every glossy on earth. I was supposed to admire her pickle knowledge. She won awards for the damned things. It got so I couldn't move in my cottage for jars of frigging pickles. She'd even tell me new pickle ideas in the middle of the night, instead of concentrating on other things. We parted after a flaming row. I'd accidentally told her the truth: Cooking is only how to fry tomatoes. She went critical, swept out with her pickles, thank God. I mean, Juney writing about pickles, while half the world starves to death. Is this reasonable? One more fashion.

Somebody slipped a hand in my pocket. Above, a girl pirouetting in plastic book-wrappers and strings of gilded hazelnuts, and somebody picks my pocket in the million-guinea seats?

I know some pickpockets who can pass you on the opposite pavement, and nick your wallet. No kidding. One subtle-monger in Bolton market could strip you clean without putting his pint down. That's class. But a woman's long fingers, painstakingly lifting the pocket flap? I sighed, didn't move. My pockets were Thekla's husband's anyway, and empty.

On the catwalk above, two sandal-shod girls in leather fronds hung with bones swished past. Thekla led a standing ovation. I stayed seated in case Fingers Malone wanted to explore further.

8

'Read it, Lovejoy,' somebody whispered, a woman.

Read what? Nobody'd given me a programme, and I'd no money to buy one. Thekla ran a tight ship.

'*Lovejoy*!' Thekla snarled down at me.

I rose to clap. The two girls above took their time clearing off, so we could admire their mauve painted legs. To me they looked covered in warts. The lights dimmed with cymbals and a thunderous paradiddle. Meekly I went deaf. The two mannequins were seen in glorious fluorescent colours against black curtains. The place erupted at such spectacular beauty. I looked behind to see who was pestering my pockets. The seat was vacant.

Thekla faced me, eyes brimming. The hall was a-chatter, people swooning at the splendour we'd seen.

'Wasn't that superb, Lovejoy?'

'Er, mmmmh.' Frankly, no. It was crud.

'Those *cherubs*! Carrying it off!'

'The, er, creations,' I murmured.

A creature, two rings adorning each digit, leaned across to Thekla.

'Thekkie, you *terrible* angel! You *stole* the *world*!'

'Thank you, Rodney,' Thekla said modestly. 'They were rather stupendous, weren't they?'

'Stupendous?' This apparition really relished grovelling. 'Globally awesome! Truly, truly!'

'The next are yours, Rodney, I think.'

'My modest little effort? Nothing compares!'

Then it came, my instant nightmare. I recoiled in horror. A stick insect paraded down the catwalk, jerking and twitching, supposedly playing a guitar she carried. Her left half wore a sheath dress made of carpet slices cobbled together with sailor's twine. Her right vertical half was bare, breast, bum and all.

The roars were deafening. The lass flirted past, spun to sustained cheers. I felt hate rise, stifled myself. As the riot diminished, I leant across Thekla. She made room, thinking I was going to be emphatic about what we'd just seen. She was right.

'You did that, Rodney?' I asked the goon.

'Yes.' He fluttered roguishly.

'You want locking up, you frigging nerk,' I said. 'That carpet was worth you morons put together.'

My feet didn't touch the ground. God knows who gave the signal. Two bruisers appeared from nowhere, hauled me upright, dragged me willynilly down the aisle. They slammed me out through the double doors, across the foyer, and literally hurled me into Sizewell Street. I didn't know which way was up, bounced, slithered to a stop.

'Look!' a toddler bawled with that miniature foghorn voice they have. 'Lovejoy!'

'Wotcher, Tel,' I said wearily, supine.

'Want him!' boomed the infant.

'Not now, dear,' Tel's mother said, hurrying the pushchair past and ignoring me with that glazed air women assume when hearing an unexpected belch. Once we'd twice made smiles, last Mothering Sunday to be precise.

Rising, I checked myself for bruises. I felt like slaying Rodney. The carpet he'd hacked to death was a Turkish nineteenth century Kum Kapou. These are priceless – well, one costs more than a freehold house, 3 bdrms, 2 rcptns, gdn & grge. This carpet looked seven feet by five, from the snatch of design I'd glimpsed. Rodney must have simply thought, Hey, nice – and reached for his knife.

See what's happened to justice? Some crazy fashioneer kills a beautiful antique, yet it's me gets ejected. Nobody in there gave a single thought to how that butchered Kum Kapou carpet felt. In life it had been gold, silver, with a dazzling prismatic sheen. The village is Armenian, near Istanbul, where the carpet sellers call its superbly fine knotting 'palace' quality. Look closely, its pattern depicts tiny animals among foliage. You can travel the world and never see a lovelier carpet. I was almost in tears. I vowed to remember Rodney, and get even.

Nothing for it but to shed this monkey suit. One thing was certain, it was goodbye Thekla. I'd tried to be pleasant. It wasn't my fault if they were all deranged.

No money, me looking a right prune, I went to wait for the bus in the Welcome Sailor at the town's east gate, hoping to scrounge a groat or three.

Where, as tragedy would have it, I met Tinker and his Australian cousin's nephew. When you're sliding downhill it's difficult to stop.

They were both sloshed as a maltster's wasp. I crossed to join them, coughing as my lungs tried the fug's carcinogens. Tinker actually doesn't smoke, having no time between ale intakes, but everybody else does except me. And Tinker's cousin's nephew, Roadie.

'Smart arse,' the apparition said, eyeing me.

'Eh?' I'd forgotten I was gorgeous. 'Sorry. This bird ... '

Normally my conversations are just the odd word, the rest being obvious. Roadie grappled in an ugly moment for Tinker's beer, lost on a pinfall, sulked.

'What bird what?'

Roadie communicates, or fails, most of the time. He's a sharp sixteen, attired in black leather with alchemic jewellery and barbaric slogans in lettering with so many serifs that you can't read it. Still, if my talk ends in dots he's every right to end his in spikes.

'Son,' Tinker explained, 'Lovejoy's been dressed up by some lady. Pint?'

'Sorry, Tinker.' He was asking me to pay, not offering. I went to the bar. Frothey was working the pump handle in an erotic manner. She fascinates me. Fair, fat and forty. I could eat her. Womanlike, she knew I'd come a-begging.

'Hello, Lovejoy.' She judged the glass she was filling, and leant forward to exploit symbolism. 'No.'

'Not even in my posh gear?' I smiled, exploiting forgiveness, tat for tit, so to speak. 'I'm at the fashion show.'

'Fashion?' Almost everything came to a stop.

I sighed. 'Dolled up, nobody to go with.'

'The regional?' Her lovely eyes got rounder. 'You've got *tickets*?'

'Aye.' I sighed again, though I often find you can overdo acting. 'I'm late. Can you get off work?'

She breathed, 'Those tickets are *gold*, Lovejoy!'

'I've a relative. Er, Rappada ... ' I'd forgotten who I'd invented. 'Still, another time, eh, love?'

Somebody called for service. She ignored him.

'Wait, Lovejoy.' She was agog, working out how to defect. Women are past masters at ditching their tasks. I watched her mind crunch possibilities.

'Well ... ' I'd have looked at my watch if I'd got one.

She pulled a pint to keep me there. 'Five minutes in the car park, okay?' She was whispering.

'Right,' I whispered. 'Can Tinker have one?'

'Yes. Be sharp!'

Women are beautiful, unless they're wearing fashion. Life's really weird. Here Frothey was, gorgeous in her black dress and phony pearls, actually wanting to see other women garbed like space aliens. And she would honestly envy those models' overpriced tatters, their showy anorexia.

Not only that, but she was urging me to get a move on, when I was the one ready to scoot. It's something to do with their certainties.

For a bloke like me, everything is simply unknowable. To Frothey, everything is obvious.

'When you're ready, doowerlink.'

She rushed off. I carried the beer to Tinker. Neglected boozers clamoured like angry infants.

'Ta, Lovejoy. No news.'

'There's another pint, if you're quick.' That made him chuckle. Like urging a ski racer to hurry. 'News?'

Roadie's missing sister Vyna was the reason he was here.

'Oh, aye.' She was seventeen, had slipped her cable three months. Her parents were frantic. Roadie wasn't. His grudges got in the way of practically everything. 'You try what I suggested?'

'He's an idle git, Lovejoy,' Tinker explained. He hawked up a gob of phlegm into his empty glass, a man with a hint. 'Does nowt but sponge and sup all day. Pillock, see?'

'Aye, well.' Clearly a family trait. I'd best be off, seeing Frothey would be down soon. I lied, 'Tell Frothey I'm waiting outside, Tinker.'

'Right.' He was already shuffling to the bar for his pint. There'd be an argument with the bartender, seeing I'd not arranged anything. 'Lovejoy? That bloody fish. Been shuffed from the auction.'

'Eh?' I was aghast. Not again? 'What's going on, Tinker?'

'Dunno, mate. You're the wally.'

A wally is trade slang, an antique dealer, in theory the moneyed gaffer who knows. Some theory.

'Lovejoy,' he said. 'What if Vyna's kidnapped?'

Roadie sniggered. I gave him a look. 'Okay, Tinker,' I said at last. 'I'll help.'

'Ta, Lovejoy.'

The bar curtain that closed off the stairs fluttered, Frothey coming. I escaped by a whisker, and darted down the alley, the most baffled antique dealer in East Anglia. Everything was awry, starvation stalking my land. I ought to decide on swift action and leap to it. Instead, I hide. But now things had become ultra odd. I had to do something urgently, or face extinction.

As I trotted through the town, I reflected. Life comes down to one question: 'What did you do in the Great War, daddy?' Like in that haunting World War I poster, the gaunt man, his little girl. Even if you only ask it of yourself. The kernel is that terrible *what*. Not when, or how, or why. 'Why' is motive, and is eternally unknowable — making love, hates, decisions to move home, gamble on divorce – so why bother asking 'why'? 'How' is only prestidigitation, the way you leave her, which bus you catch, incidental stuff. 'When' is only colouring in bits of life's picture. No, everything about everything is *what*. I was driven to act.

3

'THAT FISH', TINKER'D said, was shuffed. Translation: stuffed fish – don't laugh; it'd buy a new car – at Threadle's junk auction in Long Melford. I'd told Tinker to bribe it out of its legitimate place (sorry, pun not intended), whereupon I'd frolic in several thousands profit, a pastime that usually entails me scuttling clear of creditors until I'd managed to spend some.

And somebody else had bought it before Tinker could do the dirty deed. Eeling down Short Wyre Alley I thought, what *is* this? Who but a stuffed fish collector collects stuffed fish?

The name is J. Cooper, floreat about 1925. Buy one of his little gudgeon in a labelled glass pot, you're in clover, for he's supposed to have done only four. You can still find them, at the odd boot sale. A huge Cooper-stuffed pike will pay for a prolonged Caribbean cruise. An arrangement of dace, or a mixture of fishes, will net you much, much, more. So keep looking. They're out there.

This can happen in antiques. It's below the I-found-a-Rembrandt sensation, being down at subsistence level, among the scavengers and debris feeders where I just about break even year by year. Predators are a problem. I usually am quicker than most, because I'm a divvy and nobody else is.

Yet now I was being out-guessed. It had been going on for some weeks. I was reduced to living on nowt. Hence I'd had to accept Thekla's affluent presence. Only temporarily. I'd intended to repay her when my ship came in, honest. I don't scrounge off women without making a nearly almost definite promise to refund every penny, and I mean that most sincerely.

Which left me wearing Thekla's husband's posh suit, plodding among our town's mediaeval alleyways as inconspicuous as a rattling rainbow. I headed for the Antiques Centre, instinct guiding me wrong as usual. As proof, Aureole.

'Not one word.' I entered, raising a threatening digit as dealers drew breath to howl derision.

One or two cackled. Most wisely subsided.

A few customers drifted among the stalls. Business looked moribund, but that's antiques for you. Antiques is like war, one per cent terror, the rest boredom. The Centre was in stupor mode.

'Funeral or feast, darling?' Aureole cooed sweetly. 'Big Frank marrying again?'

People snickered. I scented grub and gave a moan. The Antiques Centre's a church hall that our ancient priory, rapaciously swapping holy precepts for filthy lucre, sold off to the biggest syndicate of crooks, namely us. (Us minus me; I was short of funds when the hat came round.)

'Or some other catastrophe?' Aureole went on.

She's a beautiful lass, the Centre's prime mover, coordinating the local dealers. It's got a dozen booths and stalls, central heating for cold days, and a tea bar.

'What you got, Lovejoy?' from Basil-the-Donkey, a bloke like a garden gnome, jutting beard and popping waistcoat. His nickname's the only one I can think of that's longer than a given, and about it I'll say nothing more. He's furniture mad, an obsessional keeper of data, photos, auction prices, who-saw-what rumours. He sells news to other dealers.

The others stilled to hear my answer. I did my shrug, tutted in disgust.

'Everything's handies these days. Makes me sick.'

Basil-the-Donkey lost interest. Handies are pocket-sized antiques. Ladies' chatelaines, theatre glasses, jewellery, miniature enamels, anything you can lift unnoticed. Aureole and others became alert. I strolled about.

'What sort of handies, Lovejoy?'

Somebody had just had a toasted tea-cake, the selfish swine. Its aroma teased the air. I went giddy from hunger. I breathed through my mouth, trying not to scent other people's calories, that cruellest of all perfumes.

'Eh?' I was near Alf's Alcove. 'Oh, some crappy Bowie knife.'

More of the dealers went back to their nefarious chitchat. A lady was being captivated by a mid-Victorian hourglass on Tick's 'Tockery For All Antiques' stall. Everybody was taking bets by signs on whether she'd buy it. I knew she wouldn't, because she was aligned at forty-five degrees to the stall, her head on the tilt. Women never buy when they stand like that. I spoke softly.

'Bet you she doesn't, Alf.'

15

He signalled across to Gumbo – 'African Ethnic Genuines To The Trade'; Gumbo blacks up like a black-and-white music hall minstrel. My heart sank. Alf'd just bet Gumbo that the customer wouldn't, on my tip. 'Bowie knife you say, Lovejoy?'

'No good, Alf. Made in Sheffield, looks too new.'

And off I wandered – to be hauled back by a suddenly frantic Alf. I looked at him coldly. I'd teach him to win bets on my say-so, and me famished.

'Get off my new suit.' I shook myself free. 'It cost a fortune.'

'Sorry, Lovejoy.' He gave his most ingratiating smile. It was ghastly, as bad as watching Tinker eat. 'Only,' he added casually, 'I've been looking for a, er, fake Bowie knife. In good nick?'

History's joke is that the old Wild West's Bowie knives were mostly made in Sheffield. Alf was jumping to the conclusion that I didn't know this. In antiques whole fortunes are founded on improbables that suddenly become front racers.

'Mint,' I grumbled. 'Rum inscription, though.' I glanced at the clock. 'I'll be late.'

'Got time for a cuppa, Lovejoy?' He did the gruesome trust-me grin that hallmarks the antiques crook. 'Only, I've not seen you lately, wanted a chat … ' He strove to think up something he wanted to chat about. ' … er, Tinker's missing lass.'

'Okay, but I've not long.' We went to the tea bar and sat at a table. Fake iron gardenware, not antique and therefore superfluous to civilisation. 'You take the blame if Thekla comes hollerin' her head off.'

'Right!' He got some teas.

Aureole came across to make sure that he put money in the till and took none out. When the Centre opened, dealers nicked the gelt, so Aureole took it on, paying herself a fifth of the takings. There was a row, of course, with Katherine – Stall No. 12, Edwardian jewellery, writes haiku poetry that gets nowhere, hates Aureole for a number of things I'll mention if I get a minute. I like Katherine. I want Aureole too, of course, but that's not the same thing as liking, is it? Aureole rules.

'You want, Lovejoy?'

My throat cleared itself. Aureole's double meanings are famous. And my chest suddenly bonged like a Mandarin's gong from something on her stall.

'Some tea-cakes and a slice of that, please.'

'Nothing more?' She started on the grub behind the little counter.

She has a woman's knack of being able to cut rolls and butter scones without looking at what she's doing. My Gran could do it, even when telling me off. They're born with the knack.

'A couple of jam butties, please.'

She strolled about, set the toaster going. Aureole does a lot of strolling. It's just a means of showing off, not going anywhere.

The hidden agenda, as folk say these days, is that Aureole runs a chain-dating service. It's our town scandal, the sort nobody's supposed to know but everybody does. It's notorious, as is Aureole. She's not done a single deal with any female dealer in living memory. The trouble is that sin pays, like crime. Aureole's worth a fortune. She just likes the heady excitement of antiques, scoring against odds. About antiques, she hasn't a clue. About people, she's cannier than most.

In case you've not heard of it, chain-dating's the rage. Law — that retard in scholastic clothing — is unsure whether to declare it illegal. Moralists fume and councillors rage. The town's two grottie news rags thunder, and reject Aureole's advertisements. Aureole? She swans on, indifferent, making a mint.

In chain-dating you simply register with Aureole. A fee changes hands, from you to her. Then, on dates you've specified, you are contacted by Aureole's assistants. Everything's clandestine, contact by pigeon post if need be.

You turn up, meet the lady (or gentleman, *mutatis mutandis* — also one of Aureole's clients) and enjoy your evening. Everyone rejoices. Okay?

Yes, because a week later, the same thing. Except this time the partner is different, for Aureole's chain has moved down a link. Every encounter counts one link. It's the miracle of chain-dating: you never, never ever, meet the same lady again. And no lady ever meets the same gentleman. Everyone slips, link by link, along the dating chain. See the consequences? Novelty is all. It's the modern way, disposable dating. In fact it's so frigging modern it's redundant. Me? I think they're off their heads.

East Anglia can't decide whether Aureole's a whore, a madam, or a social service ministering to the emotionally disadvantaged.

'Alf? The till, please,' Aureole called.

'I put in!' Alf gave back indignantly.

'Two teas, when I'm doing Lovejoy all our supplies?'

'I'll get it.' Alf went, grousing.

Aureole strolled over with some apple pie. I started to wolf it. She laughed, ruffled my thatch.

'Never not hungry, are you, Lovejoy?'

It's all right for Aureole, who doesn't eat much. I can never work out why they admire appetites so. My Gran used to admire me eating, like I was some carnival. She used to say, 'Better than a repast, watching him go at it.'

Aureole checked Alf's progress as he scoured his stall for usable coins.

'You want in yet, Lovejoy?' she asked quietly.

'In?' I was guarded. I'd finished the grub and she'd not yet brought the rest. You can't be too careful.

'You heard. In my chain.'

That again. 'No, ta.'

'Why not?' She spoke softly, enticing. 'You invented the whole system. Remember? Plant the orchard, you deserve some fruit.'

She wasn't far out. I'd been telling her, a year or so back, how some Birmingham tea-lady had been injured in a set-up car crash for stepping out of line. (A tea-lady's a dealer, either gender, who works for pin/beer money on the side.) Our town has a couple of tea-ladies, who dispense sexual favours to make up their lack of cash when buying antiques. It's fraught, dangerous, but you can't warn folk who don't heed.

Foolishly, I'd been explaining the tea-ladies' scheme to Aureole.

'Say a customer wants an Ince corner cupboard,' I'd said, making it simple. Aureole listened, wide of eye. 'The woman dealer hasn't got one to sell. A Brighton dealer, however, has. No deal, right? Now, she guesses that the Brighton dealer, who has the lovely Ince furniture, fancies her. So she meets him one dark night.'

'What happens?' Aureole's eyes were like saucers.

'The Brighton dealer sells her the valuable Ince cupboard, cheap. Because ... '

'Because she's given him sex!' Aureole cried, ecstatically inventing the wheel.

'Correct. The lady sells the exquisite pale heartwood Ince cupboard to her customer, and the world wassails. Everybody wants sex, see?'

'Of course!' she'd squeaked, dazzled.

I should have said nothing more. Except, bigmouth, I'd gone on.

'Beats me,' I'd said, 'why somebody doesn't set up a list of people. Sort of a chain, go down a partner each time so you'd never get anyone twice. You'd think,' I'd continued, gormless, 'it'd be dead obvious.'

'Wouldn't you!' she'd breathed. 'But how, Lovejoy?'

'You'd need a phone, detailed computer records, and you'd have the world's most regular clientele. Safe as houses. Folk would fall over themselves to join.'

Her gaze triggered hope in my mind. I remember saying, 'You've not got an antique Ince cupboard?'

'No, Lovejoy,' she'd said. 'Just something on my mind.'

That week she founded the Aureole Halcyonic C-2-D Agency. It's the town's honey money infamy. I've even met folk overseas who say, 'Hey, isn't that where chain-dating … ?'

Back to cadging grub.

'Stop nagging.' I eyed the counter, but Aureole doesn't take hints.

'Some women keep asking if you're a link.' She smiled, strolled. 'Any time, Lovejoy. No fee to you.'

'It's supposed to be random,' I shot back, 'and a fixed fee.'

'You mean that tourist girl?' Aureole asked, stung. 'She was trying to get away. Anyway, it was only once.'

With no idea who she meant, I let it go. Alf returned with enough to pay.

'Here, Lovejoy,' he said, indignant. 'That's a frigging banquet.'

'You offered.' I can be as indignant as Alf any day. 'Anyway, you'll win from Gumbo any minute.'

We watched as Gumbo mournfully trailed the customer to the exit, reducing his price every yard. The door closed. Alf yelped, gleefully and went to collect his winnings. Aureole rolled her eyes heavenward, buttering the toast.

'What girl, love?' I asked suddenly.

'*What* what girl?'

'The one you mentioned. Getting away?'

'Oh, some overseas lass. I'm not good on accents. South African sounds New Zealand, Aussie sounds Zimbabwe, y'know?'

'Tell me, Aureole.'

'No.' She moved, no destination. 'Marmalade?'

'Yes, please.' A calorie is a calorie, not to be sneezed at. 'Who was she, love?'

She halted, eyed me. 'Deal, Lovejoy? No fee, and you can have the pick of my antiques?'

'Any seven items?' I bargained. Outside, thunder rolled.

'Any three, Lovejoy. And six chain dates.'

'Three. Lend me the fare home, to shell this tat.'

'Done, Lovejoy. First time you've ever looked smart.' She slipped me a note as Alf returned gloating. Her features were impassive, but inside she was laughing. 'Come round tonight and I'll tell all.'

'Eightish okay?'

'Right.' She went to lay up the tea tray.

The girl could be Tinker's lost relative Vyna. I didn't want to knuckle under to Aureole's blandishments, but what can you do?

Alf plonked himself down opposite, all jubilation.

'Right, Lovejoy! About this Bowie knife.'

Oh, God. I'd forgotten. Quickly I invented, 'It's highly engraved, Alf ... '

Easy to fib, but all I could see was the precious, genuine antique on Aureole's stall. I'd just made the antiques deal of a lifetime. My heart sang.

4

As ALF AND me fenced lies, I vanished back in time. Outside the Antiques Centre, thunder rumbled closer.

People nowadays think that we invented sexual oddity. Wrong. Establishments near Bury Street in Regency London's St James's were busily proving that two centuries back. The women's flagellation club met in fashionable Jermyn Street, Piccadilly, Thursday nights. It allowed in only a dozen women. They drew lots to decide batting order. Six would strip. The chairwoman dished out rods, and they would flagellate the passives. Magazine accounts of the time say 1792 was a hit year (sorry about the pun). Lectures on eroticism preceded every club (sorry) session. The aim (I'm getting embarrassed about these puns, but can't keep them out) was to gratify, expiate, and turn milk-white skin to red.

The culmination, that century's diligent observers reported, came in Theresa Berkley's flagellation house in Portland Place. Theresa was a game girl. She had ambition. True blue capitalist, she reasoned that it was wrong to restrict this thrill to women. Also, why use only stiff Jermyn Street rods? Serious thinking was required here. Madam Berkley therefore set up her own code. Green birch wands, kept whippy in warm water, were always available. Leather cat-o'-nine tails, adorned with needles and fine wire nails, also proved popular. Slender canes from Long Acre's furniture makers, green nettles, coach-harness thongs, broom faggots, God knows what else, were ready for males and females alike. Remember, it was the age when sin was front-page stuff, notions of guilt and torment were the rage, life one enormous religious porridge.

Theresa's establishment flourished.

One problem, though. La Berkley saw that a support was necessary. Thrashing clients to ecstasy had a certain transcendental quality, but proved messy. Bed laundry cost, as the clients became bloodily replete. Her business expenses ate profit. Luckily, Georgian London was inventive, and proved equal to the task. Why not, some unknown artisan suggested, create a flagellation frame? Custom-built, faced with kid leather, covered with a single replaceable sheet. Adjustable, on a rachet with mahogany stretchers, you could thrash from any angle. Make sure there was space for the weapon, for different types of stroke, and Bob's your uncle. No beds needed! Cheap quick turnover, strong, eminently re-usable, desirable ...

The famed Berkley Horse was born.

Theresa ordered a set, and life's rich pageant rolled on just that little bit richer for the Berkley Flogging Establishment of Portland Place.

See one, you can't mistake it, unless you're as daft as the average dealer. It reminds you of an easel, a leather-covered wooden support about sixty-five inches tall. Later models extend or shrink with wooden holding pegs that screw in. There's an arched space for your head, and two rectangular openings for your belly and knees, slots for your feet. Three pairs of ornate brass rings for binding your head, chest, calves. That's it.

And Aureole had one on her stall, pristine, so genuine it chimed in my chest. God knows who'd made it. The great furniture makers of that golden age had lived only a stone's throw beyond Piccadilly. Tom Chippendale, eldest son of his immortal dad, was beavering away nearby at 60 St Martin's Lane, though plummeting downhill to bankruptcy ... I felt my divvy's malaise as Aureole's Berkley Horse clanged in me. Chippendale? I moaned inwardly.

The recent boom in erotica has taken antiques by storm. Dealers are crazy for sexy implements, paintings, working models, sexy tobacciana. It's a queer world, but you just can't ignore a 'push', as the trade calls inexplicable surges, because it's where money suddenly goes. A few years ago it was Georgian silver. Then the Impressionists. Then the Moderns, until those international sales when modern paintings didn't hook in the floating money. Antiques is an exciting landscape dotted with smoking ruins showing where dealers came to grief.

My mouth watered. Aureole was using the Berkley Horse as a stand. She'd pinned some repro brooches to the leather, silly cow. Damaging a genuine antique ought to be punishable by poverty, and serve her right.

It isn't just antiques, though. City of London companies were floated for dafter things than colours daubed on canvas, or for clay shaped by a potter's hands. It's an odd fact that if a stock exchange demands money for some loony enterprise it's taken seriously. Old does not mean honest. It can also mean tricky. 'A Wheel Of Perpetual Motion' had ancient investors flocking, as did that well-known, 'Undertaking Which Shall In Due Time Be Revealed ... ' – and you had to pay up beforehand. Don't laugh; 1,000 investors raced to buy on the same morning, the old report laconically states, that the perpetrator 'disappeared in the afternoon'. Imagine stockjobbers – the word came in about 1688 – actually having the nerve to trade in a company that merely promised, for heaven's sake, to teach gentlemen Latin, conic sections, and 'the art of playing the theorbo'. But trade they did, folk fighting in the streets for a chance to lose their gelt. Even the patented steam-operated gentleman's boot remover seems somehow sane.

'Lovejoy.' He was suddenly there, six minions in support. Not so mini, these minions. Pale, I quickly went into a fawning stoop.

This bloke – I mean esteemed gentleman – is a life-threatening enterprise called Big John Sheehan. He's one of these quiet Ulstermen who put the fear of God in you just saying hello. Our ancient saying, 'Ulster for soldiers', is true, true.

Big John's always impeccably dressed, shoes glittering, gaberdine overcoat, black bowler. He once made a henchman walk home, just for having dirty shoes. From Shrewsbury, over a hundred miles.

'How do, John. Congratulations.' I did my cower.

To my astonishment, his eyes filled. He removed his bowler, cleared his throat to disguise emotion. He glared, checking that nobody was jeering. Luckily, we weren't.

'Thank you, Lovejoy. It's a stout heart that remembers loyal anniversaries.'

Christ, I thought in panic, now what? I'd only meant his nephew getting a job in antiques at last, God preserve innocent antiques from duckeggs. Loyal anniversaries? I looked desperately at his blokes, all smiling granite, no help.

'It's only right, John.' It had better be.

'Lovejoy.' The world stilled even stiller. 'You did well getting Shaver in. You divvied some pots, did the man a favour so he would oblige?'

'Pleased to help.' I sweated a terrified sweat. Big John's approval tends not to last. 'Hope he does well.'

Shaver is John's nephew, dense as a moat. Sheehan had promulgated an edict that Shaver must become an antique dealer. Finally, I'd got him a position as trainee in Croydon. The dealer had only agreed because I'd divvied his silver collection. Ten cruets, four inkstands. Only two were genuine Georgian. He hadn't changed his labels, of course, but knowing what's fake helps.

'He will.' The world nodded. 'Want anything?'

I drew breath. The wise man asks little, accepts less. I could hardly say I'd just been flung out of a fashion show so would he please get even. But refusal offends, so accept, costlessly.

'Would you ref, John?' Which would only take a single nod. No fee, and he'd leave satisfied.

'Right, Lovejoy. Show me the reffo.'

Everywhere now, law has become irrelevant. In the dim past, laws must have been useful and quite nice. Do this, do that. Fine, everybody living by a code, transgressors getting tidily done for, all that. But happy days are gone. Forget to pay a parking ticket, the law hounds you all the days of your life. Steal gillions in some international scam, massacre a township, you get instant immunity, and your biography's an alltime bestseller. Law is for the mighty, not us.

In the antiques trade, the ref system has evolved. Ref for 'referee' in the old sense, not the football man with a whistle. Suppose I promise to deliver an antique by a certain date. We don't go to lawyers, draw up some contract that would take aeons to enforce. We ignore law, lawyers, written agreements. We go to a ref, somebody who has violence – and therefore justice – at his fingertips. It's called 'doing a reffo'. One thing first, though. You've got to have the thing there – Old Master painting, Hester Bateman silver jug, whatever. The ref has to see it. His word is law. (No, delete that. His word is better. It's fair.)

'This, John, please.' I pointed.

'This board?' He stared at the Berkley Horse.

'Aureole's giving it me.' Sheehan, I remembered uneasily, is moral. Better leave him in a state of innocence.

'That so, darlin'?'

'Yes, John.' Aureole smiled openly, plus a secretive smile inwardly to herself. 'It's Lovejoy's.'

'Fortnight. No charge.' And that, said John, was that.

He left, his men tramping stolidly fore and aft, us all fawning and hoping he'd remember how glad we were he'd called, then shakily blotting our damp foreheads. Notice one thing? Doing a reffo takes no time at all. And Sheehan didn't need to know what the item actually was. No money changes hands. Normally, the ref is paid ten per cent of its value. Simple, eh? But if you default, the ref simply inflicts what punishment he thinks fit. He can declare you untouchable, a 'nothing' who is simply ignored by one and all and instantly goes bankrupt. He can confiscate whatever he wants to make restitution. The ref's word is, well, law. Sadly, refs don't do domestic cases, but let's hope the time will come. We need laws. The trouble is we've only got lawyers. Where was I? Calling, 'Ta, John. Appreciate it, ta.'

An hour later, exhausted, I reached my cottage. Its aroma disturbed me, Thekla's perfume plus my grot. I sighed, got down to resuming life. Solitude can be relief.

The sky was black, thunder on the go, lightning cracking the eerie pewter sky. No rain yet. The estuary must be catching it. The air felt too muggy to breathe.

Quickly I shed Thekla's husband's posh outfit and had a coolish bath. I don't like heat. Summer's a pest, its sunshine making you sweat before you've gone a yard. Give me grey skies any day.

Women undo seasons. Thekla had whinged about draughts, bare flagging underfoot, no electricity, no phone, water from my garden's ancient well, et endless cetera. She had everything reconnected in a trice, so she could remind me every two seconds how grim things had been before she'd arrived, that I'd cost her a fortune. I told her they would only cut it all off as soon as she left, but women won't be told. They assume that everything's permanent when not even life is that.

So I made a zillion phone calls while the going was good, ransacked the place for stray money (found two ten-quid notes and a mound of coins; Thekla hates change, pollinates every shelf with deposits of the stuff). I hoped she'd leave her scented soaps, though they made me stink like a chemist's, because proper soap's expensive and I get sick of stand-up washes in well water using soap made of bacon fat and ashes. It's cheap, but wears you out.

The water barrel I drained and filled with clean tap water. No way to store electricity or gas. I brewed up, noshed everything I could find in a great hot fry-up, ate a mystifying jar of small mushrooms (quite good really; the label said they were truffles; I was really pleased; George III was crazy for them). I slung a jar of Gentleman's Relish because you need a whole meal to go with it and my prospects weren't that promising.

Thinking of the economic outlook at Lovejoy Antiques, Inc., I ordered a picnic hamper, instant delivery, from Griffin's Stores ('Emperor Size Hampers For Celebratory Occasions') on Thekla's credit card, couldn't think of anything else so told them to send me three pairs of socks. I'm not much of a thief. I wish I was. I ordered seven pizzas from the fast foodery but they wouldn't bike them out to the village, lazy swine. Then the credit cards were stopped. At this point I made the mistake of answering the telephone.

'Who?' I said guardedly. 'No, Lovejoy isn't here.'

It was a northern accent, restful the way your home town's broad speech always is.

'I have the right number, though?' She hesitated, laughed prettily. Did I know that voice?

'What's it for?' My confidence returned. Bailiffs lack hesitancy, and don't have pretty laughs.

'To whom do I have the pleasure of speaking?'

My heart warmed to her. Who'd she said, Stella Somebody? I'd not heard such eloquence since I'd left the north. Those Manchester-based TV sagas ignore the north's politenesses, so they get everything wrong – accents, speech rhythms, words. There was honest politeness in my native slum. Its speech just sounds rougher, if you've got the wrong ears.

'Bran Mantle.' I shrugged a mental shrug. Make up names, you don't get caught. 'Can I take a message?'

'It's the bi-centenary. Would Lovejoy come and give a talk?'

'What sort of talk exactly?' I asked. If they were rich I could cull a deposit, then not turn up.

'Why, antiques! It's his subject, isn't it?'

'Er, would there be any antiques?'

'Oh, yes!' She gave that disarming laugh. 'We've all got his little how-to book! It will be quite an antiques occasion!'

The pretty voice instantly moved from a nuisance to adorable. I went giddy with greed. A whole antiques show? With me the sole arbiter? Christmas, come early.

'Well,' I said airily, 'I might be able to persuade him. He's hoping to get to your bicentenary.'

'He is?' She was delighted. 'Stupendous!'

She gave me her name and address. I promised to corner that elusive Lovejoy.

'Er, one thing, Stella.' Time to improvise. 'Lovejoy has special rules about antiques.'

'I quite understand! We'll agree, of course!' Agree to anything I might say? I had to sit down. 'Thank you so much. The parish will really appreciate it. May I call you Bran?'

26

'Who?' Oh, me. In mutual confusion we rang off.

When you're thrown onto your own resources, you have to sink to a working system.

We once had a peer of our realm who replied to an invitation from the (then) Prince of Wales, no less, by telegram: *Regret must decline invitation. Lie follows by post.* I can't remember if Lord Charles Beresford got away with it or ended up in a dank dark dungeon, but there's a lesson in there. It's this: honesty is so rare it's always a risk, the stuff of exclamation marks.

With Thekla gone, removing my last financial prop, honesty had to go. In that next hour I rang several people, including Liza at the local newspaper, and announced that I was guest of honour at a great antiques festival to celebrate the bi-centenary of ... of where? Anyway, I said it was a prestige slot, said royalty would be there, and rang off before I was forced to invent precise details. It wore me out, so I gorged a pound of Wensleydale cheese and two packets of chocolate biscuits I'd missed, brewed my last brew, and lay on my divan to reflect on the art of sexual flagellation and the very, very valuable Berkley Horse from the stall of the exotic Aureole. It was mine!

It's easy saying I should've told Aureole the truth. But nobody ever does. Think of the mighty legend of Yamashita's Treasure in the Philippines. That World War II Japanese general hoarded a two-ton mega-ingot of platinum. Every so often this giant blob is discovered – and turns out to be an unexploded mine, ship's anchor, discarded oil drum, et phoncy cetera. Cynics note that each trumpeted finding sends platinum's market price tumbling in America, Hong Kong, London. But the legend, and its excited re-re-discovery, surges on, powered by the 'three-quarters' tax Manila imposes on treasure.

No. People who find treasure – even if they pay only tenpence in Bermondsey market – think only 'It's mine! All mine!' Hang sharing, unless you're compelled. I should have remembered that, but I was in mid-gloat.

My system arrived at, making one mistake after another, I searched that jacket, and found a message in the pocket somebody had tried to dip at the show.

It read,

'Lovejoy,
    Supper, my guest, the Quayside, seven?
Please! Reason, money.'

No signature. Woman's handwriting, more roundish than a man's. The paper was one of those sticky squares that you use to remind yourself to buy mayonnaise today by fixing it on the mound of similar self-messages ignored for months. This had a headline: Orla Maltravers Featherstonehaugh, phone number, Mayfair address. If I had a name like that I'd keep quiet. But a free meal was a free meal. Hunger stirred.

Search for Tinker's lost girl Vyna, poor thing, or go for gold with this unknown lady? I knocked guilt out cold, first round. As the thunder did its stuff I rang anybody I knew with a motor. Finally, I got Roger, who had a scheme. I pretended interest, said give me a lift to town. His greed agreed for him, said he'd be round in half an hour.

Roger Boxgrove isn't called that but isn't half a million years old, either. (I'll explain in a sec.) He'd bought a new Jaguar by pure lies. I like travelling with class.

5

'COME IN WITH me, Lovejoy,' Roger said, shooting his gruesome diamond cufflinks to blind other motorists. His motor is the size of our village hall.

'Ta, no.'

'Easy pickings. Two skulls and a pelvis yesterday. Money for jam.'

Not jam, exactly. Grave robbing is grave robbing. I didn't say so, because we weren't even at Wormingford and I didn't want to have to trudge through the rainstorm.

'Any genuine, Rodge?'

'Nar.' He's one of the few people who can do a scornful chuckle. He honked a tardy Rover on the Horkesley slope. 'Genuine's trouble. Fake is simple.'

You have to admire a real artist. Roger's scam was almost perfect, a true perennial.

He'd come across it in an old newspaper, and *kaboom*! The perfect money machine! You can try it yourself, but by the time you read this you'll not be alone.

It happened back in May 1994, when this flashy modern Roger Boxgrove was born. The original Roger Boxgrove is long dead, but still around – in bits. Half a million years ago, the prototype Roger walked out in southern England questing for food. He was everything a man should be: tall, strong, fit as a flea. He moved with brisk strides, sure of his strength.

Roger carried flint tools – a stone axe, a skinning knife. He was a highly skilled huntsman; marks on his stone axe prove it. Probably he skinned the dead prey of lions that then abounded, and made off with the meat. England was different then. Giant stags roamed, rhino, packs of small vicious wolves. Life was almost as dangerous as now. It was in Boxgrove Quarry chalk pit that Roger met his doom. We don't know exactly how. Maybe from a fall, some predator. Anyway, down went Roger – to be discovered in diggings. They've only got fragments of Roger. They called him Boxgrove, after the quarry.

He's dated from secondary evidence: 600,000 years ago water voles had different teeth; those giant deer and rhinos went extinct some 480,000 years since, those numbers that scientists talk. Sizing and sexing bones isn't hard.

These find sites are always pandemonium. Interest drives us, of course, but the main force is avarice. There are fortunes to be made there. Discoveries don't have to be wondrous troves from Troy like that scoundrel Schlieman conned and smuggled, no. Human artefacts are the front runners these days. Why? Because now we're all lost, and want to know who we are. Overnight 'Roger Boxgrove' became as famous as a pop star. Quarries were raided by night. Museum robberies soared. And a new confidence trickster was born. Guess who.

Enter no-good scrounger Napier Montrose Shelvenham, of no fixed abode. He immediately called himself Roger Boxgrove – there's no copyright in titles – and started selling bits of bone, flint chips, 'Stone Age tools' from Sussex, Surrey, Kent, and anywhere else he could spell.

So this penniless chiseller in those first few glorious months sold any bone he could get hold of, claiming they were from the world-famous Boxgrove Quarry. It's an antiques fact that fraudsters get help from God-fearing truthsayers like you and me. They also get help from administrators. Proof: some English Heritage geezer actually announced to TV cameras within millisecs of the Great Find that he'd give more details *when the skull is found next summer*! Gulp! Everybody assumed that somebody was secretly concealing more skeleton bits.

This modern Roger provided – provides – more and more bits. I've seen him sell hippopotamus teeth, any old zoo bones, suitably aged in the Piltdown Skull manner. Roger uses stains because he hasn't the patience to bury them in Pittsbury Ramparts, which is how us fraudsters age fake weapons. He sells to museums overseas. A thousand zlotniks here, two thousand there, mounts up, if you do seventy-two cash-on-the-nail sales a week. He bribes the Inland Revenue, usual terms.

'Fakery is always simpler, Lovejoy,' he was saying. 'God help my business if I ever have to go straight. Poverty's murder. Short of women, grub, gelt. Who needs it?'

'Mmmh,' I went, knowing the feeling. 'What'll you do if the museums rumble you?'

'They won't.' He dabbed the dashboard. Treacly music flowed. 'Know why, Lovejoy? Because they're only inches from fame. One bone turns out genuine Boxgrove Man, and they're on the TV talk circuit for life.'

You have to admire class, like I say.

'A north Suffolk sexton's coming in. Digs the graves, tenth-century church. I'll ship out to every corner of the planet.' He eyed me, conjecture in his gaze. 'We could make a killing, Lovejoy.'

'What could I do, Rodge?' He fought a slow Ford for the middle lane, the g force dragging my cheeks. We made life by a whisker. 'All I do is detect genuine antiques. I'd bankrupt you because all your relics are fake.'

He sighed, testy. Con merchants hate reason. 'That's the point. A Lovejoy certificate of authenticity'd bring in fortunes. My business'd quadruple! You heard of venuses?' He guffawed, overtook a brewer's dray. The carthorse shied, its driver hauling and cursing. I shrank in my seat.

'You mean the artefacts?'

'What else?'

It hurts to talk of others' good fortune, always so undeserved. These so-called 'venuses' are figures of antler, ivory, some of stone. Grimaldi, from the Menton caves, bordering Italy and France. Everybody knows the tale, how the French antique dealer Louis Jullien found some little Ice Age carvings. They weren't much to look at, just dumpy females with steatopygous bums, crude faces. But, over 20,000 years old, you can't knock them, and M. Jullien got well over a dozen. Their Museum of National Antiquities collared half as many. That's how things lay for a hundred years, because Jullien emigrated to Canada before 1900. The Peabody, Harvard, bought one delectable venus from Jullien's daughter half a century later, and that was it.

This next bit's even more painful. A Canadian lately bought a handful of these priceless Ice Age venuses – secret word is for 75 quid – in Montreal, browsing round an antique shop. News spread. Prime Ministers and governments became involved. The common danger? Only 150 such Ice Age artefacts are known for certain, and 'belong to all mankind'. Meaning we're sulking at the luck of others. Jealousy, in a word.

'Goldbricking every dig,' Roger was enthusing.

'Ta, Rodge.' I got out a strangled, 'No'.

'Provisional?' he asked, grinning.

I didn't manage any reply to that. One thing East Anglia has a permanent supply of is entrepreneurs (dunno what the feminine word is for it, but we've tons of those as well). They all drive sleek customised motors of giddy horsepower, have several addresses. They can buy and/or sell serfs on a whim, especially if the serf in question is broke.

'Thekla'll exact vengeance, Lovejoy, so watch it.'

They also hear scandals before the first blood splashes.

'Think I should scarper?' I asked uneasily.

'You're good at evasion, Lovejoy.' He belled us up to ninety on the town road, passing the policeman on point duty with a cheery wave, the bobby, Old George, saluting respectfully. If I'd done forty George would have clinked me up for a week. 'But for Christ's sake run like hell if she does the other thing.'

'What other thing?' I was mystified.

'Apologises, you pillock.'

The car's acceleration lulled me. What was he saying, that an apology is the final insult, evidence of preceding cruelty?

There were these two women I'd got to know in our village. Maxine was middle-aged, comely, buxom, married with two-point-nine children at university, rich husband commuting like mad. Her neighbour, the older Mrs Prowell, shared her husband's wary tenant farmer's eyes. Nothing remarkable, except Mrs Prowell hated Maxine. 'For no reason, Lovejoy,' Maxine told me one day when scouting the terrain before letting me out. Thirty years, no reason? We'd become close when I'd called to sell her a seventeenth century William and Mary period door lock, solid brass, complete with key and keeper key escutcheon. (I still smart, because Maxine's gleeful welcomes those warm sunny afternoons made me feel I'd be a cad to ask for the money, which I never got.)

Came one autumn morning, Maxine pruning the daffodils, whatever, when here comes Mr Prowell. Please, he begs, my wife's grievously ill, the Grim Reaper tiptoeing in Mrs Prowell's gate. She's not long to live, wants to say sorry, dear Maxine. Won't you forgive and forget? Anguish reigned.

'Tell her no,' says Maxine sweetly. 'Your wife has hated me for thirty years with such *evident* enjoyment that I couldn't *possibly* deprive her of that pleasure in her last hours.' And demurely continues snipping. With her secateurs and trug, Maxine was a picture any tourist would recognise, the charming English garden scene.

This is true, every word. I was concealed hard by, having dived into the shrubbery when I'd heard Maxine's gate go. Aghast, when the sorrowing man'd left, I asked Maxine how she could be so vicious. She'd smiled with beatific Saint Theresa rapture, and said as we'd gone upstairs, 'Thinks she can twist the knife one last time, after what she's put me through? Bitch. I hope her cancer does it on a cold wet night. Get undressed, Lovejoy.'

And she'd followed this Christian charity with hours of passion wilder than I'd known for days. Until Roger's remark, I'd thought it something exclusively female. I sighed, bucketing along the town road in a downpour on squealing tyres. I always catch up after everybody's moved on.

'Here, Rodge,' I said, suddenly. 'Do you really know Thekla well?'

'Everybody knows Thekla, Lovejoy.' He laughed. 'Ambition, she. You want my tip? Never do anything to further your own ambition when it's suggested by others. Women know this by instinct. We blokes never learn. Oh, Carmel's looking for you. An antiques job.'

'Thanks, Rodge,' I said gratefully.

'Anything for a pal. Think over my offer.'

He dropped me at the ironmonger's on North Hill in lessening rain. I cut through the Dutch Quarter – Flemish weavers lived there when fleeing persecution centuries back. A place of refuge.

Tinker was outside The Ship, by St James the Less. He looked even shabbier than usual. He avoided my eye, which is odd. He was with Roadie, watching the parade to the war memorial. Roadie still looked every inch the yob. I wished he'd close his mouth now and then. He prides himself on his belch, thinks them the soul of wit. He was calling embarrassing sex slogans at the girl drummers prancing by in their shimmery yellows and blues.

'What's up, Tinker?'

'Them social services, Lovejoy.' He hawked, spat at a waste bin, didn't make it. The phlegm slid down, sending me green. We're a god-awful species.

'No help?' I'd sent him.

'Chucked me out for being grottie.'

My vision dissolved. In a scarlet cloud I hauled him through the crowd, stormed with him down Head Street to the plush offices of the Department of Social Services – every word of that title a cause for infinite merriment. I marched in, ignoring the uniformed goons who guard affluent bureaucracy against us who finance their upkeep. I disturbed two Social Support And Care Experts – more hilarity –

who were filing their untroubled nails. They looked up, yawning. I switched their telly off. They were outraged.

'You've no right to come in here,' one said.

'It's that filthy old man back,' said the other.

'And me.' I shoved Tinker into a chair, gestured Roadie to another while my vision cleared. 'This gentleman's relative is missing. Help him.'

The girls worked out hate priorities. One whined, 'I've an urgent interview soon, Lovejoy.'

'No, Dawn.' I spoke loudly as a security man entered. 'You're booked in at Hayre Fayre, tint and rinse.' I gave her a moment not to choke. 'Barbie? You've logged a Child Support Agency visit, so your hubby won't know you're meeting Joggo near the brewery lay-by.' Lay-by is correct.

They looked at each other in alarm, glum social workers forced to act. Silence fell. I waited. The security man withdrew under my gaze. Joggo's a repossession man known for violence. He'd repossessed my furniture twice. I hadn't argued.

Tinker wheezed, 'Look, Lovejoy ... '

He went mute when I raised a warning finger. Barbie, conscious of Joggo's sexy impatience, spoke at last, eyeing the clock, a modern Garant quartz, perfect time for ever, but who'd want to give it a glance?

'Look, Lovejoy,' she tried. 'We do vital social work. The police do missing persons.'

'They sent us here,' I lied. More silence.

'Who is the child?' Dawn glared at her dusty forms, indignant at having to fill one in.

'Vyna Dill, from Australia.'

They brightened. 'The Australian High Commission ... '

'Sent us here.' I could get quite good at lies.

They sank into misery. 'How did she come here?'

Tinker stirred when my nudge nearly toppled him. For somebody desperate to find a relative he was singularly reluctant.

'Er, her parents sent her. To study.'

They brightened. 'The education authorities ... '

'Sent us here,' I capped. But, study?

'Studying what?' Barbie growled. A growling woman is a frustrated beast to be avoided. But I had my own rage and didn't care.

'Technical stuff,' Tinker said. 'Dunno.'

'Where is she enrolled?' growled Dawn and Barbie together, sensing a way back to inertia.

'Dunno.'

'Her age?' Dawn chirruped, now blowing her nails.

'Seventeen,' Tinker said. I looked at Roadie, doing his leer at Barbie's breasts. It was a revolting sight – the leer, I mean.

Relief lit their countenances, scorn rethroned.

'Nothing to do with the DSS, Lovejoy,' they said together. 'Get out ... ' etc, etc.

Out on the pavement I really went for Tinker.

'How come you don't know what she's studying, or where?'

Roadie sniggered, seeing the bands wheeling in. After his triumph seducing Barbie, he would apply his snotty leer to our marchers. God, but we're a horrible species, or have I said that?

'It's children, Lovejoy,' Tinker said, crestfallen. 'Who knows what they're up to?'

'Roadie.' I made him face me. His leer was nauseating. 'Wipe your nose. Where is Vyna likely to be?'

He giggled, a high-pitched staccato that actually made me step back. The bands came nearer, lads bugling, girls' drums pounding. Pipes skirled and banners flapped. He tried to turn. I held him, wondering how the hell I'd got into this.

'Dunno.' The grace of a social worker on the skive.

'Awreet, Tinker,' I said, unhappy. Tinker was looking at the approaching girls.

Normally, Tinker would be going on about their scanty attire, saying, 'Their parents should get locked up, they'll catch their death of cold'. It's his litany. The importance of this? He never misses a chance to prattle against modern shirkers or scanties. Yet he was avoiding my eye, not a word when our town's youth were Going To The Dogs and Catching Pneumonia before his very eyes. It was weird.

'Them birds're all right,' Roadie snivelled into his sleeve. 'I could ... '

'Awreet, Tinker,' I decided. 'We'll do what we can to find your lass. Get her picture photocopied. Send word, Big Frank from Suffolk, Little Dorrit, Aureole, Margaret Dainty, Beetroot on the Priory Church corner, Sadie. Paper the rest.'

'The photo place'll be shut, Lovejoy.'

'Do it, Tinker.' I'd had enough. There was something wrong here and I really wanted no part of it. I had a fake violin to finish before the week was out, or else. Vyna was probably fine anyway. I'd done what I could. I moved off, saying, 'Roadie, wipe your nose'. He was already calling out coarse offers to the first ranks of girls.

That old joke: When your memory goes, forget it; that's what I was doing. I hadn't any right to, but things were pressing. Tinker was a pal, but this Roadie was objectionable.

Other people, I told myself, are as you find them, not as they merely seem. Wasn't it our sensitive gentle poet Shelley who fastened his cat to his kite and flew it in a storm among the thunder and lightning? People are what they do, not what they say. That includes women, acquaintances, people you meet. And friends, even ones as reliable as me. Completely absolved, I headed down the side street for the treacherous world of sex plus antiques. Somebody ought to invent a word mixing the two. Sexanques? Anquex? It's a serious lack, for the two together are the perfect excuse for everything on earth.

God, but we're a.h.s.

I knocked at Carmel's tiny terraced dwelling, gazing wistfully at its fourteenth century architecture. These cottages form a cluster, all genuinely old. Course, they've been 'improved' by our town council, a band of overweight spoilers laying all waste before, happily, the atherosclerosis resulting from their gargantuan expense-account meals ends their game. The structure, though, is still original. Carmel was in.

'Hello, Lovejoy.' She almost wore a silk floral gown. 'Sod off. I'm busy.'

'No you're not, Carmel. You never are.'

She slammed the door.

This is average. I waited, without taking offence. She's always starting up new enterprises, but has one constant sin. It's the ephemeral world of creativity, a posh word for cadging, 'dealing'. She's made for it. I've heard her use over a dozen accents in a single evening, and that was in seclusion on her boat moored at the marina. Carmel lives for telephones, rings on her fingers and bells on her toes, to coin a song. Carmel never stops.

The door slammed open, if doors can do such a thing. She stood glaring.

'What *is* it?' *She*'d sent for *me*, note.

'Work, Carmel?'

Two lads howled by on a motor bike, whistling lust. Absently she made a rude gesture, kept her anger for me.

'You always interrupt, Lovejoy. I'm sick of you. You're never away from my door.'

Translation: How broke are you, Lovejoy? I pondered on how to reach her clinking clanking heart's locked coffers.

'We've not met for months, Carmel,' I said reasonably.

'So why this urgency? Because your cottage's repossessed, and your whorish fashioneer's ditched you?'

'Eh?' Being homeless was news. Visiting Carmel always paid.

She saw how startled I was. I could see her mind change.

'Come in. You've a minute, Lovejoy.'

Carmel's minutes are famous for their elasticity. Even I've managed to stretch one to a full day with minimal inventiveness, and I'm not up to much. Think how a tycoon like, say, her pal Roger Boxgrove'd do.

Two phones were ringing, one inside her gown. She answered it in French, pointing a finger to the living room door. Obediently I went through and shut the door. It went whoosh, soundproofed. I like Carmel. She and I met when she asked me for help stealing a filing cabinet from the solicitors Parlpley and Donnash's in St Edmunsbury. Her car had conked out and mine was miraculously functioning. She actually flagged me down on the A47. We loaded the stolen files piecemeal. Ungraciously, she'd played hell because I'd no car phone.

Waiting, I inspected her furniture, the display plates, the armchairs, none of it antique. Except one little carriage clock on the mantelpiece, Leroy et Fils of Paris. I went up to it, said hello.

'Got it, love?' I asked. 'Can I look?'

It felt all right, so I turned her round and opened her back. The alarm setting's face was white! Why Leroy wanted to hide it thus I don't know.

'You're beautiful,' I told the clock. 'Want to come home with me?'

'I heard, Lovejoy! Keep your thieving hands ... '

Miserably, I sat. There was one other recent addition, I noticed, a sepia photograph of a Great War soldier in its original ebony frame. He looked desperately young, Royal Artillery badges. Carmel wafted in.

'That soldier? My ancestor. He contacts me occasionally, in spirit. He has a fund of stories.'

'Does he now.' I rose with a litany of excuses. Mysticism is rubbish. 'Imustbegoingjustremembered ... '

'Shut it, Lovejoy.' She sat opposite, crossing her legs. I swallowed and sank, trying to look everywhere else. Carmel isn't fair. She makes it impossible for you to stare away, then blames you for gaping. 'How much for a sand job?'

Definitely no reason to leave. If I'd not called, she'd have sent Bushmen trackers out. In fact, I was probably the subject of her phone calls. Now Thekla had cut me off, Carmel had scanned her satellites. A sand job's a special sort of theft.

'Depends on where, and the guard system.'

'Is that all? What about the stripe?'

Stripe is the item(s) due to be stolen. Carmel likes to use these terms because her clients, especially the ones who finance such robberies, like to remain aloof yet are impressed by jargon.

'Think national, Lovejoy. Like Tate Gallery loans.'

A sand job's simplicity itself. Nowadays, it's all the rage. God knows why it's called a sand job, perhaps because gym plimsolls were called 'sand shoes' and robbers wore them.

In a sand job, a rich art collector, the roller, burns to possess, say, a famous Constable, Da Vinci, whatever. Smouldering with unrequited greed, he moans in disturbed slumber at the nerks in the National Gallery who won't sell it to him for threepence. Then the radio news announces that the wondrous painting is being lent to some gallery abroad. His chance! Quickly he phones his favourite thief, and orders a sand job – that is, to nick it while it's overseas, and bring it home to daddy.

Success requires two elements. First, a friend writes to the press denouncing the loan in ringing terms ('Why should our great national treasures be hawked about Europe? Will it be safe from international art theft ... ?' Curators anxiously reply that 'all precautions have been taken ... '). The second element is robbers good enough.

Please disabuse yourself of the old-fashioned Bulldog Drummond footpad-and-gumshoe image. Times are new. East Anglia's robbers, craftsmen all, don't immediately hit the ferry to Holland and jauntily steal the stripe and bring it to the roller. Not nowadays, for hoods everywhere are eager to rob on command, for a price. So if, say, the stripe is a Birmingham Gallery sculpture being lent to Bergen in Norway, Scandinavia's art thieves are telephoned (at their terribly secret Copenhagen number) and a fee arranged for them to do it. If

Glasgow is loaning stripe to Paris's Louvre, then you dial the oh-so-secret Brussels number for a French sand job.

'The stripe's incidental,' I said.

Carmel's eyes widened. 'I never thought I'd hear you run down antiques.'

'I mean the stripe is a constant. The only variables are where, and security.'

'A sand job's normally outside my creativity.'

'Oh, aye,' I said, cynicism showing. She wasn't normally this reticent. Carmel has brokered several Continental thefts, and done well out of them, meaning forty per cent from the insurers.

'No, seriously, Lovejoy.'

Then the penny dropped. 'Turners? You're going to tish that Turner robbery?' To tish is to steal something in exactly the same manner as some famous antiques robbery, a copy theft.

'Who knows?' Offhand.

But I knew, and rejoiced. This was mighty stuff, for the notorious Frankfurt sand job had already entered antiques legend.

The Tate Gallery lent two masterpieces, each worth unimagined sums, to Frankfurt's Schirn Kunsthalle Gallery. Two hoods lurked inside until the alarms were being cut from manual to auto, their chance window. They bagged a guard, snaffled his keys, nicked the paintings, and legged it. As makeweight, they took a Caspar David Friedrich (not worth a Turner, but who can sneeze at an extra two million?). The sand job's hallmark: The hoods *know where the stripe is.*

'The Frankfurt job, Carmel. You're going to copy it. Tell me where, and I'll give you a guide price.'

My heart thumped with excitement. If it seemed safe enough, I might even watch the experts actually do the lift. It might be the only time in my life I'd ever get to hold, just for one blissfilled moment, some Old Master.

'Later, Lovejoy. You'll have to be honest.'

Carmel never trusts me. I went all hurt. It beats me why women want my company. I ripped my eyes from her legs and reached the door.

'Was that true about my cottage, Carmel?' I'd best stay away if the bailiffs were in.

'You were hardly out of the gate, Lovejoy.' She shook her head. 'I said it'd end in tears. That Thekla.'

'If you decide to go ahead, tell me, eh?'

She smiled, a lovely business ending in a slightly askew pursing of her luscious mouth. I decided to forget temptation for a bit.

'Where, Lovejoy? You've no phone, nor a home to hang it in.' She laughed. I shut the door on her final hilarity. 'Lovejoy and high fashion!'

It rained, heavy and worrying. I piked into the town centre, thinking to try Lydia, recently back from a trainee course. She's my apprentice. It was time she unlearnt the expertise she'd have assimilated from the trade's professors. My mind was going, a sand job? Locally financed? Now, if I was to embark on such a thing, which robbery would I go for? And where? I'd no home, but antiques were always one lovely big promise.

6

It was dusk when I reached the centre, drenched. There was only one free place open, the chapel reading room. I'd have gone into the theatre foyer, but I'd have been stopped at the main doors and barred for scruffiness. It wouldn't have happened in Will Shakespeare's day. Gloomy with self-pity, I opted for shelter.

The town has chapels and chapels. We have a score or so still extant. Others are gone, or apologetic. The bells of St Mary's, Minehead, ring silently now, being computer controlled. Such 'progress' is daft – a mute bell is simply a non-bell. This chapel was an antique, the only sort that matter. I stood in the dry, feeling pleased. Tradition's barmy, but good while it lasts.

Light came from a couple of electric lamps. A book stood open on a lectern. I checked that it wasn't a Guttenberg or anything worth nicking, though that thought honestly hadn't crossed my mind.

A voice made me jump. 'Do you search, brother?'

'No, Jessica. It's only me, Lovejoy.'

The chapel filled with overwhelming perfume. I almost swooned. While Jessica lives, the perfume industry is safe. Jessica lives on/under/with her son-in-law – opinions vary – on the estuaries. She is rich. To become even richer she exploits every angle, not to say curve. She emerged from the shadows. Mascara, rouge, false eyelashes that knock you askew if you get close, lipstick thick enough to plough, long earrings, sheathed in silver lamé covered in Christian symbols. She was gorgeous, but not very holy.

'Heard you were in charge, Jessica. That's why I dropped in.' I hadn't and it wasn't, but showing interest in Jessica never hurts. She was Carmel's friend. 'Got religion?'

'Hasn't everyone, Lovejoy?' No answer to that, except some Augustinian complexity. She drew close. I gasped for oxygen. 'I'm glad you've left that horrid Thekla. She's no good for you.'

East Anglia wins the gossip stakes hands down.

'You're being beaten to the buy, Lovejoy?'

'Lies, love,' I lied.

'Has some new divvy hailed in? People say so.'

'They say too frigging much.' I was narked.

'Language,' she chided, cool. 'You're in church. So you'll do Carmel's sand job?' She drew scabbard-length violet nails along my neck. My middle went funny. She smiled; diamanté dots shimmered on each white tooth. 'Welcome aboard, Lovejoy.'

Ever had that feeling that you're so baffled that you feel like giving up? I once knew this bloke, Cedric. Look at him, you'd say he was staid, middle-aged, humdrum. A collector of glass paperweights, he owned a rare paperweight from the French firm of Baccarat, in Alsace. A simple ball, it held a green glass snake on white glass lace. Tip: If you come across one, steal/beg/borrow/buy it; whatever the price, you'll end up violently rich. I'd tried to buy it, but lacked money. Well, this woman Hilary came up to me at the village dramatic society play, and gave me a letter for Cedric. I'm only the doorman and sweeper-up, stand in the darkness waiting to switch on the lights at the end.

We went outside so she could sniff tears dry. I stood there like a spare tool.

'Can't you give it him yourself, Hilary?'

She'd broken down. I shushed her, in case the audience got distracted from Noël Coward. 'I must stop seeing Cedric, Lovejoy. My husband, the children ... '

My admiration for Cedric soared. From a mere run-of-the-mill aging bloke, Cedric became the Scarlet Pimpernel. I mean, Hilary was a real looker. I would have been after her myself, if she'd had any antiques. That's what I mean. I never quite know what's going on. The feeling was never so strong as in Jessica's church.

'Aye,' I said. 'Carmel's asked. I'm not sure.'

God, but she was overpowering. The scent, her closeness, the still church. Sanctuary must be like this, without the sense of impending doom.

'Carmel and I ... ' I shook my head disparagingly. Reluctance about Carmel pleased Jessica.

'I'm glad, Lovejoy. Is it true you're going on Aureole's chain gang? I should have thought that you'd have enough ... to do.'

'Stop that, Jessica,' I said weakly, through quickening breath. 'We're in church.'

'Sacrament, darling,' she said huskily. 'That's all love is. You taught me that.'

I'd only come in from the rain. I was anxious to stay unravished while I decided, but found my hands fumbling to undo us both in the aisle.

'Shagging in church is unlucky,' a bloke said.

We jumped apart, my heart thudding alarm. Jessica was equal to it, and quickly stepped past me. It's easy for women. Their frocks just drop into place, but is anything more obvious than a bloke suddenly deformed?

'Welcome, brother,' she cooed, sweet as honey, 'to sacred harmony.' I frantically tried to conceal my incipient lust.

The newcomer was vaguely familiar. Youngish, down-at-heel, leather bomber jacket, oily lank hair, six foot, mouth agape, pointed winkle-picker shoes that went out with the dodo. He was muscular, though. An iron pumper, always in and out of poses. He moved aside. I realised that he was keeping the altar in view, and recognised him.

'Wotcher, Tubb,' I said. 'Still training?'

'Lovejoy.' He came, warily rounded Jessica. 'Carmel's put me on the sand job. Sorry I'm late.'

Late? I'd not spoken to him for months. 'You?'

He went indignant. 'What's wrong with me, Lovejoy?'

Jessica's sanctity evaporated. She looked annoyed.

'Tubb's Carmel's helper,' I explained, wishing I'd not come, and that I'd not got a helper like Tubb for a robbery. 'He's just out of gaol.'

Tubb was released a day late. His sentence had ended on a Friday. The most superstitious bloke on earth, he'd clung screaming to the bars, until the prison governor wearily agreed to let him stay an extra day. Ancient lore says that Friday starts are bad luck, like not facing an altar. Here in East Anglia some old people still creak out backwards after Evensong. I'd not heard the superstition about not making love in church. If it's a real superstition, it's a rotten one.

'When're we off, Lovejoy?'

'I haven't said I'd do it yet.'

'Another time, Lovejoy.' Jessica swept off.

Sadly I watched her go. With her makeup and dress sense she could outvamp those fashioneers any day of the week. Which jolted my memory. I was supposed to be in the Quay nosh house, then meeting Aureole.

'See you, Jess,' Tubb said after her. Odd, because it's her private nickname. I'd thought he didn't know her. 'Carmel says to stick with you, Lovejoy.'

'Then no loony superstitions, okay?'

My mind settled a jigsaw piece in place. Carmel needed me and nobody else for her sand job. I was still the only divvy for leagues around.

'How much time've we got, Tubb?'

'Some days.'

Then I'd time for a free meal. I dithered for a split second. Aureole represented grub plus the Berkley Horse, but being a link in her sex chain was a definite minus. I like to choose where to lose, so to speak. On the other hand there was the mystery pickpocket Orla Maltravers Featherstonehaugh, of London's Mayfair, who stole nothing but who promised supper. On the *other* other hand, I had given Aureole my word of honour. On the *other* other other hand, had I really meant it? Orla won.

'See you anon, Tubb. My auntie's in hospital.'

Tubb accompanied me. I stepped into the Trinity Street dark. 'Don't talk to her if she's in one of them cubicles, Lovejoy. It's bad luck.'

'It is?'

'Witness, wish, or will through glass opposites what you say!' He was eager to guide me. 'Look at her through glass'll bring evil. Take care.'

'Er, right, Tubb.' I moved away from the barmy sod. Just my luck to have Tubb foisted on my promising job.

He called after me, 'And stay away from them green hospital gowns, okay?'

'Right, right.'

Okay, so green's unlucky. Has anyone ever seen a green nightdress? I knew this bird once who wouldn't go out wearing green, though the colour suited her. Tubb carries superstition too far. It was his downfall. He was burgling a mansion in Lincolnshire. His mate was chewing a hawthorn twig while jemmying the window – country folk call hawthorn 'bread and cheese'; children like the taste. Only when Tubb had shone his flashlight had he seen the twig. Superstition struck, for hawthorn indoors signifies calamity. Tubb let out a shriek, roused the household. Police caught him less than a mile off lamming along a hedgerow, which to this nerk proved how unlucky hawthorn is. Bonkers.

'Don't step on cracks, Lovejoy!' floated after me in the gloaming.

Like a fool I actually found myself trying to see the flagstones in the lamplight. It only goes to show, daftness is catching. I should have remembered that, and stayed safe. But I didn't so I wasn't. I started down East Hill past the town hall clock, with Saint Helena and the True Cross, and Boadicea glowering. Symbols. Tubb'd say they were unlucky, but he's cracked.

Lightning flashed, silhouetting the building against blackness. The rain descended. Maybe Tubb was right. The downpour stopped me reaching the Quay. I judged the traffic and dashed across to the Bay and Say pub, arriving like a drowned rat.

'Wotcher, Lovejoy.'

Sadly Sorrowing was in. He got me a drink, a record.

'Ta, Sadly. What's the occasion?'

'Sold ten this week, Lovejoy. Great, eh?'

Sadly Sorrowing makes fake Regency writing bureaus. They're not bad, but he makes too few to eke a living. He's called Sadly Sorrowing after a greeting card rhyme he made up. London firms wouldn't buy it, so he had six thousand printed – to be rare collector's items, you understand. He sends them out on every possible occasion, to get rid. So if you get married, win the lottery, lose a leg or have twins, you get a *Sincerest Condolences* card with his famous couplet that begins, 'Sadly sorrowing sinners slowly soaring ... ' We all joke, 'No, Sadly – we'll wait for the film.'

'I told tourists they were Lord Fauntleroy's.'

'Great.' I gave up. Ten was his max. 'Here, Sadly. You know Brad, eh?'

'Brad the boat builder? Wivenhoe? I live near him.'

'He ashore, or out sailing?'

'In this storm?' The rain was slashing at the pub windows. 'He'll be out tomorrow down the Blackwater.'

Good news. Tomorrow, I'd not be poor, with Brad's help. Tinker came in with Roadie. I stood them some ale with the remnant of Thekla's largesse.

'Frothey went gorilla, Lovejoy.'

Roadie sniggered. 'I told her you'd gone with that posh sheila.'

'What're we after, Lovejoy?' Tinker gazed soulfully into his empty glass. I got him another two pints, which was almost me cleaned out. 'You've got that look.'

'Carmel has a sand job. I'm lumbered with Tubb.'

'Gawd, Lovejoy. Might as well phone the Plod. His superstition'll cock it up. Hear how he got nicked? They were robbing this mansion ... '

'I know,' I said sourly. 'Maythorn indoors.'

'We broke, Lovejoy?' Tinker asked.

Roadie fell about as I hawked out my last groat. 'Some antique dealer! Evicted, stony broke.'

'Aureole might have word of your niece,' I told Tinker sourly, but didn't say she'd been on Aureole's dating agency. Tinker gave a grimace. He looked shifty.

'Big John wants you about scossing the Yank Museum.'

'Oh, dear. I've just seen him.'

Sheehan must have decided he'd been too giving over that reffo. Every so often he considers antiques as a career. That is to say, he decides what antiques he wants, and we're expected to obtain them at no risk to him. To 'scoss' is to strip entirely of spoils, for later division.

'The one in the West Country?'

It's actually the only extant American Museum in the whole of Europe. Established in the 1980s, it's still worth seeing. A great mansion filled with old American furniture, patchwork quilts, utensils. Entirely furnished, ready to inhabit, early New England vintage. Word said it had naff security. I wondered idly what the USA had done to incur Big John's wrath.

'Tell Big John I'll think hard about it.'

'And Lydia's back. There she is.'

My heart gave a lurch, a rotten sensation. I'm in enough trouble without emotion creeping in. Don't get me wrong. I'm in favour of Lydia, love, the lot. But travel light goes fleetest, and Lydia was impedimenta. Women tidy my cottage – when I have one, that is. Thekla's tender loving care lost me my home. See what I mean? They tidy everything so my few clothes are untraceable. The arch tidier is Lydia.

Another lurch. I saw her shadow on the vestibule's frosted glass. Two lads hauled in, laughing, joshing as Lydia hesitated. She'd dither there until closing time unless I fetched her.

'Wotcher, love.'

'Good evening, Lovejoy.'

There she stood, blushing prettily. Slim, but not too. Dark blue suit, smart hem, high-neck lace blouse, small matching hat, navy blue handbag, neat white gloves. My resolution evaporated. I grinned like a fool.

'You're back, then, Lyd.'

46

'Lydia, please. May I ... ?'

'Oh, come in. Tinker's here.'

We joined them. Everybody gaped, playing who's-the-looker. Women gave her the cold eye, working out how to talk her down. They'd have a hard time. She dulled every mirror. Tinker explained Roadie to her.

'Good evening, Mr Dill. How do you do, Roadie?'

'Is she real, for fu – ?'

Tinker clapped a hand over the youth's mouth and gravelled out in a whisper audible on the Kent coast, 'Shut your 'ole, lad. There's a frigging lady present.'

I smiled weakly. 'May I offer you a drink?'

'Earl Grey tea, please. Do they have biscuits?'

She drew off her gloves, knees together, ready for the sermon and offertory. Body of a sinner, manners of a saint, soul of a nun.

'Is she real?' Roadie was astonished.

This called for my bent eye. He subsided while I went to ask Prissy the barmaid for some Earl Grey tea and some biscuits. The bar lads guffawed, but even they knew that Lydia was the classiest the pub had ever had in its chequered seven-hundred year old history, and just eyed me with envy.

'You joking, Lovejoy?' Prissy asked. She was new, a Walsall lass. 'Tea and biscuits in the saloon bar? How much do I charge?'

'Make a note,' I offered gallantly. 'I'll settle up later.' Like I say, Prissy's new.

' ... a divvy can unerringly diagnose antiques, you see,' Lydia was telling Roadie when I rejoined them. 'So Miss Carmel is particularly keen ... '

'How was the course, Lydia?' I interrupted. The less said about Carmel's sand job the better. Lydia would assume it involved inspecting some cabinet in a vicarage. 'Learn all about antiques? Porcelain? Wedgwood? Paintings?'

'Lovejoy,' Roadie said. 'Your shag's telling us about some bint's sand job.'

'Could I have a word, please?' I beckoned Roadie into the vestibule. A snogging couple desisted, watched sullenly as I throttled the lad until he went puce.

'What ... ?' the nerk gasped when I let go.

'Listen. Lydia is not like you or me. We're nigh on rubbish. She isn't. Keep mum, or I'll break your arm. Understand?' I didn't know

47

if I could fulfil the threat, being a coward, but I could at least
bludgeon him and run.

'What's so special about her?' he choked, feeling his neck.

'*She's* so special about her, see?'

Enough, in case he decided to fight back. I told the snoggers sorry,
and brightly returned.

'Roadie's checking the weather.' I eyed Lydia. She smiled shyly
back. 'You're bone dry, love. It's teeming cats and dogs.'

'Mr Boxgrove kindly gave me a lift from the railway station. He
was seeing off Miss Aureole's friend.'

'How kind,' I said. Lydia talks like an abbess.

'Wasn't it?' She smiled, sun breaking through cloud. 'He gave her
a ticket, a map and everything. He would have introduced but she
was in desperate hurry. She seemed so tired. Just back from Salford,
too.'

Deep down Roger's a shagnasty. I wasn't jealous, but didn't like
him giving Lydia a lift. Change the subject.

'Tinker? Aureole owes me a Berkley Horse, okay?'

'Is that an antique, Lovejoy?' asked Lydia.

'Er, no,' I lied. She'd have her notebook out any minute. 'It's, er, a
wooden display stand.'

Tinker frowned. 'You got that right, Lovejoy? Isn't it ... ?'

'Get another pint,' I bawled, nudging him hard. I smiled at Lydia.
'Tinker always misunderstands.'

Her tea was served on a tray with doylies, if you please. The old
Bay and Say had never seen such elegance. I glanced gratitude to
Prissy, who went red and looked away. She's nice, Prissy.

Something was odd, though. Roger doesn't do kindnesses except
for money. Tinker knowingly caught my anxiety, gave one of his
spectacular coughs as cover, shaking the rafters as far as the Roman
ruins, and went for the ale.

'Sorry, miss,' he said, returning carrying five pints. I wish I could
do that. I once tried lifting three, but spilled two. His rheumy old
eyes streamed. He wiped snot into his palm, and gulped phlegm
down with relief. 'My chest's getting worse. I need a drink bad ... '

'Oh. Please, Mr Dill. Allow me.'

He swiftly vanished her proffered note into his mitten. 'Wouldn't
dream − ohwellifyouinsist. Ta.'

'Would you care for a cup, Mr Roadie?' Lydia asked, pouring. 'I
am pleased about Miss Carmel's new ... '

'No!' I shot in, then lamely added as everybody in the pub stared. 'He's allergic to tea.'

'Er, yep, allergic.'

He was learning. My head ached. I kept sane by asking Lydia about 'Antiques For Trade Experts' in Chichester. Outside, thunder stuttered, quivering the floorboards. It was a while before the din dwindled and folk started to come in shaking umbrellas.

'And now, Lovejoy,' Lydia said eagerly, coming to the end of her diatribe about Georgian furniture. 'Could you tell me of the successes of Lovejoy Antiques, Inc?'

Roadie laughed. Tinker looked uncomfortable.

'Well,' I said weakly, 'we've been after ... '

'*Successes*, Lovejoy.' She frowned. 'I insist.'

I managed to say it seventh go.

'None, love.'

Her luscious lips thinned. 'In all that *time*?'

So I explained, down to my present penury and homelessness.

That night I slept on her mother's sofa.

7

THAT SOFA NIGHT was longish, as nights go. I'm not one to lie awake fretting. If you sleep, you sleep. I usually read, or lie smiling at memories. But not tonight. Mavis warned me (a) not to move one inch, and (b) not to touch a single thing, like I was going to nick her teaspoons. (They were only electroplate anyway.) I sighed. I'm what prejudice is for.

The storm crashed and pealed. The living-room fire died. I watched the embers. Hearing Lydia moving about upstairs made me unhappy. Worse, I was outwitted.

My sparse living comes from detecting antiques, among the crud of fakes. I *feel* genuine. They speak to me, as in Thekla's fashion show with Loon Rodney's antique carpet. We divvies are few and far between. I've only heard of ten besides me in my whole life, and I've searched. The chance of meeting another divvy is logarithmically remote. Yet here I was being outsmarted, out-started. Reason? *There might be another divvy around.*

Look at the evidence. I turned under my blanket, stared at the embers. Lydia must be sleeping, selfish cow. She sleeps on her side, hands bunched under her chin, as if kipping is a sheer slog. She does her hair in a bun, olden style, except when she goes to bed. My mind wandered after Lydia, deep in slumber … Where was I? A rival divvy.

Evidence: Tinker was busy searching for Roadie's missing sister Vyna. Tied up with Thekla, I'd sent Oddly after the mazarine. And it had already gone.

More evidence: that fish, Tinker's words, had been shuffed — illicitly pre-sold. You could count on the fingers of one hand the people who'd spot, as I had, a J. Cooper display of antique stuffed fish.

Yet more evidence: lately, I'd been out-sprinted on seven genuine, heart-burning antiques. One that really grieved me was a plain flat piece of iron with a sharp angular point. It was priceless, a 1490s fireback from some country house nigh a century older than Good Queen Bess. In a scrap metal yard in Goldhanger. The yard gaffer was out, and I was hurrying to meet Betty about a silver salver so I didn't have time to wheedle the fireback out of the gaffer's bonny missus. I sent Tinker. Unbelievably, he'd come back empty-handed. Somebody had bought it minutes before.

Now, this simply doesn't happen. Never ever. I could understand losing the mazarine – everybody falls for silver, queen of metals. I could accept losing the fish display – angling is the kingdom's most frequented 'sport'. I could even believe losing a Bow Factory soft-paste porcelain mug, decorated with crude copper-plate printed figures coloured in with enamels. It had the one feature that makes collectors squeal with joy – a little heart-shaped blob at the handle's bottom. You may have to look hard to see it, but it means a fortune.

But a soot-encrusted chunk of iron from behind a fireplace? Crudely made, in a sand-floor mould, rope and sword-handle indents its only decoration?

Never in a million years.

I'd only gone into the scrap yard to ask if I could use their phone. The chimes from the fireback had literally knocked me reeling. I'd told the scrappie's lass not to sell it please, promised the earth ... Gone.

Conclusion: there *must* be an evil divvy in the Eastern Hundreds. He had a car, and money, therefore a backer. Uneasily I thought Big John Sheehan, except he is straight as a die and ferocious, yes. Devious? No. Somebody new in these remote east lands, was funding my mystery foe. It was driving me to drink.

Or it would be, if I hadn't alienated Frothey.

The rain lashed on the windows. The gale howled. The embers fell with a tiny crash. Dozing, I remembered Jessica, in her church. That conversation when Tubb arrived was phoney, some way. Two people pretending they'd never met. Like they both knew all about Carmel's sand job. I watched the embers.

Antiques are the strangest things. People think that some genius makes them, the world applauds and the antiques are fixed for ever. Wrong.

Antiques are a shifting sand. Often they're so ephemeral that they're gone like will-o'-the-wisps. Other times, they're staring you in the face unnoticed. Like poor old Vincent van Gogh's paintings that nobody wanted, and now you have to queue for days even to glimpse them under armed guard. And Lowry's once-derided paintings of matchstick people in grimy mill townscapes. And Munch's 'formless, vulgar, brutal' paintings, that caused such an uproar in Berlin in 1892 that the artist rose to fame.

It can go the other way. What is at first priceless can become cheap, like money, that halves in value each decade. A generation ago, you couldn't give old steam railway engines away. Today, whole towns turn out merely to see one puff by. We have a well-heeled woman called Fortune Phoebe, who stands eternally by the council rubbish dump. She makes a mint out of discarded dross, squirrelling a car load away every nightfall.

Like the 'lilly-narcissus', a.k.a. the tulip. Brought innocently from its native Turkey to Vienna about the 1540s, the tulip showed up in England in 1577 to no ado. So what, a different flower? Then it took off, in Holland in 1594. For forty years the Dutch went crazy. One – *one* – bulb of a red-white stripey flower fetched 10,000 guilders, the cost of a pricey town house. Dealers used diamond-merchants' scales to weigh bulbs out. The dirt cheap old flower zoomed to priceless.

Until a terrible April in 1637, when the whole inverted pyramid – paper shares of paper wealth on paper promises balancing on a tulip – toppled. Speculators' fortunes crumpled. Ruin stalked Holland's proud cities. The lesson, if only we'd hark: money is whim.

Sometimes, too, antiques can change and we forget. The worthless suddenly focuses today's lust in a new way unprecedented even though nothing about the antique has changed. Nowadays, we all boggle at the daft Victorians who couldn't see the blindingly obvious, that barmy old Turner's strange daubs are worth a king's ransom.

Sand job, but where? No prizes for guessing that Roger Boxgrove's new wealth was funding it. He'd put me on to Carmel, the instigator. But what was the stripe? Jessica, and Tubb already knew, if I'd guessed right. I knew of few museum loans, though I don't follow news much. Should I ask Lydia, in the morning? Something she'd said vexed me, but I didn't know what.

It's unusual for me not to wake about five. The wind had abated, the rain a steady drizzle. In the gloaming Mavis's garden seemed to have been put through a tumble drier. I tiptoed about, had my bath without splashing. By the time I emerged, unshaven but clean, I knew Lydia was listening. You can always feel a woman awake in bed, even with walls in between.

Toast is easiest. I managed to strangle the toaster's beeping when it popped. Mavis only had inferior marmalade, really annoying. What good is stealing a neffie breakfast? I brewed up. The house listening in silence. We're odd, people.

I stole a teaspoon, drank the milk, nicked the milk bottle, Mavis's kitchen salt, a half-pint commemoration mug, and a bottle of spring water. Off to make some free money. We homeless waifs have to.

Dressed, dry, I let myself out, walked to the bypass, where I got a lift from a returning student. I told him I was late for my fishing smack. He drove me the extra three miles to the harbour.

Brad was about to put to sea. With a cheery greeting I jumped aboard, thrilled that his lass Patsy was with him. She's the most beautiful female on earth, dark eyes, pale skin, lips you'd jump into without hanging on to the selour. She's one of these exquisite women who wears clumsy garb to accentuate the entrancing figure beneath.

'After mackerel, Lovejoy?' Brad joked. He knows I think fish come in batter.

'Ha ha, Brad,' I said gravely. 'Land me at Toosey Stone?'

'Morning, Lovejoy,' said Patsy, stopping the world.

Weakly I returned the greeting, sat in the thwarts, whatever those are. The clouds were wearing thin, the wind whippy.

'What's in the bag, Lovejoy?' Patsy asked.

Brad grinned. 'Lovejoy's broke. He's hunting amber.'

She eyed me, coiling a rope. Everything Patsy does looks erotic. We'd once made smiles when Brad was away at Birmingham's flintlocks auctions. I hoped Brad didn't suspect. I wouldn't like to fall overboard.

'Amber? *Hunting* amber? At Toosey Ness?'

'I'll show you,' I offered, and quickly added, 'Er, when you're both free.'

Toosey Ness is the local way of saying Saint Osyth's Point, after the priory. It's marked by a great stone, for sailors to take sightings. There's one each side of every estuary, predating the Romans.

'Amber's cast up on shore after storms.'

'Got enough salt there, Lovejoy?' Brad's often seen me wash for amber.

'Aye, ta. I nicked all Mavis had.'

'Mavis who?' Patsy asked, quick as a flash.

The boat pulled as the river widened and the sea's expanse showed.

'Mind your own business, Patsy,' I said. 'Have you a bowl?' Mavis who, indeed. Women are nosey.

Brad put the sails up, hauling away, Patsy heave-hoing along. I clung on. The wind tugged and shoved. Land receded. We were in the North Sea.

Half an hour later I plopped onto the muddy foreshore and was alone on a desolate sea mudbank in the dawn, with solid land two furlongs of mud away. I was lonely, but my pursuit of the evil divvy needed money, and amber was the only free money left.

My shoes sucking at every step, I ploshed along the windswept shore after the precious sea gold.

Every amber hunter's dream is the famous 'Burma Amber' in South Kensington's museums, huge at 33 pounds 10 ounces. But not all amber's immense. It's not all amber, either.

Balts favour white opaque amber, we clear honey-coloured amber. I particularly love the deep red ambers of China. On the beach, amber looks like flotsam, utter rubbish. Hunt some yourself. It's easy. It's free. You'll find a piece sooner or later.

Measure ten level teaspoons of salt into half a pint of clean water. The specific gravity of this fluid will be near the all-important 1.13. Then scour the beach. Plastic's trouble – shredded plastic's everywhere nowadays. Your magic bowl of salt solution is your secret weapon, for most plastic sinks in it. Glass also sinks. Stones sink. Rusty metal sinks. Rubber floats, but bends. Wood floats, but wood splits like, well, wood. Also, flotsam wood is pale, veined, striated.

That leaves only two things floating on your salt water. One is jet – itself a seashore thing, black, and a genuine organic gem, though fashion killed it long since except in Whitby.

The other floater is amber. Never mind what it looks like. If it doesn't sink, it's a contender. It's S.G. will be 1.12 or just less, which is all that matters.

Within ten minutes I found one scrap, then two more. Another half hour, six, one thumb-nail size. Two hours I went at it. A dilute sun started washing St Osyth's tower, which ancient smugglers' swift cutters used for guidance to the despair of the Excise. I made fresh salt solutions as I went.

Finally I had twenty pieces. The largest chunk was cindery brown, nearly an inch across. Several bits were the size of my little fingernail, the smallest a spicule. I'd got enough to survive.

Even a remote windswept shore is wondrous. I found several blobs of copperas, but left them. In years gone by, these heavy masses were excitedly sought on the Eastern Hundreds sealands by village boys.

They'd teem down at low tide to Walton and suchlike places, gathering sacks of the stuff. In one year, 150 tons.

People'd buy the copperas, which country folk still call 'vitriol', and put it into open-air tanks. Rainwater would wash its goodness into lead buckets. This horrible liquid (it stinks to high heaven, really niffs) was then reduced in a heated lead-lined boiler, into crystals of iron sulphates, your original vitriol. Once, highly saleable, but not now. It's still used by the older antique forgers, but younger fakers have no patience, too hooked on mass markets to do a proper job.

There were other things. Wood, jetsam from ships. Here, I'd once found a Roman coin, a denarius sadly honed by the sand. You occasionally find fossils, ammonites. As I hunted, I saw Wonker beachcombing three miles to the north – he's a flotsam sculptor, holds shows in London galleries. He didn't wave. Odd. I'm sure he saw me.

Elevenish, I hailed a man fishing in a rowing pram out of Pyefleet Channel.

'Caught any yet?' I hullooed.

'Not a thing.'

'Ferry me, please? Not near the oyster beds.'

He laughed. 'Squeamish, eh, booy? Brad told me.'

All in all, a good start. Ominous.

8

TO SNARE SOMEBODY I didn't even know existed, I'd need gelt and help. I headed back to Lydia's mother's place. A vintage Bentley stood outside.

'Lovejoy.' Mavis welcomed me glaring, a tribute to finishing schools, polo, and vitamin supplements. She made my name a denunciation.

'Hello, Mavis.' I gave her time to invite me in for breakfast. Nothing. 'Er, is Lydia in, please?'

'No.' Her lip curled in scorn. I like to see that, even if it's me that's being bollocked. Mavis's lips are magic. '*Look* at you, Lovejoy! Filthy, muddy. I've forbidden Lydia to have anything more to do with you.'

I didn't understand. 'I want help, please.'

'You mean you want some woman to scrounge off, to … to *use*, Lovejoy! Don't come here again!'

'But …'

'Lydia is joining Lissom and Prenthwaite – real professionals! I have just arranged Lydia's salary. Mr Prenthwaite has signed forms.'

'She can't.' I was aghast. 'She's my appentice.'

'Apprentice? For how many more years, Lovejoy? And you stole my commemoration mug! A wedding memento! I shall report you to the police!'

Oh, hell. I'd left it on the beach. 'Look, love … '

'Don't you dare "love" me!'

The door slammed. I turned, nowhere to go, with my little sack of raw amber. I felt sorry for it. Umpteen millions of years in forming, the most beautiful bio-gem in Creation, reduced to being hawked about. Rain came. I thought of Roger's posh scheme, of the aromatic Jessica, Carmel, and her superstitious Tubb. I was hungry.

Hunger means food. The card was in my pocket. I found a phone kiosk, told a sulky operator I'd been instructed to reverse the charges, and got through to the Mayfair number. She'd promised me grub, after all.

'Hello? Lovejoy, for Orla Maltravers Featherstonehaugh.'

'This is she.' Brisk, curt.

'Er, sorry about last night. I tried ... '

'Don't lie, Lovejoy. Be here, five-thirty, today.'

'I can't. I've no money, and I'm ... ' Mavis had spotted it, so all women would. 'I'm filthy.'

No question, just an amused assertion. 'Then clean yourself up.'

'I can't. My home's gone.' Even to me I sounded pathetic.

Orla purred, 'Stand or deliver, our Thekla. You weren't destitute at the fashion show. What happened?' She was falling about laughing, but hard in the voice.

'Are you a dealer?' Into the unexpected silence I said eagerly, 'I've harvested some sea amber. I'll fake you a Georgian pendant. Just give me a place to work.'

'You'll *what*?'

Well, she'd been too good to be true. When all else fails, try truth. 'I rang hoping you'd stand me a meal, love.'

'Is it really that bad?'

She was probably a fashioneer friend of Thekla's anyway. 'Cheers, love. Ta for the offer of yesterday.'

She started to say something, but I rang off. I walked into rain. Well, rain washes mud off.

Behind the town library's a derelict area. Rag-and-bone men, shoddy-and-tat dealers, assemble there. When I was little, they'd go round our streets crying 'Rag bo-o-o-o-one! Donkey sto-o-o-o-one!' For old rags or bones you got a block of white, grey, sandy rubbing stone, to do your front steps with. Donkey carts have gone now. It's all dodgy pick-up trucks with peeling number plates. The space is about an acre, weeds, bare soil, rusting cars, and a shed where Kent the Rammer sells tea and fruit cake. When all else fails, this is the place. A few people were mulling over loads of clag in the damp. I drifted to the tea shed.

'Lovejoy?' Tinker, begrimed mittens full of cake, was slurping his breakfast in his natural habitat. Sometimes he sleeps in abandoned vans, to save having to cross into St Peter's churchyard, his permanent abode.

'Wotcher, Tinker. I'm looking for somewhere to work.' I felt slightly odd, my insides palpitating. I looked about; not an antique in sight.

'Been amber fishing? Kent's got better.'

Kent the Rammer's a ram raider. He raced motors at Silverstone,

Brands Hatch, the famous places. Retired for taking bribes, he's in demand for driving rammers — nicked cars fitted with battering rams, for crashing into shops or warehouses. It's the modern way. Birmingham rammers are best, present company excepted. I'd seen Kent actually do it, and he's dynamite. He's slight, placid-looking, butter wouldn't melt and all that.

'Wotcher, Lovejoy.' Kent leant over his counter. 'Fire tigers, three sets. Poncey, but maybe old.'

Now, you used to see fire irons at house clearance sales when auntie's imbecile cousins sold her house off. Poker, fire tongs, and a little shovel is one set. Remember when everybody had coal fires?

Guess what common antiques have soared most in price over the past thirty years. Have a stab. Impressionist paintings? Tompion clocks? Georgian silver, used by the Prince Regent? None of the above.

The answer is fire irons. Once, you couldn't give them away. They were scrap, for pennies. Astonishingly, you can make your fortune from them.

Unless you're like me, able to detect the melodious chimes of an antique's secret beauty, you have to know what people want. That means learning. And anybody can learn fire irons.

Think only of the shovels. Fancy shovels are carved. Shell shapes, bell shapes, hearts, flowers, rounded shovels with twist-stem handles. Iron, of course, the first ones were. But came the age of brass. The Victorians, my heroes, put brass handles on the steel shafts. *The brass handles almost always unscrew and make a perfect fit.* Valuable tip, that.

'Got a few,' Kent staggered me by saying.

'*Don't!*' I yelped. As scavengers looked up at the fuss, I ahemed and strolled to Rammer's side door.

He got the point. Tinker came to shield me from sight. Rammer handed me a pierced bell-shaped fire shovel, steel. I started to sweat. This explained my odd feeling, for it was genuine. Twisted steel handle, matching rivets symmetrically placed to hold the undamaged, exquisitely pierced, thistle pattern blade.

'Want to see the others?' Rammer asked casually, turning to serve a vagrant motor dealer tea and a wad.

Weak at the knees, I waited until the customer had gone. 'The rest, Rammer?'

'I think there's three sets. Not much use, though.'

'The ponceys, please?' Rammer'd meant fancy. 'Any with ... ?'

With leaves twining along the handle, different colours of copper, vine tendrils perfectly preserved. And fire tongs still with their dual central tips, quite like axle caps, covering the ends of the pivot rivet. Nowadays, this Art Nouveau work may not look much, but it means wealth. Victorian craftsmen were so keen on Nature's emblems that they threw caution to the winds. Hang durability, they cried, show off your skill. So they swapped brass and steel for the milder copper. Hence, copper fire irons are rarest. Like these.

Tears filled my eyes. Perfection, a dream. And I'd begun to doubt myself. I was off my rocker.

'Here, Lovejoy.' Tinker stuffed my bag of amber into my pocket. I must have let it drop. Rammer went to serve somebody at the front of his little shed. Tinker hid the fire irons under his coat flap.

'How come, Tinker?'

He grinned with triumph. Bristly stubble improves him somehow.

'That old fireback, Lovejoy. I asked, along the road they're building. Some old houses got spliced. Where there's Elizabethan firebacks, there might be more stuff. So I tipped Rammer off. He's done rams for the navvies' ganger. But they'll cost, Lovejoy.'

'Price doesn't matter, Tinker. I'll pay.' I'd have to. I'd let myself get too dispirited. Tinker had done well, taken over, doing my job. I felt ashamed.

'Three full sets, and one matching fender.'

'No bucket?' I held my breath.

'Aye, Lovejoy. Copper, flowers going daft on its outside.'

An Art Nouveau coal scuttle, properly called a bucket, with a fire-kerb, would buy a house. Or my cottage back.

'What do we do, Lovejoy?'

'I'll have the gelt for Rammer by closing time. Cash. Tell him my price is ... ' Quickly I judged Rammer's old Escort corroding listlessly nearby, Rammer's affair with a barmaid that had cost him. His brother was in gaol. Rammer has a gambling streak. 'A new motor plus a thousand in his hand. Okay?'

'Right, Lovejoy. Here,' Tinker asked as I turned to go, 'got enough for a pint?'

'Sorry, mate.' Dealing in a fortune in one breath, not a bean the next.

'Where'll you go now, son?' he asked.

That made me pause. I ran through possibilities in my mind, then slumped at reality.

'Aureole's,' I said sadly, and went, lamb to Aureole's dating chain.

Even when I try to look posh I'm no Douglas Fairbanks, Sen. or Jun. But she had a vested interest in lending me her flat to do the amber.

As I hurried off I was hailed by Vinegar. He always has money, just enough to cue scroungers.

'Wotcher, Lovejoy. Do me a job?'

'How do, Vinegar. No. Too pushed.'

Folk like Vinegar are always in troubles of their own making. He's nicknamed Vinegar because he scooped a wondrous antique once for a song, clearing out an attic. A marble bust of Pope Sixtus IV, of unholy memory. It was mint, worth a fortune, and he'd paid cornflakes. Then he committed a cardinal sin – cleaned it with vinegar, a.k.a. acetic acid. Marble's very name is a byword for hardness ('Hard as marble,' et lying cetera), yet it's soft, as stone goes. Kitchen vinegar rots it like bad teeth. I slaved to rescue his precious bust for weeks, impregnating it with coloured waxes like the ancient Romans and Greeks did. No good. The bust was ruined.

Watch how an antique dealer approaches any marble object. He'll run a hand over it, rubbing his fingers afterwards to see if they're waxy. You can tell that marble has been 'wax improved' by examining the surface in oblique sunlight, to see wax. That's why dealers always take time studying 'improvable' marble antiques. All the marble stones lend themselves to fakery. Thus, the pretty serpentine – soft enough to cut with a knife – is often dyed to imitate jade. Plain old calcite, stained by cobalt pigments, is a famous let's-pretend turquoise. Marble itself is sometimes stained coral to fake, well, coral. Cheap humdrum magnesite subs for precious lapis lazuli. The list is almost endless. My favourite dye is indigo, dissolved in urine. Gently heat the marble, dip it in, and presto! – a precious new gemstone instead of common marble. It's a rotten trick, though, and I would never do it. Hardly ever, honest.

'I've a bit of dosh, Lovejoy.' Vinegar's droopy dogface was under an umbrella. I slowed for shelter.

'What's it to do with, Vin?'

'Sfrags, Lovejoy. A job lot. Divvy them, eh?' Sphragistics is the study of seals – the amulet and insignia kind, not those cruel nautical salmon slayers.

'Are they any good?'

'Brilliant. Romans, I reckon.'

'No, Vinegar. Ta. I'm doing contract work.'

He halted. 'You don't look in work, Lovejoy.'

'Cheers, Vinegar.' I went, plunged in despond. If word had

reached Vinegar that I was touting for work, I'd sunk really low. He was always last to get any news.

Anyway, his Roman sfrags were probably a group of eight I'd made months back from shells I'd snaffled at Brightlingsea. Forged Roman seals are quick to make, five a day, and cheap. Last thing I wanted was to buy my own fake handiwork back.

Twenty minutes later I was in Aureole's flat. She gave me the key, delighted. It's down by St Leonard's. I had a bath, got my clothes drying on her radiator. I towelled dry, brewed up, foraged and scoffed, then lay on her bed, alone. You can't have everything.

9

COMING TO, I washed the amber in cold salted water for a proper look.

Folk wrongly call it 'sea crystal'. Amber contains no real crystals at all. I nicked a lens out of Aureole's specs. You sometimes see small insects, ants, and the like trapped within. Gruesome, but ladies, and antique dealers, love them. Proof of antiquity, they think. Not quite true – a bloke along the coast incorporates live ants into copal varnish and does a pretty good fake amber. You can be fooled. Copal resin, worthless, is the only amber fake you need worry about. It comes from all sorts of hot-climate trees, and you find bits dislodged from lumber jettisoned by shipping. The famous 'electric test' for amber – rubbing it on your blouse, then seeing if it will pick up paper by its negative electric charge, is useless; almost any plastic comb will do it. The Ancient Greeks called amber 'electrum', from the sun, hence our word electricity.

Aureole has a gas cooker. Finding no paper clips, I borrowed one of her earrings, prised out the modern grotty stone and chucked it. I heated the wire to redness. With the blade from her manicure set I scraped a flake off each amber piece, touched it to the hot wire, and got a satisfying aromatic pong, a good positive sign. One or two little flies were inside. I avoided their reproachful gaze, transfixed since Eocene and Palaeocene times these sixty million years.

One good-sized piece was cloudy, whitish. I searched Aureole's kitchen for some rapeseed oil, but she had none, really uncooperative. The trick is dunk the amber in hot oil. Cloudy amber clears quickly – the oil's supposed to soak into the minute bubbles. I hate it, because it's cheating. The oil causes minuscule circular cracks, which make the amber gleam more. Everybody does it, even to valuable cuts from block amber. Needless to say, if you're offered an amber pendant, examine it with a lens. Those little fissures produce an almost sequin-like glittery look and are a give-away that the amber's been abused.

Like I was doing. Sorry.

Then a slice of luck. Aureole had just ironed clean linen handkerchiefs. I borrowed two, tore them into strips, laid my ambers one to a strip. Her whisky I'd poured into her fridge's ice tray, so the alcohol separated. Soak linen in neat alcohol, you have the perfect instrument for amber. Not only does it clean it, but it gives further proof – copal smudges your white cloth after thirty seconds.

Aureole also had a pressure cooker. I scraped the ambers clean, heated some water, bagged selected ambers in a strip torn from her skirt, and immersed the bag in the pan. While it warmed, I bent her eyelash-crimpers – horrible things, give me the willies – to make a pressing tool. She could always buy new. And why'd she muck about with her bonny eyes anyway?

Amber warmed just short of boiling water goes pliable. You just push bits together. After, heat it to about 180 degrees, maybe less, and mould it firmly. I borrowed her garlic press, which compresses amber as well as a proper tool if you hammer a flat piece of metal into its perforated base – luckily, Aureole had a modern pewter pendant I used for that. Improvised gadgetry's never easy. I took five goes, and ruined her implements, but you can't make an omelette without et cetera. So I made a lovely 'ambroid' chunk, made of smaller pieces. We cheat like this because a large piece is more valuable than several bits, for antique amber pendants, earrings, necklaces.

You can always tell ambroid, though. Look closely, you'll see interfaces – planes where the light changes, like that bobbled glass in porch windows. The only other reliable sign is that ambroid's bubbles become stretched instead of round.

After all this, I owned one large piece of ambroid, and six smaller decent genuine ambers. In celebration I brewed up, fried some eggs and bacon, borrowed her cheese, and finished her bread. She hadn't any puddings, which I thought a bit stingy. Why invite a friend in, with nothing to eat? Aureole ought to get her act together.

One niggle. Why did Wonker ignore me on the shore? We're pals. I'd done him favours. He was making an antique wall plaque for me. Odd.

Worn out, I hid the ambers, lay starkers on the bed and slept the sleep of the just.

There wasn't much grub left when I woke. I scavenged for calories. I put the telly on, and found a fashion show. I observed their antics, bemused.

The narrator's words, for instance. Frantic-alloso? Petrificationally? When he asked his third desperate question, 'Is this black zooish frondelle actually *happenish*?' I switched off. I was in enough trouble from Thekla's mob.

Hanging about almost got me caught. I was barely out of the door before Aureole's small purple motor came whirring round the corner. I ducked out of sight through the little park that backs onto East Hill. It was coming on for dark. The Ship tavern was booming. Mercifully Tinker was in, with Roadie sulking beside him.

'Wotch, Tinker. Got a sec?'

God, but he stank worse than usual. His grubby mittens looked crawling. I asked if he'd seen Roger Boxgrove. He hadn't. I told him to scout, that I was broke.

'Got the amber fancied up, though, eh?'

You have to smile. He's amazing. I've found him sloshed, snoring in a shed for two days blind drunk, and seen him wake, rub his eyes, and say, 'Lovejoy? Hear about them sofa tables at Beccles? Just gone for a song.' It's a gift, news by osmosis. I can't do it, or I would.

'Aye. Here, Tinker. What's Wonker up to?'

'Carving you that fake misericord. Why?'

'Not fake, Tinker,' I corrected patiently in case anybody was listening. 'Genuine antique misericord from an unnamed cathedral. Only, Wonker saw me on the shore. He didn't come over, not a cheep.'

'That bird, I suppose.'

Bird? I started guiltily, but couldn't remember having done anything illicit lately with Wonker's bird. She's comely, from Black Notley. People don't need evidence to blame me, I've found.

'Not you, son,' Tinker gravelled out, hawking up phlegm and spitting expertly into the pub fire over folks' heads. 'He's lost his bird to that chain game Aureole runs.' His mouth corrugated in disapproval. He's a prim old soak.

'Nothing to do with me?' I asked hopefully.

'Nar, son. Ought not to be allowed.'

Relief flooded in. 'That all? Look, Tinker. I want a place to mount the sea gold. Benjie?'

'Not Benjie, Lovejoy. Turning out Victorian jewellery like Ford motors for foreigners.'

'Hell fire.' I tried getting a pint for Tinker on the slate but the bar girls looked askance.

'There's some bird from up home's phoning Antiques Centre.' Up

64

home to Tinker means north, where we both come from. He cited, 'Stella Entwistle wants Lovejoy to ring Bran Mantle.'

'Never heard of him. Where can I work?'

'Your own workshop?' he suggested. 'It's only boarded up.'

Not a bad idea. I brightened, found Tellso playing tap room billiards and borrowed a few quid off him on the strength of having a collection of antique horse brasses for sale. I promised them by ten the following morning, bought Tinker enough ale to swim in, and hit the road.

On Head Street by the post office I nearly jumped out of my skin when a bloke yelled my name.

'Lovejoy! Don't, for God's sake!'

'What? What?' I screeched, scared stiff.

'The cracks! Have you no sense?' Tubb caught me up. 'You want bad luck on the sand job?'

We'd not need bad luck, with Tubb bawling about the secret robbery.

'Why don't you just send the Plod a frigging postcard, you noisy sod?'

'Keep our luck, Lovejoy, and we'll do a grand job.' He made a thumb and finger sign, both hands.

'Like your last robbery?' I cut back, then wished I hadn't because his face fell. 'Sorry, Tubb. Having a bad spell.'

'Spell? Portenta's a friend. Reversal of fortune's her speciality this equinox. She hexed the elections ... '

'No.' I knew Portenta, all spells and heather.

'Definite dosh and date for the sand job, Lovejoy,' Tubb said, loud enough to alert the coastguard. 'I'll call Portenta.'

Hearing that Carmel'd given the go-ahead was all very well. Portenta always uses Hedingham Castle's cauldron, as secret as our fire brigade.

'Better not, Tubb.' I invented quickly, 'Er, I've got a lady who's the best. I'm,' I added with daring, 'her nephew.'

The bus was on time. It'd never been on time before. I don't like unreliability, and played hell with the driver Diana all the way to the village. She took not a blind bit of notice. Women never do. Coming home was like old times.

Notices bragged of the law's assault on my insulted home, planks nailed over the windows, hefty wire mesh on boards barricading my porch. Stern penalties threatened anyone removing (a) seals, (b) notices, or (c) anything else.

Sad, I walked among the weeds and brambles. The thought of other people ransacking my cottage makes me feel sick. Bailiffs, burglars, it's always the way. International fraudsters hive off fortunes, pull the old bankruptcy dodge, and get millions in what's laughably called 'legal aid' to live in Park Lane. Your ordinary bloke gets his cottage boarded up.

Houses are really odd. I stood gazing in the wet garden. If I'd been on holiday, the cottage wouldn't be different. What I mean is, it would still look lived in. Now, though? I'd been evicted barely hours, and already it looked abandoned. It's as if a home actually *knows*. I shivered.

'What's the matter?' some woman asked behind me.

'Mind your own frigging business, missus.' I didn't look round. I wanted fewer people, not more.

'I'm sorry, Lovejoy. I tried to stop them.'

'Oh, aye.'

I'm never cynical, but calamity makes you wonder. Everybody 'really tries' to help, wishes you well, sends love, says they're thinking of you. Yet you finish up in the mire just the same. There'd probably be a shoal of good luck cards on the mat. Even Portenta's hocus-pokery is more sincere, and she's sham through and through. At least she believes something.

'Want a lift to town?'

'No, ta. I'll stay.' I went to the, my, cottage.

Her worried voice said, 'You'll get arrested'.

Start at the beginning, I suppose, would be best. I used a sapling lathe − 'pole' lathe, they called it anciently − in the undergrowth. It wasn't hard to find, just a couple of saplings and a string between, with a treadle and holding ropes. I searched the weeds, came up with a rusting hammer, a saw, a battered plane.

The sods had boarded up my workshop, only a garage converted to proper use. I savaged the planks, broke the law's seal and entered the cottage. I had the wit to knock up a mediaeval rope hinge for the planks once I'd nailed them back together. That way, anyone on the lane would think it still barred, while the planks became an improvised door. I put the saw where I'd found it. It would get me in by winkling it in a gap I deliberately left.

Lord of my own domain, I'd done a thorough job. Nobody outside could see a glim. Electricity, water, gas, phone, everything was cut off. I found my oil lantern, and lo there was light and the light was good, so they could get stuffed.

My workshop didn't need defences, because its door faces away from the footpath. I started work.

Amber is hell to cut, bonny to carve, and ecstasy to polish. My trick is to warm it in my mouth – it shatters less, and doesn't flake. I have an old dentist's drill, worked with my foot, and use burrs and bits for fine work. Unless you've a lifetime's experience, always fake by copying. Wedgwood's designs are best. For heaven's sake, though, use a piece of felt glued to your smoothest burr, and don't miss out any surface depressions except the deepest. I did an arbor, an urn, and added a Greek goddess because I liked her shape. Took two hours. Then I felted – polished – it by hand.

'Tea's up, Lovejoy.' Same voice.

She must have waited for me to finish before interrupting. Women persevere, that's for sure.

'Can't be. I've got none.'

'I've bought in, and a camper's Primus.'

Curious, I looked. It was Faye, lone lovely who'd got ribbed at Thekla's fashion show.

'Ta, love. Bring any chips?'

'Appetites later, Lovejoy.' She smiled. 'I've a sheaf of messages. A smelly old man says that Kent the Rammer sold the tigers. Does that make sense?'

For a moment I went giddy. A drizzle started, wet onshore wind. Kent had sold the fire-irons? But it was imposs ... It wasn't impossible. Not if somebody was following me about *seeing what I divvied*. Or Tinker. Who on my side wasn't on my side?

'Are you all right, Lovejoy?' she asked. I'd sat down on the little decorative wall I'll finish one day. But one day is none day, old Lancashire saying.

'Mmmh, ta. I've been hunched over too long.'

'A barmaid called Frothey is angry. And some antique dealers. That smelly old soldier ... '

'My friend.' I gave her the bent eye. 'Tinker's my barker, the best in the business.'

'I apologise, Lovejoy.' She went red. 'And Roger Boxgrove. And Lydia your apprentice. Tinker says phone Stella Entwistle, and how long are you going to be Bran Mantle. I didn't understand that. And a cross middle-aged lady called Mavis. Aureole is going to sue you for every last farthing for wrecking her flat.'

That last really surprised me. You make Aureole feel needed, and what thanks do you get?

'Some others I've written down.' She took my arm. We went inside. 'Look at them when we've had our snack. I have a suite booked at the George.'

The thought of grub made me swoon. 'You've … ?'

She smiled prettily, explained, 'I'm your chainer. I've hired you, Lovejoy.'

'Look, love,' I began, embarrassed.

'Please don't feel at all put out. You're paid for and above board.' She coloured some more. 'Well, not quite *that*, you understand. Arranged.'

'Who with? I've no money to go taking anybody out.'

'Aureole.' She was pleased with herself. 'I've never done this sort of thing. But I do believe you should start with the creator of a system, don't you? You *did* invent chain dating, Lovejoy?'

The place had been tidied up.

'But I didn't think I'd be anybody's link.'

'Well, let's consider that while we have supper. We can leave for the George when we're ready.'

Things were looking up. I smiled at Faye, thinking what a beautiful lass she actually was. Some women really do get it right.

10

'WHAT DO I have to do?' I asked Faye as we approached the George. I like the old place. In its day it's been everything from a brothel to a lazaro, plague hospital to a pilgrim's rest.

'I'm a newspaper columnist. There's your answer.'

She led the way through the lounge. Hardly anybody in, the evening yet young. A crusty Colonel Blimp nodded over his *Times*. The log fire blazed. A waitress swayed about, black dress, starched apron. Two ladies sat sipping tea, hot crumpets in the dish. It was all happening.

For a second I wondered whether to scarper, but chucked the idea as aroma wafted out from the carvery. News columnists and me don't mix. I never read what they make up.

'When, Lovejoy?' she asked in the foyer.

'When what?' I yelped. 'Er, sorry?'

She did the woman's non-smile, so innocent you could tell she was laughing.

'When would you like supper?'

'Now, please.' It's not my fault if women never eat. Because she'd had one chip and a lettuce last Easter, was I expected to starve?

She wanted the table moved, our seats shifted. I swear waiters like this sort of thing. She had two rushing about demented.

'Look,' I said, uneasy. 'Are you investigating that dig thing? Maldon?'

'Let's order first, Lovejoy.'

We did the menu mutter, then I got down to it. No good ruining free nosh by worrying over past sins.

'It wasn't me last October, Faye,' I confessed. 'It wasn't my fault that land got sold. Maldon authorities allowed builders to erect 450 houses right on the most valuable historic site in the entire world. Well, in Maldon,' I ended lamely. 'Can I have your bread?' Women don't like bread, dunno why.

'Please take it.' She sat, chin on her interlaced fingers, and said with wide-eyed erotic innocence, 'It isn't what folk are saying, is it?'

'No,' I said, swiftly buttering her roll in case she changed her mind. 'They *would* say that. Look, Faye. Ask why an ancient town allows a property company to bulldoze a rural site.' I glanced about, nervous. 'Not far from Heybridge. The council is only spending public money to help the homeless, so what better reason? Why *not* build in that particular spot?'

'Envelope, please,' she quipped. 'The answer is?'

'Because it's the only untouched Iron Age town we've got left, love!' Tears filled my eyes. I couldn't help it. 'That Heybridge site was a pristine mediaeval borough, on an Anglo-Saxon township, on a Roman colony, on an Iron Age town!'

'Are you all right?'

'Course I am, silly cow. It's the onion.' The soup was stinging my eyes.

Her eyes were on me. She hadn't started hers.

'Didn't folk realise?'

'It's a question of reverence for life.' I couldn't continue for a minute. 'Think. Those ancient Iron Age people, living out their little lives. They must have believed that us folk coming after, their descendants, would surely *care*. They must have sat by their fires smiling, thinking how their future children – *us* – would revere their ancestors' relics. They buried small treasures as gifts, offerings to some tree god perhaps, tokens to us who would come after. But did we?'

Her face seemed to be swimming. 'Did we, Lovejoy?'

'Did we frigging hell. Incompetent money-grabbing councillors sent the builders ripping in. Archaeologists – inept criminals to a man – hove up, started frantic excavations only days ahead of the bulldozers. The press – you – made a hue and cry: *Race Against Time!* I framed headlines with my hands.

'I'm sorry.' She sounded surprisingly lifelike for a reporter. 'Shall we talk afterwards?'

'Shut up and listen. In eleven days the archaeologists excavated quarter of a million pieces of pottery *alone*, plus God knows what else.'

'Wasn't there a Maldon spokesman ... ?'

'There always is.' I scraped my bowl viciously. 'They said, *We'd no idea.*'

'But they knew?'

'The Heybridge site's been known at least two hundred years, love.' I slurped a bit of the wine. 'It's called administrative efficiency. Or bribery.'

Her eyes never left me. 'Why does your name keep coming up, Lovejoy?'

'Look.' I was fed up with accusations. 'When councillors and magnates combine to exploit land, our Iron Age *ghosts* for Christ's sake, haven't I a right to do something?'

'So you did, Lovejoy?'

'Okay. It *was* me. I organised the gang that broke those two fellers' legs. And okay, I hired the moonspenders – enthusiasts with electronic metal-seeking devices.'

'Let's get this straight,' she said. 'It really truly *wasn't* you who injured those two men?'

'Honest,' I said most sincerely. 'Hand on my heart. What's happened to the grub?'

'We have to choose it ourselves, I think,' she said in a faint voice. 'In a moment.'

She was taking a hell of a time finishing a salad. 'Rules are rules when you're nicking artefacts, Faye.'

'Of course, Lovejoy. I see that.'

I'd recovered, smiling at a past success. 'We lifted over seven thousand items in nineteen days. I've not been paid yet.'

'Lifted? Meaning stolen?' She looked horrified.

'No.' I took her salad and finished it. Wait for her, we'd never make the real food. 'They're left by our own ancestors for us.'

'When did the men's legs get broken?' she asked faintly.

'That pair nicked stuff on the sly. It's against the rules. You pinch historic artefacts for the team. Everything went to Worcester,' I said proudly, my heart lifting with emotion. 'Every pot we lifted, every pennyweight of metal. Beautiful.' I almost filled up.

The two blokes were caught selling Roman coins from the excavation. One had a Roman doctor's probe, a straight thin instrument with a terminal midget spoon. I was called to the tavern after closing time and shown their spoils. I didn't see the miscreants, Dogleg and Chaplin, but I knew them. Furnace was their ganger, mortified. He's an astonishingly gentle bloke, who funds two children's hospital beds.

'See, Lovejoy,' he'd said in his kindly Devon. 'My lads get very hairy.'

'I know, Furnie,' I'd said back. I was frightened, because I'd once seen Big John's gang simply take a house apart. And I do mean brick by brick, simply vanish the entire place, when the owner delayed payment. It had taken fifteen hours one Friday night while the non-payer's family was in London. He'd returned Saturday morn to find the dwelling gone, his furniture auctioned off for a children's charity. The house itself was rubble under a Buckinghamshire housing estate. I was scared witless because Big John hadn't really been angry on that occasion, merely disappointed. I could remember worse times when he'd been furious, and wanted three-league boots next time. He had funded the Maldon rescue.

'The lads want Dogleg and Chaplin limping, Lovejoy,' Furnace had said, sad.

'They do?' I'd croaked, desperate.

Furnace was relentless. 'Yes or no. If no, what?'

Indeed. Sweat dripped down my face. I still feel it in the candle hours when memory won't let go. If I'd let Dogleg and Chaplin off with a slap on the wrist, it'd prove I was in collusion with them, and I wasn't.

'Do I tell my lads to break their legs, Lovejoy?'

'Better be yes, Furnie,' I said, in anguish.

'Good, Lovejoy,' Furnace was pleased the job was still being run smoothly. He has a smile a saint would kill for. 'Do the right thing, eh?'

He bought me a drink, I remembered. We'd talked of some goalkeeper being accused of taking bribes to throw a football match. Furnace thought it scandalous.

'Lovejoy?' Faye said. She was looking worried.

'Oh. You're ready?'

We rose, chose our meal. I'm clumsy spooning vegetables, always drop some. Faye did it for us. It's lovely to watch a woman; whatever they do's pretty as a picture. As we returned to our table, I caught her looking at me with a calculating air. It suddenly occurred that she hadn't wanted to ask about the Maldon steal at all. Which raised the question, as they say, what the hell?

'What the hell, Faye?' I said, whaling in.

'You guessed, Lovejoy.' She coloured slightly, but not enough for guilt. More a cocky pride from hoodwinking me. 'I want you to bring down a fashion house.' She smiled at my expression, adding quaintly, 'Please.'

'Oh, right,' I said, cavalier. Any day of the week, Lovejoy's the man to destroy a million-zlotnik trade emporium. Was she mad?

Humour them when they're off their trolley or when you want to wreak your wicked way. It's the only tactic.

'You think I'm joking, Lovejoy? Or insane?'

'No! Fashion's serious stuff. I mean, everybody knows it's ... ' I petered out. What, a con? 'It's, well, famous.'

'It's everything, Lovejoy.' She stared past me, entranced. I wondered if some film star had hove in. I almost turned to look. 'Clothes, dress. Fashion is the world.'

By now I was hurling grub down like a stoker coaling up. Time to cut and run. She was beginning to sound like Thekla. I still hadn't recovered from that.

She prattled on about reputations, money, materials, imports, fiscal overloads and amalgamations. I occasionally did a 'Mmmh,' and a 'Really?' or two, to keep her going until the pudding. I didn't understand a word, didn't listen in fact. I suppose women do the same with us. Tit for tat – pun not intended. She talked so much, quite carried away, that I had to scoff her plateful, though I felt she'd too much gravy. You can only take so much.

The lass cleared our plates. I can't resist trifle. One bird I used to know said I was still a child because trifle's for children. Faye didn't want any, but the waitress knew I couldn't stand seeing a woman go hungry, and brought two.

'I need a fashion house to suffer shame, Lovejoy,' she said, wistful. 'It *fully deserves* to.'

'Fine, fine.' Another barmy scheme to ignore through the long nights ahead. 'Which, er, fashion house, love?' I asked grimly, Bill Sykes of the Black Hand Gang. I pulled out a card. 'Got a pen, love?' I was saying when she reached across. The card was Orla's.

Faye went white. 'Orla?' she said in a whisper. 'After he almost *died*?'

I stopped eating. 'Eh?'

Her lips had gone bluish, under the lipstick. '*She all but killed him.*'

Who killed who? 'Who killed who?' I asked, glancing nervously round the carvery.

People stopped dining, to look across. Anas the manager raised his head like a wary stag.

Her voice rose. 'You and Orla, Lovejoy?'

'Shhh!' I tried to calm her. 'I'll blam her shop. Honest, love!'

'You tricked me, Lovejoy!' She stood, collected her handbag, glared. 'Deceived me! You, in with her, Lovejoy!'

The place was silent, except for her hooting and hollering. I tried a smile, nodded, shook my head, whatever this mad woman wanted if only she'd shut up and pretend everything was all right. Then I could clear out, let her screech her head off.

'Nearly murdered!' She burst into tears.

'What's going on?' Anas advanced, beckoning waiters.

Quick as a flash I stood, leaving half a trifle.

'Look, Faye. Sorry, but I've an appointment ... '

And fled up the stairs, across the lounge, through the saloon bar door. As far as I got.

'Hold it, Lovejoy.' Dinsdale stood there, the George's security officer.

For a second I was tempted. He's corpulént, fortyish, looks everybody's pushover, but I've seen him sprint after some baddie like a greyhound, rugby tackle him, then give him a good hiding.

'Wotcher, Dinsdale. I'm late for ... '

'I'm taking you in charge, Lovejoy. The police are on their way. Naughty. Who'd you kill this time?'

'Some barmy bird in there suddenly raised hell. Started blaming me, somebody nearly getting topped.'

'The lady you came with,' he corrected. 'Come along.'

'Amn't I allowed a phone call?' I tried to joke.

'That's America, Lovejoy. Here, do as I say.'

The police came and arrested me, no time for coffee. In a cell twenty minutes later, I remembered a friend whose new baby arrived home. Next morning, this friend dazedly awoke, and asked his missus, 'Jesus. Was all that Monday?' I knew how he felt. Except it was the days coming that were the headache.

11

'KILLED WHO, GEORGE?'

The police sat me on a bench. Not a proper cell, where they'd have to document me with tea, chance to lay my head. Police nicks always smell of armpit and boiled cabbage.

George is a stout bobby with feet too worn out for a real job.

'Can't say.' He tried to look like he was busy. They often pretend they can write.

'State secret, is it, saying who I topped?'

'He survived.'

So I was arrested because I *didn't* kill somebody? Then yesterday must have been a near thing, and all last week, because I'd not slaughtered anybody then either. They'd collared me for innocence.

'Got anything to read, George?'

'Sod off, Lovejoy.'

A woman's magazine lay on the bench, fashion models trying to look like they enjoyed starving so their hips and shoulders showed bones. No breasts, prop legs. The government should make them eat.

'Ah, Lovejoy? In please.'

The office held silver cups from golf tournaments, for this was the abode of one Cradhead, a ploddite of renown. Besuited, floppy fair hair, talks funny from the silver spoon in his mouth, a Chief Constable candidate if ever I saw one.

'Wotcher, Mr Cradhead.' The lads rhyme his name with Spithead. His commonest word is 'ah', but you've to watch out. 'Mr Drinkwater on leave?'

'Ah, yes.'

'Ah, pity.' Drinkwater's his boss, eminently deceivable. This smarm isn't. 'Who'd I kill, Craddie?'

'Please sit down.'

That deflated me. I'm not used to civility. I dithered. He wagged a cautionary finger. I sat.

'I got a Pascal engine yesterday, Lovejoy.' He smiled at my surprise.

'Who copied it?'

The Paradox, as it's known in the antiques trade, was knocked up about 1642 by one Blaise Pascal, a youth eager to lessen his dad's eye-strain. All France fell about laughing – a *mechanical* calculator? Zut alors, what would bank clerks do all day? But Pascal persisted. Early versions of his calculating 'engines' are rare. I swallowed, lust rising.

'Modern, I'm afraid, Lovejoy, about 1920.'

Maybe I could copy it in ivory or bone, do ebony work to convince the unwary ... I realised I was licking my lips.

'Here?' So casual I almost slid off the chair.

'I'll give it you, if you're honest in return.'

The trouble is I'm a scruff. Ask anybody. I was brought up in places where this lot'd starve. Tinker too, hence the bond. But origin's a handicap. Like, Cradhead is Oxford, Brigade of Guards, all that. If I'd his background, a chummy chat would have solved all problems. But for shoddy me Cradhead was proposing a serious contract. Default, I'd find the contract written in blood. Guess whose.

'I perceive your dilemma, Lovejoy.' His elegant hands tipped to show cleverness. 'You resent my status. Has it never occurred to you that I might envy you yours?'

'No.' I was uneasy. Cradhead was no nerk.

'Think.' He counted to ten, letting my plebeian cells clodhop to a synapse. 'You are at home with scruffs, and they with you. Me?' He chortled, really did chortle like they do in kiddies' comics. 'Layabouts clap eyes on me, they know instantly that I'm not of their world.'

Like me in a police station, perhaps? I didn't speak. This sounded like a real deal. I was the innocent non-murderer, so how come the Plod needed me?

'To pass yourself off among us lowlifes, Craddie, dress up and lurk. Sherlock Holmes did.'

'Ah, there's the rub.' He tilted his chair. I was beginning to miss Drinkwater, slug thug of the old school. 'You're the fashioneer, Lovejoy.'

Fashion was starting to nark me. I wish to God I'd never met Thekla.

'Fashion? One bird has me ditched. Another has hysterics and accuses me of murder. Oh, aye.' I was bitter. 'I'm your fashion expert. Want a frock?'

'Don't, Lovejoy. The doctors say he won't die.'

Pity. I might've got off. It was innocence landed me in this. 'The Pascal?'

'Ah, I want your assistance, Lovejoy.'

Now I knew he was up to no good. 'Me?'

'Just pass on what fashion world gossip you hear.' He smiled disarmingly, clean teeth, manicured nails glittering. Racehorse owner, probably. Maybe Cradhead had a girlfriend keen on fashion?

'That it, Cradhead? No catch?'

He opened his hands, eyebrows raised.

'Your trouble, Lovejoy, is that you are untrusting.'

Asking me for fashion tips is like saying report the apogees of Saturn. 'What if I'm wrong? I can't talk their words.'

He chortled again. I began to wish Lewis Carroll had never invented the bloody word. *Alice in Wonderland* used to put the fear of God in me.

'Yes or no, Lovejoy? Concur, and you may depart.'

'I concur. May I depart?'

A nod, more amusement. I ahemed, made for the door, ready to halt if he beckoned.

'Oh, Lovejoy.' Wearily I halted. 'A young Aussie lady's roaming about, obscure cousin of Mr Dill. If you catch a glimpse, do ring.'

'Course. Pleased to.' I wish every promise was as easily made. 'Er, Craddie? The Pascal.'

'Third drawer down. Bureau.' Already he was immersed in documents. Nervy, I went to open the drawer, apologising every inch. He ignored me.

It was ivory, with metal innards. A replica, yes, made about 1900 or so. You get toy ones from the 1930s, and demo copies. But this was a memento of a great mind, done with skill by Victorian craftsmen. I moaned.

'It's yours, Lovejoy. Sorry about the plastic bag.'

Carefully, I held on to sanity. Balancing myself, I asked, 'Eh?'

'Yours, Lovejoy. Token of appreciation from the police. Cheerio, old chap.'

Now, nobody says 'old chap' nowadays. That dated slang comes only in American thrillers trying to be olde worlde and, I've heard, as mockery in posh schools. Maybe he wanted to insult me? I glowered. He grinned, not a chortle. I lifted it reverently, tried to speak, couldn't.

He didn't haul me back. I strolled very slowly past George, giving them every chance. He snored gently. I shook his arm, asked was it okay to go. I reached the High Street, marvelling. A present, for God's sake, from the Old Bill? For agreeing I'd help them out if their organdie and lapel trims came unstuck? I made it to the door of the Three Cups by the old Saxon church.

Tinker was there. I gave him the Pascal engine, told him what it was.

'Get it to Vinegar. He's got a few quid. But don't take any antiques in exchange – especially don't take any Roman seals.'

He cackled, suspecting. 'Right, Lovejoy. Did you phone that Stella? A frigging nuisance.'

'Sell this Pascal, and my ambers, to Vinegar for what you can get. They're under my doorstep in a tin. I've a feeling we'll need money.'

We'd have had a nice chat then, but I was assaulted by Aureole, who tore in wanting to scratch my eyes out.

'Lovejoy! You bastard!' she screeched, first clue that she was near.

'Aureole! Dwoorlink!' I did my pleased smile, ducking. Trouble is, you can't clock a woman. You've just to grin and bear it while they lash and claw. It's called equality.

'You ruin my trade, get me in bad with a wealthy client … '

That's Aureole. Anything going wrong is my fault. Anything goes right, she wants praise. *I* defaulted on her system? When I'd invented it, made her a rich woman for doing sweet sod all? And Faye her client had me clinked for nothing. I backed out into Trinity Street, the lads jeering.

'Lovejoy? Pay up, pal.'

'Dinsdale?' I yelped disbelief.

The George's security officer stood there, bigger in the gloaming. Aureole screamed with delight.

'Supper, wine. You didn't pay, Lovejoy.'

'You hawked me to the peelers,' I yelled. 'And the lady was paying. Right, Aureole?'

'No, Mr Dinsdale.' Aureole was thrilled things were going her way. 'Lovejoy booked my lady friend.'

'I didn't!' I cried. A crowd stood about, enjoying the show, drinkers looking out hoping for a scrap. 'Aureole! You owe me that display stand!'

'That rare mahogany Berkley Horse, Lovejoy?' She smirked. I gaped. How did she know? I'd told nobody. Or had I? 'I sold it hours ago. You were going to cheat me!'

'This way, Lovejoy.' Dinsdale grabbed my arm and frogmarched me off. We got as far as Cutler Alley where we couldn't be seen from the tavern doorway. He said into the darkness, 'Mr Boxgrove?'

A shadow thickened under the gas lamps.

'Great, Dinsdale.' Notes crinkled, and Dinsdale marched away. 'Want a job, Lovejoy?'

'You already offered me, Roger. No, ta.'

'I've rescued you from a fate worse than Aureole.' He walked with me. 'I know where Tinker's relative is.'

'His Aussie cousin's girl?'

'In fact, I want you to follow her, Lovejoy, and I'll foot the bill. Only take you a day. She's left town by train.'

One problem, I can cope. Two, I manage. But three bend my brain. Now four? How come Aureole suddenly knew about the Berkley Horse – and had instantly sold it? Not the mystery divvy again. I couldn't stand it. My temples throbbed.

'What's Tinker's relative got to do with you, Rodge?'

'Can I explain in confidence?' He began without waiting. He strolled into the High Street. I blundered after, enjoying my migraine. 'I've been seeing a married woman, Lovejoy. I saw her off at the station.' Lydia had mentioned Rodge at the railway station. He shrugged. 'She got upset, flounced off. Know what I mean?'

'I've heard they do,' I said sourly. 'So?'

'She should've taken some bone relics for a customer, waiting for them.' He waxed indignant. 'She left me, egg all over my face. What could I do?'

'Use the train guard?' I was beginning to see. He'd palmed the phoney bones off onto Vyna Dill, as messenger.

'Guards won't, not since they changed the railways. Then I heard this girl book to the same destination. I asked her to deliver my parcel, for the fare.'

'Where did she go?' I asked, too casual.

'Lovejoy. Go for me, just check that it arrived, then I can cash the cheque. Stay there a few hours, in case, then you've earned your gelt. What d'you say?'

'Why don't you phone him?' If Rodge would only mention where the girl had gone, I could simply tell Tinker and resume my normal life of penury.

'No names ... '

No pack drill, I finished for him silently. Antique dealers never reveal a customer for nothing. Yet it sounded contrived, like he was desperate to get me out of town. Ridiculous.

'All you do, Lovejoy, is see if there's any message for Mr Boxgrove.'

'How d'you know she was Tinker's missing lass?'

'Accent. And that photo Tinker has. Her brooch said Vyna.'

Three reasons is often enough.

'Okay, Rodge. Tinker will go after her, do your job.' Then I could go and lie down in the dark. Nobody gets headaches like mine, nobody.

'No, Lovejoy.' And he smiled pityingly when I drew breath to demand why. 'Tinker always gets thrown out of hotels. Won't you do it, for your pal?'

'If Tinker wants to come too, you'll pay?' I didn't want a teenage girl on my hands. I didn't want to find her at all, come to that.

'You, Tinker, and that Roadie?' He wheedled, 'I paid your bill at the George carvery, Lovejoy. And got you off Aureole's hook.'

Who stole my Berkley Horse, I grumbled to myself. A brief journey might save my sanity, though.

'Look, Rodge. Who didn't get killed?'

'Faye's bloke, Viktor Vasho, Liverpool fashion designer. Old dresses on new crumpet.'

'Old?' My migraine lessened. Antique dresses would make even Thekla's cachectic models look attractive.

'Pathetic sod, that Viktor Vasho.' We reached the Welcome Sailor, stood outside its honky-tonk din. 'Is that a job for a grown man?'

'It wasn't me nigh killed him, Rodge,' I said. 'Honest.'

'I know, Lovejoy,' he said, amused. 'It was me.'

'You? Er, right, right.'

We went into the saloon bar. Eve flashed us ales before we'd sat. Tinker and his charge weren't in, but Kima — Regency porcelains and furniture — smiled and waggled her fingers enticingly. She's new in from Hong Kong. I'm crazy about her. Has connections in Canton, mixes genuine porcelain with fakes that are so realistic it takes a real divvy like me to suss them. She holds sales in her house in St Peter's Road near the garage. I'd have maybe got closer, if my head had been on instead of somewhere in space. I waved back.

'This Viktor Vasho, Rodge,' I said, checking nobody was in earshot. 'Er, you nearly killed him?'

'Mmmh.' He was quite offhand, called, 'Here, Eve. Any messages from Lowestoft?'

'No, Mr Boxgrove.'

'Bloody suppliers,' he groused. 'Hold us honest workers to ransom.'

'*You* tried to kill this Viktor Vasho bloke?' I wanted this honest worker to get it straight.

'Not in so many words, Lovejoy. Give me credit for human compassion.'

'Oh, sure. Why?'

'It's Faye, Lovejoy.' His face went misty, his soul – always assuming – off into dreamland. My mind went oh-ho. Love is where things go wrong. 'Me and Carmel, okay. But Faye – I'd give anything.'

It happens to me too. Women have that effect. We can't calculate like women, when passion raises its benighted head. Somehow they seem able to time the game. We can't, just go headlong.

'Faye? You're after Faye? What's the problem?'

He stared at me so long I got anxious, but he was only amazed at my imperception, the way lovers are.

'She isn't crazy about me, you ignorant prat, Lovejoy,' he said courteously. '*That*'s the problem. She's crazy about Viktor Vasho.'

'Ah, I follow.' I sounded like Cradhead, which suddenly intensified my migraine, force cubed.

'You don't, Lovejoy. Viktor Vasho's a superb designer – fraudulent, of course. Simply takes old Victorian night clothes, sex wear, and churns them out in modern materials. He's from Mayfair. Organises antique shows, ancient dresses.'

Quad force now. Migraine screwed my face up. I remembered Orla of Mayfair, and said nothing.

'So you tried to top him?'

'Well, it was reasonable,' explained this scion of virtue and logic. 'I didn't just go pell mell. That would have been wrong,' he explained with an air of injured piety. 'I'm not that sort of person.'

'Good lad,' I said. 'Got an aspirin?'

'I hired some Bethnal Green blokes to nick Viktor Vasho's design collection. I thought he'd top himself – they do that, very emotional, see? Then he'd be out of the way. It was a beautiful plan. Nearly worked.'

He blinked away disappointment. What with him choking back sorrow that his murder had gone awry, and me trying to see, we made a right pair. I vowed not to tell Cradhead this, cancelling my earlier vow, Pascal Paradox or no.

'Good thinking that, Rodge.'

'Faye found him. He'd taken an overdose.' He went all bitter. 'Another hour'd have done it. Some bastard of a doctor saved him. Why don't they mind their own frigging business?'

'Tough, Rodge. Maybe next time. He's okay, then?'

'No.' He brightened. 'Not spoken since. He's under the shrinks. Do they get better?' he asked hopefully, 'or do they relapse and pop their clogs?'

'Rodge. Why did Faye accuse me?'

'She must think you're pals with a woman who's after Viktor Vasho.' Orla?

'These antique dresses, Rodge. Who has them?'

'Mmmh? Oh, he's got a vast collection. Faye knows. He links up with museums, does displays.'

Now, turn-of-the-century dresses are in vogue, but cost peanuts. There's been a little upsurge, but nothing like what I think they're worth. Endless hours of detailed stitching, the work in each one. To see perfect *fin de siècle* evening attire sold for a few pence – I'm not kidding – at junk sales is heartbreaking. One day, folk will realise, then it'll be too late.

'The Bethnal Green blokes burned his designs on Wandsworth Common.' Roger smiled at the thought. 'Did a charity gala, fireworks, sausages, cake, lemonade.'

'Aren't people kind, Rodge.'

'Heartwarming.' He stared morosely into his glass. 'Pity it didn't have a better outcome. Now Faye's hunting for vengeance.'

'Just like a woman. Tut tut.' It was a scenario I was well out of. The safest option seemed to be catching the train to wherever it was, looking for Vyna. 'About that trip.'

'You'll go, then?'

'Deal,' I said. 'Where to, Rodge?'

'Destination and money in an envelope when I've made some phone calls.' He rose and left, pleased.

Two deals in one night. One a cinch – a valuable Pascal replica for nothing – and the other a doddle.

'Where to, Lovejoy?' Tubb perched on the vacated stool. 'Portenta says Libras will win this week's lottery. You're Libra, right? Carmel says to drop by.'

'Eve, love,' I called. 'Got an aspirin?'

'Oh, what a shame, Lovejoy. Got one of your heads?'

'No, love,' I said, broken, as Tubb began to explain about lottery odds and the zodiac. 'Three.'

12

TUBB FOLLOWED ME to the railway station. I wouldn't say where I was going. He stood with me on the platform.

'I'll pay on the train,' he explained cheerily. 'Carmel'll courier us the sand job details, where we're staying.'

Ever secreterer? 'Tell Carmel I resign.'

'Will we be hunting antiques as we go, Lovejoy? Finding antiques is just luck, right?'

His superstitions. Why do people believe in luck, when there's no such thing?

'There's a million ways to find antiques, Tubb.'

He intoned his creed. 'Luck.'

Much he knew. Waiting, I tried to explain.

Finding them's the battle. Sometimes they come wholesale. Like, years ago the space shuttle *Challenger* beamed out radar shots and pinpointed the fabled lost city called Ubar, astonishingly in Oman. Archaeologists are going about saying that these ancient places, heaving with theft-worthy antiques, became windswept ruins because Dark Ages climates went berserk. So if you've an *Endeavour* shuttle handy, find the exotic lost cities on the Great Silk Road, beat the Yanks to it.

That's one way. Or you can thieve, with fewer resources. Knowing where that Rembrandt portrait is in Salisbury, Wiltshire, you steal up with a seventeen-foot ladder and smash the wooden shutters ... except it's been done. The smash-and-dash. Incidentally, trust to speed, never mind alarms.

Burglars have three friends. One's carelessness – leave your window open, tell tipsy friends about your priceless Chippenale Chinese-rail chair. Another is those sophisticated electronic alarms, that kid you all's secure. Third is insurance – is it *really* wise to tell strangers exactly what treasures your Auntie Nelly's got? Local antique dealers like Suffolk Frank (silver, multiple bigamist, thick as a plank, friend) love insurance – for everybody else, because they've all got insurance clerks on their payrolls. Bribery's cheap; it's work that comes dear.

Or you can have a notable ancestor. Like Lord Northesk's, whose illustrious forebear was Nelson's sidekick at Trafalgar. This provenance is valuable, when you finally sell that lock of Nelson's hair, your ancestor's sword, his gold Trafalgar medal, and the rest. Your certificate triples the antique's auction value.

Or you can invent any of the above, bake a fake porcelain, daub a dud Leonardo, whittle a mediaeval carving. Everybody does it. A local yokel called Stats is our numbers guru. He says that thirteen times as many antiques are sold each year *as were ever made in history*. Get it? The world's awash with forgeries. I help, make plenty.

'See, entrails show life's magic forces.' Tubb made a flowing gesture as the train bucketed in.

'Entrails means something's dead.' My headache had gone, leaving a lightness, everything at a distance.

Tubb nodded enthusiastically. 'But forces are captured! You spread entrails ... '

Entrails, all the way to Norwich? 'Wrong train, Tubb,' I said. 'It's the next, ten minutes. Look. Get us a cuppa. The buffet's there.'

He pondered, was superstition against it? The train squealed to a stop. Doors banged.

'It's bad luck, starting a journey without a warm drink,' I told him. 'My grandad was adamant.'

'Is it?' He was shocked, thinking immediately how many times he'd taken that fearsome risk. 'Christ.'

Off he went. I got aboard, ducked, and didn't sit up until the train was well out of the station. Another week before Carmel's sand job, was it? Plenty of time. And Roger had promised I'd be home in a day. I closed my eyes, alone. Bliss. My headache faded as the town, Aureole, Carmel, Faye, fashion, Orla of the fancy surname, Thekla, Oddly (failure), Tinker (failure), me (failure), faded from consciousness.

Norwich is a pleasant city, give or take areas of vandalism executed by the city fathers. Dunno why, but every new batch of councillors instantly hatches some plan to flatten the town's middle for a new mega-storey car park. They instal vast supermarkets. This eliminates all known vegetables from everybody's diet because they've eliminated the greengrocers. You don't believe it? Go to any town centre. Park your motor on some seventeenth floor. Wander, listing the shops. Then answer this: what is missing? It's the poor old green-grocer, with his spuds, cabbages, carrots. Buy a lettuce now, it's been flown in plastic from Africa.

Norwich has car parks, a castle, a weighty history, a football team (its fans allege), and ancient hotels bravely enduring against the odds.

And Tee Vee Rydout, who owed me a painting of the Norwich school, or the money from its sale. He lives with a yodelling banjo-playing uncle on the river.

At the railway information desk, I asked Roger's question of a wizened old duffer. 'Any message? Mr R. Boxgrove.' He told me no.

'No young lass, Aussie accent, leaving a packet she'd failed to deliver for Boxgrove?'

'No, sir.' That was that, then.

So I booked in at a hotel, anger on hold.

Up at sixish, I bathed, shaved with the little razors hotels provide, didn't use their corrosive sublimate of aftershave that peels your chin skin, used their folding toothbrush, and had a ton of breakfast.

It's not far to Tee Vee's boat, a mile or so. I approached the *TeeVee* from downstream. A dog barked, dozily uncaring, from the line of moored boats. The *TeeVee* was a highly decorated longboat, 'barge' as folk wrongly say, a truly clever disguise for the best counterfeiter in the Eastern Hundreds. No banjo being plectrummed in the dawn, so I clambered aboard and stomped on the cabin by way of greeting.

'Jesus Aitch frigging Christ! Who's that?' And up glowered Tee Vee from below. Mane of a lion, features almost acromegalic, prognathous jaw, immense body, you could clothe him in Bond Street, he'd still look off the road. He said, 'It's only Lovejoy.'

Only? He'd rue that. 'Morning, Tee Vee. Got it?'

'God, Lovejoy. Let me wake up. What time's this? Come in. I'll brew up.'

'Ta.' Stooping, I entered the fug. What's with these nautical blokes? Maybe it's our island air. Everywhere in our creaking old kingdom's seventy miles or less from the sea. Whatever, boats are as boring as tennis and golf, which is saying a magnitude.

For a start, there's no space. The cabin's airless. Cook anything, the pong lingers. Also, rivers are unpleasantly rural, go through leafy countryside, and I love only towns, where antiques come from.

'Er, morning, love. Sorry.'

'What bleeding time d'you call this?' the gorgeous girl on the bunk said. Blonde, without visible attire.

On another bunk Tee Vee's uncle snored. He's banjo mad.

'It's urgent,' I explained. Nowhere to sit except on the bunk, and friendliness can be misconstrued.

'If we're not on fire, it's sodding well not,' said the charmer. She belched. My mind reverted to purity.

'Got it, Tee? Third time of asking, note.'

'Got what?'

He flopped down, making the girl abuse the world in blink-bleep lingo. She huddled, snored immediately.

'The money, Tee. For that Norwich school painting.'

'That was fake,' he said piously.

'So were your American dollars.' I raised a hand to forestall interruption. 'You commissioned a fake. I didn't commission counterfeit money.'

'It's frigging hard, Lovejoy,' he grieved, scratching his belly. He wore pyjamas, gold, pink, yellow, orange. 'Them Yanks don't play fair.'

'Meaning what?'

'Counterfeiting's hard, Lovejoy.' He was narked. 'Them swine've started putting mixed polyesters in dots and strips. When you counterfeit, the frigging ink doesn't take.'

'How unfair,' I said politely.

'Un frigging *fair*, Lovejoy?' he cried. 'Every sodding image blunts! And the USA's experimenting with different polyesters. And trace elements!' He almost wept, the American Treasury so unsporting.

They did a survey a couple of years back. Russia, China, Latin America, and sundry punters round the globe held – the US said – up to 30 billion dollars in untraced accounts, tin cans buried in the yard. Wrong. The figure's well over 70 thousand million. Any Russian, or anyone slipping from the Baltic to our fair East Anglian shores, pays in bundles of 20, 50, and 100 dollar notes. Whatever the US government estimates is wrong times three.

'You owe dollars, Tee,' I said. 'There's nigh on 400 thousand million *genuine* dollars about. No hard feelings. I'll take coin of the realm.'

He wheedled, 'There's two hundred million fake dollars about, Lovejoy. What's a few more?'

'Pay,' I asked, calm. 'Last chance, Tee.'

'Haven't got it, Lovejoy. You could have it.'

'Dear me.' I went and hauled Uncle Bat awake. He roused, reached for his banjo. I'd just have to bear the din.

86

'Morning, Lovejoy.' He was instantly awake. His frame showed only bones, his face infolded. He rummaged in the bunk, found his teeth and shoved them in so his face expanded and I recognised him.

'Morning, Bat. Do you sleep with those things on?'

He had plectrums on all but the last digit. Name a tune, Lovejoy.'

'*Give Me A Ticket To Heaven*. Know it? By way,' I added, 'of farewell.'

He strummed a chord, and eyed me. He didn't sing instantly, an all-time first.

'Farewell, Lovejoy? Whose?' He knew me.

'Tell me, Bat.' Tee Vee was listening hard. Reckoning time had come. 'How come your nephew looks like a movie monster, yet pulls these exquisite birds?'

He chuckled. 'You're the same, and pull as much.'

'Here, Bat, nark it,' I said, indignant. I'm grotty, but spotless underneath.

'And he's got money, son!' Uncle Bat fell about.

Not quite true. Tee Vee has phoney money. Antiques is merely his cover. He's a foomer – buys only forgeries, and sells as real. Like, he'll buy a fake Norwich school painting from me, sell it somewhere on the Continent as genuine.

Uncle Bat, skeletal and toothless banjoist of Norwich's waterside cafés, is Tee Vee's counterfeiter, brains of the outfit. Tee Vee's his natural son. Uncle's only 'Uncle' because he was a pawnbroker.

'Counterfeiting going well, eh, Bat?' I felt sad on account of what I was going to do, but I was getting tired with being bollocked for nothing. Not long ago I wasn't homeless or penniless. Now look.

'Pretty well, son,' he said. 'I'll have this polyester blot problem ironed soon. I'm working on a modified shedding screen – image refraction, o'course.'

'Of course.' As if I understood.

'It re-melds the electronic focus by light resonance, gets the picture back. I know what you're thinking, Lovejoy.' He was dead serious. I tried to look like I was pondering electronics. 'That it should be a purely chemical elution process.'

'Well,' I said, lost, 'first things first, eh?'

'Wrong, son. Sod microscopic techniques. It's *got* to be image refraction. Wouldn't work with us – we've too many different notes, see?'

'Good thinking. Glad it's all okay. Toodle-oo.'

'What about your song, son?'

'Sing as I leave. Cheers, Tee Vee.'

'Cheers, Lovejoy,' he said warily, from underneath his bird's blanket. How the heck he manages to fit in (I mean the bunk) I can't imagine.

Jumping down to the riverbank, I undid the mooring ropes. On board, I heard the banjo strike up. Uncle Bat's voice warbled, '*Give me a ticket to heaven/ That's where Dad's gone, they say ...*'

It was two furlongs to the boatyard. Hardly anybody awake on the river, though a woman splashed a bowl of water over the side of a craft downstream. I chose a moored boat, sleek with a high prow. It looked tough enough. I gave its nose a shove and hopped aboard. It started to drift with that laziness only boats manage. I searched it for people. Fine.

Drifting's quite pleasant. No more peaceful holiday than on a boat, though tranquillity wears you out before you've gone a mile. This thing had an engine that promised molto action. It had an easy starter.

The sound of Uncle Bat's plink-plonk came over the water as my boat drifted close to Tee Vee's barge.

'*My Daddy worked upon the line, but when I went tonight/ To take his tea, he lay there ...*'

I sang along, filling up at the Victorian song. There was a great pole thing. I dug it into the river bed, began slowly to bear onto the *TeeVee*. Even if you slip a longboat's mooring it moves inchwise, even on a river like the Yare.

Counterfeit's not bad, when you think. I mean, what is inflation but a secret change of money? We ordinary mortals don't inflate the dollar, yen, dinar, whatever. Governments do it.

'*I ran here – I hope I'm not too late ...*' I warbled the little girl's plight.

Look at the Donations of Constantine, dated 30th March, AD 315, by which Emperor Constantine gave to Pope Sylvester the Holy Sees of Alexandria, Constantinople, Jerusalem, and all the churches in the world. For good measure the Emperor chucked in Rome, all Italy, and the regions of the west. Saints were beatified on the strength of it, countries swapped or given wholesale. Then it was proved a forgery, done by a Lateran priest for Pope Stephen III. It was exposed by a brave papal aide called Lorenzo Valla in 1440. Its political effects are with us yet. That's the trouble with forgery; do it big, you can get away with it. Little, you're doomed.

Look at sex, I thought, busily poling. There's Aureole, making a great living from chain dating. Those sex surveys they're always doing say that men have three times as many lovers as women. How come? Do women underestimate? Do men exaggerate? See what I mean: phoney truth, fake research, or what exactly?

I poled my drifting boat towards the *TeeVee*. Remember that Leonardo da Vinci hand-written Codex – 72 pages written in Big L's own lillywhites? It was knocked down to a secret bidder for over a cool 30 million US dollars. The bidder's identity was kept under wraps. (It was Mr Gates, the American computer wizard, but pretend he's still incognito. It's his own business.) No, pretence is fine.

Unless you don't pay up.

Then things happen. If you have a banjo-playing uncle – a genius counterfeiter, who works under cabin floorboards in your longboat – to pretend that you're a lucky antique dealer, then you are vulnerable in ways that, say, Roger Boxgrove isn't. Or Aureole. Or crazy Faye. Or, even, me. Because some annoyed bloke like me might nick a high-powered boat, tie your mooring rope to the stern of said powerboat, and, singing a sentimental Victorian melody, quietly hot-wire his engine into life.

'The station-master said, "Come, little one, I'll see you right" ... '

The engine boomed, settled to a steady thrumming. I shoved into gear, moved forward until my boat took up the strain, then headed into mid-stream.

Faintly I heard somebody yell. I creamed along as fast as power allowed, singing the joyous ending.

'Though injured, Dad'd not been killed! And oh! her heart was glad ... Come on, Tee,' I bawled. 'Join in.'

He was trying to claw his way forward, in his glitzy pyjamas. I waved, friendly.

'She said, "If I lose Dad again, I'll come to you and say ... " Chorus now, Tee. Show the townsfolk, eh?'

Houses began to appear. We passed a little school, children in the playground stopping to wave. I waved back.

'Mister,' one yelled. 'Why's he got jammies on?'

'Er, his mother's not up yet,' I yelled, all tact.

'He'll be late!' they shouted. They love others' disasters. 'He'll catch it, won't he?'

'He will that!' I bawled. 'Likely from the Excise.'

'Lovejoy!' Tee Vee bawled. 'You can't!'

I carolled back, *'Give me a ticket to heaven/That's where dad's gone, they say ... '* and steered towards the weir.

With average luck I could maroon his ponderous longboat

crosswise. The hull would crack. Which would call out the fire brigade or whatever. Whose report would astonish Norfolk's authorities, at the vast array of counterfeiting machinery. The river authorities would be angered by 100-dollar notes bobbing among their ducklings. The Customs and Excise would perforate their morning ulcers ...

'Please, Lovejoy! Please ... '

The boat slowed a little when I cut the engine. They don't have brakes. Ocean liners have to simply go round and round until their motion peters out, I've heard. The *TeeVee* loomed closer. I'm not scared of boats, much, but didn't want the longboat running me down. Moving fast, a speedboat's great. Slowed, it's thin-skinned.

'Can't hear you, Tee. Sorry.'

'I'll pay you,' he screamed. His beauteous bird appeared, screeching her head off. 'Real money!' He waved handfuls of conviction.

Easy to tow a longboat to block a river. A policeman cycling on the bank called, 'What's the matter?' I pointed to Tee, ask him. The bobby tore his eyes from Tee's bird, and asked. Tee began some tale. Uncle Bat played us out as Tee cast off. He handed over a load of zlotniks. I examined them closely, did a count, waved to the Plod.

'For helping,' I called over.

'Isn't that Donard John's boat?' the constable shouted back, suspicious.

'Kind old Don,' I answered airily.

'He's a stingy old sod. And why's he still in his 'jamas?'

'Dunno, constable. Better ask the lady.'

Snapping into gear, I zoomed off leaving Tee wailing. His engine's been dud these three years. I paid no heed. Honest, people'll have me carrying the pots and pans. Is it my fault? I rounded the curve, moored the boat, and started my search for Vyna.

Mistake. I should have stayed aboard, cleared the bar at Great Yarmouth, and sailed into the sunrise.

13

TAXI NUMBERS CHALKED up in rural phone boxes mislead. Jokes, malice, company rivalry, take your pick. The first I tried was a frosty lady. Second, a temptress wanting to massage my exhausted frame. I was narked, not having exhausted my frame yet. The third taxi number was a taxi number, a first for Norfolk. It took me to a supermarket.

They detect dud money by clever pens – stroke the watermark, it goes black and you're under arrest. I went in synthetically angry.

'Look,' I told the manageress when they dragged her down from her office slumber. 'I paid good money for, er, goods. You forge-changed me.'

'Allow me, sir.' She wearily subjected my note to a trillion tests. 'It's perfectly good. What goods did you buy, sir?'

Suspicion is unfair. 'You sure? Okay, then.' I marched out. Tee Vee's payment was genuine. Norfolk was on the mend.

The antiques game has gossip like others have weather. You know what's happening, like you know if it's raining. I phoned Chessmate, an intinerant gossip-monger in bric-a-brac who works the 'attic' circuits. He told me there was a beaut, this very day. So it came to pass that I taxied to the august Thornelthwaite family mansion. Attic debris, please note, is where human hate and love combine. (Skip this next bit if you're sensitive, because it's exactly what will happen to all you own, right down to your pot teeth.)

Many folk resent fame, fortune, and nobility. I rage against nobody, except people who kill antiques. What law says the rich, the ex-rich, or the would-be rich, must be saints? Add those up, we're all in there. The viewers ogling the Thornelthwaites' possessions were of two sorts, antique dealers and sour locals in various stages of glee. I was the only one a-sorrowing, because house sales break my heart.

An auction viewing day is a psychodrome waiting to happen. When the auction starts, it's 'Game On!' for psychodrama. The entire psychotic arena fills. Carnage begins, and with it triumph for the lucky few touched by the stars. For the rest, dismay.

As usual, the auctioneers had rigged up a marquee. Somebody was unfolding chairs, setting a dais and podium, microphones, phone sites, the paraphernalia of a flog-off auction. When a family is submerged in double-entry accounting and sells up, the attic dealers – a right circus – home in on human misery. They're not so bad – walnut brains, looters' morals, but dealers are dealers. The ones I can't abide are the gloaters, the ghoulish grinners who only come to jeer. They don't buy, only finger and sneer at crumbling aristos. Who the crumbling family is, was, doesn't matter. The ghoulists park their motors and saunter in, copycat conquerors. They snigger. We all do it, you, me, emit that serves-them-right cackle of the jackal and the carrion bird. I'm ashamed of us. Then I think what saints people are. It's a paradox. Same with religion, really. I believe in God, but His earthly sales force is crap. I believe in antiques, but people ... ? Sensible answers, please.

For an hour I wandered, feeling the ancient house's pulse. It was a lovely if faded Queen Anne mansion, but essentially undamaged. They had loved it, those old folk whose portraits hung on the stairs. Dealers were pricing furniture, carpets, Sheffield plate, cruets – don't know why, but to me cruets are saddest, truest symbols of a death-sale sell-up.

As I ambled, a middle-aged lady without a coat was near more often than chance allowed. So? On I went, sensing the loveliness of age. I recognised the odd dealer. Chessmate soon arrived, a short ambitious Geordie 'of climbing habit' as gardeners say of plants too aggressive for their own good. I gave him the bent eye and he cleared off. The last thing I wanted, him seeing what I divvied as genuine. I felt on holiday, scouting on my own with gelt in hand. Yet it also felt odd, a betrayal. Tinker was ultra-loyal, right? But every time I sent him for an antique he returned empty-handed. This was new. I put it firmly from my mind.

You drift anywhere in a house sale, as the marquee's trestle tables stack with household items. The house is always open to viewers, in hopes that they'll come with wallets and purses a-bulging. The nervous coatless lady stalked me ineptly. Security agent? Paintings – ancestors, Italian scenes from the Grand Tour, nothing special but old. I smiled with pleasure, the antiques warming my soul and them smiling back. A brass-banded walnut case, size of an elongated fag packet, beamed at me. The wood had 'C.C.' marked on it. Nobody was about. I found it in my pocket, a lovely feeling, beautiful. I felt seventeen again, brilliant, in love.

From the withdrawing-room I entered the long hall.

'Wotcher, Lovejoy.' Tubb pulled me forward. 'Never stop in a doorway. It causes earthquakes.'

'How ... ?' I didn't complete the question. He'd bribed the old wrinkle-faced information man at the station, then simply phoned round the Norfolk dealers promising a few quid to reveal what sales I asked about. No wonder Chessmate had dropped by – he was just collecting his thirty pieces of silver.

'Tubb,' I said wearily. 'Leave me be. D'you hear?'

He beamed, not taking a blind bit of notice. 'What d'you reckon of this? Seventeenth century?' He poked a pipe, carved as a naked woman in an erotic posture. 'You stuff tobacco into her head – it's the bowl, see? And you suck ... '

'Ta, Tubb, but it's not that old.'

Meerschaum, 'sea foam', is a clayey silicate of magnesium, supposedly minuscule marine creatures plonked down by a retreating Ice Age. Turkey was the main supplier. But until Count Andrassey took a chunk to Karl Kowates a mere 200 years back to make the first meerschaum pipe, there was really no such item. By a historical fluke, Mr Kowates was a Budapest cobbler, his hands leathered from years of shoe polish. That prototype meerschaum pipe became a mustardy-gold. The meerschaum pipe was born.

'What d'you reckon it's worth?' Tubb trumpetted.

Deafening secrecy. I turned quickly, to see at least seven dealers suddenly spin away and pretend frozen interest in furniture, mirrors, rugs. They were following me. I'd been sussed as a divvy. Or had Chessmate sold the news?

The edgy middle-aged woman wasn't making it easier. She was homely tweedy with round features. Heaven knows why she was traipsing after me. I stabbed a warning finger at Tubb, and drifted on.

I started taking notice, blood boiling.

There are ways of 'breading' the stock, as dealers say. Just as anglers throw bread bait into pools, antique dealers go about making disparaging remarks to improve their buying chances. Like, 'Here, Fred. Look at this!' Snide laughter. 'Think they'll get a fortune for it? Never seen worse!' Chuckle, chuckle.

This, note, for a beautifully chased American silver table-water jug. It stood tall on a table, waiting to go to the marquee. From a distance it looked warty, with such high relief engraving it hardly seemed shiny at all. Experts, that talkative lot, say always trust that 1850s–1860s Yank silver with such prominent chasing. Well, time races on, so look at the engraved picture. Flowers, country churches, churchyards, with the church looking as if it's trying to appear English *and not quite making it* is the best tip. The marks, of course, you can look up. Americans think little of their own antiques, yet pay fortunes for our dross. Beats me.

Ignoring the dealers with difficulty, I drifted on, followed by a straggle of seemingly indifferent dealers. They even took notes, lot numbers that I couldn't help smiling at. Despite my growing anger, I found myself talking to one or two antiques. You have to be polite. Some furnishings were beautiful.

There was a lovely mantel clock. It didn't look like one at first sight, being marble and porcelain. It was a mourning figure leaning over an urn on a plinth. She was draped, Greekish, exquisite. No more Ancient Greece than you or I, but some skilled artisan had copied from the London maker Benjamin Vulliamy's pattern. The two rims, where the urn and lid meet, rotate. They're numbered – usually Roman numerals below, ordinary above. A snake, twining horribly up the urn, leans over to point the time with its tongue. Grimly funereal, but see a genuine one like Lady Lever's at Port Sunlight and you'd sell your granny for it.

Admittedly a Regency fake, but that only made it genuine to me, if you follow. Some poor, yet immeasurably skilled, craftsmen in Georgian London must have seen Vulliamy's original, and copied every brilliant detail in their workshop dungeons. Find me the bloke who can do that today – please. I blinked my admiring eyes.

And heard a clink.

In a mirror – modern wall glass, so ignorable – I saw an overcoated bloke, moustache, homburg hat, pocket a small something, the pig. I heard a snigger.

The sorrowing maid's heel was missing.

For about a second, or hours, I stood trying to shake my fury. He'd deliberately chipped the heel. Soon he would loudly point out that the clock was damaged, virtually worthless. Then at the auction he'd buy it for a song, restore it using the heel he'd nicked, and sell it for a fortune as complete. Some dealers carry brass tools to inflict this destruction. I swallowed my rage. They don't think of the antique, just greed. Tonight this elegant lout in his bloody homburg would brag how he'd fooled everybody, looted himself a mint.

'Sorry, love,' I said mentally to the now-damaged leaning marble figure. She'd been perfect for a couple of centuries.

'Beg pardon?' somebody asked.

'Nothing.' I must have spoken aloud. I'd have to watch that.

Poor Benjamin Vulliamy. He passed on his love of clocks to his son Benjamin Louis who in 1820 invented a clever dead beat escapement – the clamped pallets can be adjusted. It caught on among continental makers, not much here. But, honest to God, what must Ben be thinking, watching our rotten antics from his cloud?

From then on, I got angrier.

The auctioneers' whifflers – think bribable scene-shifters – were in on the scams, as usual. You could see the money passing as the dealers filched openly and laughed about it. I saw a shabby bloke nick a nail file from an etui and blatantly do his nails with it as he strolled. Dealers don't steal like this simply to sell. They steal so that they can go to the eventual successful bidder and offer to make up the etui's complete set of manicure implements. The bidder's glad to buy, because he'll have paid much less in the auction for the incomplete George the Second lady's gold-mounted manicure case. The whiffler who doesn't work this scam has yet to be born. Such thieves are called 'toppers' in the trade, and form an elite clan where sleight-of-hand rules. (Don't laugh – these sly tricks will be played out on every single one of your own possessions sooner or later.)

Stifling rage, I went upstairs. By now I was judging faces, appearances, remembering the rogues. I listened for names. There was Pill, Duddo, a pretty woman in green called Gelina, a sour-faced hulk they all seemed to know called Calleon, and Mr Skanner, who was Homburg himself.

Skanner was particularly busy. I went by as he inspected a three-foot bronze. Even though it was a fake, I felt instant fondness for this Nubian bust. Cordier's original was nineteenth-century. There ought to be two, African 'noble savage' images of the Victorians, man and woman. A genuine pair would buy a Kensington house. The female is striking, imperious with her downward glance. Once seen, never forgotten. They're forged the world over now, best from Turkey, Taiwan, Italy. This was an early fake.

'Is it marked?' I asked innocently.

'Yes. The famous Cordier.' Skanner chuckled loudly. 'A gooseberry trying to be a grape!'

And the bastard actually scraped the figurine's shoulder with a file. He wore gloves, a common trick, his file hidden in the middle finger.

He'd have a second one along the ring finger, always on the preferred hand. He then had the gall to inspect the scratch he'd made, using a loupe, ten times magnification. I wagged my head to show how I admired the rotten pig, and oafed about, bedroom to landing, staircase to kitchen, raising my eyebrows, sharing in the general ribaldry.

Sometimes, human beings make me wonder what we think we are actually doing. If you stand before anyone on earth – the most powerful dictator, the seductive woman – and laugh at their wisecracks, you're a friend for life. The thickest nerk to the proudest emperor wants to be liked. Some comedian once said there were only six jokes; the rest is winning approval. Yet we all crave admiration, somebody to laugh when we trot our tired old six. We *know* that the person who laughs truly admires us, thinks we're great.

Which itself is a laugh. I mean, Skanner in his posh handmades does the old scag trick on a bronze bust and positively swells with pride when I, a passing tramp, grin at his cleverness. I almost puked. Hate edges you close to murder, a frightening thought.

To stay calm I started looking for honest collectors among the growing crowd. I found one or two examining a box of old toys. Nowadays, they're all after an uninteresting tiny aluminium triangular R.A.F. V-Bomber that Dinky made in 1955–6, in its dull little box. It will virtually buy you the town hall. (The No.992 AvroVulcan, just in case you do come across it, wears the number 749. God knows why.) Not even an antique, mind-bendingly dull, yet you can retire on it. That's collecting, money mad. It's not reasonable, like antiques. Those Chelsea porcelain 'masqueraders', two little 1760s figures holding masks, bring the same price as any small Art Deco by a named maker. And that endlessly copied Art Deco lady, so shapely between two borzoi dogs on her onyx base, made by D. H. Chiparus in bronze and ivory, will fetch seven or eight times as much. There's no accounting for money, and that's the truth. The Chiparus craze took off like a rocket when, inexplicably, pop stars started buying them sight unseen. Collecting's like shooting an arrow into a rotting orchard and hoping you'll hit the one good apple. Madness, because ...

'Excuse me, please. Can I have a word?'

The flustered lady, never far from sight.

'Are you security, missus?'

'No. Yes. I mean, not really.'

Was that a negative? 'What about?'

'Please.' She wrung her hands. I realised that she'd chosen her moment. There was nobody else near, by some miracle, though I could hear them all breading away, such merriment. 'Could we come to some arrangement? I'd make it worth your while.'

Me? I looked. Did she mean me? 'Are you a punter?'

'A ... ?' Her brow cleared, we had contact. 'No. I'm ... ' She took a run at it, launched. 'The vendor.' Like she'd just learned the word.

'The vendor?' I said, amazed, then went red. 'Sorry. Rude of me.'

She spoke bitterly. 'You mean why is a worn-out frump selling off a mansion?'

'Sorry, missus. I've had a long day.' It was not noon. The auction was two o'clock. 'What can I do?'

'Please. This way.'

Leading off the spacious landing was an oak door. Only Japanese or American heartwood, as most of the nineteenth century, but honest wood's a rarity. These modern kiln-dried days leave a nasty tenth of moisture in wood, to warp and crack as soon as you turn your back.

'There's a place here. Do sit.'

An alcove, such as servants used attending on the mistress's summons. Two small cushioned stools, modern junk. I sat obediently.

'Arrangement, missus?' Was she her ladyship?

She disposed herself, knees together, blue eyes apprehensive. Less frantic, she'd be more attractive.

'Would you take your gang away, please?'

Gang? I stared. I'm only me. In a flash, my brain screamed *Quick! Exploit!*

'Gang?' I'm pathetic. 'There's only me. Lovejoy.'

'Please don't. I'm not altogether stupid. They hang on your every look.'

To somebody innocent, it might actually look as if I was leader of a wolfpack.

'Er, seeing you've realised, missus, what arrangement were you thinking of?'

'I'll give you a fifth of the profits,' I heard her say. 'But you must leave the auction in peace.'

'Fifth?' I said, stunned.

'Quarter, then.' Her bottom lip trembled, driving a really tough bargain with a master criminal. 'It's my last offer.' Straight out of the poorer grade of 1950s black-and-white rep-actor films. 'As soon as I get the auctioneers' accounts.'

She had as much chance of seeing honest accounts from this

shambles as I had of making cardinal. I know auctioneers who compete, see who can falsify most each week. They actually bet on the result. I've been going to auctions since I was born, and I've never seen an honest one yet.

This malarkey was getting out of hand. 'You don't live here?'

She relaxed and actually said thank you. 'This house is my sister's. A widow, passed away recently. No children. I'm to dispose of everything.' She peered about our alcove. Answers were everywhere, could she but see.

'I might, love,' I lied, but I'd have to leave her to her fate. I had my job to do, Tinker's missing relative, get my life back on the rails. After all, I told myself righteously, this was a diversion. I'd only come to celebrate recovering my non-counterfeit owings from Tee Vee.

'It's kind of you.' She smiled, minuscule. It took twenty years off her. 'I ran a fish-and-chip shop.'

'A chippy?'

'In London. This country area is so ... remote.'

My feelings warmed. Anyone who mistrusts countryside deserves help. And chip shops sometimes keep me alive.

'I'm like that, love. I love a town.' I smiled back. One born every minute, usually me.

'You know how I feel, Lovejoy.' She sighed. 'Kate's death duties are huge.' She looked wistful. 'Do you know what I want?'

Did another gangster-type deal loom? I hadn't escaped her first one yet. 'No?'

Her eyes went larger still. 'Have my chip shop voted the best in the whole kingdom. Can you imagine anything better, Lovejoy?'

Ten billion things, actually. Clearly a nutter.

For aristocrats and strangers, I ought to explain that a chip shop, whether it calls itself a Fried Fish Emporium or Joe's Chippie, is basically a grub take-away. There's a counter. You queue. Servers fry fish, chips, cook mushy peas. Salted and vinegared in newspaper (trad) or grease-proof (posh), you scoff them on the hoof. There's no better food. The poor man's nosh, it flourishes defiantly on. They sell burgers nowadays, curries, vegan fry-ups. I didn't know there was a world ranking. Like cricket?

'Toff's, of Muswell Hill.' She spoke with envy. 'They have it in their window, *Voted The Best In The Kingdom*. Like the peerage, Lovejoy!'

A woman after my own heart. Anyone who spoke in such

hallowed tones deserved a smile from Dame Fortune instead of that goddess's usual nasty smirk.

'Deal,' I said before I could think. My belly rumbled in total agreement. 'I'll help. But first, a gypsy's warning. Listen, okay?'

Sitting there, I told her about The Case.

It's mostly boring, so skip it if you have strong ideas about honesty. If you read on, don't blame me.

Antique dealers call it The Case. Some years ago, a lady in Switzerland bought an Egon Schiele painting. Call her Marie, protect the innocent. She was so lovely it makes you wonder why she collected art at all, having herself to look at. But collect art she did.

To a famous London auctioneer (phew! Almost said Christies. Narrow escape from litigation, eh?) Marie paid half a million. Add the auctioneer's repellent ... (fill in the dots with any horrible adjective) 'buyer's premium' and it becomes even less trivial. Still, where's the problem? Lovely lady buys painting, we can go rejoicing and brew up.

But suspicion raised its head. Was it *really* by Egon Schiele? The alluring lady sued. London's lawyers girded.

The Case hung on this: the painting was original, yeah verily by Schiele. But some 94 per cent of it had been overpainted, and the famous Egon Schiele monogram ES added. The auctioneers' lawyers wept that honestly they'd honestly been honest, because the painting underneath was by Schiele, see? So it must still be, see? And bonny lady was simply too cruel saying it was wrong to flog her an overpainted daub, see?

The pretty lady's mob didn't see, not they. Stone of heart, they glared across the High Court. What bloody good's (I'm paraphrasing) a painting that you can only love six per cent of? They howled, *Make them give our lady her money back, m'lord*!

Now you and I, being pure, might believe auctioneers' catalogues. Auctioneers, however, have a nasty habit of welshing when accused of falsehood or mistake. So never mind the auctioneers' posh London address. Don't believe a word. An antiques auction's the only place where you can buy a cabbage, discover that you've in fact bought a rotting melon, ask for your money back and get told to sod off.

Enter the famous Clause Eleven, which releases auctioneers from responsibility. It says they've no real interest *in their own honesty*. Sorry about the italics, but I fume about it. You'd see how interested auctioneers are in honesty if you paid them in counterfeit money. Even the High Court saw the problem. The judge was especially baffled about the iniquitous premium that the auctioneers charge. Charging for zilch is what I call cheating, robbery, interfering with Magna Carta and weather and pinching toffees from infants. I hope they sue. I used to know a posh bloke whose vintage car was stolen by a friend. This fine gentleman drew himself up, shot his hand-stitched Bond Street cuffs, and said quietly, 'The cad'. That's real education, the sort I've never had. I have to resort to mere abuse, not half as good. In that single word, generations of breeding registered utter contempt. I wince just to think of it, and it wasn't even me who nicked his motor.

By some miracle of mismanagement, the High Court got it right. Marie won, could return the Schiele, get her money back plus interest. The morning the news broke I danced with delight. But the sombre fact remains. 'Auctioneer' means don't believe everything you read. It might be wrong. It might be right. But it might be wrong right, or right wrong.

Time to cool down.

'How terrible!' she said, not quite overcome by the tale. 'But my auctioneer is reliable, Lovejoy. He used to play golf with Kate's husband.'

'Oh, good.' She hadn't heeded a word I'd said. I could do no more. Time to scarper.

'Right, love. I've to see a pal nearby. Watch Kate's furnishings, okay?'

'I promise, Lovejoy.' She coloured some more. 'Briony.'

'Eh?' I halted, narked. Just when I'd escaped. 'What's Briony?' Some sort of daffodil?

'Me. I'm Briony. Briony Finch.'

'Oh.' She was so vulnerable I had a last try. 'One thing, love. You should have auto-cameras rigged up. Your stuff's being nicked right, left and centre.'

'Stolen?' she said. 'It can't be. It's all marked.'

See what honesty's up against? 'Use your eyes, silly cow,' I said, narked.

'Of all the … !'

Outrage leaves me cold. I'd myself to think of, explanations to find. I collared a lucky taxi at the gate, feeling let out of school, and went the dozen miles to the ultimate antiques gossip.

14

FLORSSTON VALEECE WAS in his outhouse, complaining about the cold. Nicola is demure, worried, and petite. She left her husband for this apparition.

'You're worse than a bird,' I said conversationally from his doorway.

'It's chilly and wet, Lovejoy.' Florsston didn't bother to look up. I'd not seen him for years. 'I *hate* damp. Why doesn't somebody tow this kingdom to the Med?'

'Lovejoy!' Nicola exclaimed, coming to buss me. She's always delighted, except when telling you how she's getting on with Florsston.

'Florssie. What's the game?'

That drew a shrewd glance. 'What've you heard?'

Florsston Valeece was a giant in every direction, so immense that you stop thinking of him as fat at all. He's just that shape. We have euphemisms for whale size: large, well-built. Daft, really, because fat's fat. Beside him, Nicola was a pretty sparrow. The outhouse held racks and stacks of material.

'Nothing, Florssie. I'm worried. What's pulled the money lately?'

'In antiques?' He was playing for time.

'If I'd a problem with machinery, Florssie, I'd have gone to a wheelwright.' I walked down his workplace. 'How many different stuffs you got?'

Every inch was cleverly used. Display panels, hinge frames, rolling shelving on welded rails. No wonder he was the best paid materials man in the Eastern Hundreds.

'Eight thousand, not counting solids. Solids means woods, metals, elements for alloys. Solvents and the like are spoken of with contempt: "chemicals". You duffed up Tee Vee, Lovejoy. Very uncalled for.'

'He paid me in wad, not wadge. Doesn't do, Florssie.'

'We aren't married yet, Lovejoy,' Nicola said, as if that had been the sole topic so far.

'Congratulations for the happy day,' I responded.

Florsston's eyes brightened. 'All my life I've loved stuff, Lovejoy.' He sounded wistful. Nicola smiled fondly, recognising his monologue. 'It's mankind's rampart against war, the ... '

... miraculous conviction that Man can create just as God can. Material – down to the cheapest linen – is a living substance made in our own image. It excels empires, the Stock Exchange, and proves ...

'That we too are gods,' I finished with him.

He wiped his eyes on the handkerchief Nicola passed. I always wonder when I see this couple. To me, she was wasting her time, or maybe that's what women do? He was examining a cloth fragment with a complex binocular miscroscope.

'Robes,' he said, misty with rapture. 'Doesn't the name sing?' He snapped at Nicola, who instantly whipped out a notebook, 'Tell her it's robe, printed twill cotton, of course.' He looked at me, dreamy. 'They were made from 64-square printing cloth for wraps, mostly Cashmere effects. From the Edwardians on, they became furniture coverings and curtains.'

'Sounds brilliant.' He talks like this for hours. I've heard him. 'What's on, Florsston?'

'Zephyrs.' He was still dreamy. 'That's a lovely old fine-cotton. I like astrakhan. It's got a fleecy look. All that uncut pile, Lovejoy. And people actually prefer plastic. Can you credit it?'

'No,' I said, because I couldn't.

'What's lovelier than an embossed velveteen? And I *do* mean cotton, Lovejoy!' He pointed to his great stacks. 'I've stuff there to melt your heart. Get me a drink.'

I'd almost turned to obey before realising he meant Nicola. She shot out with an apologetic bleat. He checked that she'd gone.

'There's a fashion scam in the north, Lovejoy. Arranged from here in East Anglia. You ever hear the like, tail wagging the dog? It's being funded by somebody who died half a million years gone.'

'I've heard.' I hadn't, but why admit ignorance?

'That Thekla's scouring the earth, wants you back. And there's big money in, for nothing.'

That stumped me. Money, pouring for no reason? 'Money is always *for* something, Florssie.' I asked cautiously, 'Who in the north? Where?'

He said, 'I know what you're asking, Lovejoy. Nobody's defaulted on payment for my invaluable services in identifying antique fabrics. And nobody's hired me for the northern job either. But Spoolie dropped by this morning, asking if you'd been here. He'd just come from Thornelthwaite. It's a mansion house viewing. Said you'd not turned up on time.'

Well, I thought, antique dealers' paths do cross sometimes. I'd have to contact Spoolie.

'Ta. I'm obliged.' Nervy now, I paused. 'Florssie. I might need you for a special, okay?'

He thought. 'Would you take Nicola off my back?'

'Eh?' I went blank. I couldn't imagine anything better than having Nicola on my back. 'Er ... ?'

He sighed, woebegone. 'I'm no het, Lovejoy, never will be. She knows it, but is obsessed with the challenge of curing me.' He winced, indignant. 'Doesn't she think I've tried – well, maybe *wondered*? I keep telling her to get lost.'

'And me do what with her?' I asked, worried.

His eyes closed in horror. 'I can't *begin* to imagine, Lovejoy. I thought you'd *know!*'

'Silly sod. I meant, what then?'

He grew wistful. 'In the olden days you could sell a woman, even a wife, in any tavern.'

Nicola returned carrying a tray, whisky, ice. I got none. Florsston has a terror of people spilling booze in his workshop.

'Who's that work for?' I asked.

'Carmel. She's selling might and main lately.'

'Well,' I said, heart in my boots from panic, 'everybody raises cash.'

'Seems so.' Massively he slurped his drink, held the glass out to Nicola for a refill. 'Don't be late at Thornelthwaite, Lovejoy. There's word that stealing from the viewing there's as easy as scrumping apples.'

'I heard that,' I said, casual. 'Cheers, Florsston.'

He wouldn't let me go. 'Is it a deal, then?'

'Eh?' I eyed Nicola as she poured him another drink. What choice had I? I might need his expertise. And my agreement might turn out to be a lie. I sometimes find that. 'Oh, sure.'

'Thank you, Lovejoy,' he said fervently. 'I'll do you a grand job. I pay in full. Agreed?'

'Agreed.'

The taxi found me a roadside nosh bar in a discarded cattle wagon. It had a clientele of lorry drivers, cow men, and dogs. I hired a driver's hand phone, collected quite an interested audience as I struggled to find help, cursing under my breath.

Sometimes I think I must be on another planet. Then common sense takes hold and I *know* I'm on another planet. It's women who straighten me out, even crooks.

Take a look at the news, I thought, phoning away. Any day of the week, there's things you could never invent. Pick any three items. Do you get sanity? All news is completely mad. Today's random three: a special discount is announced, on giant hissing cockroaches, everybody's favourite pet. Next, astrophysicists admit that they've 'lost' – their word – nine-tenths of the universe. Third snippet: some loon's taking on Parliament for ignoring some ancient law that fines you for jumping a bus queue. They're true, just this morning's lunacy. News is the reason I live in antiques, even if it's daft and dangerous.

But sometimes a particular idiocy's strangely hard to find. Like policemen, crooks are sometimes never there when you want them. It galls me. Nine phone calls, and all I'd got was scatty wives, bored boyfriends, irate assistants. Soon I was in a blazing temper, very unusual for a patient caring bloke like me. Then I struck oil, in the person of Wanda Curthouse.

'Wanda?' I sweated relief. 'That you? Lucky me! First number I try!'

'How sweetly you lie, Lovejoy!' Wanda purred. 'In what desperate straits are we this time?'

'That's unkind.' I was hurt. 'You've forgotten.'

'That we were friends, until a young tart strolled by? Then you were off like Dick Turpin on *his* mare.'

Wanda made me feel bad for nothing. It's not fair. I put a high quality smile into my voice, trying to ignore the packed nosh wagon.

'I hoped for a better welcome, love. I'm trying to make amends. How's business?'

'Excellent. My husband Bertie does my accounts now.'

'Good!' I really meant oh hell fire. When you need a crook, go for the best, even if she hates you. 'Above the old antiques lark now, eh? Never mind, love. I'll get Fribble from East Mersea. He can shift bulk at short notice. And he's not crossed swords with ArtWatch. So-long, love.'

She tried to answer but I rang off and waited breathlessly. The lorry driver wanted his phone back, but I clung to the gadget. It rang, Wanda, enraged. 'Lovejoy?' she shrieked.

'That you, Wanda?' I went all innocent. 'How'd you know my number?'

'I have the right electronics. You mentioned ArtWatch. Is it that big?'

'Sorry, love, but there's some Gloucester lads ... '

Her voice went seductive. 'Darling, we're friends ... '

In half an hour, I alighted at Briony Finch's gates. Nothing for it but to live a life of phoney honesty for a little longer. During which time, I'd see why I was expected here in the first place, especially as I'd never heard of the blinking manor until today. I found Briony, advanced smiling, my hands outstretched, and drew her into solitude.

'Hello, love. Sorry I was so long. My friend was ill with, er, sickness. It's all going to be okay. I've hired a friend who leads an auction team.'

Briony didn't smile. 'I've been told all sorts of hideous things about you, Lovejoy. The minute you left the dealers became extremely frank.' I'll bet they were, I thought, but stayed mute. 'Some of them were *very* charming, Lovejoy, and most anxious to help. Why did you tell so many lies?'

'Fibs.' Smiling, I took her arm. 'It's code. She's bossy, a bit scarey.'

'Then why did you hire her?'

'She's got the right electronics, love. Anything else been pinched or whacked while I've been busy?'

'No,' said this innocent, pleased with herself. 'I've had to be vigilant, though. One gentleman was actually paying a dealer for one of Kate's chairs! As if he actually owned it! Can you imagine?'

Well, yes. I sighed. Moncing's the oldest trick in the book, to distract while thieving, at an auction viewing.

'Get near the door, Briony. Try to be a deterrent.' I was worn out. With Briony's vigilance we'd be lucky if there was anything left to auction. No sign of Spoolie, but I'd have to get hold of him and ask what the hell.

Please, God, I prayed, bring Wanda Curthouse on swift angel wings even if she still hates me. An enemy in need, friend indeed.

15

E VER GET THE feeling that your head's so filled with clutter you're demented? I found a loo, went in and sat. Solitude is restorative. I'll bet that half the Venerable Bede's parchments came to him when he was on the loo, maybe Shakespeare's too. But even there you're sometimes not safe. I babysit for the village women. For sanctuary I once sat in the toilet, but the infants battered in hollering for me to come out and play. I kept hearing the dealers' mutters as they passed the door. One deep voice, Brummy accent, showed his temper.

'That casting's stinking the bloody place out. Warn Brady to cool it.'

'Can't be cooled, Vet,' somebody snickered.

'Fewer effing jokes, you,' Vet growled.

I almost smiled. The trick when casting white metal is the temperature. You test it with a burnt match. Touch the end into the molten metal, it emits a wisp of smoke. No smoke, don't proceed. Too much smoke, give up. But just a wisp, pour the molten metal into your quick-set mould, and you have a good replica. Very few circuses — antique dealers in scarey numbers — bring their own delly men. A delly man's a faker who'll fake anything on the spot, moving with his hirers, day to day. They're pretty rare. Each has his own modus op. One I know does it mainly in a van, a mobile lab. They were probably dellying a lovely silver vinaigrette. I'd seen it in a cabinet pathetically labelled *Please do not TOUCH*. It was worth stealing, for vinaigrette collectors spell money.

Back in the eighteenth century, such was the stink in London's streets, and of unwashed bodies in fashionable assemblies, that the more sensitive gentry carried silver containers of herbs soaked in vinegar to defeat the offending pongs. Collectors go wild for vinaigrettes made as likenesses — Byron, Nelson.

The real risks to the delly man's activities are in the auction room. The auctioneers might not let you hold the item, for example. In a country house auction, though, it's simple. It might be necessary to hire a slip man. They're around still, these archaic entrepreneurs, though like lamplighters they're dying out. You pay them fee-for-item. Describe the item to the slippo, and he'll hand it to you in quarter of an hour. Pay him instantly. You make your mould, and return it. Later, maybe even after some days, he'll find you, smiling. You're expected to 'dash' him, as the trade still says in 1880 Gold Coast lingo. (Never use that horrible word 'tip' to a slip man; he'll be mortally offended, being a true gentleman crookster.) The 'dash' is half what you paid him before. Fail to dash him, you'll never hire a slippo again as long as you live. A close and sophisticated lot, they. Here, in this innocent house you could have nicked the entire manor, no slip man needed.

When it seemed quiet I left the loo. I'd already made up my mind to stay and see the auction through. I had to find Spoolie, who had known I'd be here when even I hadn't known that.

More people were in now, casual 'women' – meaning stray gapers, male or female – and swarms of dealers on the merry round of picking and nicking. The auctioneers arrived. I knew none, thank God. They looked right prunes, two oldies and a bossy youth they called Lionel. Briony welcomed them like conquering heroes.

She told me, glowing, 'You can relax now, Lovejoy.'

'Eh?' I stared at her.

'You've been on tenterhooks! Should we have tea?'

'No, love. I'll stay here.' With me by the door, some dealers had at least hesitated. I shuttled between the exits, but it was like those school problems about a forty-gallon bath leaking from different holes. The dealers nicked stuff, stowing the loot in their parked motors and coming grinning for more.

The auctioneers conferred, glanced my way, sent their toffee-noser across.

He tapped my chest. 'Okay, squire. Piss off.'

'Are you sure, sir?' I went servile.

A sour featured whiffler with a hand under his left lapel tapped his shoulder. 'Sure, Teazle,' Lionel said.

'Ta, Mr Lionel.' Teazle gave a triumphant smirk.

'Er, excuse me, sir.' I was narked, seeing Teazle stealing with that old trick. He didn't even pause, went on down the wide steps. He'd be gone in minutes. I could feel the sweet clamour of the antique concealed under his collar. He'd been hiding handies in his gloves. He'd examined several pieces of jewellery, got two in his trouser turn-ups, one in his hat's leather brim-lining. One was a pearl pendant, only mid-Victorian but, I was sure, Fabergé of St Petersburg.

Lionel took my arm in a tough rugby grip. 'I said piss off.'

'Really?' I said, 'Briony said to list the thieves.'

'To *what*?' Lionel couldn't believe his ears, bawled, 'Jasp! Get Al and Mack! We've got a right one here.'

'I've counted eleven thieves, sir. Including you.'

'You ... ?' Three whifflers approached. One hung back, an elderly geezer in a waistcoat and watch chain. Somebody with sense, then. I'd an idea I'd seen him before. 'You cheeky sod. Out, lads. Mind the brickwork.' His joke. He gestured, and the ignorant pair advanced.

'The donty'll cost you, Lionel,' I said, less servile, 'if they lay a finger on me.'

The whifflers halted. Lionel didn't understand.

'Donty? What's a donty?'

'Tell him, old man.' I spoke only to Waistcoat. 'And tell him how I know.' In the distance, I heard an engine chopping the air, growing louder. My spirits rose. Could this be Wanda, arriving at last, in style? The old man spoke with serfly diffidence.

'Donty, Mr Lionel, is when auctioneers mark antiques down, to deliberately sell to their own planted bidders.'

'And ... ?' I prompted.

'And have hirelings selectively remove items that might attract bidders.'

Mr Lionel acted furious. 'I'll have the police on him! Slander! Get Inspector Derrick, Jasp.'

Derrick? I groaned inwardly. If the worst happened, I could still hoof out and leave this mess to poor Briony Finch. I knew Derrick, and he me.

'For ... ?' I asked Jasp.

'For the auctioneer staff to buy themselves ... '

An elderly austere auctioneer joined us as I finished for Jasp. ' ... at a private ring auction afterwards. Thus stealing six value equivalents, the going rate for a donty.'

'What's a value equivalent?' Mr Lionel demanded.

This is ignorance for you. There should be a university degree in ignorance, B.I. (Hons), Bachelor of Ignorance with Honours. Post-graduate courses, M.I., then finally a Ph.D. in it. Maybe they already have?

'What's going on here?' the old auctioneer asked the air. I like the officer class's pretensions. Like old jokes.

Lionel seethed. 'This tramp's making accusations, Mr Stibbert.' Stibbert was the name on the vans, leader of the pack. 'I'm evicting him.'

'What accusations?' Stibbert spoke to a distant throng, Adam's apple yo-yoing.

'Of a donty. It's some trick or other.'

Stibbert gave a wintry smile. 'Then he's read my book, Lionel!' He lowered his gaze to me. All ex-officers are thin, over three yards tall. 'The donty is an auctioneer's confidence trick. The word was coined by one Lovejoy three years ago. You'll not find it in dictionaries, only in ... ' he twinkled, ' ... my glossary!' He snuffled, the ex-officer version of a laugh.

'Rotten book, Mr Stibbert,' I remarked. 'Make your staff read it, though.'

A helicopter landed in a paddock about four furlongs off. Through the window I saw a lovely figure alight, shake out her blonde hair. I was astonished. How could Wanda have done so well without me? She'd prospered mightily. Three other birds dropped to the grass. Well, I'd hired her. I wondered if her husband was a big bloke. Wanda stretched, and signalled to five cars coming through the ornate gates. As organised as ever, Wanda. I smiled the smile I'd been keeping in reserve. Relaxed, I strolled away as old Jasp whispered to his elderly boss.

The marquee seemed placid after that. Sundry folk were drifting in, reserving chairs near the auctioneer's podium.

'What're you after here, son?' an old lady asked me. 'That silver teapot? Just like my old mother's.' She dabbed her eyes. 'Will you bid for me? Only, I've never been to an auction before.'

'You thieving old bitch,' I said. 'Knock it off or I'll pull your teeth out.' She gasped with outrage, but boxers are always indignant. A boxer is somebody on a dealer's payroll, hired to inveigle innocents into bidding for an antique on her behalf. During the bidding, boxers make a fuss, withdraw bids, start arguments, create confusion. The public is deterred and the exasperated auctioneer scrubs the item entirely. Boxers are usually frail crones or old soldiers, plucking on heart strings with their bony scavenger fingers. They're paid a flat rate.

Time to watch, not to do. I heard the helicopter cough aloft, and smiled. Wanda's team could outdo a brigade. I could have killed for a cup of tea. I wondered what stunt Wanda would pull. She never lets you down – when moved by her own special brand of greed and carnal lust. Old Jasp woke me minutes later. I'd dozed off from excitement.

'Lovejoy? Mr Stibbert says please join him forthwith.'

'Ta, Jasp. Forthwith no.' I smiled into his worried face. 'If I were you, I'd clear off before it happens.'

'There's no way out, Lovejoy.' He'd sussed me all right. Wanda's hooligans must already be legion out there. It was what I wanted to hear. I reclined. I'd need all my energy later. And if Spoolie was so desperate, he'd find me, and I'd no need to search at all. The murmurs of the growing crowd lulled me to sleep.

16

WHEN YOU DOZE, questions begin. Out of nowhere come queries nobody can answer. Like, why *did* they murder Mario Lanza? And how can whole populations starve when there's a food glut? Why do poinsettia branches all pup red leaves when you've only hooded one branchlet – they need sixteen hours of dark for redness. Or why is everybody daft about Victorian Penny Blacks when they're ugly as sin and they printed 72 million of the damned things anyway. No answers.

Except sometimes there comes a glim called hope. When it does, it lights the world, fills the heart.

'Lovejoy!' Somebody shook me awake, whispering.

'What?' I whispered in terror. 'Is he back?'

Then I came to. I was in the auction tent, not cavorting in secret sin. I put my head between my knees until my mind landed. People were crowding in, dealers gaily swapping IOUs.

'It's time! Isn't it exciting?'

Briony Finch. I like older women, but she was a pest. 'Aye, gripping,' I said. 'Briony, don't create a fuss. D'you hear?'

'Of course I won't, Lovejoy!' She actually hugged herself. I had to smile. 'It's all going perfectly! I gave your lady friend tea. Isn't she sweet? Her own helicopter!'

'It's not fair to interrupt,' I said. 'Stay by me, okay?'

She went frosty. 'I don't need reminding how to behave, thank you.'

'Sorry. It's just that I'm excited.' I was sleepy. 'I hope the auction goes well, for your chip shop's sake.' That set my mouth watering. How long since I'd eaten, days?

'Ladies and gentlemen!' Stibbert ascended the rostrum, adjusting the pince-nez on his proboscis. He glared, restraining righteous anger at the naked avarice before him.

'Auction rules are in the catalogue,' he intoned. 'Please remember that strict attention is paid to the law.' I honestly didn't guffaw. 'Prices on the fall of the hammer.'

No, really. I didn't fall about. Stibbert made it sound as if his firm was as honest as the next – which, come to think of it, it probably was.

'Lot One,' Stibbert intoned, as Lionel's minions took station. I was beginning to wonder what Wanda was up to. I'd expected her troops to be mingling or mangling. So far there was nothing. Not that I'd been vigilant. Briony squeezed my hand.

'It's really sweet of you to be so *worried*, Lovejoy.' She smiled, embarrassed. 'I appreciate it. I'll try to repay ... ' She coloured. I looked noble, because it actually was magnificent of me.

'Lot One showing here, sir!' the whiffler's traditional cry.

Old Jasp, poor chap. He held up the motoring leathers, straight Edwardian. It lacked the helmet and goggles now. Somebody had nicked them. Stibbert hesitated as he realised that his own catalogue listed the old motoring set as complete. Professional skill came instantly to his aid, so he disregarded honesty.

'Motorist's garments, Edwardian. Offers ... '

The bidding started, rose to a moderate sum. Briony squealed excitedly, gripping my hand. I wished she'd turn it in.

'Going ... gone. Lady?'

'Lissom and Prenthwaite,' said Lydia's cool voice.

Which made me shrink. She must have sailed in with the throng as I'd dozed.

'Lot Two,' intoned Mr Stibbert, peering at us like God from a cloud. 'A tribal African stone carving, Benin, with the name *Nigeria* engraved under its base. Start me at ten thousand ... ?'

Gasps from the public, plus hooded grins from the dealers. I looked about. More anxiety, because still there was no sign of Wanda. I trusted her, though. And I'd seen her arrive, hadn't I, in her whirly?

It was knocked down for a song, a mere three thousand. I almost wept. It was genuine, some memento of Nigerian colonial days.

'Name, if you please, lady?'

'Lissom and Prenthwaite,' sang out Lydia, joyous.

'Lot Three. Collection of Royal postcards, dated, showing portraits and scenes, seventy in all. Who'll start me? Can I say ... ?'

'Quid!' one dealer guffawed, to general titters.

Briony was scandalised. 'Lovejoy! Those ... '

Sadly I shook my head. 'They're a drug on the antiques market.'

Early postcards of old aeroplanes, buses, vehicles, would have been a different matter.

It happened just before Lot Ten. Wanda entered, even more beautiful than I remembered, walked down the aisle, choosing to seat herself at the front. She took her time crossing her legs, to stifle progress. Mr Stibbert graciously waited, then ahemed back into action.

A reserved man, a carnation in his lapel, walked to the rostrum and with a sad nod to the astonished Mr Stibbert tapped the microphone.

'Excuse me, please,' he said in measured official tones. 'All right for sound, Mr Shepphard?'

'Just right, sir,' somebody called out gravely.

My spirits soared. I could have married Wanda on the spot, fell in love with her all over again, that genius of crookdom and hoodery who was saving the day, the scam unfolding before my very eyes. Dealers began to whisper, heads down. I saw at least three rise and start to edge out, only to halt and sink back. I saw one dealer in front of me bend to stow a brown-paper parcel under a neighbour's seat, getting rid of evidence.

'You dropped this, mate.' I retrieved it for him.

'Ta,' he said, murder in his eyes.

'Lighting, Mr Shepphard?' called the carnation man.

'Exact, sir,' said the same voice. 'Still rolling.'

'Thank you.' The man said something under his voice to Mr Stibbert, and turned to us. We were frozen, agog. 'Ladies and gentlemen. I want to thank you all. This auction was the subject of a special TV Roving Reportage. For the past six hours, all cars, auction items, and yes, even your own conversations have been faithfully recorded. Our Looming Lenses will be familiar to those who watch Channel Zen.' The man smiled. I saw Wanda's head tilt slightly, checking every word, giving orders. This must be Bertie. Grudgingly, I had to admit that he was playing really well.

'That's illegal!' somebody called angrily.

'No, sir. We *saw* a deal of illegal conduct, but *our* procedures are quite legal. You, sir, for instance, removed a certain item and stowed it in your car. Check that, Mr Shepphard?'

'Yes, sir. Rewind tapes?'

'We'll see it on TV,' Bertie decided. He smiled at the protester. 'You might like to see if I've described your theft correctly.'

The audience was rising, dealers bellowing with fright. Then quiet descended as a file of four uniformed policemen advanced to the rostrum, and several plainclothesmen came after. Now I did look.

'Does that mean we'll be on telly?' a woman next to me asked brightly.

'Looks like it,' I answered.

'How exciting!' she exclaimed. 'Why is everybody so cross?'

'Can't fathom some folk, love.'

'I do apologise for this,' Stibbert was saying, lost. Bertie was implacable.

'This whole auction was false, ladies and gentlemen. We at the TV authority believe in fair play. So we set this up, recording the entire viewing with our hidden cameras, to show how crooked *some* dealers are. We took the precaution of sending certain honest dealers in. Those will of course hand in the antiques they have purloined. When every motor and person has been cleared, everyone will be allowed to leave.'

'William!' exclaimed the lady to her husband. 'A real sham!'

'Scam, missus,' I corrected politely. 'Thrilling.'

'Slowly, please, ladies and gentlemen.' Wanda's hubby pointed. 'Tables are at the exits. Those who willingly return their concealed items can be escorted outside. Their vehicles will be searched. Is that understood?'

'Understood, sir,' minions called.

'And keep filming. I want every face, every number plate.'

'We already have most, sir. Just one or two.'

The lady near me tutted, 'They should have *told* us! I'd have had my hair done. Straighten your tie, William. I don't want Esme criticising.'

'Lovejoy,' Briony asked, puzzled. 'There's something I don't quite ... '

I got in first. 'I was just about to ask you.'

'Excuse me.' The woman was doing her make up. 'Can we buy the video?'

'Yes,' I replied gravely. 'I'm a TV agent, so I can take your order. For an unbelievably small sum you may reserve your copy, post free ... '

'Lovejoy?' Wanda's man was looking over heads to me. 'Ladies and gentlemen. We have obtained the services of a divvy, that human scanning machine. He will stand by the exit, and ensure by his miraculous infallible sixth sense that no-one has any concealed antique.'

You could have heard a pin drop. Everybody turned. I rose, made my way along the row.

'Lovejoy?' I heard Lydia gasp. She pushed towards me, blazing. Usually she apologises every inch.

She stood before me, bosom heaving, eyes glittering. 'I might have known!'

'Sorry, love.' Every dealer in the tent wanted to marmalise me.

'You're *always* sorry, Lovejoy! You've ruined a whole auction!'

Humility evaporated.

'You silly mare.' I felt done for. 'That chap, remember? Wrote you a note after you bought Lot One? He's offered to find you a matching motorist's helmet and goggles. Am I right? He's nicked them. They're in his car.' I hadn't seen anything, but it had to be so. On cue, a bloke bolted towards the exit, but got wrestled to a standstill.

'A note?' Lydia, pale, rummaged in her handbag. That would take a fortnight, so I spoke on.

'And your Nigerian stone carving. Notice that hardly anybody bid?'

'Because I judged my bid to perfection, Lovejoy!' she shrilled. The crowd was our silent audience.

'No, love. Because a dealer had just engraved the word *Nigeria* underneath.'

'During the viewing?' Still furious, but bewildered.

'I was to be distracted by an old dear who wanted me to bid for her, the Auntie Masie trick. She's over there. Her partner'll be the culprit.'

'But why deface an ancient carving, Lovejoy?' Lydia was almost too angry. She'd tell her mum tonight, 'Oh, the *shame!*'

'Nigeria wasn't called Nigeria until a British colonial's wife actually invented it in 1914. You see, Lydia?' I said sadly. 'You've forgotten everything I've ever taught you. An ancient Benin carver *couldn't* have inscribed *Nigeria* on anything. Possible bidders would have tried to make sure of the date, and would then suppose the carving a fake — and not bid. See?'

'They'd not bid?' she said in a small voice.

'Anybody fool enough to buy wouldn't be able to sell the defaced carving. So you'd have to sell it to somebody who'd pretend to be taken in. You'd sell the genuine piece for a song, and be glad.'

'Be glad?' she repeated, eyes huge.

It was no good. 'Think, love. The whole auction's off anyway.' I made my way to the main exit where Wanda's men were stationed, and wearily started listening for the faint chimes of a wondrous – and better – past.

The excited couple who'd sat next to me smiled chattily when their turn came, smiling coyly up at Mr Shepphard's cameras. It'd do no good. They were all phoney, cameras, sound booms, the whole Wanda gig. But they invited me to come and stay in their bungalow at Wells-Next-The-Sea. She promised that I'd lack for absolutely nothing. I said ta, I'd be along a week on Tuesday.

When the marquee was vacated, one hundred and thirty-six small antiques were found hidden under the chairs, and another forty under the dais. Deterrents work sometimes. Wanda came over, smiling.

'Lovejoy? Meet Bertie.'

'Wotcher, Wanda. How do, Bertie. You did superbly.'

'Naturally.' He was not glad. 'Hurry out, Lovejoy. Take up station.'

'Eh?'

'The gate. You are needed to search cars.'

'Right.' I left the marquee with Briony. Mr Shepphard's team was already among the Plod.

'Lovejoy,' Briony said. It started to drizzle. She tutted in annoyance. 'There's something I don't understand. My husband was in the police. Are those uniforms correct?'

Halting, I raised my gaze to heaven. Why me?

'Are you well, Lovejoy?' she asked. I'd just saved her bacon, and she quibbles about duff police?

'Feeling God's rain on my face,' I invented. 'It reminds me of childhood, before I realised I was born to be an antique dealer.'

'How perfectly charming!' she said, misty.

The cars were queueing at the main gate. I resumed walking. 'Now shut your teeth, you silly cow, and do as you're frigging told. Understand?'

'Lovejoy!' She trotted after me on the wet grass. 'What a horrid thing to say!'

'Write all names and car numbers down,' I told Shepphard. 'No good relying on cameras alone, okay?'

'Already got the lads at it, Lovejoy,' he said. 'Mr Curthouse said that was essential. Legal reasons.'

'Mustn't forget those,' I said. 'Anybody brewing up?'

Nobody was. They'd got hot flasks, not for sharing with the likes of me. And everybody was going to earn a mint. I beckoned the first motor into the gateway, ready to suss it out. *Why* me?

And came an answer from on high: Nick a motor, Lovejoy! Sleekie's not far away. Remember those motorist's leathers? A heavenly brainwave. When in doubt, bring on theft. Smiling, I realised I'd been far too honest lately, altogether too kindly. Ta, God.

'In the boot, Mr Shepphard.' I smiled down at Skanner's apoplectic face. 'And something under the bonnet. Step out, please. Strip off. I want that statuette's heel, Skanner. And you can pay for the repairs.'

I told Briony, 'Bring me some grub, love. This'll take some time.' She argued, but I told her that food and hot tea was a rule of the Amalgamated Divvies' Union. Still no sign of Spoolie, East Anglia's film maniac. The only cameras here were pretend, under black cloths. Yet was it why I'd been somehow got here, to wreck this simple country auction?

'Next, please,' I called, trying to look confident that my excursion wasn't going tragically wrong.

17

Briony finch was solicitude itself. She had an elderly lady hard at it when I came in.

'Thank you, Mrs Treadwell!' Briony kept saying in that get-lost tone by which women rid themselves of nuisances. The old dear plodded on.

'Is there nothing stronger?' Wanda asked outright.

Briony got flustered. We were in the main dining room. You could hear the shouts of Wanda's lasses cataloguing. At least they had sense — weighing items, measuring paintings, the obvious tactics that museum curators overlook.

'My sister kept a bottle of sherry. Kate loved a glass at Christmas-tide. It seems to have disappeared.' Briony flapped her hands helplessly.

Among antique dealers alcohol has zero life expectancy.

'It possibly got accidentally thrown out,' she said. 'I'm so sorry.'

'Let us be precise, Mrs Finch.' Bertie wanted the deal closed. 'One third, adjusted for value-added tax, of all incomings from your forthcoming auction, once arranged, will be Wanda's. The balance will be declared openly. You receive the money in thirty days.'

'She accepts,' I said. 'Ta, Wanda.'

'Can you not send out for a proper drink, for Christ's sake?' our leading lady asked irritably. 'My whirlybird army of scholars, and not a flaming drink!' Scholar's the in term for a hired crook, 'soldier', a hood taken on for a scam.

'Whatever the level of sales,' I told Bertie.

'That's axiomatic, Lovejoy.' He didn't like me. I was happy with that. Maybe he'd heard lies about my honesty. I couldn't imagine him and Wanda ...

'Axiomatic or not,' I said, 'Briony wants it.'

'Very well.' Efficient, but sour as lemon soup.

'Wanda?' Sonny, her leading whiffler, interrupted, dragging in a terrified uniformed man. 'Listen to this.'

'Tell.' Sonny cuffed the prisoner by way of prompt.

'Lovejoy spotted the ship,' the bloke said.

Wanda stared at me. 'Ship?'

'Toy. Model of the *Lepanto*.' My hands showed its size. 'Only tin, but valuable.'

'How valuable?' Bertie's voice rose to falsetto. So he did feel passion, money his trigger.

'Small house, freehold, garage,' I said.

'Worth a *house*?' Bertie drained before our eyes, swayed, lips purple, and fell forward in a slump. Sonny made a grab, managed to hold him. Mrs Treadwell trundled off for some sal volatile, recognising a true faint when she saw one. Wanda belted me round the head, screaming.

'Bastard, Lovejoy! He's *delicate* about money!'

Briony was stunned. I fended Wanda off. Sonny said, 'Wanda,' and she calmed instantly. I understood. Bertie only loved lucre. Marrying Wanda was simply the acquisition of an asset. Needing physical solace, she had Sonny to help in more ways than paltry. Anybody less like a Sonny I'd never seen. Stonily malevolent of eye, and angrily fast with aggression. He'd give Wanda solace all right.

Bertie moaned. I watched, fascinated. The prisoner, a fake bobby, stood limply by. Mrs Treadwell wafted a bottle under Bertie's nose. It seemed to lift his head off. He shot up, sneezing and gasping. Good old Mrs Treadwell, I thought, eyeing her little green bottle. I hoped the Victorian courtesans managed to come to with somewhat more elegance. Bertie was now belching and retching.

'See what you've done, Lovejoy?' Wanda yelled. 'Bertie's *fragile!*'

'I didn't do anything, love,' I explained patiently, pointing to the prisoner. 'It was him.'

Wanda's eyes narrowed. 'What'd he do, Sonny?'

Sonny said, 'He let himself be vamped by some young tart. She nicked a toy ship.'

'I didn't think, Wanda,' the man bleated. 'She said it was for her little brother. I let her out through the walled garden.'

Wanda went quiet. I griped, looked for the exits. Wanda noisily belligerent, or in the throes of passion was one thing. Those I could cope with – have done. But Wanda going quiet is a frightener. As the air chilled to sub-zero, Briony voiced her chintzy cheeriness, seeing her little tea party running into difficulty.

'I'm sure Lovejoy has it wrong,' she gushed. 'That tin toy was only a copy, made by that London sculptor, a friend of Kate's at art school.'

She smiled, benignly passing the biscuits. I took a handful, calories where you can. Sex is the same but different. 'For a cinema film.'

'Shhhh, Briony,' I tried, but she went on digging the miscreant's grave.

'It wouldn't even float!' She trilled a gay laugh. 'So they never used it!'

'Film?' Bertie slumped back into his faint. We were all mesmerised by Briony's saga.

'Yes!' she prattled gaily. 'They made one of those terrible war pictures here. Because of the lake, you see. Was it *In Which We Serve*? Terribly sad. How they managed to photograph toys instead of real ships, heaven knows!'

'Briony,' I said, as Bertie whimpered in and out of coma. 'Please ask Mrs Treadwell to bring her sal volatile back.'

'Of course!' she cried, and tripped happily out.

Sonny instantly let Bertie slide to the floor. He downed with a thump. Wanda didn't bat an eye, still ominously silent, staring at me hard. My cue.

'Look,' I said, trying to save a life or two. 'Auction prices for Germans, the trade's term for tin toys – vehicles, vessels, horses – have soared. The *Lepanto* model – I think the Maerklin firm – was on this table. It's big, three-footer. Four funnels, two masts, red keel, black hull, five lifeboats a side complete, twin screws, 1909. I told one of Stibbert's whifflers to guard it with his life.'

'Lovejoy. What price?' Wanda's voice became sleet on a window about to give. 'A film prop. Mint, provenance guaranteed?'

'Enough to buy a six-year world cruise, Wanda.' Barmy, but true.

Wanda winced, a pretty sight under the right circumstances, but not now. 'Jim?' she whispered to the frightened man. 'The whiffler tipped you off that the tin model was valuable. Did the girl pay you?'

Sonny, unbidden, felt in Jim's pockets, brought out a wadge of notes, chucked it on the table.

'Wasn't worth it, Jim,' Wanda said. 'Who was she?'

'Some Aussie blonde, young,' he whined, shriller. 'I didn't think. For Christ's sake ... '

'No, Jim. For mine.' She dabbed her eyes, but making sure her heart-felt pity didn't ruin her mascara. 'It's your legs, Jim. Lovejoy, go with Sonny.'

For one frightening second I misunderstood. Sonny frog-marched Jim out. He was babbling, 'Wanda. Please. I've got children ... ' I followed, my mouth dry.

We went round the side of the house. Sonny took Jim across the gravel, pushed him against an outhouse wall. My legs were shaking more than Jim's.

Sonny stood away. Jim said a wobbly, 'Can't we come to something? We're mates, right?'

A car drove slowly up. Sonny replaced the driver, gunned the engine, raised his chin to me as if in mild exasperation at the carry-on. I wondered how to get Jim a remission of sentence, and didn't say a word.

Sonny moved the car an inch. Jim doubled in anticipation. Sonny called advice. 'Keep straight, mate.' Jim came erect, closed his eyes.

The car moved slowly, suddenly accelerated with a spray of gravel. It drove at Jim, crunched his legs against the brickwork. He whoofed forward, his forehead slamming on the car bonnet from the impact. Blood spurted up the wall. Why up? I thought, sickened. The motor lethargically dragged itself away, idled.

'Get an ambulance, Forkie.' Sonny emerged, slammed the door. He beckoned me. We walked back inside. 'You know the rain, Lovejoy.'

Rain and hail, tale, rhyming slang, the story for when the police came. An accident, somebody tried to nick the car, nobody saw. Jim, poor Jim, got in the way.

Not long back, I loved a lass who worked among antiques periodicals. I persuaded her to list the 'WANTED' adverts. Know what collectors, dealers were screaming for most? Answer: pond yachts. No kidding. Little old sailing models. Plus bits of ocean-going anythings. So if you've any photos of defunct liners, old portholes, lengths of the *Mauritania*'s hand rails, you are undoubtedly in the money. Who knows how these craving epidemics start? Maybe it's the boom in air freight, bulk carriers, the dwindling-to-nil of our shipbuilders. Or maybe nothing we know.

Wanda saw us come. Bertie dozed on.

Until now I haven't described Wanda Curthouse, because it wouldn't have been fair, plus I wanted to show how trustworthy I am. You'll see why. This is Wanda:

Two inches above medium height, skin like an English peach, lips full, eyelashes a foot long, natural blonde in her late twenties, walks like a trained dancer, shapely legs ascending to heaven, her figure a dream made for lust, as near as any form can get to perfection. I was there once, and ruined it by consorting with her younger sister. Wanda is an aggressive grabber, but what man would care? Any bloke who strayed from her was a nincompoop. I have an excuse, being a pushover.

'In a way, I was glad when you called, Lovejoy,' she said, as if the Jim episode had never been.

'Ta, love.' I heard Bertie gag. 'He's breathing funny.'

'He's dreaming of lost money,' she said offhandedly. 'Know why I was glad?'

'About me calling?' I thought, blank. 'No, love.'

'Because you're straight, Lovejoy, though weak as a kitten about women. I put her in charge of an hotel, Blair Atholl.'

No prizes for guessing who 'her' was. 'Oh, right.' I added lamely, 'Wanda. About Geraldine. It was all my fault. Can we start again?'

'Lovejoy. Do me one thing?'

'Owt, love. Give or take,' I added quickly. Wanda expects you to keep promises, a horrible habit she was born with.

'Find where that tin ship goes.'

That astonished me. I mean, here was this brilliant woman, beautiful beyond belief, who I'd taught antiques for the best years of my life – read three weeks – and she didn't have the sense to see that Basil-the-Donkey would know its whereabouts in a day.

'Right. It'll take a couple of days,' I lied.

She gazed at me so long from her position by the bright window that I felt as faint as Bertie, but less limp, as it were. My throat went thick. Women make choices vanish. 'What's between this Briony bitch and you?'

'Eh?' That also surprised me. 'Never clapped eyes on her before. Wants to run a chip shop.'

'And you just blundered in?'

'Honest, love.'

She said, insulting, 'She's just your type – breathing.'

'Ha ha,' I said evenly. 'Want me to stay?'

'Yes. Here will do. But no fiddling. I don't want Bertie fainting every two minutes.'

'Hand on my heart. Wanda.' I hesitated, checked he was still blotto. 'Is everything all right? Don't want to pry, but … '

She smiled. I weakened further. A woman's mouth changing shape makes your mind change shape too. I clung to the subject, whatever it was.

'You always could tell, Lovejoy. It must be the psychic in you, the divvy bit.'

'Psychic!' cried Briony, coming in with Mrs Treadwell. 'That's the word! I knew it! Lovejoy is psychic for old antiques!'

'Briony!' I said sternly. 'You've taken ages.'

'I'm so sorry,' Briony said, flustered. 'Mrs Treadwell had put the sal volatile back in the box and misplaced its key.'

We got Bertie round by the old dear's waft-explosion technique. As I propped him up, I found Briony gazing fondly at me.

'You know what I think, Lovejoy? I think you are really embarrassed deep down, to feel so lovingly about things, that you mask your psychic nature.' She smiled at Wanda. 'Mrs Curthouse, does it run in the family?'

This was getting out of hand. The important thing was to keep my suspicions about Tinker's lass Vyna from Wanda. I didn't want to get smashed against some wall like Jim. The important thing was to find out how Vyna had got ahead of me, and made another fortune.

'Lovejoy? What is it, dear?' Briony asked, a hand to her throat. 'You look positively ... cross.'

I laughed a swashbuckling laugh. 'I was imagining being on that tin steamer, if it had been real, Briony. That's all.'

'Honestly!' she exclaimed, laughing. 'Little boys, aren't they, Wanda? I expect Lovejoy was the worst!'

'That's true, Mrs Finch,' Wanda said. Her voice had gone quiet, her eyes unwavering. 'Absolutely the worst. Can he stay here? I could adjust the fee ... '

'Of course he may, Wanda!' Briony cried. 'It's not the slightest trouble, after all you've done! Not another word! Lovejoy will be our guest.'

'That's settled, then. Thank you, Mrs Finch.'

'Briony, please. Unless you think I'm too forward?'

God give me strength, I thought, exasperated. We'd be ironing the anti-macassars next. I was glad when Bertie awoke with a snort. By then, Wanda was talking urgently into a mobile phone, and Briony was instructing Mrs Treadwell about airing beds. I couldn't catch what Wanda was saying but I heard my name.

Quiet voices are a nuisance. I've often found that. The sal volatile bottle drew my eyes. It was silver mounted. I desperately wanted to see what locked box it came from. If I guessed right, it was worth me. Give or take.

18

'Don't say psychic.' I argued with Mrs Treadwell much later.
She was doing vegetables. I'd made a couple of phone calls.

'That's because you're psychic.'

Arguing with old women is like arguing with young ones,
hopeless. I once had a row with a three-year-old lass, who reckoned
toothpaste was made from horses. I ended up believing her. Even
now I'm queasy about cleaning my teeth.

'Psychic's balderdash. Antiques just give me flu. Sweating and
suchlike. Gets better as soon as I move away a few yards.'

'That's psychic all right, Lovejoy.'

She washed some white stuff and started to dice it. Watching an
older woman preparing vegetables is really calming. They must have
done it in Ancient Rome, and in the famous Iceni tribes hereabouts.
In my own county of Lancashire, our great pre-Roman Queen
Cartimandua must have lain on her fur rugs idly watching her serving
women doing vegetables for her dinner – in the rare minutes she
could spare from snogging with her standard-bearers while her King
snored his head off. (Terrible to relate, the one occasion he did wake
she had him executed.)

'Anyway, it wasn't an antique. Not old enough.'

'Excuses. Are you Mrs Curthouse's friend?'

Danger. What was Wanda's story, cousins or something? 'We're
vaguely related.'

'That's right, Lovejoy. Invent.' The old lass swished things in a
colander.

'Where's your apothecary box, love?'

She laughed. '*Thought* that's what you come for, Lovejoy! Your
sort wants woman's company for what you can get.' I won't tell you
the rest of her affable onslaught. It's all wrong. I'd honestly visited the
kitchen to cheer the lonely geriatric up. But that exquisite bottle,
reduced by Mrs Treadwell to a sal volatile sniffer, deserved a good

home. 'Your one saving grace,' she ended, 'is that you're stupid. Women wrap you round their little finger.'

'Nark it,' I said. 'That box.'

She stopped work, not an ounce of trust in her. 'It's beautiful. And yes, it's complete. Every one of its square-sided bottles, stoppers, original lining. The old lady gave it to me. It's my one and only heirloom.'

These apothecary boxes are worth a king's ransom. Every grand house had one, from the seventeenth century on, until Edwardian times. Travelling druggists and apothecaries topped up supplies as the families' potions, simples and unguents depleted. I hate – *hate* – the modern trick of turning these lovely boxes into cocktail cabinets. I was pleased with old Mrs Treadwell. She would preserve it. That's all a genuine antique asks.

'You'd do better with somebody else, Lovejoy,' she rabbited on, 'instead of that hard bitch.'

'Here!' I exclaimed. Their instant hatreds astonish me. 'You mustn't say things like that!'

'I know her sort, fur coat and no knickers. Men are magpies. Anything with half a shape and her own teeth, you lose control. Briony Finch is the woman for you.' She wagged a chiding potato peeler. 'Nobody misses a slice off a cut loaf, Lovejoy. Remember that.'

An old saying, straight from my childhood. I smiled. 'Suddenly decided I'm eligible?'

'Suddenly decided you're soft in the head. If you'd an ounce of drive you'd charm that mahogany apothecary box off me quick as a wink. But you give up, once you see I mean to save its life. Soft as putty. You don't stand an earthly with women these days.'

She started dicing some meat. I rose in a hurry. You can only take so much carnage. I'm all for soya bean. The silly old sod laughed, holding her sides.

'Well, it's raw,' I said feebly.

'Of course it's raw, silly! It's not cooked, so it's raw. When it's cooked, it's not raw.'

Her laughter receded as I made the safety of the hallway. I could hear Wanda's mob organising the items, covering them with dust sheets. I found Sonny.

'That Aussie girl. You see her?'

'I think so, Lovejoy.' He was checking lists. 'Lovely bit of crumpet. You know her?'

'No. Odd that she homed in on some pricey toy and lammed off through the bundu, though, eh?'

'Made herself a tidy fortune,' Sonny said sarcastically. 'That a clue?'

'Why here, though?'

'Because it was today.' He paused, penny finally dropping.

'Among others, Sonny. Big, easy pickings, sure. But would this have been the biggest local auction? Not by a long chalk. There's three. One today, over at Holt.'

'Dealers go where it's easiest. The bigger the stately home the greater the profit. She'd go for the simplest, right?'

He still wasn't quite there. I helped.

'See, Sonny? You knew all that straight off. But would a girl fresh off the boat? A lone teenager, new into lipstick, roaming the countryside?'

'Teenager, was she?' Sonny said evenly, eyes hard.

Oops. 'The way Jim described her. See my problem?'

'No, Lovejoy.' He was cool. Wanda's girls stopped working to listen, Wimbledon style, heads switching side to side. 'I see one single problem. You came in out of the blue and raised the game here. Why? It makes me wonder if *you* aren't the problem, not some stray tart whizzing through.'

That's where logic gets you, nowhere. I shrugged, accepted defeat, and went to look at the grounds. Briony found me.

'Lovejoy.' Stern, facing perdition. 'Those policemen weren't true policemen at all, were they?'

'Special constables, love,' I lied. 'Security firms have their own uniforms. Wanda hires them.' The uniforms were from theatrical costumiers.

'Oh, that's all right then.' She hesitated. 'Did you hear about Jim's car accident? One of Mrs Curthouse's men drove him to hospital.'

More lies were called for. 'Jim'll be fine. I talked to him. He was worried nobody would feed his pet dog.'

'Really? Will they?' I gazed blankly at her. She explained, 'Feed his dog?'

'Oh, yes.' I improvised. 'A labrador spaniel.'

'A what?'

I grew impatient. What right had she to cross-question me for heaven's sake? It's no wonder she narked me. 'I'm off to Norwich, love. Where's the bus stop?'

'Three miles off. The bus comes tomorrow.'

Odder still. I thought of a girl carrying a three-foot long metal model. I'd looked at the kitchen garden from Mrs Treadwell's domain. Beyond, fields, grazing herds, woods, a river. Now no bus.

'Love, would you let me use your phone, please? And I need a lift to Norwich.'

Spoolie arrived at the railway station buffet as it got dark, full of grumbles. I cut him short. I was knackered.

'Lovejoy. I've come a million miles.'

He meant sixty; I'd put a threatening message on his answerphone. First thing he did was walk round looking at film adverts. I watched. He's just seeing if the posters are nickworthy. He runs The Ghool Spool, a small antique shop between two tottering pubs in Mistley. Movie ephemera, stars' autographs, starlets hair-bands, old newsreels.

'Nothing much here,' he groused, going to ask the counter lady if he could filch a couple of her posters.

There were very few passengers about at this hour, sipping tea, waiting for trains. Spoolie had that look, a typical ex-con with a mission – to get the whole world hooked on the film industry. I know for a fact that he's been trying to buy the 'H' from that Hollywood sign in California. His wife left him, annoyed when his obsession took priority. Now, Spoolie had known that Chessmate told me about the Thornelthwaite auction – and was worried sick when I'd been slow to arrive, Florsston said.

'Here.' I shelled out a little gelt. 'That's your lost trade, Spoolie. Business good?'

'Good?' he growled, splashing tea into his saucer, an old prison trick, to drink up fast before somebody else gets it. 'It's terrible. I went into feminism. Hopeless. Not worth a light.'

That startled me. 'Feminism?'

'All the rage, believe magazines.' He tapped the Formica. 'How many movie titles start with *Woman*, Lovejoy? Forty-seven, compared to 153 that start with *Man*. See what I mean? And *Mrs* and *Mister* are as bad – 13 to 59. *Princess* titles outnumber *Prince* titles, half as many again. Frigging movie business.'

'I know.' I thought of poor Nanook, that genuine eskimo who'd starred in *Nanook of the North*, 1921. When the documentary achieved mega status, the news media gleefully beat a path to Nanook's igloo to announce his sensational world fame and endless riches – to find that Nanook had starved to death in the ice. The movie makers had simply forgotten him. Once they'd used him and made fortunes out of him, of course. For them, a movie success story. To me, I think it's creepy.

'Tell me where a German tin toy'd turn up, Spoolie. Made for an old war film. Mint.'

'Tin model?' He quivered, a huntsman's pointer. Acting that he'd not known of it at all, of course.

Only giving him the bare bones, I told him about the *Lepanto*. He moaned so loud I had to kick him under the table.

'Every collector's dream, Lovejoy. Two catches, see?' A catch is a mob of collectors interested in a particular antique. 'Models are so in you wouldn't believe. The movie manics would compete. Oooh.'

Another kick shut him up. I hate over-acting. I'd got his point. 'Who'll it go to, Spoolie?' I had to follow the trail he was to lay.

He licked his lips. 'A deal, Lovejoy. I'll promise a hundred thousand, from a collector I know. We'll split fifty-fifty, okay?'

'Spoolie.' I went sad, genuine. 'I haven't got the model. But sure as God grows trees the toy'll turn up in forty-eight hours. Pure cash sale, highest loot on the nail. Where, though?' We waited. I said, 'I'll ring you every few hours, night or day, Spoolie. Be there. I don't want to be chatting to a recording as hoodlums batter my door down.'

My manner – fright mixed with anger – got through.

'What's in it for me, Lovejoy?'

'Maybe the odd letter, photos perhaps. Copy of some old war picture.'

'Let's have your phone number, Lovejoy,' he said, pulling out a pencil stub, but by then I'd gone. Some folk think you were born yesterday.

The missing girl Vyna was not far ahead. I was learning. She knew me better than I her, but I was close. She must have been at Thornelthwaite, seen me spot the valuable item. She was cannily fast, and had accomplices. Somebody had paid Spoolie – supposedly scouring for film relics – to keep watch for my arrival. So Spoolie knew the backers, if not the scam. Chessmate probably knew much less.

In a way it was quite exciting, now feeling the hunter instead of the hunted. When I caught up with Vyna, she was in for a piece of my mind. But where had she gone?

Tinker. I'd have to contact the old soak, my one reference point. I got a taxi back to Briony's. In the dark it looked like something from the Baskervilles. Luckily Briony was up, and Mrs Treadwell for once wasn't sawing up the corpses of massacred creatures. She'd made a vegetable curry.

'And you got the rice right!' I said, whaling in.

'He's nothing but trouble, this one,' Mrs Treadwell told Briony. 'Likely to get worse.'

'She's trying to marry us off, Briony,' I said. 'Watch her. Haven't you proper bread, Treadwell?'

The old lady clipped my ear. She'd made a lovely batch of flour cakes and loaves, still warm. She sat to watch me eat, as if seeing me gorge somehow filled her. I was full afterwards, first time for days. I told Mrs Treadwell she was learning, and told Briony to take her on the staff. We bickered. Then Mrs Treadwell got reminiscing, the old days when there were cinema parties for London folk at the mansion and all was gaiety. Film folk were such nice people. Aye, I thought, listening dozily, tell Nanook's ghost.

19

'IT COMES DOWN to money,' I told Briony Finch next morning, getting ready to go, and I was explaining what would happen. The day dawned cold, bright.

'It shouldn't,' Briony said, wistful.

'Nothing should,' Mrs Treadwell said. 'More, Lovejoy?' She'd chopped coddled eggs up in a cup. I'd thought the art had died out when I was little.

'Ta. Look, Wanda will empty Thornelthwaite. They'll give you a list – furniture, everything down to the last cufflink. Don't worry,' I put in quickly as Briony made to interrupt. 'Wanda is trustworthy. I've said she can shell five per cent.'

'Shell?'

'Steal from the accounts,' I explained patiently. 'Anything more, I'll be cross. Bertie, her numbers man, will render the sale figures two days before the auction.' I grinned, pleased. 'Auctions don't usually end so neatly!'

They looked. 'End?' Briony gave Mrs Treadwell a glance, comparing bafflement. 'Sale figures *before* the auction?'

'Of course.' I sighed. 'It's called a jumper – no, love,' I interposed as they drew breath, 'a jumper *auction*. Wanda'll give the summary to you, because I'm going. You can have it checked. It gives prices a bad name.' Translating every inch was giving me a headache. 'Here. An example.'

The small wooden case I took out was walnut, banded, very like some homemade cigarette case, 'C.C.' marked on the outside. You wouldn't give it half a glance. I opened it. A tiny abacus lay within, polished ebony beads on metal rods.

Mrs Treadwell accused, 'That's Mrs Kate's knitting counter. Why isn't it with the other things?'

'Because it's valuable, love.' I opened my palms, like a conjuror about to con the public by his *Positively no deception*! 'Positively no deception. Antiques give money a bad name, and vicky versy. I lifted this from the living-room to stop it being stolen. They were nicking everything not nailed down. In future, lock up every small thing. They are the first things that strangers steal.'

Briony cried, 'But it would look as if we didn't trust people!'

'Isn't it terrible?' I said, dry.

'Valuable?' Briony was curious.

'It's two years' rent on a shop, love. Clockmakers Company of London.' On the inside of the case was pasted a paper, instructions in old copperplate. 'The maker's name will be somewhere. Take it.'

'Why didn't you steal it, Lovejoy?' Briony asked. 'Bertie said you were a cheap thief. Who,' she added nervously, 'kills people.' She went lamely on, 'Please don't think I'm being critical.'

'Jealousy, love. They're all like that.'

'It's being psychic,' Mrs Treadwell said comfortably. 'People are jealous.'

'Will you shut your tripe!' I yelled, losing my rag. 'Stop batting your gums, you silly old trout! Psychery's quackery!'

'Your eggs, Lovejoy.' Unabashed, she plonked a cup in front of me. 'Don't feel bad about your third eye. Just take care.'

See? Women and children take not a blind bit of notice. Some blokes I know can frighten people with a glance. Me, women just shake their heads smiling. Nothing I can do, except pretend they're thick. I addressed Briony.

'Wanda knows I have a notion of what your furniture and movables should bring. She'll give you a list, with money totalled, before the auction. Post-dated, see?'

'No, dear.'

Headaches have no business coming. It's not fair.

'Can you imagine any better guarantee,' I said, eyes closed, 'than reporting that this made a thousand quid *before* it'd been sold?' I patted her hand, the one with the abacus. It must date from our Great Civil War period, if not earlier. It had broken my heart to hand it back. But Briony Finch, would-be proprietress of the kingdom's Number One fish-and-chip shop, would have been a lamb to the slaughter. And I'd got back on Wanda's good side, assuming.

'Guarantee?'

'It's Wanda's written promise, love. That she'll obtain *at least* those prices for you. Anything above, Wanda splits fifty-fifty with you. Anything less, Wanda will have to make up.'

'Jumper sale.' Briony repeated it, learning.

'That's it. Not many antique dealers will do one.'

'They might lose a lot of money?'

'Got it! Mrs Treadwell? Have you any bread organised?' I didn't smile. She came with a mound of cut bread and butter, touched my head like *she* forgave *me*.

'Wanda,' Briony said. 'Why so willing to take risks, for me?'

'They'll make a fortune, love.' I noshed fast. I hate being asked for my motives. Motives can't explain murder or honesty.

'Or lose heavily, Lovejoy?' Briony said slowly.

'That's their business. I can't help inefficiency.' Quickly I made sandwiches of what I hadn't finished, and bussed the pair of them. 'See you. Better get on. I'll phone.'

'Lovejoy.' Briony came with me. Mrs Treadwell stood watching. I made the top of the front balustrade, but I'd guessed right. A police car was coming in the gate. I drew back. 'Won't you stay until it's all done with?'

'No, ta, love. I wasn't here, okay?'

Her mind clicked into gear. Her eyes widened. 'You want me to lie to the police?'

'Aye, love. I'm in trouble if you don't.' I scooted out of the kitchen door, past Mrs Treadwell, hared across the walled garden and into the field beyond.

There was an ancient trackway between hedgerows. After a furlong, it opened into a lane. Marks in mud showed where a motor had waited one drizzly day.

After ten minutes of plodding, I got a lift from a horse-drawn cart. For seven miles the driver narrated the problems of cattle feed. I went, 'Mmmmh,' because where's the difficulty? Cows eat grass. I've seen them at it, fini.

The city hadn't changed much, but I had. I phoned Roger Boxgrove, reported semi-truths to his answerphone. I'd been hoodwinked too long. I was sick of being mucked about. I suppose losing the abacus did it, but I wanted to kill somebody for treating me like a fool.

'Spoolie?'

He was edgy, his voice squeaking high D. 'Lovejoy?'

'Me, Spoolie.' Should I ask cryptically if he was being hounded, or what? But not only Wanda has technology. We might be bugged. 'Any news? I'm in a hurry.' I opted for falsehood, the way one does. 'I'm after a different antique, er ... ' I invented, rollercoaster, 'I don't want to waste any more time on that model.'

'Honest?' Then he gasped. My worried mind noticed that he reacted with eagerness to my fantastic lie *then* gasped. As if he'd been reminded by a blow.

'Aye, Spoolie.'

Silence. Somebody'd cupped the receiver. He came on, panicky casual.

'Lovejoy? The Maerklin model's in Brum. I know where she took it. Meet you there?'

'Why can't you tell me now, Spoolie?'

'The vendor's shrewd, Lovejoy. Won't let me say.'

My heart was banging. Poor Spoolie.

'Tonight, Lovejoy? Station?' The line went dead. Then, 'Not the International Centre one, the other. Tennish?'

'Okay, Spoolie.' Sickened, I put the phone down. I almost said farewell. I hadn't told Spoolie the maker's name, but somebody else had. And he couldn't find a Maerklin with a map.

I phoned Briony Finch, told her I'd ring from Birmingham station after ten o'clock. Then I gulped my egg butties, grumbling because there were only three. Birmingham, ten o'clock on a cold frosty night? Some hopes, Spoolie, I thought. I needed a car. I went and bought some cheese rolls, hoping they weren't sogged to extinction with mayonnaise. I got a taxi to take me to Sleek's village. Seven miles, and thirteen quid. Is it any wonder nobody goes to Norfolk?

She was pretty. Grief filled my heart. Everybody's got a gorgeous bird but me. I smiled, hoping I'd done my teeth.

'Hello!' I said. 'Mr Sleek in? Sorry I'm late.'

'He isn't back. Have you an appointment?'

Appointment? To see a card sharp? God Almighty. You'll need an appointment to go to the loo next.

'Yes. His motor. Rejuvenation time again!' I was poisonously jovial. I'd have liked to have been sincere with her, but I was scared Sleekie would hove up. 'The new car wax is in! We have it ready at the ... ' Christ, what was a car polisher's garage called? I invented, 'At Car Cosmetics, Inc. The wax starts going off after thirty minutes. Can I have the keys, please? The usual place?'

'You came by taxi.' She was doubtful. 'From a garage?'

That narked me. Why women don't trust anybody is beyond me. As if they're on the lookout for deception. Here I was, a hard-working car restorer, come all the way to this one-dog hamlet just to polish her bloke's motor, and she mistrusts me. How did saints manage?

'Even I can't drive two cars at once!' I laughed merrily, but could have strangled her. Would you believe it, but still she stood there, doubting away.

'Sleekie's very particular ... '

'Of course!' I said soberly. 'Security is everything with these old Braithwaites. Did he see to the hand throttle?' I frowned accusingly. Women love to deny an accusation, clear themselves.

Her brow cleared. I knew its name. 'Oh, he's always out there!'

'Good, good.' I smiled, glanced at her quaint little floral village, a scene of stuporous dullness. 'Sleekie has all the luck. Lovely cottage, lovely motor, and beautiful ... ' I tried to blush, but they never come when you want. 'I only wish I was half so lucky.'

No ring on her finger. She followed me, noting my look.

'I've still a chance!' We laughed a merry laugh. 'Will you be here when I return the car, er ... ?'

'Ruby.' She undid the garage padlock, swung back one leaf of the door and darted inside, tapped some alarm control. The gleaming roadster was in racing green. 'It's ... ?'

Oh, hell. 'Me?' I paused to look into her eyes. How do blokes like Sleekie, an aging card sharp, get birds like Ruby? I'm loyal, sincere, straight as a die, and on my tod. 'I'm Jig,' I said. 'Pleased to meet you, Ruby.'

You can only hold a meaningful look for a few seconds. It becomes too pushy. I busied myself, checking that the chains weren't on the hubs. Sleekie's a mistrustful sod.

'Have you the key, please?'

'Yes. Here, Jig.'

She unclipped it from her waist. For a millisec I stood as close as morality allowed, my breathing funny. You get times like this. I was torn between this exquisite creature, or making off with Sleekie's massive vintage motor. Fear won. Sleekie's sly. He wouldn't exactly brawl, but sooner or later I'd finish up poisoned by an unknown hand.

'What time will you bring it back, Jig?'

Hopes rose. 'I'll phone, Ruby. Will you be in?'

She nodded. 'Yes. He does evening performances at the Tolbooth. They send a taxi.'

'Marvellous.' I swung into the leather driving seat. 'Perhaps we'll have time for ... ' I displayed a brief wrestle with conscience.

'Maybe.' Pert smile, a definite plus.

A quick prayer to the god of engines. I pumped the petrol knob. You can flood the damned thing and it takes a day to clear. A woman called Sheila had showed me the manoeuvres, but that was long ago. I'm still not sure whether I was glad when the motor fired. I'd have to go. I'd forgotten how high these old bangers are. You seem miles off the ground, on a palanquin. I released the handbrake, rolled the old car forward. I halted.

'Ruby. You wouldn't like to come along?'

'Get on with you, Jig.'

Jig? Me. 'Have the kettle on, love.'

'Perhaps.' Her smile lit the village.

Easing the clutch in, I moved the monster forward onto the road.

A lovely lass, Ruby. Did she truly know the effect she had on a bloke? No. Women don't, or we'd never do anything but grovel around them all day. Lucky old Sleek. I've never seen him with the same woman twice on the trot.

20

O LD MOTORS ARE a nuisance. You never feel in control, like the damned thing's letting you sit there but don't get too cocky. Also, they're strong. Touch the throttle, and your neck jerks, clings to some tree you passed a mile back. The wind howl deafens you. And other motorists salute, applaud, hoot, expect a wave. Old motors are absurdity on wheels. No wonder they never caught on. And costly? The thing needed filling up every two yards. I stopped at one garage and got surrounded by enthusiasts asking about axle ratios and carburettors. I hid the gleaming hulk behind a tavern's trees when I stopped for nosh in the early afternoon, but it was no good. Some maniac actually asked if I'd let him slide underneath for a gander, as if any car's interesting. I'd sold this old crate to Sleekie five years before. It had acquired a load of trophies along its front bumper, I noticed, this rally, that procession, like war medals.

Driving, I pondered. 'She,' Spoolie had let slip, took it to Brum. 'They' wouldn't let him say more. Plural, of foes? And somebody had told him the maker's name, Maerklin. Poor Spoolie. The nasty thought kept recurring. Spoolie wouldn't keep our appointment. Despite my promise, I turned at a roundabout and headed south on the A45. The opposite direction, save you getting the map out.

The only time in my life I ever gambled for a girl, I lost to Sleekie. He'd eyed this Alana I was trying to inveigle. She had a collection of bat-and-ball implements – racquets, battledores, table tennis bats. She had a couple of old shuttlecocks. They aren't worth a lot, and she wouldn't budge. I'd decided to slope off when we met this man waiting for an illegal auction ring to finish in a tavern. He started doing card tricks. Alana was fascinated. My hopes rose that she might leave me, if she was fascinated enough.

'It's the eastern shuffle,' I told Alana airily.

'Shush, Lovejoy!' she'd cried. Sleekie produced four aces from the pack. Then, surprising even me, a fifth.

Sleekie had smiled. 'It sometimes works by chance, sir. That's why nobody ever gambles on that trick.'

'I'd gamble,' I said recklessly.

He said, 'Play you for your lady, then?'

A joke, but with pretended anger I grabbed the cards. 'Right!'

'Lovejoy!' cried Alana, but thrilled.

'Then I too will stake everything I possess,' Sleek said gallantly. Maybe that's why he always gets the bird, having more outrageous lies.

We cut the cards, the highest card in five. He was determined to lose, of course, after which he'd entice me and gullible boozers into a game. I'd end up losing, and so would everybody else. These card sharks are ten a penny. On auction nights they go from tavern to pub, work the football trains. I played silly, of course nicking the top card. He knew, but couldn't accuse me outright of wanting to lose Alana. His eyes went glassy. He had no time for legerdemain. I kept the pack by my elbow, in case a tentacle reached that far.

He won with the ace of spades I'd given him. Tight-lipped, I bussed Alana. She stared with horror as I offed, obviously to blow my brains out from grief. In fact I went to a dance at Benignity's, only hiding my heartfelt sorrow, of course. It was Alana's own tight-fisted fault, her and her rotten collection.

A twelvemonth later, I met Sleek on his way to Newmarket races. We had a laugh, old times. He didn't harbour a grudge. Alana had turned up trumps (sorry), helped him in sussing out marks in taverns, did a few games of her own. He'd ditched her in Southampton, a cruise ship. I sold him the Braithwaite, brokering for Big Frank from Suffolk, our local bigamist, trigamist, umpteenamist, who still owes me for my cut. It had belonged to an old colonel with a gammy leg in an old folks' home.

I'd have gone for more legitimate means of transport, but I needed to blaze a trail. Reason: the old crate thundering away was unique. It was made by one Braithwaite, inventor of no renown. Very few people knew of its existence, except me, Sleekie, sundry ex-Sleek women currently recycling, and a few antique dealers. They alone would know what, and who, they were following. And one or more of them would know why.

Whoever came a-hunting me had hired the rival divvy, who was destroying me. It had begun when Tinker's girl called Vyna arrived, instantly to go missing.

That too was an uneasy thought. I lost concentration, frightening a motorist into hooting. Then he forgave me with a salute and a grin. I waved, fixed my eyes on the road, enthusiast of the sport of kings.

There's a village called Birdbeck so small that everybody misses it. Go through in second gear, you won't even know. It's within striking distance of my own village. It has two other attributes. The first is it's the unlikeliest hideout on earth if you want concealment. The second is Lizbet.

The hideout is a sweetpea farm. No kidding. Far as the eye can see, sweetpeas all colours of the rainbow. People come miles just to be photographed against the hues, scent the perfume. To me, see one sweetpea, see all. But Lizbet sends out catalogues by the million every year, sweetpeas this colour, that shape, this fragrance. You'd think people'd get fed up, but every year it's onward and upward.

'Wotcher, love. Lizbet about?' I parked beyond the forecourt. A quiet time. No queues, only women packing shipments.

'Up at the big house.'

'Ta.' I walked the rest, met Lizbet in her estate wagon before I was halfway.

'Lovejoy.' She cut the engine. 'How long this time? Two minutes? Ten?'

'Don't, Lizbet.' I hesitated. 'On your own?' She wouldn't have stopped otherwise.

'Don't pry. What do you want?'

Lizbet can force you into honesty.

'I am in trouble, love, but just passing.'

'Does it involve the police?'

My disclaiming chuckle would have appeased anybody else. It didn't even change her face. And it is a lovely face, smooth skin, eyes like jewels, fair hair, lips that tell you more than red wine. I felt myself pulled.

'I asked about police, Lovejoy.' She closed the car window a little. We talked through the slit. What did Tubb say about talking through glass?

'Of course not, love. I nicked a motor, without.' She knew without what. 'Can I leave it here till eventide? How's Jonto?' She has this infant.

'Not so little. Started school now.'

'Oh, er, great.' School? He couldn't have. Wasn't it only two years? But Lizbet was an obsessional timekeeper, so probably knew Jonto's age. I felt dispirited. Time would be more likeable if it'd only give it a rest for a month or two. 'Look, Lizbet. If it'll queer your pitch, I'll move on.'

'I'll let you, Lovejoy.'

'Right, right.' I was relieved, though I'd have still left the Braithwaite even if she'd said no, in a coppice you can reach from the main road.

Something caught my eye. A stick bearing my name, near a wide swathe of the most beautiful blossoms you ever did see. Magenta – no, more a purply scarlet. Exquisite. Take back what I said about sweetpeas being all the same. This one was magnificently shaped, wondrous. The throbbing hue stretched over the main field, deep, perfect, flowers from outer space.

'What's that, love?'

'*Lathyrus odoratus*,' she snapped. 'The plants we grow. Forgotten that too?'

My name was on the stick. *L. odoratus*, var. *Lovejoy*, it said. I went to look, touched petals. Lovely. I cleared my throat. Me?

'Lovejoy,' I read dully. I'd have looked at Lizbet, but flowers make your eyes run. 'Rotten name for a species.'

'Variety, not species. Is that it, the extent of your visit?'

'How's the farm?'

'Hard as ever, Lovejoy. Competitors, money for expansion, the usual. Lucky we're the best.'

'I heard you won again. Prizes, in the paper.'

'Naturally. You?'

We were fencing like Basil Rathbone in some mediaeval castle, but I was out of snarls. I kicked the soil, finally met her eye.

'Lovejoy Towers not been repossessed yet?'

'Yes.' I gauged the daylight. 'Look, love. I'd best be off.'

'Get in. I'll drive you, overtake the bus.'

And the whole journey we made what my Gran called spoon-and-saucer conversation, anything but what mattered. She dropped me off ahead of the Bures bus, drove off without a word.

Late afternoon, I reached town, lurked in the bus station's grotty nosh bar until twilight, then marched to battle.

An American gambler once said everybody ought to gamble, in case they were secretly lucky and never found out. That's like the belief in antiques. Sooner or later, we're all going to find the missing Old Master, Robin Hood's famous Last Will and Testament, or that stupendous Hope Diamond's non-existent twin. Look at the numbers who turn up at the 'antiques road shows' that flood the nation every weekend, carrying bedspreads, old – indeed new – chamber pots, desks made last week, porcelain figurines churned out in Taiwan. The truth: most is trash, utter dross. The fiction? Why, we *know* our thing is Gainsborough/Hepplewhite/Wedgwood/Lalique/Ming Dynasty. Anybody who says different is obviously trying to cheat us.

In other words, the con. But in antiques we con ourselves, as if we want to save dealers the bother. The hope in folks' eyes breaks my heart. There's a proverb: Guard against your enemies, but not even Heaven can save you from friends. There's truth. Our biggest friend is ourself – we think. We're our own worst enemy. This explains what follows.

The possibilities in any town are endless. But here, Thekla was gunning for me. Oddly was all right. Tinker should have been my first choice, but I'd got that strange feeling about him. Basil-the-Donkey, Alf, Gumbo and his ilk at the Antiques Centre? Well, hardly. I owed Alf that non-existent Bowie knife. Roger Boxgrove no also, because I'd got that strange feeling about him too. Carmel? I was hired to do some sand job for her, now lost in my labyrinthine mind. Tubb, her superstitious helper, I'd avoid, because God knows who he was phoning every stride. Jessica wasn't really up to this, and anyway'd sort of got religion, or not.

I crossed the road, keeping to the shop doorways, still working it out. I could fail on my own without Sadly Sorrowing's help. Lydia had declared independence. Mavis her mum had it in for me. Brad and Patsy were civilians, not in the game. Kent the Rammer, the rest, had jobs. Portenta, Tubb's stargazer, would be casting runes. Faye had had me arrested for not killing her bloke Viktor Vasho. Big John Sheehan only gives orders, never accepts them. Cradhead the Bill would gaol me for whatever crimes he suspected the world of.

Unerringly, I picked my one proven enemy. With a dangerous woman you know where you are, safety rule.

Aureole had left no lights on. I still had her key. She'd still be out, to see to her chain-dating quota. I just turned the key and went in. It's strange going into a place you intend not to burgle. It's as if it raises its eyebrows in astonishment, what are you doing here? I have feelings about houses, just as they have, if we'd but listen.

The kitchen, bedroom, pantry, where I'd washed the ambers. The fail-safe computer was in the wall of her bedroom. Her chain-date code word was AUREOLE, about as original as people get with access codes. She'd not used her birth date, though oddly I knew it from when we'd made smiles, two days before mine at the end of September.

The console came on easy, just the one button underneath. I didn't put any lights on.

I can't work those computer mouse gadgets, being clumsy, and they never click when you want. I used the keyboard. God, I pity folk who tap away at those things all day. It took me, I swear, nearly an hour's blundering to get the simple alphabetic list of chain-date clients. I couldn't find the actual dates. Aureole, clever lass, had blocked access.

The list seemed endless. It scrolled up and down, me wildly mixing right, then wrong, instructions, then having to start again at the beginning. I had to get up and take deep breaths. The computer wearily started firing instructions at me. I meekly obeyed. Finally it listed the names, sternly ordered me to go One Page Down At A Time.

Which is how I came on Boxgrove, Roger. I stared at the name. A number against his name, 007164. After long negotiation I persuaded the console to sequence the numbers. Grumpily, the screen rolled them before me at breakneck speed. I pleaded with it, and found 007164's date.

I sat staring. '007164: Dill, Vyna'. Tinker's missing relative. There was a 'Catalogue Reference' file, but I couldn't find it. Possibly details of each client – age, preferences, availability days, where not to go in case of meeting husband/wife/neighbours.

One thing narked me. I came across my name – me, for heaven's sake. Against Faye Burroughs. She had a number, I didn't. Against me was the word *Reserve: Aur.* So I was put aside for Aureole? A titbit for afters, when the great lady could be bothered? I seethed, almost told the damned thing to ablate its memory. You can do that, except I didn't know how.

By the time I got out it was latish. The chances of meeting Spoolie by ten were remote. I had no illusions. Spoolie had set me up. He'd be going over his old films in his pit at Mistley, not in Birmingham at all. Now I was really motoring.

Only one thing to do, make sure that Spoolie was home in his cinematic heaven. If he was, I'd know I was being flushed out to track me all the easier. I walked to the town's fly-by-night taxi rank outside Marks and Spencer's. I checked that I didn't know the driver, and told him Birdbeck.

By ten-thirty I was struggling to hold the Braithwaite on the

Mistley road. I smiled as I drove, working out phrases for Spoolie when he saw me. I was sure how it would turn out.

21

SPOOLIE'S SHOP IS on a slope in Mistley, between two black-and-white Tudor taverns that lean together confiding, like they do. I left the Braithwaite in a little square, otherwise empty, that opened to workshops for potters and arty-crafty activities, and a pair of old alms-houses endowed these 600 years. Lights were on in The Ghool Spool, I could see from the fanlight.

That really annoyed me, him so cool. Then I thought, oh, well, the poor blighter was being bullied. If everybody kept to the truth, the world wouldn't be in such a bloody mess, right? I rang the bell, a yank-and-clank tugger. No answer. I peered in the letterbox flap, and grinned at a ghostly flickering on the stairs. No hard feelings, Spoolie, I thought. Run your old films. You'll gape when you see me – you think I'm in Birmingham.

Startle him? But I hate practical jokes. You need a sadistic streak. But I mistrust humour. Even laughing at a comedian's jokes takes nerve.

I pulled the bell louder. No answer. I went round, found the back gate open. There's a yard with slate walls.

The back door into his storeroom wasn't locked. This was a bit unusual. I entered, calling, 'Spoolie?'

Maybe he'd just gone to answer his front door? I went through the corridor curtain. No sign. Upstairs I could hear that clipped speech, grating black-and-white films. Not sure whose voice, somebody once famous.

The front parlour is Spoolie's shop. Counter, stacked films, posters, boxes of postcards, past claims to past fames. A loo off the corridor. Spoolie always checked movies for props – guns, handbags, cigarette brands, clothes. Two movies a night, fourteen a week, cross-checking cars, shoe styles, jewellery, hats, anything to sell to film buffs. A barmy career, but fans are nearly like real people.

'Spoolie?' I started up the stairs.

He lives upstairs, with his projector. I'd only been up once before, three years back. He'd been looking for a partner in his money sink of a trade. I'd listened politely while he brought out his prize possessions. I'd thought him daft, and declined. The trouble was Spoolie always set his sights too low – he'd wept when he'd been outbid for a dress allegedly worn by Marilyn Monroe. Beats me. Addicts never listen.

On the landing, I knocked, the door slightly ajar. The projector was whirring away on a cut-down bookcase. Before the window stood a screen. No light otherwise. The projector did its muted clatter.

'Wotcher, Spoolie,' I called. Then I saw there was a gleam from under the bathroom door. Very cramped, though with my cottage I should talk.

Sighing, I relaxed in his armchair, from where Spoolie watches these grainy old films. He says it's from *Casablanca*, but it's not. I gave it him, a throwout. He paid twenty-eight quid for forged sale certificates to back up his preposterous claim. Derrin on the Walton marina churns them out for a pint. Spoolie thinks he boxes clever. Like I say, Spoolie's no brain.

'Spoolie?' I yelled. 'Get a move on.'

Old films are great sometimes. When you're all of a do, and your infant's playing up, feed and change him, pull the phone out, then watch some old re-run. You'll laugh with scorn for two minutes. Then you'll be engrossed, and wonder why you've wasted your life watching TV sitcoms. Like this, *Madonna of the Seven Moons*. I like Phyllis Calvert. It was up to where the gypsy makes love to the elegant lady who inexplicably appears in his encampment. Stewart Granger was doing his stuff. Spoolie would start hunting the gypsy caravan in the morning.

By the armchair Halliwell's reference book, with a scatter of notes.

'Spoolie? Jean Kent's doing her jealousy.' Tempestuous, sultry. 'I once saw her in a stage rehearsal. She kicked over a chair in a temper. God's truth.' I chuckled. 'Want to sell it? Personal True Star Reminiscence?' That's Spoolie's own product, a typed tale. He charges a fortune, guarantees that nobody else gets a P.T.S.R., but invariably betrays his guarantee. A real trouper.

He'd scrawled, *See Halliwell*. I hefted the book. *Novelettish balderdash killed stone dead* ... Halliwell'd written. 'Hey, Spoolie! See Halliwell's judgement, the rotten sod? Nothing wrong with film romance.'

No answer. These old black-and-white films are lustrously lit. Colour killed them, technology exterminating art. Colour films haven't quite got it yet. I really hope they succeed. The bathroom was silent, except for running water.

'Hey, Spoolie,' I bawled. 'List your top pre-colour pictures. You're not allowed *Double Indemnity*.' Everybody says that first, get crime out of the way.

No answer.

'I can't accept Anna Neagle, Spoolie,' I shouted. 'Nepotism. I'm sick of her brave face.'

Not a word. Shouldn't Spoolie've been shouting that I was wrong again? A *scatter* of notes. Spoolie was obsessional about his jottings.

'It's dawning on Stewart Granger now, Spoolie!'

Nothing. I cleared my throat. Voices aren't reliable, not when you want.

'Produced in the wartime,' I said, two attempts.

Odd, how the armchair was placed. I had to lean over to get the screen full face. Spoolie sits directly in front. Now, I don't really know Spoolic, only as a pattern, the way you know somebody who's always on your bus, the characteristics unalterable. I concentrated on Patricia Roc.

People don't change.

'Hey, Spoolie!' I called, higher pitched. 'The Yanks got upset because Patricia Roc was too flagrant in that James Mason highwayman picture.' I've loved Patricia Roc ever since *The Wicked Lady*. I gave a falsetto laugh, unconvincing, my hands clammy.

'What was that song, Spoolie?' I hummed a few bars of *When Love Steals Your Heart*.

Not a word. The film now could have been anything, *War and Peace*, the news, *Lawrence of Arabia*. I'd never had difficulty concentrating on Patricia Roc's breasts before. Why had a bloke gone for a bath in mid-obsession, leaving his watching chair askew and his notes scattered?

Scattered. Out of reach.

With a yelp I leapt up. The reel had ended. I hadn't even caught the screen blob that signals the switch. The picture whitened out, clack, clack.

'Spoolie?' I whimpered. Then I caught myself and smiled. Of course! He wasn't even in! He'd had to rush out, maybe to the pub.

Spoolie didn't drink.

Then I chuckled. Of course! He'd had to phone!

He'd a phone right here.

'Spoolie?' I said. 'Hell of a bath you're having.'

Then thought how stupid I was being. For God's sake, I'd only to try the bathroom door handle. It would be locked, which would prove he was inside, hiding from me. I relaxed in relief. The explanation was there all the time! Obvious! I chuckled at my own folly. I'd shout through the door — tell me who'd put him up to luring me to Birmingham, and I'd know it all. Q., as they say, E.D.!

He must have seen my arrival in the old Braithwaite. He'd guessed I'd be disappointed in his betrayal, setting me up. Well, sure, who wouldn't be narked? But I never really get mad, only sort of sad. And even God does that.

So he'd scarpered into the bathroom, was pretending not to hear. Hence his leap from his chair.

'Heavens, Spoolie.' I crossed to the bathroom and tried the handle. 'You had me going there.'

My scream deafened even me. I stood by the open door. Water touched my shoes. The light was on. I was stupefied, but not enough to prevent me seeing Spoolie lying in the bath that overflowed with reddish water, taps fugging the place up with steam.

That noise was intolerable, making my mind spin, my senses blanking out in the racket. I stopped screeching. The din ended. It'd been me, recoiling and howling and going, 'U-u-u-ughhh' or something and being sick on the carpet that was wetting as the bloodied bathwater followed me. I was vomiting and trembling because I'd been talking over old pictures with a dead thing, a corpse which was Spoolie.

For a horrible moment I found myself sitting in Spoolie's armchair while the celluloid went clack clack and the white screen gleamed pallor all about, perversely turning the whole room into a silent epic with shadow and light shoving each other for attention.

On its own the bathroom door slowly closed on Spoolie, lying there in his clothes in the red water. My non-brain went daft, asked, Hey, Lovejoy, what old film ended like that, a door closing while the camera withdrew? Spoolie once argued it was *Escape to Happiness*, the hero's wife coming slowly downstairs saying, 'Welcome home, John,' to Leslie Howard as the music swelled. I retched onto my shoes, realised I was being sick in dead Spoolie's chair and leapt away with a cry that almost choked me, my throat burning and my belly griping. I'm never cold, but found myself shivering like a thrashed dog. I whimpered and keened, made a dash down the stairs, falling on the second last like a fool.

The darkness was trouble, even though I wanted to be out there in the cold. I wanted rain to wash my hand where I'd touched the door. I wanted to splash in a gutter puddle, wash the bloody water from my soles, wet me all over so the death would go from me.

Without a thought I ran to the motor, cursed it for stupidity when it wouldn't start, groped for that weird pump thing without which it won't get going. It boomed into thunderous life. I'd driven four crazed miles before some motorist flashed me for no lights. I switched them on as his tail lights dwindled to nil.

Some time later, I stopped trembling. I realised I was on the Great North Road, by then coherent. I filled the Braithwaite up at a garage, I think near Norman's Cross. An admiring motorist came over, said affably, 'I expect you want to raise, eh? Need help?'

'Ta, mate,' I said. Reflexes can be useful.

'I'll do it!' Eagerly he raised the canopy. It was only then that I realised it was teeming cats and dogs, and I was wet through. 'I once had an Allard!' he said, like I was expected to kneel.

'Good heavens. You must be an expert.'

'Well ... '

Other motorists came to poke around the old crate. Christ, I thought, is the whole world off its trolley? I went to the loo, bought some grub and swigged some tea, I think. Then I drove off in a chorus of admiring shouts from yet more maniac motorists who sprouted in the night. I drove like an automaton, thinking nothing. I must have been going a couple of hours when road signs developed meaning. I played back the memory of those helpful motorists. Different accents, slidey up-and-down, sentences ending in a falling tone you don't get in East Anglia. Next sign, I made myself focus on the lettering, spelled it out as I trundled past.

Birmingham? I put my foot down harder. You will wait for me, I thought, you rotten swine. You won't let me lose the trail. If Lydia had stayed loyal instead of listening to her mother, or if Aureole had seen sense, if Thekla hadn't been vindictive just because I'd ruined her life's work, I'd have had a woman along to help. They're more practical, and see the obvious quicker because our male noddles are always chock-a-block with irrelevances. (Don't let on that I think this. I wouldn't like it to get about.) I'd made Spoolie ... I blotted out the verb to suffer, and changed emotional gear. I was sorry that kindly motorist had put the car hood up. I deserved a cold drenching. That bathroom stank. The hot water had discoloured his skin.

I pulled onto the hard shoulder, vomited a bit more for old time's sake, then drove on. I wondered who it would be. Not Spoolie, that's for sure.

22

NERVOUSNESS CAN DESERT you, when it ought not. Suddenly you're too calm, and don't care. I was like that. I parked the great engine at a hotel and booked in. I walked to the station.

Normally, I like railways, even the new rehashed terminals. And even at night, after the witching hour, when there's maybe the odd wino, and one tired dad checking the platform where his daughter's express will come batting in. Our main line stations always have a nosh bar, machines challenging you to combat space invaders. I got tea and a cheese roll damp with mayonnaise that stared me out and I chucked away.

Nobody I recognised. I watched two young up-tight lovers arguing in that silent head-shaking ritual that we developed in the caves. They left not speaking. I read the posters. They only reminded me of Spoolie, who would never do himself in. Okay, everybody gets downhearted, hears of a friend driven to extreme measures. But Spoolie, halfway through a film?

Cradhead's number gave me a yawning policewoman, poor thing.

'Cradhead, please.'

'The office is closed. Can I be of assistance?'

'Tell him The Ghool Spool. Somebody died.'

'Your name and number ... '

They think you're stupid. I went back to my place. Somebody'd removed my tea. I had a row with the server, so-called, and had to buy another. I watched the entrance. Nobody I knew. Passengers ambled tiredly. Three blokes stood by platform 6A's steps, waiting for the early newspapers, race addicts, different horses to lose on today.

Whoever came to meet me here was the enemy. Whomsoever sticks his hand in this pot ... Except I believe Judas was volunteering, faithful supporter to the last and the churches got it wrong. My foe was the traitor. Okay, I'd somehow got Spoolie topped. I ought to have guessed. Or maybe I really had, deep down, thought, well it's only Spoolie.

But I'd made sure he wouldn't ever publish his book that had occupied him ten years, *Film Props and Items*. It was an annotated list of all the movie gear used since the dawn of time. Even in clink Spoolie worked on it, had the prison arguing what Garbo wore, even about the window glass when Moose Malloy's reflection shows up in *The Big Sleep* and Dick Powell ...

Poor Spoolie, the horror of it.

The tea made me choke, rotten railway tea. I snuffled. The prison governor must've been dismayed when Spoolie got parole and the inmates reverted to crime. If I'd been the chief warder I'd have hired Spoolie as visiting recreation officer. *Spoolie, the Film Man of Dartmoor.* It'd have made a brilliant story, intercut with scenes from his favourite oldies, better than Burt Lancaster and his bloody spadgers.

Know what hurt? I hadn't really known Spoolie. Had I just used him up, to identify the rival divvy?

The traitor came in. I saw the reflection. It hesitated, drew breath, came closer. Stopped.

'Evening, Lydia,' I said.

'Good morning, Lovejoy.'

She sank opposite. Silly me, not keeping my eye on the time. Lydia, Miss Precise. So all that defection business was a fraud. I eyed her, curious. At times of treason you don't see the woman's shape, her luscious form, feel the slightest pull. It was like she was made of sawdust. I couldn't even register beauty. Women are creatures of love and betrayal, somebody once said, or should have, but quotations only work against a backcloth of understanding. Like, somebody worked out that Thomas Hardy used over 900 different poetic metres instead of the usual 300. So? Who knows the significance of that, but some dusty old dons cranking word engines?

Times like this, I wished I still smoked my pipe. I might have felt in control, instead of a twig floating towards rapids.

'I've come to apologise,' Lydia said. I watched her lips move and marvelled at my absence of hate.

'Apologise for what?'

'I've had a long talk with Mrs Finch.' She set her lips. Disapproval was coming. 'However, I have to explain something first, Lovejoy.'

Here it came: *I caused death, but in a good cause.*

'Spit it out, love.'

'There's no cause for vulgarity, Lovejoy.' She steeled herself, went for it. 'I *dislike* Mrs Treadwell.' She inhaled, settled. 'There! I've said it. She has far too many frank opinions for one of her station.'

The server came to steal my tea again. 'Finished?'

'Mind your manners!' Lydia didn't raise her voice, but heads turned even out in the concourse. Lydia invented a laser voice, and deserves royalties.

The woman flinched, wiped her hands on her apron. 'He's been here hours. This isn't a doss house.'

'*Did you hear me madam I will not tolerate such insolence …* ' Et Lydia cetera. I waited the storm out, trying to gee my mind to a synapse, make sense. Lydia sounded straight Lydia.

The woman slunk off trying to look as if she'd won.

'You dislike Mrs Treadwell?' I clung to the wisp.

'She revealed that she advised you to … ' She took shallow breaths, leapt. ' … to *cohabit* with Mrs Finch. Mrs Finch's type is the salt of the earth. But she is a middle-aged widow who operates a fish and chip shop. Doubtless she has merit … '

Why had Lydia come? If I was wrong about Lydia, then what was I right about? Maybe she'd explain. Owlish, I blinked, waited for her to … I was going to say 'come clean', but Lydia is testimony to Water Bright From The Crystal Stream.

She glared at me with the self-satisfaction of a woman having had a row.

'Now, Lovejoy. What is your problem?'

'Problem? I thought you'd tell me.'

'I?' She wrinkled her brow. It cleared. 'Is it that Wanda, Lovejoy? I also dislike her.'

My head sighed. Lydia solves everything by finding some other bird to hate, whereas I find that women are best liked. My difficulty is finding enough time to like enough, if you follow.

'I'm not sure, love.' I found her shape had reappeared a bit. Warily I watched her mouth, can't be too careful. 'I'm lost.' But not so lost that I couldn't prompt her into revelation. 'Tinker's cousin's girl Vyna. I'm trying to find her. I'm worried about the poor child getting into bad habits.'

'Go on, Lovejoy.'

A glimmer of mistrust still, not enough to justify stopping. I showed a bit of mannish loyalty, those irrelevant sentiments that Lydia knows simply don't exist. I worked up to it.

'It's my childhood, Lydia. I grew up in a northern town. Tinker's the same, a generation ahead. He knows what it was like.'

'So?'

A shrug. Apologies go a long way with Lydia, especially if they're for nothing. 'Tinker had to stay in case Vyna showed up in East Anglia, see?'

She hesitated. 'All the antique dealers know about Tinker's relative, Lovejoy. Vyna should have stayed studying fashion.'

'Fashion?' I said. This was supposed to be me, explaining. 'Vyna?'

'Of course. She'd been touring fashion exhibits in museums. Didn't I say she'd been to Salford for that purpose? You don't listen. But you haven't the resources to find her, Lovejoy.'

'No, love.' I was patient. 'I went to the police. Cradhead's doing nothing. People won't give Tinker the time of day. And the girl could be anywhere.' Noble, I girded myself. 'You might not be aware, Lydia, but a teenage girl is still a child.' I waxed lyrical about me, the brave rescuer, battling to save a forlorn maiden. Lydia halted me.

'Hasn't it occurred that she might be evading you?'

'Lydia!' I went stern. 'No cynicism. Until this girl is rescued ... ' Straight out of Richardson's *Pamela*. Lydia was miffed. She regards bollocking as her own personal ploy. 'I feel responsible. Tinker is my friend,' I ended. Maybe, my sluggish cortex cautioned me, the spy is somebody else, not Lydia.

'Why here?' She looked about, swept her fingers along the table surface with disapproval. The server woman hated it.

'I was to meet somebody here at ten last night who would say where Vyna had gone.'

'Who?'

'Dunno. I was late. They didn't show.' I looked at her. I've never known her lie without blushing. 'But you did.'

'My secretary rang round all the dealers.' She coloured slightly. 'I still have your address lists.' My ex-apprentice. 'Chessmate, Mrs Finch. And my firm has the Mercia franchise for hotel foyer displays. The Braithwaite, Mr Boxgrove. *And* that gentleman I simply do not trust.'

'Who, exactly?' I thought I'd been invisible.

'Tubb, they call him. And Carmel.' She leaned close, a secret in the offing. 'Tubb works for Carmel.'

'And Spoolie?' Hard to stay casual.

'Certainly not, Lovejoy.' She bridled. How Lydia manages to do it I can't fathom. 'Break off *all* contact with him. He has been *in gaol*, Lovejoy.'

She was innocent. I stopped acting, just nodded. Anybody could have traced me. Or had I deliberately left a spoor an anosmic dog could have followed?

'If you have no idea who was to meet you, Lovejoy, then there will be a message.' She went to the counter. Voices rose, Lydia's laser. She returned, replete as ever after a scrap or sex. 'Come, Lovejoy. Aldridge street market, eleven a.m.'

'Eh?' I looked at the server. 'Get some grub.'

'Not here, Lovejoy.' Lydia swept out, head high. I'd have tried it, but would have fallen over the chairs. She told me when I caught up, 'That woman thought you too unkempt for an antique dealer, Lovejoy. The description of you – via a newspaper vendor – was imprecise.'

We breakfasted at a greasy nosh place round the corner. Bread fried in fat, eggs and bacon, stale bread a foot thick, porridge stiff as glue, tea strong as sludge, rock-hard marmalade, black puddings you could bounce. Thank God some places know how to cook. Lydia didn't eat, must have breakfasted on the train.

'Vyna,' I said in the Braithwaite. 'In fashion where?'

Lydia's lovely lips thinned. Her luscious figure had returned.

'Little minx,' she said, holding her hat on one-handed. 'Supposed to be studying at Viktor Vasho's. The fashioneers have a student register.'

'Well, it must've been hard for her.' I set the great Braithwaite booming uphill, heading for Walsall.

'Everybody has difficulties, Lovejoy!' Lydia said sharply. 'That's the trouble today … ' etc, etc. Now, Lydia's not quite twenty-four, and was gunning away at a lass not much younger.

But Vyna Dill, in fashion? Viktor Who?

'How come you know so much fashion stuff, love?'

'You sent me on a course to the V & A Museum, South Kensington, on materials in antiques.'

'Er, aye.' I'd forgotten. I'd wanted to get rid of Lydia for a while because of Janie Markham. 'To educate us in fashion.'

We made the street market with half an hour to spare. I was past concealment.

23

ALDRIDGE MARKET IS long and thin, fifty stalls petering out
between shops. We parked in a place marked *Deputy Mayor
ONLY*. I nicked a 'Disabled' sticker from another car ('Lovejoy!
How dare you! Such wanton ... !')

'Who in the market, love?'

'It was verbal only, no names, no note.'

'Look,' I said. 'Pretend you're not with me.'

She muttered, but obeyed. I walked down the crowded market.
No shops names I recognised, no decent antiques, no Maerklin
tinner. I saw Lydia at a haberdashery, ignored her, drifted on, felt my
chest. Eleven o'clock came. Nil.

Only one thing to do. I did a despondent shrug, asked a few
stallholders if they'd any antiques, the usual. Still nil. There's a market
clock, the only antique in the place, but too solidly stuck to be
nicked.

Then, moving off, I saw it. On one of the stalls was a photo of the
Lepanto, my tinner, propped against some wellingtons. It definitely
hadn't been there minutes before. I pushed through, looking.

'Is that for sale?' I asked the stallholder.

'Eh? No, mate. Young lassie left it, said her brother would come
for it. That you?'

'Er, aye. Ta.' I gave him a note, took the picture. 'Sure it was her?'

'Blondie, a bit of all right.' He grinned. 'Got your work cut out,
the boys after her, eh?'

'True, right enough.' I did a lot of grinning. On the reverse, *Sold
today. M/CTM. tomorrow.*

The tinner had been flogged, then. M/C is Manchester. TM,
though? I went through the market, saw Lydia look sharply at the
photo in my hand as I passed. Then I ran to the council offices
cursing. Vyna would be watching to see I'd got the message.
Nobody.

Lydia had arranged to meet me in Aldridge library, if all failed. I went into a tavern facing. The barman glanced at my photo, smiled.

'Lot of them about today.'

I feigned surprise. 'Bought it off a barrow.'

'Girl had one just like it, waiting here for her brother. Aussie. I'm good with accents.' Vyna, lurking here, peering.

'I collect old pictures. She still about?'

'No. Notice dolly-birds go for older men?'

It took time, but I got it out of him. She'd been with a flashy older bloke. No, the barman hadn't caught his name. He ended up being suspicious. I told Lydia all this when we met up. I got a newspaper. It seemed that somebody was dead, half a column inch, a fill-in by a tired stringer. Foul play was not suspected. The deceased ran a film enthusiasts' shop. That was all the world could manage for Spoolie, *requiescat in pace*. We left Aldridge.

Manchester, not a million miles from where I was born. Odd, but the wayward lass had travelled north-west. Map the trek, it pointed to Lancashire. Hadn't she just been there, though?

'She could've just asked Tinker. He'd have gone north like a lamb. So why this obliquity?' I wasn't sure of the word, but it sounded sly.

'Lovejoy,' Lydia said. 'I am fatigued. Can we sleep in a decent hotel?' She caught my stare and quickly corrected, 'Hotels, near Piccadilly Square. We can walk to the museum.'

'Museum?' I pulled the old motor to the verge.

'Manchester Textile Museum,' said this wonder. 'The message on the photo.'

'Right.' I pretended to have known all along. 'Sorry. Thought I saw somebody I knew.' And drove north.

Here's a tip: Never go back, never *ever* cubed. Old schools, old loves. Never.

That old girlfriend you once loved to distraction. *Should* you ring her after all these years, suggest you meet, hoping for the same old passion? Don't do it.

Or you're now maybe a respectable housewife, remembering that bloke, some past holiday. And you've accidentally (ho, ho, ho) kept his address. Temptation nudges, you're at a loose end. Children off to school, you can't settle. Why not phone, casual, oh good heavens, I must have dialled the wrong number, can it really be you? Then it's, 'Well, I *will* be near the Haymarket tomorrow ... ' And your heart's a steam-hammer as you put the phone down and what'll you wear and

where *is* the Haymarket, how long before the family get home ...
Exciting stuff? Don't do it. It'll end in tears.

Please, I don't mean don't have a fling. I'm all for love. Wherever
it flourishes, let it be. But that's love. It's not nostalgia. Nostalgia's
fine in its bottle, but don't ever take the cork out.

Example: this housewife. Married eight years, thirty-two. Sees a
gorgeous actress. Hey! I was at school with her! She broods. Is she
missing out on life? Recalls a bloke she once knew. Out comes that
old address book (ho, ho, ho), arranges to meet him, lunch at the
Royal Academy, posh nosh should-auld-acquaintance-be-forgot. An
enjoyable encounter is had by all *three*. For, horrors, the uncompre-
hending Adrian brings his missus, who (of course she would be, the
cow) is an attractive expert on Tiepolo ... See? Catastrophe. Will our
housewife ever sleep again? Unlikely. Her ghastly error was mistaking
nostalgia for passion, and uncorking nostalgia.

Example Two, though, is happier: this housewife, and all that.
Married, etc, sees actress. Hey! School, broods, missing out on life,
etc. Thinks, sod this for a game of soldiers. Joins a library/rambling/
study/music club. And guess what? Shares cars, club outings.
Friendship blooms, a bloke she fancies. Soon it's passionate rejoicing
with dot-dot-dot and waves on the sand and heavenly violins. She
isn't past it at all! High marks for cool.

Just before you dash off a vitriolic letter to the Archbishop of
Canterbury saying I'm advocating unbridled promiscuity, I'm not.
I'm saying be honest. If you're going for it, go with care. Let a
thousand fragrant flowers bloom, sure, but don't talk yourself into
something that isn't. Love is not nostalgia. Why not? Because
nostalgia's nostalgia. Love is love.

The implication is never go back. Your school's changed. Streets
have gone. That lovely girl's now a hateful woman. The scraggy little
specky lass you scorned is now a famed beauty. The yokel you
laughed at owns the county.

It's the same in antiques. There's a current move to send every
antique back. Where to? Why, to its roots! The Elgin Marbles,
Leonardo's works, Egyptian artefacts, Russian ikons, French Impressionists to Paris ... Politicians, noble as ever, jump on the band-
wagon, hoping they're creating an impression, which of course they
unerringly manage.

It's gaining ground, this back-to-roots. I mistrust people yelling
that their idea's justice, right. Political rectitude has a foul record. I

don't know the rights and wrongs of things, because I'm basically thick, but *should* antiques go home?

Sometimes, yes. Like, the Israelis pinched whatever they wanted between 1968 and the early Seventies, and then gave them back to Egypt. Good. I'm glad the tombstones they nicked from Sinai in 1956 are going home too. Those funereal lamps, vases, steles are worth a mint, but back they've gone, those 1,000 crates of Sinai Peninsula antiquities. Gold stars to all concerned. Mamluk, Nabatean, Roman artefacts, the lot, representing from about 4,000 BC to the Middle Ages. Some regarded those antiques as sheer loot. Others pretended it was legitimate archaeology aimed at finding proof (they failed, incidentally) of those tiresome blokes wandering the Sinai Desert for those yawnsome forty years. There are two dozen peaks that Moses might have strolled up, the day he did the deal, but so?

It's not always clear-cut. Is Holy Mother Russia of the Czars the same country as Russia now? If not, can contemporary Russia claim all the Fabergé eggs, so famed, so craved? If Fabergé'd stayed in St Petersburg they might well have executed him. How can we say where his original loyalty should lie? I can understand the New York Metropolitan Museum of Art cleverly settling out of court, after that terribly bitter legal joust, and reluctantly sending back the Lydian Hoard of priceless gold and silver artefacts to Turkey. Receivers of nicked goods don't want legal precedent hanging round their gallery's neck, right? Turkey is stubborn these days, has its sights firmly set on those wealthy New York galleries that display looted relics. And everybody knows where they were ripped from their moorings in South Turkey.

There's an International Convention, to prove that comedy isn't dead. The hilarious Hague Convention of 1954 ('for the Protection of Cultural Property') is a laugh a minute. Occupying powers must, it avows, protect antiquities and not sell, steal, loot, remove, pinch, or allow to be nicked, any and all. Good, eh? So nobody must do what is currently happening in Thailand, Cambodia, South America, the USA, Russia, the former Soviets, South-East Asia, the Middle East, Central America, Italy, Cyprus ... Stop it, everybody.

Political nostalgia is the enemy of common sense. The priceless Dead Sea Scrolls belong(ed) to Jordan, but the Rockefeller Museum hasn't given them back. Fine to argue that the Elgin Marbles should 'go back' to Greece, but they were bought originally from Turkey. And legitimately paid for. Return them, to corrode like the ones left in situ? It's a problem. God knows what the answer is, except He doesn't. If we all stopped secretly paying tomb robbers to nick antiques, there'd be no argument.

As long as money is the prize, everybody's in there. Not long since, headlines blazed *Four Countries Tussle For Priam's Treasure!* because the archaeologist Heinrich Schliemann was a lying rat. He whipped priceless chalices, breastplates, death-masks, from ancient Troy in western Turkey in 1873, and gave King Priam's treasure to Berlin, Prussia. He said he'd paid the Ottomans 50,000 francs. In 1945, the 9,000 priceless gold antiques were entombed in concrete beneath Berlin's Zoo station, and got collared by the Soviets. Greece lays no claim. Turkey does. Germany does. Russia does, and has them. They could settle in an afternoon over a cup of tea, but no. That would be a precedent, *then* where would loot be? Loot gives theft a bad name.

Glad that's settled. Where was I? Saying never go back to your past.

So I did.

24

A TROUBLE SHARED is a trouble halved, they say. In antiques, a trouble shared is a trouble doubled. If it's with Lydia, quadrupled.

My part of the North is stolid, grimy, impervious to analysis. The South regards it as uncouth, inescapably grim, always raining, a subnation of crude comics whose intellect is par with amoebae and whose wit is lavatorial. The North, to some, is football hooligans and brash shabby girls squabbling in slums between murky mill walls.

That's one view. It's wrong.

Lydia's opinion was expressed as we thundered up Trinity Street past the railway station of my home town some miles from Manchester. It was dark.

'Lovejoy, how depressing. Can't we find somewhere else?'

'I'm looking for a place to hide this crate.'

'Why don't we simply park it in Manchester? That's where we've to meet this wretched girl.'

Left then right, and into Nile Street. Jesus, but they'd obliterated the dark satanic mills' great chimneys. They'd shifted the station clock tower, but this? Most of the houses were gone. In the bleak neons the area seemed utterly stark.

'Thank God. Still there.'

The derelict garages where we played football were intact, rickety doors askew. I picked the padlock, old habits dying hard. I drove the Braithwaite in. Lydia squealed.

'Lovejoy! Something's squeaking!'

'Probably you, love.' I'd had enough. 'Places have mice.'

We went out into the night. I padlocked the door after me. I could get to Manchester early, meet Vyna Dill, have a parents-want-you showdown, then suss out some local antiques. We started walking, Lydia working up to cut out. If she didn't, I'd ditch her.

'This town, Lovejoy. It's the Mass Observation place, isn't it?'

Here comes the second view.

Back in the Thirties, some academic Yanks searched the world for 'the archetypal slum'. They found one, perfect. They trumpeted their achievement, got a 'research' fortune. They developed this technique. Get people to write in about themselves, year after endless year. They compiled a masterpiece, tell the world 'about slum life'.

It's all nonsense. I was nearly adult when I came across it in a library one wet afternoon. They meant my home town! I asked my Gran. She sniffed, 'They asked me and Gramp. They couldn't understand us not having stamp money for a fortnightly letter.'

'See?' I explained this to Lydia as we walked. 'The research is worthless. Only the affluent could afford to write in.'

'It's still not very savoury, Lovejoy.'

For just a second I paused. She too halted.

'Yes? What, Lovejoy?'

We were plodding in drizzle. Some countries would pay God for a single day of our wet. It was no use. Lydia saw only gaunt factories, skeletal rafters where streets were being obliterated. Terraced houses clung together begrimed, barely a window lit. Her opinion was a predetermined vision. But where Lydia saw ugliness, I saw only beauty. It's as people view a woman. Lydia thinks Aureole a slut, and I don't.

'Nothing.' We resumed. 'Mind your footing.' The pavement was tilted where an excavator's great wheels had crushed the flagstones.

'Imagine, Lovejoy! People must have *lived* here before they started redevelopment!'

Not they. We, me. Not scores, thousands. The area was the size of ten football pitches. I said nothing more, just walked on, her arm linked with mine, into the bright lighting of Bradshawgate. Very soon, there will be a northern archaeology boom bigger than anything since the Egyptology explosion of the 20th century. Back then, every museum worth a groat had to have a mummy and a slice of Pharaoh's hieroglyphics. Yet before long, they'll go berserk with aerial photography, topographical surveys of fantastic precision – to pinpoint our streets, mills, sawyers' yards, all our industries that progress couldn't get rid of fast enough.

So dig out your great grannies' baubles, your grandads' bowls, pipes, clogs. Better yet, look them out now, while your Nellie's not slung them in a mad-mood spring-clean. Write down everything you can remember, their workplace stories, their boring tales, dances, songs, what they paid for food. You'll weep tears of regret otherwise, and regret is the most useless human emotion.

An hour later, I was in the Man and Scythe. Lydia, in the Swan. I didn't sleep, just sat listening to the dialect from the taproom below. Even if I couldn't have Lydia, selfish cow, I was in a state of bliss once-removed. Home. Mistake, but here I was.

Come morning, I'd get shot of Lydia. Lovely, but now a liability, a thousand leagues away while I lay alone. I'd not had a bird for years. Well, less than that, but I couldn't help thinking of Lizbet among all those blossoms in East Anglia's fair land.

Yet in a way I was crazy over Lydia, estranged as we were. I once knew a middle-aged actress, pretty famous, and said ta when leaving. She fell about.

'Silly!' she laughed. 'I was forty before I realised that it's not how you look when you say your lines that matters. It's how you say your lines when you say your lines.'

'Oh?' I'd responded, puzzled. She was voluptuous, dreamy, worn out.

'It's what a woman *does*, not how she looks. Don't tell other women. They'd hate me for saying it.'

This particular night, God, but I believed her.

The only remedy for woman-hunger is an antique, and vice versa. The ideal is both together. Try to do without women, you starve. Do without antiques, you die anyway. I'd discovered that when Amy took me in hand.

Dreams are worse than dreams. My mind seized its chance, surrendered to memory. I was in a great house, long ago doing my first robbery of my first antique.

Once, there was childhood. Nowadays, there's no such thing. It went out with innocence.

Amy was a thin little lass in my class. It was those days before nuns grew legs, hips, and handbags, when you could understand adverts, when drugs were teaspoons of medicine for Grampa's chest. Girls dutifully went backwards at dances, and sober lads danced forwards. In clogs, we lads marched into school with Sister St Union playing the *March of the Slaves* from Aïda. The little girls threw non-existent flowers from non-existent baskets, tripping lightly through non-existent forest glades. School, my infant mind instantly registered on my first day, was pretence. My first morning, a grey-haired old teacher, Miss Best, told me she'd taught my mother and my grandma, same school. I didn't believe her, because I was four years old, and Ma and Gran were, I'd supposed, older. Pretence!

We evolved. Morality being morality, sex was a threat to the authorities. Segregated at seven, in case any of us matured early and went ape, we got Miss Smith. She thrashed desks with a cane, thundering, 'Do you want to starve without a job? Then *learn!*' Came teens, we dispersed to earn our crusts. My first slurpy astonished kiss came complete with Amy's instructions ('Lips together, now suck'). My very first robbery also came complete with instructions.

Thirteen years old, give or take, Amy met me coming out of the pictures. She'd been smoking, jauntily going to the bad. She now looked smiley and mischievous. She asked if I'd help her to 'carry something'.

'We have to get it first,' was her tale. 'From Scout Hey.'

'Is it okay to?' Cowards know when something's not right. Moorland was fearsome wilderness, without streets, foundries, civilisation.

'Course it is!' she said. 'My uncle said I am to. He's in Africa.'

'Whereabouts in Africa?'

She said crossly, 'I don't know. Stop picking!'

She promised to teach me how to suck tongues. My doubts evaporated.

We went up the moorland road. Houses petered out, and lights. Back then, you didn't mind walking an hour to somewhere. She chatted. I went, 'Oh, aye.' There was a shifty moonlight.

Scout Hey was a sombre house, grey stones, an overgrown garden within tilted iron railings. Stones had fallen from the drystone walls. Nearby, a disused chapel. Amy stumbled ahead to search near the door. I recognised pretence, all my schooling.

'He's forgotten to leave the key. Climb up the drainpipe.'

I obeyed. It's no mystery why the truly imperious monarchs in history have all been female. Good Queen Bess, Catherine the Great, Victoria, Cleopatra, Amy.

'You took your time!' She came in, shut the door behind her. 'It's somewhere downstairs.'

'Don't you know?'

'Stop picking!'

The painting was on a wall. I managed to get it down. In an unlit house you can see more by shafts of moonlight than you can outside in open moonshine. Artists took 300 years to learn this trick of contrasts. I learned it in seconds. The painting was of a small boy standing watching his mother play a foreign-shaped piano in a tiled room. I felt suddenly ill. I tottered into the hall carrying the picture. It felt hot, burning my chest.

'What's the matter?' Amy whispered. 'You're shivering.'

This was her uncle's. Why was she whispering?

'Nowt.'

I stepped away, went to the door. And recovered, quick as that. I looked back at Amy.

'Come *on*!' She was narked, but I was wary.

'That painting made me poorly.'

'How can it?' she whisper-cried, stamping. The hall echoed. 'Carry it!'

'All the way to Great Lever?'

She finally admitted, 'To the open market.'

I went to the picture, instantly felt sick and dizzy. I stepped away. Ten paces, right as rain. It was the old painting. I was feeling something special, new.

'I can't. It sends me funny.' Tongue suck or no tongue suck, I could never carry it. 'I'll leave it outside. You can find it tomorrow.'

She argued, but cowardice ruled. I carried the painting out, reeling with instantaneous sickness, and erected a lean-to of fallen stones against the jungled garden's drystone walling to hide the painting. It took a hell of time. My hands and knees were raw.

We walked off the moorland in silence, Amy furious with me. I was ashamed. I didn't know what had happened, told myself the painting must have had some chemical on it. In my heart I knew it wasn't any such thing.

About three days later, I was playing street football when Amy came running.

'You're wanted!' she commanded. 'At the station.'

'What for?'

'Somebody wants to give you something.'

A man was waiting for us. The way things have altered, a man nowadays chatting to teenagers in a station concourse would be arrested. Back then trust hadn't yet died.

''Lo, Amy,' he said. 'This him?'

He was the first man I'd ever seen with a beard. He looked unkempt, bedraggled. He wouldn't get admitted if he knocked at my Auntie Agnes's. She would call him Feckless And Footloose, to her a hanging offence.

'This is Lovejoy,' Amy said.

The man seemed good humoured. He inspected me. 'A titch,' he remarked affably. 'Thought you'd be older.'

'I'm nearly fifteen,' I lied.

'Ta for helping with the picture. You still poorly.'

'Never been poorly.'

'Course not,' he said quickly. 'Just want to pay you.'

He gave me a grubby brown envelope. I said ta. He said ta.

'You ever sick in the art gallery, son?' he asked.

'Never been in.'

'Things in the museum make you feel queer?'

I shuffled on the spot. 'Aye. Some.'

'Like what?'

'Roman things,' I admitted, watching him truculently for the first insulting sign of laughter. 'Two pictures. That funny desk.'

A few lads passing saw me and shouted me to play footer. I started off.

'Listen, son,' he said quickly. 'Ever you're stuck for a job, ask after me with Amy's auntie. Awreet? Not posh, but honest.' The antique dealer's slogan.

He called after me. 'Just ask for Tinker, son. Tinker Dill.'

He tried to explain what being a divvy was, failed miserably. I often wonder what would have happened if he had been less perceptive.

That night I gave Gran my envelope. She drew out a five pound note, awed. Then she was furious.

'Tinker's feckless and footloose,' she sniffed, proving where Auntie Agnes had got it from. 'A rag-and-bone man.'

Later, there was trouble over some furniture that went missing from some mill-owner's mansion. I left town. Later, I returned to find my world gone. I followed a girl I liked to East Anglia, where I got a job in an auctioneer's. Within a week I was dealing for myself.

There Tinker bumped into me, taking a load of antiques to the Continent through Harwich. He became my barker. From that nothing beginning I rose to extreme penury. It was called the antiques game. I've often thought of Amy.

The hotel room was lovely and ancient, beams, bed, whatever. But an empty bed's for getting out of.

Nothing for it. I couldn't go on like this. I'd not last another day. So long, Lydia. Hello Amy. It was barely eleven o'clock at night.

Middle of the afternoon, with my sidereal clock. I was out of the tavern like a ferret.

25

For a second I stood in the drizzle of Churchgate, wondering whether to get a taxi, the Braithwaite, a lift. Then I walked it in minutes. Home towns shrink. Returning once before, I remember staring round at our two-up two-down loo-in-the-yard terraced, and thinking, Is this it?

Right onto Chorley Old Road, I could virtually see Sally Up Steps in the street lamps. Facing the ancient hostelry was Amy's Excellency Antiques among terraced houses, shops trying to look special, factories masquerading now as supermarts.

Except the Braithwaite was parked outside Amy's.

My pace slowed. The Braithwaite was unique. Nobody could possibly know where I'd only just shelved it. And who'd nick a valuable old tourer, just to abandon it? Amy didn't even know I was here. Lydia didn't know about Amy. Tinker, though, knew me, my old haunts, and Amy. So Tinker was in town. And Roadie?

A metal grille thing barred Amy's glass-fronted shop porch. I rang her bell. I looked at the huge old motor. It looked at me. I still had its keys in my pocket. I banged on the door. It opened.

'Amy? Hello.' I stood and shuffled, embarrassed.

She stared, stared more. Then, 'You're gone years, and I get hello?'

'Just passing,' I said, red.

'You'd best come in.' I entered the warmth, expecting some huge bloke to rise and thump me. 'Sit you down.'

Minuscule room, coal fire in a grate, hob, oven, tiles by Mason's showing horses on the chimney breast under the cornish, a one-piece iron Lancashire fireplace, six feet by six, gleaming copper and black-grey iron. Say, 1840. Any dealer would give ...

'Stop valuing my grate, Lovejoy.'

'I was doing nothing of the kind!' I said, narked. 'Just having a warm.'

'You're never cold. And you like the wet.'

'You always pick me up wrong.' No sign of Tinker. Did she know the Braithwaite was outside?

She laughed then. 'You don't change, Lovejoy. More theories about women than the parson preached about.'

'You have. Changed.' We sat, Darby and Joan by the hob. 'You're bonnier.'

No longer the scrawny Olive Oyle stick-legged lass. Rounder, waisted, smart. Old friends, new enemies. I ought to've asked Gran what it meant. My remark coloured her face.

'What do you want, Lovejoy?' she asked.

'Nothing,' I said indignantly. 'Just thought I'd call ... ' I petered out. She clasped her knees the way she used to.

'I've two children now. Chet's a good man,' she put in quickly. 'Works on the motorways.'

My remaining muscles relaxed. She carefully didn't smile. A small stack of little leather boxes was on the TV. Cufflinks? Medals?

'You're still dealing, then?' I asked outright.

She too relaxed. 'After you, how could I not?'

'What in?'

Amy examined me candidly. I don't like women doing that. It makes me think they're not going to believe me.

'Don't, Lovejoy.' Barely in the door, and twice she'd told me stop it, don't. 'You've looked me up. You know I'm a syndicator. And in what.'

'Look, Amy.' I went into frowning aggression. 'I'm making a respectable visit. If you can't take me at face value, I'm very sad.'

She leant forward and poured tea. (Incidental note: these old hobs, the kettle is always hot.) I finished my rant.

'You're at Man and Scythe, Lovejoy,' she said, like I'd not spoken. This town. 'And her?'

'Dealer. It's her motor. She's staying,' I added pointedly, 'at the Swan.'

'Tinker's at the Pack Horse.'

She sounded indifferent, but Amy can be sly. Secrecy was unknown. Like, everybody born here knew that it was one of my ancestors who opened the town gates to Prince Rupert's army in our Great Civil War allowing the Royalists to massacre us wholesale. Gran always pretended it was long forgot.

'The town's full of collectors,' I said. I'd passed several shops, each devoted to a collecting theme.

166

'It's the North, Lovejoy.' She sounded defiant. 'Fashion's moving in our direction. We're people with good guesses.'

That was Amy's way, the oblique remark that stirs you to reach out and grab. Just for once, I'd like somebody to *give* me something. Take that lass Cécile. About 1926, she was playing, when her dad came home. 'Guess what I've got in my car!' he cried to the four kiddies. 'It starts with C. Whoever guesses right can keep it!' Cécile won. 'Cézanne!' she yelps. Which was how *Les Baigneuses* got Cécile de Rothschild hooked on collecting. Okay, she was mostly unhappy, got treated like dirt by her bossy pal Greta Garbo. But, she always had a few coppers to spend on her mania. I don't honestly believe she murdered Garbo's friend Georges. And I don't think Garbo did it either. No, honest, I really don't. (Though why *did* Cécile hide Garbo in her flat in rue Faubourg St Honoré after the body was found?) The point is, collecting afflicts where it will, and is a disease for life.

'The town's into medals?' The nearest I could get to fashion. Amy was as quick as ever. 'I passed two medal collectors' shops.'

Amy sighed. 'God, is it! Most are phoney, but they're going like gongs. That *Medal News* started it. Homemades.'

Well, fair enough. I watched her warily. No evidence of her trade here, though. Less than a dozen years back, *Medal News* innocently asked its readers what a Bomber Command medal should look like, were one ever made. So interested were people, that somebody actually struck one, unofficial. It sold like Friday duff, started a fashion. Homemade medals became epidemic. A National Service Medal got sponsored for charity. The Voluntary Service Medal, General Service Cross, Foreign Service Medal, others, came tumbling into collectors' cabinets and onto veterans' beribboned chests.

'I like the Normandy Medal,' I told Amy, working onward. I'd given her enough chances. 'And the Bomber Command.'

'Finding the dealer's the problem.' Amy was casual, but fencing away. 'Like that Machin business.'

My mind was going. Why mention that?

The Machin business was a shocker. It earthquaked the collecting world almost into oblivion. Arthur Machin had sculpted Queen Liz's noddle for postage stamps. Out of the woodwork came collectors, like train-spotters and bird twitchers suddenly there in obsessed thousands, cheeping for Machin stamps like hungry fledglings. Dealers flourished, supplying the demand, as it were. One especially rose in swift splendour. Let's call him Al the Machin specialist. He supplied rare variants, every collector's dream. Each stamp was guaranteed, reliability his watchword. Philatelists beat a path to his door. Then it happened.

Al went honest.

The galaxy imploded.

One ghastly day, Al walked into the cop shop, and confessed. Forgery, deception, special inks, adding dyes, swapping the gum like I used to, altering the surface – yes, constable, he'd done the lot. Worse follows. Not only did Al admit every fraud, *he made restitution*. A *dealer*? Giving his ill-gotten gains back? Nobody could take it without psychotherapy. But Al came clean, repaid every groat. The phosphor strips that sort your letters, can be changed – and Al explained how. The Plod of Luton, Bedfordshire, had never had it so good, for here was a true-blue criminal who not only listed his crimes but solved them, wrists out for handcuffs. It's a wonder Al didn't offer to wax the floors, nip out for a pizza.

Al's sudden honesty ruined the collecting world. Second of June, it's 'Good day constable … ' Third of June, all collecting's down the chute, dealers waking to the sound of popping ulcers. It was night-marish. Why did Amy mention it?

'Who's the chap, Amy?'

There was a photograph on the side table of Amy smilingly receiving a trophy. I'd seen the celebrity before.

'I won an award.' She sounded proud. 'Last year's competition.'

'Eh?' I was all innocent. 'What's that banner say?' Lettering, NFD 'You won? Congratulations. What for?'

She put her cup down, rose in that smooth women's movement. I stood awkwardly, my man's legs and trunk going through angled sequences to reach the vertical. 'I'd better show you, Lovejoy. You'll never stop otherwise. Come through.'

She went to the wall and slid a part of it aside. These terraced houses are basically two up, two down, that's it. She'd just done the impossible. Lo and behold, we were suddenly elsewhere.

'You've knocked through into next door?'

'The whole terrace.'

She stepped aside. I gaped. Dresses, racks of shoes, coats, hats hats hats. I'd never seen anything like it. The vibes nearly knocked me flat. I calmed my clamouring chest.

'Waistcoats upstairs. Gentlemen's militaria. Boots, riding garments, uniforms, downstairs back. Ladies' dresses – costume, dance, crino-lines, gowns, accessories – upstairs front. I own all ten houses.'

'That award, Amy.'

'For fashion, Lovejoy.' She faced me, calm. 'Now can't you tell me why you've really come? And why you've checked up on me?'

It's enough to make anyone bitter. So what, if I look up an old flame? Somebody must have phoned her.

She finished my thought. 'I heard the minute you copied my address down.'

'Bloody charming,' I groused. 'Spying.'

'Spying, Lovejoy? You were in the paper. The *Journal and Guardian* quoted your assistant Bran Mantle. You're going to do the bicentenary charity auction at this year's fashion show.'

'Bran Mantle?' I said weakly, cornered.

'Yes! You'll divvy all the antiques that everybody's donated.' She added nastily, 'Free of charge, Lovejoy.'

'Me? I think there's been a mistake, love.'

'Day after tomorrow.' Her smile was sweet innocence. 'For certain.'

'Look, Amy.' I got up to bluster better. 'If you think I've come all this way for a charity you're off your nut. I'm due in East Anglia ... '

She got madder than me. 'Default, Lovejoy, and our newspaper reporters will hound you to death. I'll make them! That's a promise.' Her last shot was, 'Think of the antiques, Lovejoy.'

Carrot and stick. Together they make a chain. I could always run for it, if I got nowhere with Amy.

'This bloke.' I stood in front of her picture. She looked so proud among the accoutred beautiful people, smiling and applauding. Rodney, who'd had me thrown out. Thekla next to him, smiling hard at the camera. My heart squeezed from memory. The bloke, though, presenting the trophy. The same trophy was here, in a cabinet, with a framed signed photo, 'To Amy the Champion with love', and an illegible signature. 'I've seen him before. Is he famous?'

'Was,' she said sadly. 'Viktor Vasho's in hospital. Manchester's most famous fashion designer. He's not mending.'

'Manchester? I thought he was that Mayfair bloke?'

'Fashion is a Mayfair address, but a Manchester business. Poor Viktor Vasho. I studied under him before I went independent. Antiques and modern fashions.'

'Are you famous too?'

She shrugged. 'Hereabouts. But not like Viktor Vasho.'

'You won the Northern Fashion Durbar.' I wanted no mistakes. 'And Viktor Vasho came to present it?'

She sat before the fire. 'Three judges. Rodney's all right. Thekla's a bitch.' She raised her eyes. 'Isn't she, Lovejoy?'

'Thekla?' I croaked. 'Er … '

'She wants you to phone her. If you happen by.'

Small world, or has somebody already said that?

'Let her mangle somebody else.'

In vague hope I gazed at Amy. We'd been really good friends. I gave my most winning smile, and was asked to leave.

26

AMY DIDN'T LAY a finger on me. I was really narked. Close as any two human beings could be, and now she didn't even ravish me. So what's the use of an old flame? She could have had me on the spot. Not even a grope, when I'm as easy as a grape.

Do women, I wondered, as the soft rain fell on me in the town's gloaming, long for a man as badly as we feel woman-hunger? Doubt it. A man deprived is blind to food, weather, work. But women can keep going, blithely indifferent. I was unbelievably sorry for myself. Maybe there'll be sex in heaven.

Here I was in night drizzle, lonely as a monk. But purity's stupid. At least, I was no longer baffled.

Wondering, I stood staring at the old car.

Who knew the mill garages, who knew Amy? It had to be Tinker. I stared across at Sally Up Steps where I used to meet mates, claiming legal drinking age. Except, if Tinker'd wanted to let me know he'd arrived, why not stroll over and say so? The town knew I was back – those bits interested, anyway. So why this trick? It reminded me of Spoolie, who'd watched one old film too many – actually one too few, but you follow. I didn't want to activate some bomb as I cranked its handle.

There was a taxi, motor still going, a hundred yards off. A familiar figure by it. My spirits soared, and I gladly advanced.

'Lydia, doowerlink!' Life was generous after all.

'So it *is* true.' She was immobile. 'Roadie phoned me your old flame's address.'

'It's not like that!' I blurted.

'I'm leaving, Lovejoy. Do not communicate with me again.'

'Please, love. I've forgotten how to start the car.'

'Let me, *wack!*' The taxi driver was out in a flash, fondling the crate and aaahing with wonder. He had it firing in a moment, as I stood well away waiting for the uuumph of the explosion. He said

171

thanks to me. I said ta even more fervently, and watched Lydia's taxi's lights recede. I stood alone, replaced, rejected.

But I had wheels. I drove to the Royal Infirmary. They couldn't refuse me entry, relative of a patient at death's door, could they?

The main carriageways had changed so I had to keep an eye on the signs. Salford, then Central Manchester. Daft to have Salford in another city. Salford City, c/o Manchester City sounds barmy.

The hospital had free parking.

'I'm here to see Viktor Vasho.' I tried to put on a camp air, but the receptionist smiled.

'Viktor V. Vasho? The second visitor!' She clattered her keyboard. 'Relative?'

My feeble artiness was sussed. 'From his firm.'

'Name?' She entered my fictions, phoned. 'You can go up, Mr Mantle.'

'Ta, love.' I hesitated. 'Who else came?'

'Confidential,' she said, glad to refuse.

'Ta, love.' I followed the baffling signs. No wonder hospital visitors all get lost.

Hospitals are horrible. It's their preoccupation, nurses rushing while you blunder, the pong of disinfectant telling you more about mortality than any number of gruesome diagrams.

The intensive care unit was set aside. The gloomy dungeon-like nook was crammed with scary instrumentation, screens made only for cartoons trailing lines, bleeps threatening imminent silence and termination. Tubes drip, corrugated cylinders gasp and collapse, things inflate with a ghastly sucking. And the object of these glowing lights and miniature tides lies somnolent in a plastic capsule, face wedged in a transparent cup. It comes to us all, this last wretchedness. My frightened heart went out to this Viktor V. Vasho I'd never known. I stood there, one foot to the other.

'Er, hello, Viktor?' When I'm being stupid, whatever I say comes out a question, though he wasn't going to say much. Can you talk with a mask on your phizog? Where would the words go? His corrugated tube led to a glittering machine. I went closer, nervous of somebody who looked a goner. I didn't know if he was, but he wasn't going to marathon for us in the Olympics.

'Viktor?' I found myself whispering, began again louder. 'I'm Lovejoy. Just a … ' How to describe myself to a famed fashioneer? 'A layabout, really,' I said, rueful. 'Antiques.'

My hopeful pause got no response. I ahemed, watched his eyelids.

Shut. Was he registering? Can you hear, if you're cocooned like that? Doctors tell you nothing. Why wasn't there a notice saying, *It's hopeless trying to chat with the bloke in this thing*, instead of those daft warnings about cleaning babies' belly buttons and renewing deaf aids?

Disheartened, I forged on. 'See, Viktor, I was shacked up with Thekla.' Nothing. 'I met these loonies ... er, I went to a fashion show. Thekla ditched me because I didn't understand.' I was thirsty, dripping with sweat. Hospitals are hellish hot.

Two nurses zoomed past, neither looking in. Fine, I thought bitterly. What if this poor sod croaked while they swanned off to their coffee?

No response, Viktor still as a board.

'Viktor? I'm searching for a missing girl. Vyna. I thought she was nothing to do with fashion, see?'

Christ, but it was stifling. The special unit was more of an alcove, no doors. The sister's desk was obliquely across, nurses checking drugs. I looked away. Whatever they're doing can't be good for you, can it? Ampoules put the fear of God in me.

Was it worth saying any more? Was he secretly listening? He might be all glad in there, first chat for days. I felt such a prat.

'It's dawned on me that I've been led,' I told him. 'You know why I was asked to chase her? Because I didn't take the bait. An auction in my home town, coupled with a fashion show. I got a pal to help. Spoolie. He got topped.'

Viktor Vasho didn't stir. Could I lift the edge of the plastic tent? You never know what's right in a hospital. Anything could be vital.

'I don't know what's going on,' I told the still figure. 'An old girlfriend's running a fashion show. You know her, Amy. I'm hosting the auction. A double thing.'

Maybe he was thirsty? How could he ask, when he couldn't move?

'Look. Are you okay? Want some tea?' I went across to the nurse's desk.

'Excuse me, sister. About Viktor Vasho.' Even his name sounded on the blink. 'Might he want something? Only, he's lying, er, stillish. Not saying much.'

'He won't,' she said crisply. She rose, starched apron rattling, streaked in to dart a practised glance through the gloom, emerged. 'He's fine.'

'I mean, can he hear me if I talk? Will he get better?'

'We don't know.' She looked at me, then into the greenish aquarium gloaming. 'It's day to day.'

I exhaled and went back in. Viktor Vasho was a weird centrepiece in a pool of faint luminescence.

'Viktor, mate.' I hunched down, avoiding his tubes. 'I think this is all one scam, see? I came to ask why you got ki- er ... ' Something less final, perhaps, for tact's sake? 'Attacked,' I capped, proud of my word power. 'What's it all for? They could have simply hired me, if they'd needed a divvy.'

My whisper trailed away. I hadn't come when they'd asked. That Stella Entwistle had tried to entice me with antiques, when I was broke. So the real essential ingredient was me.

'My own barker – can you believe it? – is in on it too.' Maybe it was worth asking. 'Is there anything you can tell me? I even got accused of blamming you.' That didn't sound right. 'Damaging your frocks, I mean that spring collection.' Wasn't that what they call it? 'If – er, *when* – you get better, would you mind telling them, please?'

He said nothing. A green screen gave an ominous bleep. I looked anxiously at the sister's table. Her head raised, lowered.

'And there's a right miserable bitch called Faye who believes the same. Please give her a bell, put her straight. And some Orla bird, a suspicious hoary old cow. Tell her too. If you make it.' Harder still. 'If you get a minute.'

You never know how to say so-long to someone in that state. I flapped a hand.

'Cheers, Viktor.' I hesitated. 'Get better, eh?'

And left the poor sod alone. I felt ill. Somebody did that to him, for sewing frocks?

'Yes? What is it?' the sister demanded. They always glance at your middle, possibly checking something isn't going to fall out of you onto the table.

'Viktor Vasho,' I said when her eyes returned to mine. 'Do you know much about him?'

'Famous fashion designer. Do you mean his family? But you must know that, Mr Mantle, being his staff.'

'Course I do, sister. Ta, then.'

That was all. Nothing. The canteen had shut. There were only those machines that keep your money and give you the wrong drink. I returned to the car, narked.

No sooner was I in when this lass got in beside me.

'Sorry, love. Ask for a taxi at reception.' I couldn't see her face in the dark.

'Drive on, Lovejoy.' She didn't look at me.

'Faye?' I yelped, scrambled out.

'Yes, Lovejoy. The right miserable bitch.'

'Er, look, Faye. If you're going to scream ... '

'I'll behave, Lovejoy.'

Safe? I got back in. The motor took ages to start. I drove out of Manchester heading for the Man and Scythe, lay my aching head. The Earl of Derby had slept there the night before we executed him after the Great Civil War. Travellers actually ask for the same bedroom. God, but we're a horrible species. As we went I found Faye's knees catching the light. Horrible species, Faye excepted.

'I was sitting in the ICU while you talked to Viktor, Lovejoy.'

'Sly cow.'

I actually saw her smile, as the lamps flicked. Was she proud of being devious?

'As you seem the only honest one among us, Lovejoy, I've decided to trust you.'

To my dismay I said, 'Don't, Faye. I'm lost.'

27

As I drove, I asked Faye about being a fashion journalist, but I didn't really listen to her answer.

Fashion's odd. Why do we follow it, when it's only deviating from a norm to get shrieked at? It's too changeable. Birds who hie into my cottage are all at it. One, a married woman who ought to've known better, actually chucked my clothes out and had the nerve to be indignant when, naked as a neonate, I reproached her. 'They were rubbish, Lovejoy,' she shot back and added, 'Move with the times, Lovejoy.' I'd said, 'Why?' but only got, 'Don't be ridiculous … ' I'd have already solved this mystery in nanosecs but for fashion – Spoolie's death, the missing lass, this looming auction-cum-fashion jamboree.

Concentrating on not gaping at Faye, older failures came to mind. Nostalgia tricks you. That Berkley frame was still owed me. And I'd never got a tin token out of Aureole for inventing the chain date.

'*Who's* a rotten cow, Lovejoy?' Faye asked. 'Aureole who?'

'Sorry. I thought I was thinking.'

She smiled in the neon-black-neon light sequence. 'A *what* horse?'

'An antique sex aid. Now, people don't need them.'

'Will you be running this auction, Lovejoy?'

'Suppose so. Dunno. Why are you here?'

'I came to see Viktor. We trained together, same college. And the fashion show.' Reasonable enough. 'The fash thrash has an historic theme this year.'

'Amy Somebody's doing that,' I said, guarded. 'The Last Victorians.'

'How long have you been here, Lovejoy?' I didn't reply. She said, 'A day? Two?' I let her blag that one also. She spun in her seat. 'Why are we stopping?'

'A mo.' I let the motor drift to a halt, the old Farnworth road. Daylight, you'd see St John's spire. My great-gramp and great-gran were in its churchyard. I sat. What an odd thought, but for fashion, I'd have had this solved in nanoseconds. I looked at Faye.

'Not here, Lovejoy,' she said, misunderstanding. 'I'm exhausted. And I've work tomorrow.'

Chance'd be a fine thing. A police car was parked nearby to watch for illicit copulators.

'Do you know Aureole?' I asked. She expostulated, for heaven's sakes and that. I put a fist under her nose. 'Stick to the script, love. You say you trust me, but the question is, do I trust you. Aureole, yes or no?'

'Never heard of her,' she said sulkily. 'It's a stupid name.'

'Thekla?'

'Thekla?' She hooted derision. 'That prune? I met you at her show! The fashion mags ran a competition for Thekla's most apt nickname. Spittoon, moo, itch-bitch. She's paid people to find you, Lovejoy, to get you back.'

'Naheen? Dovie?' I strove to think who'd brought me into this. That pill who'd massacred the antique carpet. 'Rodney? Carmel? Tubb the body-builder?'

'That Carmel's a cow. And her friend Jessica.'

Struck oil. 'Why?' I still didn't drive on.

'Once a doler, always a doler.'

Had I misheard? 'A dollar?'

'Dole-er. A bitch who steals designs, markets them as her own. You know?'

'Really,' I said, polite. 'Does it matter?'

'Does it *what*?' She stared at this extraterrestrial beside her. 'Are you off your zonk, Lovejoy? Fashion is multi-mega-billion business.'

'No, love. Look.' I pointed through the windscreen to houses, factories, a school. 'They take no notice of it, except to laugh.'

Faye's face could have dowsed fire. 'You're stupid. Those people may buy only one coat a year, two skirts, a few blouses. But they choose the colours fashioneers decide. They buy styles that fashioneers create. Tot it up, Lovejoy. Jewellery, cosmetics, textiles, logos, toys. Add record sales. Add holidays, hordes round the globe. Add exports, advertising. Got the picture? Throw in the motor trade, the wedding industry ... '

She went on for about three hours, or maybe minutes. I listened, for the first time thinking, Jessica of the cloying scents, whose eyelashes raked your bare skin in bed?

'Which Jessica?' I asked when she paused for breath.

177

Faye said, 'Lives with her drifter son-in-law. Got religion. Once worked for Viktor Vasho. Wicked witch of the east.'

My Jessica, then. Worked for Viktor Vasho?

'Carmel?' I asked.

'Jessica and Carmel backed Thekla's last show. *Such* good friends.' Said with vitriol. I ought to have come to Faye first, but how do you know which path leads anywhere?

'Tubb was her driver but wouldn't travel on Fridays, touch-wood, green for danger.'

'I know Tubb.'

'Has second sight. It's all put on, a joke. Believing him ruined Carmel. She used to be a big backer. Lost everything on investments, taking Tubb's psychic advice. That's why she's desperate.'

'So everybody's in fashion?' My head was spinning. I felt I'd been speaking the wrong lingo.

'Of course! It's why there are whole fortunes up for grabs.'

Frocks? Vital? Though I could see that getting dressed can be important. Fashion and antiques were to meet at Scout Hey. I had a bad feeling, the sort that's never wrong.

'Spoolie?' I said the name with care.

'Spoolie? I don't know any Spoolie. Unless she's that Bristol designer into tree bark?' Not bad, as negatives go. I relaxed.

'Let's find you a place to stay, Faye.' I drove on.

Cavalier, I put her down at the Pack Horse. The most desolate feeling on earth is seeing a gorgeous bird leaving. I went to Man and Scythe, whose publican told me a Mrs Thekla Somebody'd left umpteen desperate messages, all saying ring, do nothing, please wait until I arrive ...

Plus one other, a scrawl in an embossed Pack Horse envelope:

Lovejoy,

Be in the ghost's arch, 5 o'clock a.m.
Cheers. Tinker.

They sent me up a good nosh. I wolfed it, and slept for some seconds. Then I rose, had a bath, shaved blearily, collared a few addresses, and made my way to the scene of an ancient crime so old that time's almost forgotten it.

Which bought me a few moments to consider antiques, which is where I really belong. Why did I keep forgetting that? Other people I suppose.

28

IF IN DOUBT about going somewhere – go anyway. Four in the morning – and I don't mean five – I went to the ghost's arch.

The town looked somnolent. Square and Roman, of course, the town centre, like everywhere, but now dwellings sprawled out to those chilling empty – now not so empty – moors.

Lights more or less on, one motor droning somewhere to somewhere else, nobody about. Bobbies don't patrol beats any longer. They're above all that, have their illicit fags and chips in parked limos and snooker halls.

We'd played a game, us mill children. God, I thought, hesitating by the ghost's archway, was it years since? A year when you're little seems a lifetime. When you're grown, a year multiplies to several in a blink. I honestly believe that Time gets it wrong. Time should go like clockwork, but never does. As I stood, it was blowing dank off the moors. I can never bother with overcoats and scarves, not having either, but now I wished I had. The bit of night before dawn is chiller.

Our game was to creep into the archway, escaping just before the ghost got you. The darker it was, the riskier. My cousin Glenice, always brave, went farthest in before running out squealing, which really narked me because she was female. And therefore, that now-vanished world instructed, less brave and likely to end up subnormal to boot. She currently owns a chain of hotels. I felt that old fear, stared at the ghost's arch.

A long time since, a poor bloke was murdered there. It's solid stone, leads nowhere. Carved in the keystone is 1826 under a carved barrel, *MCD* above. The great iron hinges are still there for nothing now.

The town hall clock struck quarter past four. Stupidly, we throw our archaeology away. I honestly don't know if that Greek lass who's lately excavated some unique limestone tablets at the Siwa Oasis really has found Alexander the Great's burial place. She was guided

179

by 'a sort of feeling ... ' Sure, her site's near the Temple of Zeus-Amun. Sure, too, Big A wanted to be buried at Siwa, home of the Oracle. When he died, he was encased in a golden Alexander-shaped sarcophagus in a temple on wheels, no less, and then wheeled ... to where? He was finally entombed inside an alabaster sarcophagus which, carved thin, you can see through. But other places lay claim to the Great One, as many as claim St Patrick in Eire. So even the world's most famous archaeology can get lost. We shouldn't discard what we have left.

Standing in the early morning, the universe asleep, unnerving thoughts come, like images of past loves.

My feet were cold. I shifted about. That distant sky glow must be Manchester. Behind, north and west, blackness of the moors. I walked to look at the railway. Why move the station clock? Silly sods. I strolled back. This, the ghost arch, was where Tinker divided the money, Fagin-like, among us young rapscallions who shifted his purloined antiques. There'd been three of us, me the only divvy.

You've to be careful, thinking. Lost archaeologies frighten me. TV programmes about the cosmos also scare me, trillions of galaxies with, likely enough, umpteen gillions of long dead civilisations floating in black space ...

'*Aaaargh*!' I went, my screech echoing down the empty streets as something stroked my leg. I'd leapt a league, but it was only a cat, tail up, purring.

Bending, I growled, 'Stupid moth-eaten moggie. Do that again and I'll marmalise you.' It came for a fondle. I stroked it in despair. That's me all over. I can't even bollock a cat without giving in, even when I'm the injured party. I was waiting here secret as a moon in a mine, not even the sense to bring a flashlight. But would I need one? The street lights were enough. The archway was recessed a few gloamy paces. Its single gaslight, placed there 150 years ago, was a gnarled relic. I felt so lonely. I thought of Wanda. She'd be doing Briony Finch's auction soon. Knowing Wanda's shrewdness, she'd hold it somewhere other than Thornelthwaite Manor, another symbol of lost greatness.

Just as some things get sickeningly lost, some can be found. A French official lately discovered some caves near Avignon. Why does it never happen to me? This lucky bloke delved into a Palaeolithic cave. Saying it means hardly anything, because most caves are Palaeolithic or that way on. But this contained staggering paintings of Ice Age animals. Naturally, the world went crazy. Well, 20,000 years, or more. Bears, reindeer, the woolly rhino, owls, leopard and ibex, even a bloke's hand outlined in red, 300 Cro-Magnon animal pictures wondrously preserved. But not every cave is honest. The Avignon find might turn out to be brilliantly authentic, like Spain's Altamira find, and France's Lascaux of 1940. There are supposed to be nigh on seventeen dozen Stone Age caves with authentic paintings in the bottom bit of Europe alone, and over a thousand dozen Australian aboriginal rock art sites on the Arnhem Land plateau, some a cool 40,000 years old.

When the Chauvet-Hillair caves were discovered, I scoured every report about Vallon-Pont-d'Arc, spoke to every expert. They all sang the same dirge. 'Just think,' they sobbed, 'how many undiscovered caves, whole city-equivalents, cathedral-equivalents, are lost! Basic sea level, back in Upper Palaeolithic times some 12,000 to 70,000 years gone, were three hundred feet lower than now. The great polar ice caps were enormously vaster.' One archaeologist had been to Cosquer in France to see the cave paintings – but chickened out, because you can only reach them now by swimming underwater.

Other experts try 'recreating' the Cro-Magnon art. Know the best way? It isn't with brushes, but by taking the colour into your mouth and spitting it onto the cave walls. Sadly, it's where fakery begins. Waiting by my arch, I didn't want to think of faking, until the world put its daylight head on. Dark sinister caves are horrible, like those magicalised paintings in red ochre, and dangerous manganese oxide black. This latter stuff can send you insane. But it wasn't that. The Cro-Magnons who painted at Vallon-Pont-d'Arc were probably our true ancestors. They came drifting, brawling, out of Africa, overrunning Europe some 35,000 years ago. That wouldn't be so bad, if they hadn't simply replaced the Neanderthals of Europe. No peaceful coexistence. Ice Age Europe said survive or die. The Cro-Magnons had the knack of trading, and got organised in houses for up to fifty folk. They hunted mammoths. Fine, eh? Not if you're Neanderthal it's not.

The town hall clock struck four-thirty. The cat had given up, gone.

Worse, why did those Cro-Magnon cave artists leave an animal's skull on a rock, a few piles of pigment, a fragment or two of bone, and nothing else? Whose caves *were* they, one over 200 feet long? Priests keeping the shrine sacred? Most of the animals depicted were terrors, not food, not domesticated. So why go to the trouble of protecting the Combe d-Arc caves, teaching young Cro-Magnons your ceremonies?

The frightening question is always there, waiting for when you've examined every antique ever made. It can only be asked when you're alone and cold and wondering what frigging cosmos and God are doing and why some innocent bloke's lying perilously linked to life by a thousand tubes in a hospital. It's this: if what you were doing was so vital, so life-enhancing, so beautiful, why stop?

Because some new tribe rubbed you out?

Once, I knew this bird. She was exquisite, titled, wealthy, young, had everything. Her husband was handsome, ditto, and had everything else. She used to visit me when he was away, then, worryingly, when he wasn't. Well, I was really proud of this lady. I tried to borrow money, have the electricity switched on, pay my water rates so she wouldn't have to carry water from my well. I honestly tried to haul my cottage into the light of civilisation's bright beacon. Know what? She went berserk, threatened, 'If you do, Lovejoy, I'll never see you again'. This, note, from a noblewoman used to satin, central heating, grapes in aspic, ten maids per hankie. She'd never known anything except luxury and subservience from adoring regimental officers.

Baffled, I asked, 'What's got into you? I thought you'd be pleased'. She lay there shivering in my damp cold cottage, no light, no grub, no cooking thing, no hot bath. Beside her I must have looked like some, well, Cro-Magnon. She said, 'Don't ever stop being stupid, Lovejoy. Promise?' She actually made me do that cross-my-heart. I did it, to shut her up. Immediately she was right as rain.

Twenty minutes to five.

Fakery only compounds this problem. There was a similar cave found in the Basque country. It had everything, paintings, extinct animals, red ochre, the blacks, renderings of our ancestors. A mistrustful researcher discovered small fragments of manmade sponges underneath the cave drawings – sponges on sale at modern supermarkets. The whole thing was sham. I often see slices of limestone sold from cars, allegedly from 'cave paintings in southern France', three feet by four, mounted on fibreglass. I've never seen a genuine one yet.

I looked down the arch's narrow ginnel. A few paces. Can you trust anything, like messages from lifetime friends? The bobbies of my youth smoked their secret cigarettes in this recess before plodding on. Down there, the ghost of the murdered man lived. I could feel him.

The wind was blowing colder, mizzle enough to soak. A sensible bloke'd shelter down there and wait for Tinker, stay dry. Not me, and I don't believe in ghosts. What was Tinker doing, saying to meet here? He'd know I'd be scared. Almost as if he wanted me not to be here. Barmy old soak had probably been sloshed.

I decided to see what the old place opposite had turned into. It had once been the Queens cinema, all velvet seats and thick guide ropes. I crossed over. A single motor came slowly from Manchester, accelerated gently at the traffic lights' promise.

Suddenly tired, I leant against the old cinema's wall. I used to queue here for the cheap seats, hoping for a snog with some sceptical lass. The cat purred round me. I stooped to stroke it.

'Bloody moggie.' I stroked it. 'Chiseller.'

The building now seemed to be some sort of supermarket. You can never tell these days ...

A *whoomph* almost knocked me over, more light than blast. I tumbled back, not trying to save myself. I slid a yard, glass shards scratching and raining onto the wall.

'Christ!' I remember yelling, looking round.

The motor car had no lights I remembered, now it was no use noticing anything. It accelerated off along Bradshawgate. From there, Halliwell and the moors quick as a wink, or Blackburn. I lay still, the cat lying on my feet, scared out of its wits, poor little sod.

A purplish blue light was flickering from across the street. From the ghost's arch. I strove to recall, but couldn't get things in order. Had there been a crash of glass, just before that ominous whoomph? I vaguely thought so. But the flames died quickly even as I watched, and I knew. A bottle filled with petrol, a rag down the neck. Light it, and chuck. Crash goes the glass, splash goes the petrol, and whoomph goes the Molotov cocktail. And the person gets crisped, screams, burns to death.

No cars about. I reached to stroke the moggie, felt it sticky on my fingers, yelped, looked in the street light of Station Brough, and spewed on the cat's entrails and my blood-soaked trousers. I screamed, shuffled myself feverishly along the pavement away from the dreadful thing. A large shard of glass had penetrated its soft form, slicing and slitting as it went. I found myself staggering away from the dying flames, seeing Spoolie all over again, and began walking steadily, steadily, as if I had somewhere to go.

Between spells of reeling in and out of terror, my mind demanded, who'd want me crisped when I'd done nothing? The act of a madman. Madmen? Madwomen? Aureole, Carmel, Faye, Lydia, Sheehan, Roger, Tubb the bodybuilder? Not poor Viktor Vasho. Not poor Spoolie. That moggie had only wanted to be friends. Death comes to my pals.

Tinker had known where I'd be. Tinker knew the ghost's arch. He'd asked me to be there.

Ta, Tinker, I said fervently. Ta, for having saved my life. I owe you, my one trustworthy ally, thank God. More than I could say for anyone else. Get de-filthed, then to Manchester. The show at Scout Hey was tomorrow now, coming too quick for tricks.

29

THE MANCHESTER TRAIN was only half the size it used to be. Two coaches, no engine to speak of, cramped as hell. I envied the Pack Horse's morning burden, Faye waking there. And Lydia, frosty. Maybe there'll be sex in heaven, or have I said that? I needed speed.

The textile museum didn't open until ten. I seethed in a nearby nosh bar. What in God's name do curators do, until they can be bothered? Museums are a bobby's job. I wandered to the delivery entrance.

'What's want fert see, mate?' a friendly old uniformed bloke asked. He was on the soot-blackened gate while a massive lorry finished loading. Two blokes in overalls were wheeling out the last case on a trolley.

'Is there a special display?'

'Theh't a day late, lad.' He was quite jovial. I stared in alarm. 'This is it, just going.'

'Late?' I pulled myself together. 'Can I see?' One of the loaders undid a latch of the canvas covering. It was a glass display case. Inside, a life-sized dummy, wearing an 1880s dress, complete with trinkets, hairdo, that scary smile dummies wear, maybe come alive when you're not looking. I stared trying to remember every detail to tell Florsston, the shawl, the browny silk, the pink glass brooch, the jet necklet.

'Ta, mate,' I said dully. They fastened it, racked the case onto the pantechnicon.

'The Victoriana.' The old man wore soldier's ribbons. '*The Empire's Textile Wonders*. Rotten name, eh? I remember my dad ... '

'What was it, exactly? All like that one?'

'Oh, long frocks, special materials. On dummies – they were Victorian too, heavy as lead. Wools, cottons, made overseas in them days, shipped home in windjammers for fettling in Lancashire.' He beamed, proud.

'Where's it going?'

'Don't tek on, lad. Catalogues at yon kiosk, full of pictures.' He pointed to the museum building. 'You can still catch it. They're doing a special show at some old church not many miles north. Scout Hey. Never heard of it myself.'

He waved the huge vehicle outside, locked the gates and beckoned me in via the rear entrance. It was exactly ten o'clock. A party of schoolchildren arrived, noisy starlings in the foyer. Two other adults came in. One was a middle-aged woman, headed upstairs, knew where to go. The other was a lovely lass, schoolmarmish among the children, hair dragged back into a bun behind formidable hornrims. Wish they'd had teachers like her in my day. But no Vyna. The commissionaire chuckled.

'That lorry driver was an interesting chap. His dad used to play football for Accrington Stanley. See these little bairns? Half'll lose themselves unless ... '

'Ta.' I left him, bought a catalogue for a king's ransom. No use – what catalogue is? – but it was psychotherapy. I felt the chiming malaise from the museum's antiques, but resisted. I had a journey to make. The image of what I'd seen in the display case burned in my mind's eye.

Scout Hey I knew. I had to discover Stella Entwistle, suss out her auction. I'd evaded all my helpers. Now I had to decide where Amy's fashion show began and La Entwistle's antiques sale ended. I stuck the glossy under my arm and went out into Manchester's rain.

'Lift, Lovejoy?' Tubb called from a car.

'How come you don't get fined, parking here, Tubb?' I was narked. I get wheel-clamped if I slow down.

He grinned. He was gripping palm springers, Popeye forearms flexing. 'An auspicious day, Lovejoy. I couldn't get a parking ticket if I tried. Nothing can go wrong. I've done runes, tarot, the lot.' Confidence oozed out of him. 'You're a swine to find. I've spent a mint on phones.'

'Lift where to?' I asked cautiously.

'Where you're going.' His grin widened. 'Don't tell me. Bet I put you down at the door.'

'I've a bird to meet.' His face clouded, so I supplied an extra lie. 'Off the London train.'

His grin returned. 'Hop in.' He cut into the traffic, missing a lorry by a whisker. 'Who's the girl?'

'Nobody you know, Tubb,' I said, cool. Nobody I knew either.

She was imagination. I could escape once I was past the station ticket office. 'Rotten motor you've got, Tubb.'

'This?' He tried to seem narked, like any owner. 'Bought it six months back. Sixty m.p.h. on the sniff of an oily rag.' It was hired, its licence-holder said.

Tubb dropped me at the kerb. I stro-o-olled in among passengers. I'd have casually looked at my watch, if I'd had one, the waiting-for-a-passenger image. Once out of sight, I darted past where they never have your luggage when you've paid them to mind it, and peered. Tubb had coolly parked where it says you shouldn't. He stood to watch the exit. I went and caught a train, alighted in my town in no time.

Stella Entwistle's address was in Halliwell. This suburb is named after St Margaret's Holy Well, now godlessly built over. I found the stone cottage. The old square still had its old gas lamps. Once a village, it became immersed in Victorian mills. I knew it well, before the chapels became electrical shops and the great mills were sliced into printing firms.

The door opened. I turned with a fraudster's smile.

'Stella Entwistle? I'm Bran Mantle ... er.' Something was wrong. Her face.

'Lovejoy, isn't it?' She stood there smiling.

Did everybody know my every move? She shook an oldtime finger.

'I'm sorry.' My words trailed away. 'Miss ... ?'

'Miss Renson *was* the name, Lovejoy.' Dimples just as I remembered them. But, grey hair? 'Mrs Stella Entwistle, now. Parish fund-raiser.'

Last encountered clipping my ear for misbehaviour in class, my ex-teacher. I gaped. Women change more than men, though we sling our hooks sooner.

'Laughter lines, Lovejoy,' she said, wry. 'Except life isn't that funny. Do come in.'

She went ahead to a living room looking out at the Falcon mill. I'd played football on its cinder pitch. I felt in church. Teachers always scare. I once knew an elderly professor, collector of octagonal chairs, who once got sloshed and wept over how he'd been told off in school, aged twelve. I watched her warily, not wanting my ear clipped.

'You gave me a dud name,' I accused.

'Snap, Lovejoy! Marriage is *my* explanation. Yours is merely your natural criminal bent.' She gestured me to a seat. 'I *thought* it was you on the phone. Who's Bran Mantle?'

'Washington State in America puts a risk warning on its marriage lines,' I said nastily. 'So watch it.'

Teachers look younger than numerical age suggests. Or do women teachers hold their youth? I'd give it serious thought.

'The Americas are noted for marital violence.'

'Toosh-ay, Miss. I'd forgotten that teachers of your vintage can read.'

'Still dreaming, Lovejoy? You've never grown up.' Not a smile, so she'd invited me for grim reasons. 'Would you care for some tea?'

'Please,' I said politely. 'This antiques sale for the old parish. It's above board?'

'Scrambled eggs, toast and marmalade?' She went to the kitchen. A cat strolled through in disdain, I looked away, guilty. 'Mixed cereals?'

'And fried bread, please, Miss.' I looked at the furnishings. Not too bad, for disgusting modern gunge. There were photographs. Her, younger, beside a bloke with a tash and lank hair in a porch. Our church. 'Where's Mr Entwistle?'

She rattled pans. I'm sure women make an unholy din just to punish us for making them snap into action. 'He's not here.'

'Oh?' I brightened. I'd never got close to an ex-teacher. She might clout me for suggesting that my education was incomplete.

When I cook I'm really quiet. She sounded like Agincourt. 'I'm afraid he's missing, Lovejoy.'

'Missing where?' Stupid people always say that. Tell me you've lost your purse, I'll go, 'Where?'

'I don't know, Lovejoy.' She was weeping, busying herself at the grub. 'I wish you could find him.'

From one missing-person triumph, hunting Tinker's lass Vyna, to another. The aroma made my belly rumble, so I moved to ogle the photographs.

Finding things isn't me. Last year, a Surbiton dealer bought a Georgian mahogany fall-front bureau, only forty-two inches wide. The Farnham piece was lovely. It was even lovelier when an investment bond was discovered in a secret drawer – these drawers were quite usual, for hiding passionate letters. The bond was worth a mint, plus interest since Adam dressed, well over four times the bureau's price. It's always somebody else. I'm the expert at losing, not finding.

The cat eyed me reproachfully as I tiptoed out. 'Shut your face,' I told it. Gently, silently, I reached round the speer, opened the door.

Tubb stood there. 'You're a bugger, Lovejoy. Any more of this, I'll take out insurance.'

'Look, mate,' I said, whispery. 'Get lost. I'm in with a chance here.'

'Who is it, Lovejoy?' my old teacher called amid kitchen war sounds.

'Salesman,' I yelled over my shoulder.

'They'll be narked, Lovejoy,' Tubb said. His runes had let him down.

For just an instant I almost sensed what the game was. I stared at Tubb like he'd landed from Andromeda. He was threatening me. I caught myself. He'd said 'they'. They who? Carmel? Abrasive, true, but no physical threat as such. And she was a lone operative, except in the fashion world.

'They who?' I asked.

He became shifty. 'This is once too often. Best do as you're told, or it's curtains.'

'They who?' He was behaving really lifelike, unprecedented. Even ordering a pint Tubb has to divine some tarot, work luck out. Just for that one fleeting instant he'd been himself.

'Please yourself, Lovejoy. I've warned you.'

And he went, shoulders humped, a tough with a faulty oracle. I watched him drive away in his hired non-hired motor. I shut the door, went to the photographs. One or two really interested me. I thought, aha. Terence Entwhistle at a card table. Terence on holiday, on his tie dumb-bells, acorns, leaves, hearts – German playing-card emblems. Terence in some club spinning a Victorian 'random clock'. It's a collector's item nowadays, picks out any digits from one to ten. Was Terence that all-time loser, the gambling addict?

She finally called. I went, fell on the grub.

'First I've had for two days, Miss Renson.'

She managed a smile. 'Stella, Lovejoy. I'll not tell you again.'

'Teachers never had first names.' I'd feel like when I went round a palace and saw the Queen's loo.

She watched me scoff. 'Terence has vanished, Lovejoy. But not alone.'

Which froze me. 'Who with?' For one terrible instant I dreaded she was going to say Vyna.

'Some of the antiques we're – you – will sell for us.'

Well, I laughed until I choked. Tears streamed down my face. She stared, thunderstruck. It took five minutes to come to.

'What is funny, Lovejoy?' That metronomic staccato teacher-speak has chilled and stilled children down the ages.

'Is that all, love?' I was cheery for once. 'I thought you meant he'd howffed it with some bird. Antiques, I can do something about. What were they, and how many? I'll pin him by teatime.'

'You will?' She was so relieved. 'Oh, thank you, Lovejoy. Terence is not the most worldly person. He *tries* to be commercial.'

'Any brown sauce, love?' I asked for the list of antiques her hubby'd nicked.

'Those I don't know, Lovejoy.'

Up one minute, down the next. 'You don't *know*, you silly cow?' I raged, spluttering valuable calories on gusts of anger. 'Who's in charge of the list?' God Almighty, out of Briony's frying pan into Stella's fire.

'Vulgar language,' she scolded automatically. 'I am, Lovejoy. We had no idea which were antiques. Folk just brought things in.'

My quiescent temple artery woke with a start and began to pound my cortex. My plate blurred.

'You didn't even write the antiques down?'

'Of course not. They're only going to be sold.'

'Not now they're not, love.' I moaned softly to myself.

She decided to get on her high horse. 'You are decidedly unhelpful, Lovejoy. Terence was really quite good. He only stole one load.'

See? Her bloke steals the whole shebang, and he's being 'really quite good'. If I'd nicked a light, the Plod would have me clinked. Selective thinking.

'Aye, love,' I said bitterly. 'Captain Blood only wanted one sackful – of the Crown Jewels.' I cut in as she drew breath, 'Terence'll have nicked the most valuable. He'll not have grabbed a pencil and taken to the hills.'

She said with asperity, 'You always were a grumbling child, Lovejoy. Grumble, grumble. The point is, the sale's tomorrow. *Do* something.'

'Do what, exactly?' I was relieved I'd eaten. Doom loomed.

'Bring Terence back, with the antiques he's borrowed. And sell our antiques.' Terence, arch thief of her charity, had now only 'borrowed' the stuff, so I must solve her fiasco. She said it like I had to wash up.

'That all?' I said, peeved. 'Got any cake, love?'

'I have some parkin.' She fetched it, cut a wafer-thin slice. It's our local cake, mostly for Bonfire Plot, a real filler. I helped the next chunk to be bigger. It's oatmealy, sticky. 'Can I see the remaining antiques?'

'Whenever you are ready, Lovejoy.'

So we hit the road. Her motor was toy size. I sat, knees to my chin. Neither of us touched on one difficulty. *Why* had her husband Terence nicked the antiques? Gambling fever, or something worse? I didn't ask, and Stella was not for telling. Motive's crap anyway, only made for Dame Agatha and editors, not real life. The questions in antiques are who, how, and what. You can forget why. So I did.

30

WHO SAID NEVER go back?
Scout Hey was still an old moorland chapel, sort rich visitors buy to turn into grand dwellings with cocktail cabinets where the pulpit once was, alarm boxes in the eaves. Me and Amy had robbed its great manse, now in ruins, much of the mansion's roofing reduced to a skeleton of charred beams.

A housing estate had spread over the moors. The stunted hawthorns, wind stoopers all, were distant now. Civilisation had come. Prefabricated garden sheds, Japanese cherries blooming in the wrong season, one-eyed TV dishes trained on infinity.

There's always a wind. I'd forgotten. Below, the coast road at Blackrod. You'd see the Isle of Man on a clear day. The town looked undressed without its pall of black smoke, oddly flattened without its chimneys.

'Lovejoy? What's the matter?'

Maybe a couple of dozen cars, lots of women with children about the rear entrance of Scout Hey chapel. Where me and Amy had come a-stealing was a sloping car park. Several vans stood by, marked with fashion college logos. Arty students in shawls, cowbells, clothes made of odd strings, chatted and smoked strange substances. Artistry had come. The chapel was apologetic, the way of all defrocked chapels. Its entrances were busy.

'Who're they?' I wasn't prepared for a jamboree.

Stella was puzzled at my reaction. 'Why, my helpers. Bringing antiques for sale, setting out. Those fashion students are planning their show.' She was exasperated. 'You'll do the auction. The fashion's afterwards.'

'It's an odd place. Miles from anywhere.'

She went all hurt. 'Fashion colleges do their displays here. The chapel costs nothing, not like hiring hotels.' She saw I was unconvinced. 'Seats hundreds. And it's secure.'

Secure? When her husband nicked a lorry load?

'Okay, then. Everything's money nowadays, agreed. Let's see what you have.'

She was anxious, went ahead saying, 'Hello, Mary. Did we do those notices? Hello, Betty. We arranged the parking with the police?' Boss organiser stuff.

We went into the chapel, a late Wesleyan boom building. Lovely, gallery symmetrical, pillars Mr Wesley's church at Moorgate would be proud of. The volunteers greeted us shyly. I'd been given quite a build-up, earned applause just walking in.

'Everyone!' Stella called, voice quavery. 'This is Lovejoy. Some of you remember him. He'll do our auction tomorrow!'

'How do,' I said, time and again. Smiles were everywhere. East Anglians don't smile.

Some came forward for a word. I was pleased, recognised several, one third cousin. It was difficult being friendly, because I could see only tons of dross nearby.

'We know you'll be pleased, Lovejoy,' one bashful lady told me. 'We've been collecting for ages.' Risking all, adding, 'I knew your gran.'

'Hello, Mary. I knew yours.' I bussed her. She'd been born four doors from me. I eyed the heaps of gunge, managed, 'You've done wonders, love.'

Trestle tables were set out, women busy at them. Blokes were hauling in more. Furniture, discarded clothes, mirrors, paintings you wouldn't shake a stick at, trinkets on a stand, a reproduction screen, rusting garden implements.

The whole lot was crud. I was broken.

'Well, Lovejoy?' Stella clasped her hands. What had she told her teams about Terence's vanished vanload?

'Can I have a wander, love?' I said brightly, not bursting into wracking sobs, for the sake of morale.

'Of course! People, listen! Lovejoy is going to examine our antiques!'

'And somebody brew up,' I added. 'I've not had a decent cup since I were a lad.'

Amid cheery calls, I ambled. There was volume, but no substance. Piles of old newspapers – but they have to be in pristine condition to sell. The clothes no collector would give a second glance. The furniture was soiled wartime, with sliced part-circle *Utility* emblems. Firewood. Electrical fittings, old boilers, decrepit bicycles – the entire sorry mass was unsellable. Great in a thousand years, for some Third

Millennium PhDs to write a How They Lived Back Then. But now? I feigned enthusiasm, paused for people's reminiscences. Pretended excitement at the throwout rubbish while furtively planning escape. The quicker I did a Terence the better. Maybe what he'd taken was also duff? And did it matter, if he was already in Monte Carlo?

They'd made a pleasing archway with great double doors. The chapel was one great space.

'Lovejoy!' Amy greeted me, flushed with exertion. She was marking the wooden flooring with yellow sticky tape. Students lounged in artistic attitudes. One lass tried to look pre-Raphaelite, wasn't even close. 'Here to see the antiques?'

'Hello, love. Is this where your show happens?'

'Yes. They're setting the lighting. We'll soon do an Italian run – that's a fast test rehearsal. The models drill early tomorrow. We go after your sale.'

Minus me, I thought. 'Do you need a rehearsal?'

'Of course!' She trilled a he's-not-real laugh.

Rehearsal? To walk about in different frocks? I kept silent. Three blokes carried in enormous wooden pallets. The students looked tired.

'Oh, good,' I said. 'Glad it'll be, er ... '

'Meet the mayor, Lovejoy.' Amy pulled me to be introduced. He was an affable, smiling bloke, thick-set. I'd seen his WH-1 registration limo outside. 'This is our Lovejoy,' she said proudly. I felt sham.

We made polite noises. Mayor Enderton said how pleased he was, etc, and I said etc likewise.

'We haven't money, son,' he said gravely. 'If things you auction sell well, we can make this a permanent centre. I donated my grandad's paintings to it.'

'Oh?' I said, bored. 'Your gramp painted?'

'No,' he puzzled me by saying. 'His three pictures were Mr Lodge's, his old friend. Only birds, but nice detail. Odd shine, they had, like dried cream.'

Dementia woke me. Mayor Enderton had just given a word picture of the great George Edward Lodge's birds-rocks-moss-bark natural history works. This genius died in 1954, but was in his eighties before he did his renowned bird series of 385 paintings for David Bannerman's twelve-volume book. His life shows why some artists soar and others don't. Aging fast, arthritic octagenarian George Lodge, a true hero, realised he needed detail in his pictures, against the fashion – note that please – of the times. Only one medium would do, the ancient and virtually extinct method of egg tempera painting. So he learned to separate fresh egg yolk, rub in pigments, and painted. It's lovely to paint with. You use fine brushes, line by line, over and over, on parchment or sheet copper. And you can actually buff up the painting with a cloth to a radiant gleam. Think of cream. Mediaeval monks used egg tempera to illuminate their parchments. Go to see the Lindisfarne Gospels, and you'll never forget. *Odd shine, detail, Lodge.* Fortune.

'Anything else, Mr Mayor?' *Three* Lodge paintings? Unrecorded? Sell those, he'd have his centre.

'Oh, couple of old mirrors.' He gave a sad chuckle. 'My grandad loved them. Silly; you could hardly see your face. They'd gone sugary. Nice carving, like faded gold.' He added, 'It were only wood. A bit was chipped.'

'Frame spread over the mirror?'

'Aye. Hardly room for your reflection. One was crumbling bad, dry rot.' He eyed me. 'Any value?'

'Don't sound so,' I lied. 'Look, Tom … '

He startled me by suddenly perking up. Stella joined us. He began to babble incoherently about his hopes for developing Scout Hey. I couldn't help looking from him to Stella, and from Stella to him.

They were astonishingly alive, in a way that can only mean what I think. 'Oh, good,' I kept saying. He'd fetched architects' drawings. I was shown them, peered without comprehension, did my Oh, good. They were on a loser. They'd not raise enough for the nails, let alone total rebuilding, from auctioning the garbage here. But his mirrors and Lodge funny-shine paintings …

'Stella,' I said, startling her back from gazing into Mayor Enderton. 'Who's boss? I mean, when does the auction end? Do the dealers get chucked out and the fashioneers brought in for the frock show?'

The mayor answered for her. 'The auction's yours. The textile show goes later.'

'Oh, good.' The affinity between Stella and Mayor Tom was charring the air. I asked to be let go. He said he appreciated my help. I said I was really glad. Sickening.

The mounds of debris had meanwhile risen. Old – read modern worthless – books, none with a single vibe, were being stacked amid exclamations of pleasure. Other loads of clag were approaching. I crouched for a sprint to freedom out of this hell. Could I use Tinker to nail Terence Entwistle, then scarper with Mayor Enderton's few antiques? I'd get away scotage free. Terence couldn't very well report *me* for *his* theft. Not without exposing himself as the ultimate rogue. It was beautiful.

'That you, love?' an old lady asked. I looked down. She only came up to my shoulder.

That was another thing. I'm exactly average, but I'd noticed that I was a bit taller than most. It felt odd, because I'm not.

'Aye, it's me, love.' I stared, and melted. 'Miss Dewhurst?'

'Yes, love.' She beamed with shy pride at the women nearby. 'See? I lived next door, didn't I, son?'

'Yes.' I hugged her. She only weighed a couple of ounces.

Old Alice, as we called her, had a wind-up gramophone and taught me music. Beethoven, Italian arias, folk songs, the lot. She had cats. She alone had managed to grow some trees – okay, two stunted, sooty privets that never got higher than the slate-slab yard walls – but still a miracle of gardening. She'd worked as a cotton piecer, still wore her ankle clogs. I could swear they were the same ones. She'd knock sometimes, just to show me pictures, pretty women, handsome men, landscapes painted long ago. She lived in a fantasy world of romance and colour, when our world was grey.

'You'll help us, luv?' she said.

Once, I'd been reading. I was seven. We'd just lit the gas mantle, pulling its chain to make it pop into light when you held the match to it. Old Alice knocked with her clothes prop. Neighbours summoned each other like this, reaching the prop up next door's steps.

'Come and look!' she'd cried. 'Front steps! Quick!'

We rushed to see, Gran puffing, and peered out, wondering. There was Old Alice in the street.

'See?' She was exultant. 'The sunset!'

Curious, I'd looked. The sky was a mass of scarlets, golds, rose hues on deep cerulean blue. I stared, too polite to ask. The sky often did change. Alice was looking at it, tears in her shining eyes.

'Isn't it the most beautiful sky anybody's ever seen?' she said longingly. Gran instantly went back in.

'Aye, Miss Dewhurst,' I said. I didn't mean it. But, standing there, a sense of seeing what she saw slowly grew. I went down the steps to stand beside her, to test if it looked different from the pavement. All was as I saw. It was just that Old Alice saw beauty above, where I'd seen only a flat plank. I stood an hour with her, watching the colours, learning more then than in all my schooling.

'Help?' I asked, uneasy, remembering escape.

'They're trying to buy this chapel, luv,' she explained. 'There might be music! And a place folk can stop for their tea on the way to the Lake District! Maybe dances!' Her old eyes shone. 'A pool for childer! Flowers, paths for young folk to walk hand in hand!' She turned to me. 'Oh, son! It'll be beautiful, won't it?' But her old cracked voice, with that absurd lisp she always did have, didn't hold conviction. Nothing ever did, for wistful old ladies like Alice. But her dream would be lovely while it lasted, a hope. And hope was the thing. When that hope came to nothing, then Old Alice would somehow discover a new one, and keep on.

'Aye, love,' I said lapsing. 'I'll help.'

Signalling to Stella, I smiled and chatted my sorry way outside into the macadam car park. I walked onto the one remaining patch of bare moorland grass towards the ruined mansion.

'Where are we going, Lovejoy?' Stella asked.

'Out of earshot, love.'

We entered the stone-walled garden, derelict and overgrown. The roses had reverted to wild, to stay alive, a lesson for us all. For a moment I felt a familiar strangeness come into me, stared about, looked up at the gaunt ruin. The sills were fragmenting, the walls bellying out. It was all crumbling doorways and sagging brickwork, and we ought to be ashamed of ourselves. But the feeling made me narked. I rounded on her.

'It's all crap, Stella.' I could hardly see from fury. 'Your Terence nicked the only genuine antiques.'

She recoiled. 'He took a few paintings, a pair of old twisted mirrors, Lovejoy. What Mayor Tom donated. That's all.'

'He's owffed the only valuable items.' I got angrier. 'What have you told the helpers?'

'I said Terence had removed them for safe keeping,' she said miserably. 'To a secret location.'

'The rest wouldn't sell at a jumble.'

'That's impossible, Lovejoy.' She'd gone white. 'We're depending ... '

'An auction tomorrow's out of the question.'

'It can't be!' She filled up. 'Oh, Lovejoy, they've worked so hard. And people've given everything. They hope Scout Hey will bring jobs ... '

'Aye.' I interrupted rudely. 'So you let Terence steal anything valuable. If the dealers that you've invited even see that shambles, they'll torch the bloody place.'

'But … '

My hand on her mouth, I went on, 'Do you know what you're dealing with? Dealers are maniacs. If they think they've been had, they'll assume that you've been paid to decoy them here – so they won't go somewhere else where the real money's being spent! See?'

'No, Lovejoy.' She spoke in a whisper, ashen.

'Listen, Stella.' I leant against the bonnet of a motor, hands in my pockets. I felt done for. 'A bloke I knew accidentally got the date wrong for his field auction. He'd sent out cards, got it together. Dealers came on the date printed on their invitations.'

'What happened, Lovejoy?' I felt like a stoat dancing round a rabbit, but she had to learn. That's why I'd chosen a true story, always the worst.

'They put all his belongings into his garage, car and all. Made him set it ablaze. His antiques they stole, auctioned off among themselves. Then they set his house afire. He was left naked, not even shoes to stand up in.'

'But the police, Lovejoy!'

'Stella,' I said wearily. 'For God's sake shut up.'

Well, she'd said it to me often enough.

'But it's too late to cancel now, Lovejoy.' She flapped a hand towards the chapel. 'You can't leave us in the lurch.'

Why not, exactly? Then I surrendered, habit of a lifetime.

'Give me a lift up the Scout moor, love.'

I started towards her motor, adding over my shoulder as she gasped in alarm, 'Don't worry. I'll not escape.'

31

PART WAY UP the hill we call Scout there is an ancient hall, the sort newspapers call baronial. Town buses turn back there. There's a phone box. I told Stella to hang on a sec, phoned, then we carried on to the empty moor.

'Are you sure, Lovejoy?' She didn't want me unsupervised.

'Sure, ta.' I perched on a drystone wall. 'I used to come here, stare at the town.'

'Fishing in the lodge, more like,' she said cryptically, indicating the small upland lake. Shows how wrong teachers are. I'd been taken fishing when I was six, and caught a gudgeon. First time, last time, never, as the girls chanted skipping. That poor gudgeon's reproachful gaze. Bad as a cat's any day.

'Who'd you phone, Lovejoy?' She couldn't drive off without knowing.

'My auntie,' I lied. 'Narked I don't visit.'

'Mmmh.' She drove off, looking in her mirror.

Twenty minutes I sat. The wind was rising, but no rain yet. Motors went past. One would be Stella, checking. The town's boundaries were defined to the eye. There shone flashes of water even. Nearer, moorland rising. Left, the road ran along the precipitous Whimberry Hill, sic, where whinberries (also sic) grew. Girls gathered them for the best pies on earth. Right, the road went to Blackpool's gaudy seaside.

Sea. Morecambe Bay, where horse carriages cross the sands on the ancient pathways at low tide. I've the mind span of a pilchard, but for antiques.

The sea made me think of that famous diver bloke. Dorian, was it? Hunted for a dozen years, dreaming of sunken galleons. I imagine him trudging between banks, asking for loans, getting chucked out. Until in 1993 he finally found the great 350-ton ship *Diana*, lost on the way from Canton home to Madras – stuck on a reef in the Malacca Straits in 1817. With his Malaysian mates, Dorian recovered over 24,000 precious pieces of unspoiled Chinese porcelain. I like thinking how the bankers must have changed. Christies auctioned the loot in Amsterdam nigh 180 years after she sank, and money came washing over the gun'ls. Mind you, rarity's only relative. With the *Diana*'s, 227,000 Chinese porcelain items were auctioned in those Amsterdam auction rooms from four sunken ships all in a few years. It staggers the mind – and bankrupts anybody who'd bought stupen- dously rare blue-and-white Chinese porcelain *before* the wrecks were found. It happens.

So treasure isn't just rarity. In antiques it's things like 'signature', that identifying craftsman typicality. It's also condition, appearance, provenance, the material of which the antique is made. With so many duff antiques around, provenance has galactic importance. It made me think of Briony Finch. Her antiques had stone-solid provenance: never moved from her old sister's manor of Thornelthwaite, until I'd brought Wanda to the rescue. Now, even as I sat in the cold wind, they were being got into order by that harridan's team and her dry- as-dust Bertie. Wanda would go galactic if I wanted any more changes, especially impossible ones.

The town lay in its moorland bowl.

Woman or man, never go back.

The town was the only town whose police force was imposed by Parliament. So violent was this huddle that Queen Victoria's Royal Charter in 1838 was simply sent by post, so terrified were Whitehall mandarins of visiting. In spite of the Chartist riots, genius flowered. Thomas Mort, 1816, went to Australia with some notion about making the holds of ships cold, to begin an international meat trade. Cheerful Bob Whitehead invented the torpedo.

But not everybody was a merry genius. Some were a mite eccentric, or frankly daft. Another Bob – Leach – bobbed over Niagara Falls in a barrel, and lived to brag. Municipal baths began here – well, first since the Romans left the Isle of Albion. And possibly the greatest brain of them all, poor Samuel Crompton. A sickly musician, composer, in 1779 he invented the spinning mule, that overnight hurtled cotton out of the Dark Ages and into a new phenomenon called the Industrial Revolution. Naturally, he was cheated into penury. Sir Robert Peel, a swine, called at Crompton's house while he was away and bribed Crompton's little lad George to show him where his clever daddy worked on his secret new machine. Later, rich merchants persuaded the trusting genius to simply reveal it to one and all. Peel brought his own wheelwrights to steal Crompton's design. The great Member of Parliament had the frigging nerve to offer Crompton sixpence. Poor Crompton died in penury, and his son George finished up in the workhouse. Sir Robert Peel naturally became chief of everything, and sang Samuel Crompton's hymns in church on Sundays.

. The town was the last to give up working pregnant women and little children to death in its coal mines, appropriately at Chain Pit, Hunger Hill. Public hangings for nicking cloth weren't unknown, as poor James Holland discovered the hard way. Stern values ruled. George Marsh had the nerve to preach his *own* religious ideas, the bounder, and got burned at the stake for his insolence. More riots per square yard occurred here than anywhere else on Planet Earth. No wonder that some emigrated, and did quite well. Like 'Our Jim' Gregson, who with a mate in 1848 found some specks of heavy metal in the USA, and started the Gold Rush. And our Sir Arthur Rostron bravely took his *Carpathia* to help the *Titanic*, instead of ignoring the stricken vessel — unlike that other ship I keep not mentioning.

How did I get into all that? I remember. Never go back.

Not even to Thornelthwaite?

Could Wanda hack it? Worse, could I? I decided that Tinker'd had long enough. I set off downhill among the sheep, as scared of them as they of me. The only building between me and the town was the tangle of stone buildings of Brannan Hey farm. Edgily I went into the yard, knocked, shouted, poked about. Nobody. They used to ride horses here, which also are wild beasts like sheep, to be given a wide berth.

'Wotcher, Lovejoy.'

I yelped with fright, quickly made it a cough. Tinker was sitting on the stone steps that climbed to the upper storey, grinning.

'Frigging lunatic! You scared me.'

'Thought I was a sheep, Lovejoy?' He fell about, cackling. I sat on the bottom step. It's all very well to joke. The drunken old sod'd been born here at Brannan Hey among brutes. I only knew towns. 'You've got to get over it, Lovejoy. Animals are natural.'

'Your Roadie, Tinker. Am I right?'

He sighed. 'Aye. I'll brain the little bugger, so help me. I didn't cotton on at first.' He spat hugely to his lee. 'That's why I said inside the ghost arch. I knew you'd never wait there. Scared of everything.'

His guffaw was a mite apologetic. His relatives, not mine, after all, were our traitors.

'You were right. I lurked by the Queens cinema.'

That really did make him laugh, so much he fell down a step and clung to the rail. I looked at the crumbling wood. The North's old buildings were going to ruination. Like the old house by the chapel at Scout Hey. That odd divvy feeling I'd had when talking to Stella had only come when I'd been near the derelict mansion.

'Who were they, Tinker?' I asked without much hope.

'Who chucked the firebomb? Dunno, son. Not local, or I'd have heard. The radio's on about it, police.'

A clink, glug, squeak of corked liquid calories. He didn't offer me a swig. 'What do we do, Lovejoy? We can't stay here, if somebody's going to crisp you. Do we go south? Stella's sale is all gunge, eh?'

'You've seen it?'

He said simply, 'I can't divvy, but it looked crap. Did you see them young ponces? Ought to be shovelling clinker, grafting on the canals. And them lasses dressed in tat. There ought to be a law.'

He meant the fashion students. No use reminding him that canals were now leisure waterways. And nobody shovelled clinker any more. Fashions do change.

'Lovejoy. Want to know what Roadie's up to?'

'Motive, now, Tinker? I've never believed in it.' I'd have sighed again but was too tired. 'No. He doesn't matter. The Braithwaite parked outside Amy's told me enough. I worried Roadie'd wired it somehow.'

'I wouldn't've let him, Lovejoy. You know that.' He was hurt. 'I saw your old flame Amy with her two kiddies. You could do worse than shag her, Lovejoy.'

Chivalric to the last, a knight in shining dross. But he'd reminded me of a transient lust. 'Your Vyna. Is she bonny, big specs?' I described the teacher at the Manchester museum.

'That's her. Down Under she modelled. Seen her?'

'Maybe. Where's Roadie, this minute?'

Tinker thought. 'He'll be meeting Vyna somewhere secret.' He heaved a chuckle, set himself off coughing. 'He doesn't know this town's really a village, every brick and stick a megaphone. It'll be in the Octagon bar.'

For five full minutes I pondered. Old Alice, the tangled tale. Tinker coughed, spat explosively.

'This place still yours, Tinker?' I asked at last, indicating the farm buildings. For the first time, I looked up at the old soak there on the steps, unspeakable, unutterably frayed and aged. He was surprised, gazed about.

'The farm here? Was family once. That Shacklady. Right-half, went queer, married my cousin Marian.' Translation: Shacklady, ex-footballer, was now a wildlife artist of international reputation. 'Leased it for grazing.'

'He lives here?'

'No. Lake Windermere.' His voice went into contempt. 'Know what, Lovejoy? He paints flowers. Him a grown man! Can you imagine? Our Marian *helps* the daft bugger.'

'Then we'll use here.' I looked at the gaunt buildings. 'Distract Roadie, okay?'

'Give over, Lovejoy,' he said with disgust. 'Already done it. Look, son. Why stay?'

Who has answers to that? 'We've to buy a chip shop.'

'Oh. Reet.' One thing about Tinker. A filthy old wino, true, but you don't get many friends like him in a month. 'Who from, Lovejoy?'

'For,' I corrected. 'A widow, Briony Finch.' I rose, dusted off my trousers like you do for no reason. 'We'll cut downhill. I need a phone.'

'There's a bar at Smithills.' He forced a theatrically phoney wheeze. 'I'm dry. Fancy a pint?'

We ambled towards civilisation, Tinker shuffling along reminiscing. He'd loved some mill girl from Astley Bridge who'd sung like Jenny Lind. He'd wed her when he'd been drunk. He was still indignant. I whiled away the paces thinking up tall tales to tell Wanda, and what percentage she'd accept not to club me insensible.

The nosh place was almost empty. A few parents, babes, children. Why does everybody eat crisps, that Yanks call chips? Fashion. Chips reminded me of stern duty. I bought Tinker three pints, went to phone, and got Bertie. He sounded the way you'd imagine the extinct dodo would, given the opportunity.

'I really wanted Wanda. It's Lovejoy.'

'She is not available.' He hissed it with hate.

'I need a chat, that's all.'

'That is untrue, Lovejoy.' More hissing. 'My wife predicted that you would soon importune, and try to wheedle the best antiques from us.' His voice rose to a treble, the male dodo's tweet.

'Arrangements cannot be changed. Mrs Finch's antiques are cata-logued. The auction will be held at Proudhomme Fortescue in King's Lynn.'

'Bertie!' I screamed just in time. He hadn't hung up. 'Who sicked the Metropolitan Police Antiques Squad onto me about that blue lac cabinet?'

'The what?' Bertie whittered.

'The blue japanned piece,' I bawled, howling so many lies that I frightened myself. 'I don't want to get involved. I'm out.'

Lying always makes me sweat. I was drenched, and turned – to face the silent gaze of the entire caff. They'd heard every screech. The only sound was Tinker's glugging as he swilled the third pint and hurried over at shuffle speed.

'Tinker.' I smiled, cool Lovejoy fresh from a light-hearted joke call. 'Have another?'

'It's just lies, eh?' he boomed, the soul of secrecy. 'Christ Almighty, Lovejoy. I thought we were on the run again.'

Chortling worse than Cradhead, I induced him to booze. 'Shut it, you noisy burke,' I said with quiet fury.

'Eh?' he bawled. 'Oh, I get yer. Nod's as good as a wink. Three pints, love, and one for my mate.'

The phone went as I paid. The lass held up the receiver. I strolled across.

'Lovejoy?' Wanda's voice didn't sound like an extinct bird. 'Be precise. You have two minutes, after which ... '

'There's no Antiques Squad, Wanda. And no blue lac japanned cabinet. I said that to get your attention. Will you do the impossible, sweetheart?'

'No, Lovejoy.' She waited. I waited. 'What?'

'There's something truly important here. I know where, but not what.'

'How many pieces?'

'Maybe five.' I was really down. The worst moment of my life. I could only think of Old Alice's features.

She thought for so long I asked was she still there. 'What's this "impossible", Lovejoy?'

'Fetch Briony Finch's antiques up here. For auction tomorrow.'

'You're off your fucking head, Lovejoy,' said Wanda, ever demure. 'It can't be done. My drivers alone ... '

'I'll give you ... ' Desperate, I lowered my voice. 'I'll give you me, Wanda.'

'You, Lovejoy?' It wasn't as daft as it sounded. Any dealer would give their fingers for a genuine divvy to work free, tell them which antiques were faked a week ago. To my astonishment, she hesitated. 'You in trouble? Only, two thickos came by, asking. Blanks. Even Bertie was alarmed.'

'Me? No, love.' Peter Pan could put the frighteners on Bertie. Blank means unknown. Some chance creditors, I expect. 'Honest. I'm clean. You ask ... ' I could hardly give Cradhead the Plod as a reference. 'Anybody,' I finished lamely.

'These antiques, Lovejoy. You've really no idea?'

'Honest,' I said, hoping I wasn't lying again. 'They're not mine to give, Wanda.' Heart sinking further at the thought of slaving in Wanda's galley, so to speak, I explained about the fashion show, the 'precious antiques auction' that was tat.

'Never get involved with fashion, Lovejoy,' she said sharply. 'They're plonkers. That Thekla's combing the world for you like she's on heat, silly mare.'

'A beautiful shared thought, Wanda.' I didn't want past failures. I was knee-deep in new ones. Were those two investigators Thekla's hirelings? It'd be my cottage. Mortgage people never give up.

'Tell you what, Lovejoy. I'll do it, on one condition.' Here it came. 'Mrs Finch's terms stand. I get your five cached antiques. Understood?'

My soul peered hopefully out of my boots.

'Thanks, Wanda, love.' I felt really true honest love for Wanda. Her beauteous spirit was what made women divine.

'Plus you get me a blue lac cabinet. Deal?'

'Deal,' I told the vile scheming bitch. I gave her the address. I'd have to kill her, or something. A blue lac Shrager cabinet or the Koh-i-Noor, I'd have tried to nick the Mountain of Light diamond any time. I was now bound to Wanda for life.

Tinker went spare.

'You mean that Shrager cabinet?' He actually said Shraggy, as we all do. 'You're frigging mental.'

'Don't.' I despaired. 'I'm papering an auction, supporting a fashion show, funding some centre. I'm broke.'

'There's only one blue lac, i'n't there?'

'Yes and no.' He inhaled, barmy suggestions on the way. 'Some Connecticut Yanks bought it, last anybody heard.'

The Shraggy is one of the classic cases in antiquery. Like the Great

Dud Fabergé Egg, like Piltdown Man, or the infamous Lorenzo Lotto trick, some are transparent frauds. Some, though, are ugly, murky. However famous, they're in that grey area where angels fear to tread. The ultimate nasty tale is the notorious Shrager Blue Lac Cabinet.

Once upon a time, in 1922, when flappers in cloche hats raved in Mayfair, a bloke called Adolf Shrager moved to posh Westgate (where folk still tell tall tales). Posh manor down by the Isle of Thanet, Kent seaside, all that. Off goes Shrager to buy antiques. But once he'd got them, he sulked. Lovely antiques, sure, *but all that money*! He'd over-spent.

So he decides to sell off a few, to raise the £25,000 he still owed. Shrager asks Herbert Cescinsky, greatest antiques celebrity of all time, to tea. 'What's this blue lacquered cabinet worth?' Shrager asks, casual. Cescinsky the expert says, 'Fake, old bean.' Shock, et stunning cetera, because the dealer who'd sold it was the famous Basil Dighton, Savile Row's poshest.

Lawyers manned the ramparts. Money was at stake but, ghastlier then, that other fraud known as gentlemanly honour. Suddenly, millions who'd never heard of blue lacquer were devouring the trial's lurid details. Shrager sued the antique dealer Dighton. He'd been sold a fake, he claimed. Dighton polished his finger nails and sighed, nonsense! Savile Row dealers simply *don't*.

The question was blunt: is the Shraggy blue lac cabinet fake or genuine? It was bonny – slots for letters, drawers for pens, 'oriental' decoration, the whole monty as they say. But was it a true Queen Anne blue lac cabinet, or dud?

Fake? Genuine? Sir Edward Pollock KC, the 'Official Referee', gave Dealer Dighton the verdict. Shrager was condemned, his reputation in tatters. Antique dealers everywhere preened themselves and toasted justice, ho ho.

Why is the Blue Lac Cabinet Mystery so famous? You hear such stories eighty times a day. Even back in 1923 when Pollock delivered his stern summary disputes were ten a penny.

Well, Sir Edward Pollock was an honest judge, but should his smart-aleck nephew Ernest *really* have been Dealer Dighton's counsel? And how come Sir Edward suddenly leapfrogged the queue of judges? Somebody definitely tampered with the list.

There are two other rather sick questions. Was the Blue Lac mystery a case of society's grandees ganging up on this outlander? And, two, wasn't Shrager the millionaire who'd made a vast fortune in cowardly Great War profiteering, whom society ought to punish as a dastardly cad? Me, I think it's none of the above. Everything simply comes down to antiques and the people who love them.

There's one moral that maybe outweighs all. It's this. Herbert Cescinsky, who remained resolute – the Blue Lac was a fake – smouldered on. Through 1923 and the frolicking Twenties, through the Great Crash, our Herbert furiously gnawed his cheek. Finally he could contain himself no longer. He wrote a famous book. Everybody should read *The Gentle Art of Faking Furniture*. A mint copy of the 1931 original will cost you an arm and a leg. I love it. It's crammed with common sense with acid stirred in. The dedication alone's worth it: 'To the memory of the late Adolf Shrager, who acquired a Second-hand but First-rate knowledge of both ENGLISH LAW AND ANTIQUE FURNITURE by the simple process of PAYING FOR IT in 1923 ... ' And Cescinsky adds caustically, 'READER DO THOU NOT LIKEWISE'. Meaning the Blue Lac Trial was a fix.

I'd promised Wanda a Queen Anne blue and gold japanned cabinet exactly like the notorious Blue Lac itself.

'I'll think of something, Tinker,' I said.

'You don't pay Queen Anne prices for Mary Anne,' the old soak groused.

'Shut your teeth. Have I ever let you down?'

'Don't be frightened, son,' he said. 'We'll get by. One thing. That Thekla's got some blanks trailing you. Two turned up here, asking.'

Typical of Thekla to hunt me. Women know vengeance best. I sighed. 'Deflect them, Tinker. I've had it.'

'Right.' He spat downwind. 'Don't be scared.'

That made me wild. I yelled, 'Shut your gums, you daft old bum. I'm not scared.'

'No, course not.' And we went our way. I'd a long journey.

32

TINKER LISTENED TO my instructions as I boarded the old Braithwaite before dusk. I was sick to death of telephones, so told him to make three calls. The vital ones were to Baz and Florsston.

'Basil-the-Donkey will know where a blue lac fake is available.' I ignored Tinker's protests. 'He's the records man. Pay him,' I said airily, 'with an IOU.'

By now low on money. I booked out of the Man and Scythe. Dobber, who I'd been at school with, told me Aureole was in town hunting me. 'Great, Dobber,' I told him. 'Tell her I've gone to Leeds, eh?'

The one thing that's improved in this creaking old kingdom is the road system. An unbelievable four hours later I roared into the garden of Florsston Valeece, materials expert.

The giant was humming, pleasantly arranging flowers in a vase. His workshop lights were on.

'Lovejoy!' he cried, no preamble. 'It's in hand!'

'Er, what exactly?'

'That utterly *hideous* fake blue lac Japanese bureau. If that's Queen Anne, then so am I! Your barker Tinker phoned from some *ghastly* outpost near Hadrian's Wall *whimpering*. Baz located it. I've perspired *fountains* of *gore*, and got it here at *no notice*! Take it *away*. Who on *earth* could *live ...* ' etc.

'Great, Florssie. You're a pal. I owe you.' I ignored his sharp glance, because I had a question. 'I saw a Victorian dress in a museum display case.' I described it as best I could. 'The material was marked *Tuss* and *T. Ara*. High neck, fitted bodice, brownish, shiny.' I passed him the catalogue I'd brought. He ignored it. 'There's no photograph of that one.'

'Shiny, was it?'

'The shawl wasn't, much, except for threads in it.'

'Say no more. It was tussore silk, Lovejoy. Always fawnish to chestnut, brought in from China and India. That shawl sounds rather a risk. Arachne, they called it, or tulle arachne, from 1831 on. Has frightful gold threads in silk.'

My throat thickened. This was it. There had been a brooch on the dress.

'Pretty valuable frock, eh, Florsston?'

'Lovejoy,' he sighed. 'Excellently preserved Victorian dresses like that are hardly worth the price of a decent meal.'

'Is that so,' I said. The cheap brooch, pink glass? I was suddenly desperate to see the whole display, frantic to get onto the north road.

Then Nicola called from the kitchen. He beamed, Ollie Hardy quadrupled, whispered, 'She's been victualling the fridge, poor cow'.

'Er, why, exactly?' I was lost. The blue lac piece stood there, clearly Victorian, caused a dullish chime. It had started life a dull mandarin red, with gold highlights. Probably Elston, faker of Penrith.

He simpered roguishly. 'Before you take her.'

'Look, Florssie ... '

His face grew so savage I recoiled. 'No, Lovejoy. *You* look! You wanted a cabinet. I got it. Our deal stands. The deal was, I do your rush job, you remove Nicola.'

'I didn't mean *this* job, Florssie! I meant a scam to catch a rival divvy.' Nicola was calling, the casserole's for Thursday and suchlike.

He went impassive. 'In the antiques game, Lovejoy, you promise, you deliver. Your barker speaks for you, you pay on the nail. Want me to send a hundred faxes? Everybody from Mr Sheehan to Rozzar? Every dollop broker, auction house?' I swallowed. Rozzar's a psycho. Big John Sheehan's a neat churchgoer. Both are good – as friends. 'Five minutes, you won't be able to buy a pasty with a gold ingot.'

'What must I do, Florsston?' I asked humbly, hating him. I'd only wanted a fake cabinet, for God's sake, and somehow started a global anti-Lovejoy creed.

His smile mellowed. 'Simple. Take Nicola. Sound in mind and limb, an unused bargain.' He closed his eyes, swayed, a wobbly Alp. 'I can't stand her a minute longer. Poor bitch actually *likes* Laura Ashley curtaining.' He moaned. 'I've *suffered*, Lovejoy.'

'What happens afterwards?' I really wanted to know. Sooner or later Aureole, Thekla, Faye, the rest, would catch me. I wanted fewer complications, not more.

He carolled gleeful culinary reassurance to Nicola, then whispered, 'For me a little Italian holiday, with a friend.'

'I can't take Nicola. Wanda has ... '

His glacial silence chilled me. He purred, 'You *create* difficulties, Lovejoy.'

'Please don't lumber me, Florsston. I'm in real trouble. Somebody's tried to do me in. Like Spoolie.'

'Nicola!' he trilled, angelic. 'Lovejoy's ready!'

She entered, flustered. 'Yes, dear. You *will* look after yourself? I'll only be gone two days.'

'Nicola, don't *fuss*!' He waggled sausage fingers at me. 'Be warned, Lovejoy. Our deal *insists* that you take *complete* care of this little dear! Understand?' I said nothing. He boomed, 'Understand?'

'Aye, Florsston.' It took me minutes to load the blue lac and cover it. I hefted Nicola's case.

'Go now, both of you.' He shed tears, admiring himself in a mirror. 'I can't *stand* goodbyes.'

Nicola waved at the house. Florsston slammed the door.

Tact was called for. 'Er, he's probably sad, love.'

'I know,' she said, misty. 'He conceals his emotions. He said the quicker I left, the less pain.' She glowed. 'Isn't that sweet, Lovejoy?'

'Really, er, sweet. What's he told you to do?'

'Oh, this sideboard?' She opened her handbag. 'I've Mr Baz's invoice ... '

'Ta, love.' I took the paper, let it blow out of the window, and away.

There was a light in Brannan Hey. Nicola shivered, but she'd been doing that all the journey. I pulled in among the outhouses. Moorland quiet rushed at us.

'Is this it, Lovejoy?' She alighted, exclaiming at the squelch. 'It's very remote.'

'It's the only place we've got.'

'You *live* here?'

'It's a friend's. That'll be him.'

Tinker opened the door, grinning welcome. He could hardly stand, and stank of ale.

'Wotcher, Lovejoy. This the bird we've got to dump?'

'No, Tinker,' I said quickly. He and Florsston must have chatted some more. 'Florsston Valeece's lady Nicola is here to help.' I smiled weakly at Nicola. 'Mr Dill, my assistant.'

'The place smells *musty*!' She moved timorously in.

Tinker had lit oil lanterns. A peat fire burned smokily. White dust sheets covered what furniture had been left, but the farmhouse's rafters, stonework, ancient beams and the living area's wooden flooring made it a deal better than I was used to. And draughts are refreshing. I leant on the jack spit's iron hook to poke the fire.

'We *stay* here?' Nicola quavered.

'We'll go over tomorrow's business. Brew up, Tinker.'

'Here, Lovejoy.' He ignored my request, somehow uncapped a beer bottle with a flat palm against a wall. I try doing it, but it hurts. He whispered so loudly I swayed in the decibel-riddled alcoholic gale. 'Wanda's on her way. A bird called Mrs Finch is here. And Aureole, she's rowed with Amy. Those two thickos want you. They're at the Swan.'

'Ta, Tinker.' For the headache, and the new brutes. 'Nicola, brew up, love. There's water in the well.' I was done for.

'From Lydia, Lovejoy.' He gave me a letter, watched me open it.

Dear Lovejoy,

Despite my precipitate departure, I am apprised by my employers Lissom and Prenthwaite that I am contractually obligated to attend your auction at Scout Hey. My attendance does not alter in any way my attitude towards you and the nefarious dealings in which you are currently engaged. My rescission should not be taken as a wish on my part to resume any relationship with you. It arises solely from Mrs Wanda's decision to change the venue of the auction to Scout Hey.

Yours faithfully.

For Lissom, Prenthwaite, Co, plc (registered for Value Added Tax) Lydia.

What the hell did it mean?

'Just a love letter,' I explained to Nicola, chucking it into the fire. 'That tea ready? I'm famished. Got anything to eat, Tinker?'

'Nowt,' he said. 'Got anything to drink?'

'Well?' Nicola asked. 'Water? In a *well*?'

'The loo's in the yard.'

'*Loo*?' she gasped faintly. 'In the *yard*?'

'Give me a sec, love. I'll drop you off at a hotel. They've a vacancy at the Man and Scythe.'

I sat in front of the fire and closed my eyes. I'd had enough italics for one day. I wanted to work out which fears to use most tomorrow.

Homecoming's aren't. As Nicola muttered, I kept my eyes shut, heard Tinker's gravelly voice explaining how he'd obeyed my orders.

He'd done all right. But had he stayed sober while doing it? We'd find out on the morrow.

33

AT FOUR O'CLOCK – cold, frost, breath solid in the garish lights – I was near the old Burnden football ground. The town's grotty stream runs nearby, in a grottier hollow. Lads going down there are Up To No Good, committing the giddy sin of Getting With Girls. Chance'd be a fine thing. I stood standing, as local idiom says, until a sleek red motor hummed up. It halted at the kerb. I knelt.

'What's the point of a motor this flat?' I said.

'It's fast,' Wanda said, her voice in double-whisky dawn pitch. 'No, Lovejoy. Don't get in.'

'It's not exactly secret, is it?'

'You burke. Some cars have a pose index.'

'Mmmh.' Who but Wanda could afford a one-off special tooled in Oxfordshire?

'And it's kitted out. Here.' Her hand thrust out a black box that piped nervously, 'Hello? Lovejoy?' I hadn't even seen Wanda properly yet, and here I was talking to a matchbox.

'Good morning. Briony, is it?'

We exchanged reassurances. I hung on to learn that she would be 'with me soon, dear, to take up where we left off.' I quote.

'Er, where, Mrs Finch?' My verbal unravelling.

'I'm already here, darling. Mrs Wanda is arranging the auction at your site. Her staff have been contacting buyers ceaselessly. Her printer is working non-stop.'

Real news. Printers have only one rule: everything takes nine months. I said, 'Er, why are you here, exactly?' Superfluity has ruined everything from murder to evolution and the ozone layer. It even ruins rarity. 'I hoped you'd stay at Thornelthwaite until it was over. Be less ... ' Of a problem? Simpler to milk her money? ' ... tiring.'

'How sweet.' Her voice softened. 'Mrs Wanda thought it best. So did I, after that frantic Aureole came. And that Thekla. There are some disagreeable women about.'

Wrong, but you can't disagree. Briony had the bit between her emotional teeth. 'The antiques, Mrs Finch?'

'Briony, please. I'm to vouch that it's all there when the auction starts. Mrs Wanda is most proper.'

'I'll hand you back to Wanda.'

'Over and out, Finch,' Wanda snapped. 'Happy, Lovejoy? Get in.'

'Er, the antiques?' I had to know.

'In my pantechnicons, at ... ' She waited, then made me leap a mile by screaming, '*Wake up, you idle bitches! Where where where?*'

'Yes, Wanda!' the frightened dashboard blurted. 'Affetside! Waiting at Affetside! You want the map reference?'

I nodded to answer Wanda. 'No.' Wanda's charm is strictly utilitarian. '*Keep awake!*'

'Yes, Wanda.'

Getting seated in her motor felt the reverse of being born. I wondered if there was a word for it. Unparturition, perhaps? Undeliver? Wanda gunned us into orbit.

'Know what that little cow's bonus is?' she yelled over the engine's howl. 'Dance class, two *years*. Ballroom English waltz champion year after next, she reckons. Am I a walking charity? Which way?'

'Straight on. The town's mostly one way now.'

'What thanks do I get? Lazy mare. What's the game?'

'There's junk, loosely described as an antiques auction, at a disused chapel called Scout Hey. And some fashion show. Both widely advertised. Telly, newspapers, dignitaries, the lot.'

'Fashion awards day? Antiques the attraction.' She gave a wintry smile. I could see her face sideways on in the flickering lights. A female Big John Sheehan. 'Which I have killed myself to catalogue, Lovejoy. For peanuts.'

'For money, love. And,' I dismally reminded her of the plum in the pudding, 'me.'

'At last! Which way?'

'Left fork. It's the old toll gate. In 1827, the toll charge for six sheep ... '

'Lovejoy, shut it. What's your angle?'

'Trying to keep clear of falling objects, love. Anybody been sniffing around?' I meant police. She surprised me.

'Some tart wanting her feller's wheels back. Gave *her* short shrift.'

Vernon Sleek, sending Ruby after his Braithwaite. People really exasperate me. Okay, so I'd borrowed his motor. What was it, a crime?

'There's one difficulty, love,' I said, still horizontal. 'Those five good antiques I promised you. The organiser's husband Terence Entwistle has nicked them. I can get them back.' She accelerated up Scout Hill in darkness. 'Only ... '

'Only they're not yours to give?'

'They're the mayor's. He's donated them. True lust will out. He's daft over Mrs Entwistle.'

'And, Lovejoy?' she prompted. 'Don't forget I *know* you.'

'I'm in trouble.' I told her about Spoolie, sprinkling multiple disclaimers. She listened in silence, a novelty.

'Cradhead?' she guessed. 'He's been perched in my driveway for yonks, comes in for a cuppa. Quite a lady's man, him. Says nothing. Smiles at my girls. Into fashion.'

Cradhead? Lady's man? Fashion? Smiles? Worryingest of all, silent. 'Turn right.'

'Here?' She protested, steering round the farmyard searching for a way out, 'Can't be. It's an empty farm, Lovejoy. Ugh!'

'Brake, when you feel inclined.'

The rain was sweeping off the moors towards the town. Wanda alighted, rushed up the steps calling hatred of weather. Tinker had left a lantern. I followed, daring myself to think. I mean, a massive town in the bowl-shaped vale, an eighth of a million folk. In the entire kingdom, thousands engaged in antiques. And I finish up on a bleak moorland with Wanda. I'd asked help from several bulk dealers before phoning Wanda, that day at Briony's manor. Had I been lucky to get her? Or had she put the black on everybody else, thus guiding me into her pen? She had the communications to do it. Maybe she'd engineered her own enlistment, when all along I'd been thinking how lucky I'd been to get so perfect an ally.

'Who else is coming, Wanda?'

'Bertie. My team, girls, seven whifflers, drivers. That idle cow in the commo van.' She stood shivering before the peat fire, trying womanlike to prove it was perishing. Our voices echoed. Tinker had gone. I stood, hands in pockets, wondering what felt so wrong. She misunderstood. 'Commo van? Communications mobile link-up. Are you always this thick, or just having a bad night?'

'Is that how you contact Carmel?' A guess.

'Yes.' She said outright, then she realised. 'Among others.'

'Who others?' I heard my voice shake. 'I was molotoved a few hours back.'

'Not my doing, Lovejoy.' She hugged herself, glared sourly about. 'This *place*. I'm freezing.'

'Was it you, love?' I asked, chilled to the marrow.

'No.' She chucked the shivering act, cool. 'I didn't even know. If they'd asked me, I'd have vetoed it.'

'Ta.' I checked myself. Thanking her for not having bothered enough to prevent my being executed? 'You're in on it, though. Who with?'

'You'd know soon enough, I suppose.' She tried to sound weary, finally letting me in on their game. But if she knew me, I knew her. Wanda has been acting so long she can't stop. 'Carmel once worked for me. She's always been into fashion. She had an idea of pinching designs. It's massive business, Lovejoy, if you guess right about next season's styles.'

'Isn't this show too small to bother with?'

'Yes.' She smiled. 'But fashion has to be hunted, not followed, Lovejoy.' I told her I didn't understand. 'Think hard. Suppose a fashion diva is interested in a newcomer. What then?'

'What what then?' To me fashion's an invented whim. Dig below the tinsel, you find tinsel. Wisely I didn't share this with Wanda.

'Then that diva would sponsor his display. Right?' She drifted close, in firelight silhouette. 'And make sure he triumphs.'

Wanda stroked my face with a fingernail. Was it, too, synthetic? 'So?'

Well, she laughed until tears streamed down her face, helpless. She clutched at me for support, which I gladly lent.

'Sponsors provide the judges, Lovejoy. So she'll decide the winner. Who is ... ?'

'Her boyfriend?' I guessed, shrewd. 'So Carmel is only somebody to front the sponsors?'

'Thank God you got there, Lovejoy. I'm one backer for the fashion show. The charity auction's a smokescreen, like they always are.'

'Who're the others?'

'Does it matter? One was poor Viktor Vasho. Thekla's another. Come to bed, Lovejoy. Is it aired?'

'Er ... ?' I asked.

'Aired.' She was exasperated. 'Dry, warm, clean.'

'It's straw, in front of the fire.'

'*Straw*?' She moaned. 'Bolt the doors, Lovejoy. And windows. Make sure there're no draughts.'

Fastest ever draught exclusion. I made up a straw pallet – God, sleeping on straw's noisy – and found eleven blankets.

With those, the warmth of the fire, and me, Wanda made it through the night. Until seven o'clock, when her gadgets started pinging and talking. I had the grace to say thanks, in case there'd not be time later, and also in case I'd been lied to.

One thought kept recurring. Roger and his archaeology had no real reason for coming north. Local archaeology wasn't worth much. Two old mills survived as museums. We have hundreds of ancient stone circles. Nothing else.

Tinker came at half past with some beans, eggs, bread, for an elegant repast. He didn't comment on Wanda's presence, and she did not notice his. Dreaming after Wanda and me'd made smiles, I'd thought about what antiques had chimed my bells in the derelict mansion at Scout Hey. Terence's stolen mirrors, Lodge paintings, for sure. There were simply no others. Terence would be keeping watch, so I'd have to time it right. Then Wanda roused and chimed some bells of her own, and that was that.

Calm, I told Tinker to find me a rot hound. By then Wanda was outside in her car, yammering.

'Rot hound, Lovejoy? They're rare.'

'Then get going. Don't let on to Wanda.'

A rot hound is today's reverse technology. Insurance firms and surveyors use electronic devices to trace woodrot. Silly old them. Modern technology finds dry rot with amazing accuracy, a triumph of science. A trained dog, your actual rot hound, can accurately case any building for dry rot *ten times faster*. Also, a manky old dog can be a pal, ally and guardian. Electronics can't be anything but a yawn. I gave Tinker four hours.

34

THE SCENE WAS from a crazy *Wuthering Heights*, with frivolity. Me and Wanda arrived in her horizontal motor, eeled out vertical, breathed again.

Not yet nine o'clock, a blustery wind trying to extinguish a fitful sun under scudding cloud. Children gay as garlands practised country dances. Fifers rehearsed with that where's-the-beer look marching bands have. Drummers paradiddled with the ribald competitiveness of their kind. Television crews were in, trying to outdo each other's smart-aleck sulks. A few radio mouthers were being ashamed, jealously admiring the TV technicians' braggadocio. Helpers putting trestle tables in the wrong places were laughing explosively at their mistakes. The whole forecourt was given over to preparations for the great day.

Further along, Wanda's pantechnicons stood in a sloping field. I was thankful. No sign of Tinker and the big motor, thank heavens. I was uneasy. Good news, bad omen.

There must have been about four hundred people milling about, with more arriving every second. Some nerk was barking scratchy incoherence, his tannoy cutting out every other sentence. Bunting was being tacked up. Banners flapped on poles, gangers erecting marquees. Refreshment tents had burgeoned on the two fields. The nearest paddock was covered in fashion college pantechnicons, gay folk idling or sprinting hysterically according to status. Cries of dismay rent the morning air. Why are women frantic when getting ready? I mean, they've only to put a frock on and that's it. Amy'd said there'd be over three hundred dresses at her fashion show, but they had hours yet.

'Worse than Portobello Road on a bad day.'

'Better.' Wanda was enjoying the excitement.

A team of diminutive girls danced past, harassed mothers trying to keep up. Behind me, I could feel the derelict mansion staring down. It was probably wondering what the hell. Stella showed in the main doorway of the chapel where the auction would be held. She smiled, waved, issuing decisions to a chatter of helpers, calling up to men on ladders, hurry that painting.

The poor charred mansion was being ignored. Its crumbling walls were perhaps two furlongs from the encroaching housing estate. Greeting half-familiar faces, I ran the gaunt manse's image through my mind. The estate children had probably roamed the ruin, like some sort of adventure playground, the more delicious for being forbidden. I kept my eyes off it. It was agony.

'Good morning, Lovejoy! Isn't this thrilling?'

'Wotcher, Briony. Aye, smashing.'

She smiled on us both, but Wanda got less than a tithe. 'And we're partners, Lovejoy! Your friend Amy is fashion convenor!'

Partners? 'It seems so.' I flapped a hand. 'Who'd think so many people did nothing but make frocks.'

'Shoes. Accessories.' Briony went down her printed programme with a finger in reproof. 'Cosmetics. Jewellery. Materials. Sportswear ... ' I switched off. Did people keep telling me this because they wanted a convert? She took my arm. 'Come. Show me Mrs Entwistle's antiques. How do they compare with my sister's?'

'Later, perhaps.' Wanda smoothly amputated Briony. 'Lovejoy has work at the commo van. We'll not be long.'

'See you inside, Briony,' I said. I've never had the knack of cutting women, or the nerve. It's best left to other women.

Leaving Briony in the maelstrom, we joined the mob. Tubb was there, talking to a couple of dealers, still posing, flexing his lats or whatever. He yelled a hello. Carmel was seated at a trestle table in the thronged yard, speaking earnestly with a girl. I looked closer. No specs, mousy now instead of blonde.

'Lovejoy!'

'Aureole?' She looked desperate. She must have read her Brontë this windswept moorland morning. I shied away, putting Wanda between us. 'Look, love.' I struggled for excuses. 'That amber. It wasn't my fault your flat got untidy.'

She gaped. I gaped. Astonishment ruled.

'What are you on about, Lovejoy?' she cried. 'For Christ's *sake*.' She looked imploringly at Wanda, gave her up, turned to me. 'Lovejoy. Please. I didn't mean what I said. Honest to God. Setting Dinsdale on you was a *joke*. I'll do anything. Just say it's all right. I'm begging you, Lovejoy.'

Her words came in a torrent. Folk started looking.

Mystified, I shook my head, nodded, anything to shut her up. She looked like she'd not slept for a month.

Wanda cut it. 'Listen, madam.' She hauled me aside and planted herself before the frenzied Aureole. A morris team belled up and started concertinas and uillean pipes around us. Wanda deliberately made it the cutting Continental ma-*dam*, not our mellower madam, which meant she knew all about Aureole's agency. 'Piss off, or my gangers'll lose you in some folly. Un–der–stood?'

Our county has follies – beautifully built towers, facades, castles even, as phoney as the previous three centuries could make them. They were to create an image of Arcadian artistry. Now in a state of neglect, every so often one totters into mounds of rubble. Stories abound, though, of hoods who deliberately make such wobbling uninhabitable towers fall – upon unfortunate opponents. It was quite a threat. Aureole sobbed and moved off heartbroken into the crowd.

'Avoid her in future.' Wanda asked if I understood. I said I did when I didn't.

Wanda went to speak to her commo van. The bloody woman never stopped yakking into electronics. Even on our makeshift straw she'd had three miniature phones. Enough to address the College of Cardinals in mid org. Casually I took in the distant view of the old mansion while pretending to admire the stalls springing up all about. I watched a carousel being assembled, heard its first faltering gasps as it worked itself up to wheeze-and-parp music.

'Thought you'd be here, Lovejoy. Everything set?'

'Wotcher, Tinker.' I scanned the multiplying mob. 'Mrs Finch's items will be moved in soon for the viewing, then there's nothing more to do except get a box lorry. A three-tonner, no smaller. Park it on the road side of that carousel, where there's space.'

'Right, Lovejoy.' He grinned, a miscellany of teeth and gaps. 'Shag her all right, did you?'

'We shared experiences,' I corrected sternly. I've never betrayed a woman's confidence yet. 'Roadie about?'

'Not seen hide nor hair, since he tumbled that we've sussed him. I'll kill the little bleeder.' Roadie was twice Tinker's size. 'But Vyna's here.' He was peeved. 'I've spoke. She said, what's all the fuss, like she was never missing at all. Little cow.'

'Was that her talking to Carmel?'

Tinker was surprised. 'You seen her afore, Lovejoy?'

'She pretended to be a schoolteacher in the Manchester museum.

Checking I was following the trail as planned.' Yet now I was here, she ignored me. 'Any more thoughts, Tinker?'

'On who sparked you in the archway? Nar.' He was agitated. 'See, Lovejoy, Roadie's not got the nous. He's lucky to get dressed of a morning. Vyna's a different kettle. I asked her. She said who's Lovejoy, pretending she knows nothing.'

'Roadie learned from you that I'd be waiting in the archway, and told Vyna.' We'd gone over this. Except, Vyna was everywhere, leading me on.

'She could do it, Lovejoy. She's got the bottle. Sorry.'

A fashion shoal came by. One cried out, 'Fashion back to classics, oh world!' to helpless laughter. The girls were bonny, but looked clemmed. A wild-eyed youth grabbed me. He was all earrings.

'The model Amy's given me has no tits,' he shrilled.

'Er, good.' Praise indeed, among skeletons.

'No! How can she wear the S-bend? I've reinvented it! My crinolette in heliotrope watered silk! She's got no arse either!'

Good? Bad? He swooned. Worried, I sat him on the ground.

'I know the problem,' I said. The S-bend dress lifted a Victorian lady's bust to achieve an emphatic S figure, but you had to have something to start with. 'Er, wait here, mate. I'll straighten it out ... ' Wrong image. 'Sort it out. Okay?'

'And the shoes!' he wailed. 'My recreations are *exact*. Amy's girls have yards of horrible toes!'

Victorian hostesses wore silk shoes you couldn't fit a modern ten-year-old girl into. Cinderella's prince would have had a hell of a time. But these things also weren't my fault. Me and Tinker left him forlorn.

'Why, Tinker?' I asked. I faced up the slope, to where the old mansion's charred rafters scagged the sky. 'What've I done? Why have me blammed?' A fair question.

'It's not something back then. It's because of what you are now.'

I still didn't get it. 'Being a divvy? No, Tinker. That doesn't wash.'

A couple of rousters panted past hauling some fairground organ. We helped for a few minutes, shoved the wheeled thing into position between a black-pea booth whose cauldron was gushing aromatic steam. The most appetising scent on earth. The organ was sadly new, and therefore pointless.

'It doesn't wash,' I resumed quickly before Tinker got his breath back. 'If anybody wanted a divvy, they could've called me. If I like folk, I'll divvy their antiques.' We separated to let a band straggle past, a riotous rehearsal on the hoof. 'They didn't need to make up that missing-lass pantomime. Was it that simple?'

Tinker was heartbroken, almost leading me to doom. 'Simple's always best. Every time you okayed an antique find – like those fire tigers, remember? – and sent me after them, Roadie must have told Vyna. She got somebody to snaffle it, or did it herself. She's helped somebody to clear thousands.'

'Easy, keeping me on the trail.' I looked at the sky as if questioning rain. Other folk reflexed the same, the county's pastime. 'Whatever it is must be here.'

'Some wanted you to stay in East Anglia.' His rheumy old eyes streamed. He barked a cough, momentarily quelling the carousel's flutes and an organoleum's tune. 'Aureole and me didn't want you to come.'

That made me stare. The enemy wanted me north, and the saints didn't?

'Don't you see?' He was a figure of sorrow. Holman Hunt should have painted him, a *Light of the World* in tat. 'They got you here, where you'd divvy some antiques. Then they'd nick them.'

'But why try to … ?'

'Because they're scrapping among themselves. That's the twist, Lovejoy. They torched you because they thought you'd sussed their plan. One lot now wants you topped, in case you spoil their theft, Roadie must be with them. The other lot wants you to walk away safe. That's it.'

'Two bad lots, one with hearts of gold?'

A six-year-old tugged at me, ordered me to tie her dancing shoes. I stooped, laced them, asked if she remembered her steps. She said, 'Mind your own business, Lovejoy.' I said she was a cheeky little devil. She said she could cheek me all she liked because she was my second cousin. I said, 'Oh, that's all right, then,' and rose, sighing. Definition of home.

'It's the only explanation, Lovejoy.'

'But I've not seen any antiques here. It's junk. Stella's husband's offed the only worthwhile ones.'

'I'm right, Lovejoy.' Somebody called my name. Wanda signalled that I was needed by the beautiful people, and got her nod. The mob surged. The tannoy did its white noise. Music pounded, frolickers rehearsed frolicking. I shoved through to Amy.

She was even bonnier, vivacious. It was her day.

'One thing, Amy,' I said, smiling at her two children. 'How about we postpone the fashion parade?'

'*What*, Lovejoy?' she screamed. People in earshot laughed, shook heads. One said, 'Honestly. That Lovejoy!'

'Leave it clear for antiques.' I explained that I was becoming more uneasy as the crowds grew. Amy said my wish was crazy. The world wanted its fashion durbar, and was going to get it. I said okay, fine, hadn't thought, right.

'The Victorian dresses are ready, Lovejoy. I want you to say a few words before we start. There won't be time before the walk.'

'Walk where?'

'Catwalk.' She strove for patience. 'Before the dress parade. Victorian garments first, of course, *fin de siècle*, that we borrowed. I explained it the other evening.' She ran a hand through her hair. I knew that gesture. It was to stop herself from taking a swipe at me. 'I *knew* you weren't listening, Lovejoy.'

'I'll do it. What do you want me to say?'

'Oh, hello and thanks to all. A fashion journalist will do the walk talk.'

Anybody I know? Could only be Faye. 'Can I see the, er, old frocks?' My big moment.

'Of course. We'll have to hurry.' She had only half a day, but like I say, women getting ready.

We went through the poor and huddled masses. Caravans, trailers, every type of wheeled home you could imagine, now crammed the slope, spilled into the fields. Vestals were howling at men who were laying a board gangway, green canvas canopy cloistering against the elements. One girl was having hysterics, shredding cloth with savage ripping movements. A scene from a graduate school sci-fi, only no-one would believe it. I thought, all this, for frocks? Nothing wrong with hysteria that a little quiet embarrassment wouldn't cure.

'In here, Lovejoy.'

There are grades of caravans. Amy's was extra huge and coloured a quivering purple, a temple on wheels. It seemed to expand as I climbed in, into three half-partitioned rooms. The floor was disturbingly on a cant. Girls were frantically sewing, rushing in the confined space. Dresses were everywhere. I could hardly see or think for the noise. I swayed, covered my ears.

'What's the matter, Lovejoy?' Amy pulled at my hands.

'It's the ... ' Noise? There was no noise. Only the girls' muttering.

223

The commotion outside was hardly deafening. 'Sorry,' I said. The noise, the deafening non-existent din, was in me.

'Sit down for heaven's sake.' Amy had the woman's innate anger at somebody having the effrontery to be taken poorly. She sent her children scurrying for cold tea and biscuits. She always was into traditional remedies. I was lucky she didn't have a jar of leeches and a phlebotomy handy.

Within minutes I'd recovered, came to sitting among old dresses, coats, berthas, lace, hats, veils, in every material the nineteenth century could create. Florsston should have come after all. Handbags, gloves, ladies' boots, chatelaines, reticules. Racks of boxes had labels bragging of breast and wrist watches, jewellery, brooches, rings. I really like those laburnum-wood ring trees, that you occasionally still find on bedroom tables. Fruit wood, pear or apple, have the best feel. You can still buy them for mere pence.

'Nice frocks, love,' I said eventually. Amy was watching me curiously.

'I know you, Lovejoy. Is it like that time?'

'What time?' I challenged. She looked away.

'I thought something here gave you a funny turn.'

At the far end of the caravan two girls were kneeling between rows of Victorian dresses. Each long dress was covered in plastic. The jewellery — brooches, pendants, earrings, lockets, necklaces — was in labelled bags looped over the mannequins and hangers. My brain was like a clanging lighthouse. I made myself look away. I remembered the old commissionaire at the textile museum, what he'd said. I saw the brooches, the pendants, all cheap metal alloys, pinchbeck, copper, tin. And knew it all. No wonder they killed. They'd have thought it cheap at the price.

'It's Aureole,' I invented. Blame a woman to a woman, you can get away with murder. 'She upset me. I'm sorry.'

'What's the matter?' Rodney said, swishing in. Then screamed, 'Oh, *no*! It's *him*! That vandal!'

Rodney now? My least favourite carpet slayer.

'Look, Amy,' I was all apology. 'I'll be outside.'

'At a distance of miles!' Rodney cried.

'If you're sure, Lovejoy.' Amy was still doubtful. 'We can't have you keeling over on my stage.'

Charming, I thought, narked. Never mind me, think of scrawny birds tripping down planks. As long as your priorities are right. I left, bumped into Nicola. She had this dog. Labrador? I don't know enough about them.

'Lovejoy! You're here! A man called Maurice simply *gave* me this *dog* for you!' She was so relieved. 'Jodie? Go to Lovejoy.'

'Ta.' I took the lead. Jodie must be my rot hound. 'I'm, er, good with dogs. Hello, Jodie. Okay?' I walked with Nicola. The dog kept looking up at me, tongue lolling. Why do they lick air all the time?

'Let me show you round, Nicola,' I said loudly, blithe. 'That old house over there — see it? — was the chapel manse, then a mill-owner's mansion ... '

Stroll pace, we went through the mob. The caravans thinned. We passed people having fry-ups, dealers talking prices. Wanda's auction catalogue was on sale, stacks in bright yellow covers. One dealer called, 'Hello, Lovejoy. Interested in ikons?' I called back, 'Wotcher, Trallee. Nar. There's no market ... ' An in joke. Dealers laughed, expressions woebegone. There's always a market for genuine Russian ikons. Italy and Turkey are the fake masters, Moscow itself nowadays. Cost, less than a paperback. Profit — if you find somebody daft enough to trust your 'genuine 1750' ikon of St Nicholas — enough to buy a good corner shop.

'These old mansions were in stark contrast,' I told Nicola loudly, for others' benefit, 'with mill workers' hovels.' Jodie, sensing a serious job, tugged at her lead.

'Can we go back, Lovejoy?' Nicola asked, doubtful. She looked at her shoes, the overgrown yard, the wonky gate.

'It's interesting.' In case of listeners, Terence Entwistle in particular, now we were close to the ruin, I said loudly, 'Yes, we can go in. Nobody here.'

The house looked even worse close to. A fire had gutted much. The sounds of the mob faded. The bands' clamour receded. We could have been miles away.

The house seemed reproachful; why have you let me get like this? I felt heartbroken for the poor thing. Once so grand, now with its rafters showing, patches of wall fallen into the weed-choked gardens. Clumsily I released Jodie's lead, whispered 'Find, mate'. Wood rot doesn't survive a fire.

Prattling folklorish nonsense to Nicola about the locality, I strolled casually after, whistling. Jodie vanished. Nicola asked doubtfully if Jodie would be all right.

'Eh? Oh, fine. She, er, likes a stroll.'

At maximum decibels, I told Nicola that Florsston was on his way.

'Oh, Lovejoy! How sweet!'

'He's keen to help, love.' A lie can postpone truth, and Florsston by now had reached Italy. I heard a frantic barking from the wonky landing. Jodie had gone up its charred struts like, well, a whippet. It was from up there that the hullabuloo came. I had to call her a number of times before she returned, disgruntled. I got her lead on, patted her head. She shrugged me off. I was really pleased with her, but she'd gone off me.

We went towards the first swaggers of the fashion models. Nicola stayed to admire them, while I cadged some tea from Amy's children in exchange for letting them pat the dog. A thin balding bloke was there. Jodie seemed to know him.

'You Maurice?' I asked. He nodded.

'Just give her her head, Lovejoy. She'll find dry rot the size of a penny in a palace.'

'Ta, Maurice. She's already done her trick. Pay you tonight, at Brannan Hey.'

Maurice took some snuff, waggling his pinched thumb and forefinger up his conk. God, but we're a rum species. 'Already?' He looked at Jodie. 'She's pissed owff, Lovejoy.' He shook his head. 'Dogs are workers. Give them a job, they're happy as pigs in muck. You didn't work her.'

'She performed brilliantly, Maurice. Honest.'

'Sure?' He looked as sorry as Jodie. 'If you say.'

Jodie went with him, giving me a glance of utter disdain. I didn't know dogs could sneer. Her lope after Maurice was an indignant lope. I was narked, bollocked by a frigging mongrel. I'd patted her, hadn't I?

'Ta, Jodie,' I called weakly. 'You were superb.'

And she was, finding the rot-laden antique of Mayor Tom. I couldn't shout that, though.

35

'THE AUCTION,' WAILED the tannoy, 'begins with the grand quiz. Get those answers in, everone!'

Tinker had placed Florsston's blue lac fake on a makeshift stand. You paid a zlotnik, guessed its value. I never understand why this is such a stunning attraction. The money was in brimming buckets, which only goes to show. (I'm not sure what, but it does.) Nicola was being enthusiastic, applauding the bands, helping children to get ready. She even danced a reel with the uillean pipers. Pretty lass, Nicola, going to waste.

Wanda was there, smiling hard. And Bertie, calculators poised. I couldn't walk far from Amy's purple caravan. By now it was a centre of activity. The canvas-cloistered catwalk leading to the chapel was a busy thoroughfare. Each model who did her test trot was greeted with ecstatic oohs and aahs. I leaned towards the purple trailer as if sucked.

'Fair old mob, eh, Lovejoy?' Roger said.

'Roger?' Roger Boxgrove, as ever suave, debonair. 'This far north?' Nothing here for him. I could only think of Pete Marsh, the Bog Man sacrificed thousands of years ago in a Cheshire peat marsh, but now reposing in a glass Roger-proof exhibition case in the British Museum.

'Just seeing a friend.' When I looked disbelieving, he leant conspiratorially close. 'Still hoping for Faye.'

That was a relief. What with Rodney, Vyna, Roadie's sudden vanishment, the distraught Aureole – still being deflected by Wanda's Praetorian Guard – I was too worn out to take on more suspects. Carmel I could trust, Tinker said. Faye? She was there, avoiding me, talking fashion into a dictaphone for her newspaper.

'I sold Thekla's fashion friends some palaeolithic artefacts once, to dress up a display. Costly, but brilliant!'

'I can imagine.'

'How much, Lovejoy?' Roger nodded at the blue lac. In the cold light of day it looked lack-lustre.

This is people for you. I sighed. A new millionaire, yet still corrupting away for pennies. 'That's it, Roger. You have to guess.'

'You here, Roger?' Wanda, steaming up. She demanded, 'What's he been saying, Lovejoy?'

'Nothing. Just do one thing, Wanda, eh?'

'What?'

'Buy a guess for the cabinet.' She made to snap, but I gave her my foulest eye.

She glanced doubtfully at Roger, and did as she was told. I headed for the beer tent where the whifflers were having a final pint before the auction. On the way, I got accosted by Nicola.

'Lovejoy,' Nicola said. 'Florsston isn't coming, is he?'

'Eh? Course he is, love!' I did my best optimism. 'I've had a message! He's on the M6.'

Tears streamed down her face. 'No, Lovejoy.' That loon was still announcing the quiz, rasping it out. 'Florsston's in Italy, isn't he? You *knew* he was lying.'

Typical. Florsston lies, so I get the blame.

'Listen, love.' I get desperate. 'I only wanted ... '

'I suppose I knew, Lovejoy, deep down. He wouldn't even sit beside me, let alone ... '

So why become obsessed by a misogynist in the first place? Things were getting too much.

'Excuse me, love. The charity.' I hurried to the beer tent where I assembled some whifflers by the simple act of rubbing my thumb and forefinger together. If I'd actually had any money, I could have started a new religion. Free range whifflers go in sixes. I stood apart.

'Any of you locals?' I asked. Heads shook, no. 'Or work for Wanda? Amy? Stella Entwistle? The mayor?' No, no. 'Then you're hired. I'm Lovejoy. Who's boss?'

'You are, wack. You're paymaster,' a beery bearded sloven said. The whifflers made a faint huffing. They never laugh outright. 'They call me Total.'

'Right, Total. You get the ganger's bonus, depending.' He nodded, knowing what the money depended on. The ganger's bonus is a third. I walked off. They followed, gelt apostles. I didn't point. 'Total? See that old burnt manor? Top floor – Christ's sake be careful; it's nigh gutted – you'll find a few antiques. Mirrors, paintings, not much. Bring them all down. Load them into a lorry my mate

Tinker'll have by the carousel. Covered, please. I don't want anybody to see them. Okay?' For me to drive away, as personal fee for my trouble. I didn't say this.

'Right, mate.'

'One thing, Total,' I added. 'You might bump into Mad Terence. Ignore him. He's crazy. Your pay's double standard rates, plus half, if you don't damage any. One mirror's badly dry-rotted.'

'Sooner we get started ... ' They made noises of approval, walked off with the whiffler's hunched amble. Solemn, grasping, do the job, amble to the next. They're a rough lot. Not one asked whose antiques they actually were. A whiffler's job is to shift antiques from A to B, then preferably to C at a higher hourly rate. I watched fondly. Isn't dedication grand? I got an ice cream, sat to watch the morrismen dance, tapping my foot to the ancient music, and thought of what was in the purple caravan.

A diamond is a diamond is a diamond. Ice-colourless, harder than granite, rare. 'Pinko' diamonds are something else. They are rarer even than 'pure' – meaning colourless 'white' diamonds. Years ago, you could hardly give them away. The only reason people ever bought a pink diamond was that it might be mistaken, in bad light, for a ruby. Rarest of the rare, the pink diamond was the poor relation nobody wanted to know about.

Recently, there came a revolution, the quiet kind. An important statistic happened in good old Oz, Australia the Beautiful. In 1985, Oz overtook the then USSR in diamond production. Why didn't this news send the world shrieking into the streets? Because Oz was a relative newcomer, its diamonds being mostly titchy small, industrial grades, peanut diamonds. The gem world sniggered behind its hand. If you want to make grinding wheels, go ahead, use diamonds from Kimberley in Western Australia, see if we care. These workaday fragments are mundane. What did it matter if Kimberley grubbed up another seven or eight tons of them a year? Plenty to go round. Dirt-cheap dirt is cheap, the great diamond centres quipped, chuckling at that 1985 statistic. Since time immemorial – well, 300 BC – everybody's been daft over the 'white' bobby-dazzler. Coloured diamonds were third-class gems. Then the penny dropped. Oz realised that it was virtually the world's *only* source of pinkos.

Quick as a flash, Oz went public with every erg it possessed. In 1990–1991, it won the silent war. Its yellow diamonds and even its tea-coloured browns – 'Champagne Diamonds' to the newly admiring public – leapt into the magazines. De Beers had always bought and sold coloured diamonds, of course, but returned the boring old pinkos to Oz for disposal.

Think rarity to stay on beam. In, say, the prodigious Argyle mine of Kimberley, you'll weigh some 42 million carats of diamonds a year. Question: how much tonnage is the elusive pink? Answer: a mere 42 carats. Dozily putting my head straight, I worked it out. You slog for a year, dig up millions of carats of diamonds, mostly industrial granules. Painstakingly sieving through umpteen tons, you find less than one-third of an ounce of pink diamonds. Always assuming you've kept awake and not missed any.

They are clandestinely marketed by the diamond world (in Geneva, that secret upper suite in the Beau Rivage Hotel, but keep it under your hat). The world's merchants, under armed guard, humbly pay through the nose for the privilege of buying. Never mind that they get only a few minutes to decide, that they're not even allowed to haggle for what's in those little Perspex containers. And never mind that the cost will be in heartbreaking millions of dollars. The pink gems will change eager hands. Everybody will rejoice.

See the difference? Aeons ago, pink diamonds were not worth bothering with, mere diamond trade 'glassies'. Now? The world's most valuable gem known to Man. The difference, Back Then, and Now. And Back Then's where antiques come from.

The tannoy startled me with a shrill whistle.

'Lovejoy, please! To the Grand Mega-Prize Antiques Auction Quiz Competition immediately!' I dropped my ice cream, got up to do my duty.

The fake blue lac was only wood and a daub of colour, not like a genuine antique. But I went, pushed through the crowds thronging the entrance.

Inside, the babble almost deafened me. Where the altar had been was now an improvised stage with a podium. Stella's tables of crud were relegated to the sides, thank heavens. But crammed on the stage and in a thick crescent before it were arranged Briony's possessions from Thornelthwaite Manor. Wanda's lasses and her men were acting as clerks and guards, occasionally warning off dealers who wanted too close a look because sudden last-minute inspections from dealers are the bane of auctioneers and suggest neffie goings-on.

Briony was on the stage, sniffing with pride. No chairs. The dense crowd had to stand. There must have been seven hundred, the balconies rimmed with enthralled faces. I was moved. Everywhere, as I started edging towards the stage, folk were smiling, saying ta for coming, good luck, thanks Lovejoy. Old Alice started excited applause as I reached the front. Folk even patted my back, like you do heroes.

'Ta, loves,' I found myself saying, feeling daft as a brush. 'Ta.' I made the stage, got hauled up, and faced the sea of expectant faces.

Scorn's easy to bear. Threats are my norm. But being clapped onto a stage is hard to take. I felt a stupid cold coming on, coughed a few times. All I was going to do was say who'd made the best guess for the fake, then clear off with the antiques Mayor Tom had donated. Betrayal's only fair. I deserved something for my trouble.

The precious 'dress and features furniture' – as fashion calls jewellery – was none of my business. If Manchester's pundit curators couldn't be bothered to keep pace with the times, when cheap old antiques soared from farthings to fortunes, that was their lookout. I didn't want any more wars. I'd accidentally got Spoolie topped. But do accidents really exist? Maybe the ancient Greeks were right. Everything is fate, so put up with it. Vyna, touring the textile museums of the North, had spotted the pinkos, wondered if they might be real. She'd seen my response to the one brooch I'd seen on the crated dress at the textile museum. That had been good enough. Wasn't that it?

A jolly bloke, charity badges all over him showing that he was holy compared to us, boomed, 'Ladies and gen'men! Here's Lovejoy! Thank you, please!'

I feel a duckegg at the best of times, let alone doing a Sermon on the Mount. A microphone was thrust into my hand. I looked at everybody. They were so pleased. Why? The town had had its day, was left behind in the tide race of modernity, a historical footnote. Even our speech was the failed comedian's joke, to get a bored audience going.

The little lass, my second cousin who'd made me tie her shoes earlier, was there, waving, shy. I tried to give her a wink. I saw Tinker signalling among the crowds squashing in. Cradhead was ahead of him, smiling a surprised smile at the scene.

My feet were treading water. I wanted a lass, a quiet drink, maybe make love watching a sunset, not tell a crowd how well I'd done on their behalf.

A small eddy among the spectators between two laden trestle tables. Total, giving me the job-done sign. It's a nape scratch, while looking at the hirer. Tinker's lorry now contained Mayor Tom's antiques. All I had to do was scarper.

The crowd quietened, stilled. I looked along the faces on the balconies, the ocean of smiles below.

'It's smashing to be home,' I said. Riotous applause. 'Home,' I said, sick within, 'is where the heart is.'

The crowd actually cheered. I stood like a lemon, a fraudulent one, as the racket subsided.

'Listen, pals.' I didn't know how to say it. 'Times are new. It's not like yesteryear. Morality's new. You have to be aware who the frauds are.'

'Hear! Hear!' cried the announcer. 'This is the very reason we have the prestigious firm of Lissom, Prenthwaite and Co's lovely Miss Lydia ... '

Lydia's letter. She came onto the stage.

'This is the very reason,' I cut in, and I had the microphone, not him, 'that I've decided to agree to Lissom Prenthwaite's request.' I overrode, seeing Lydia's sudden dither. I thundered, 'I'll do the auction myself. Miss Lydia has generously agreed to step down.' Into the applause, I called out the result of the Great Quiz. 'The winner is Mrs Wanda, of Sutton Coldfield, who priced the blue lac cabinet at sixty-eight thousand. Congratulations, lady!'

Before questions could get going, I yanked the auction list from the announcer's hand.

'Miss Lydia, auctioneer of the famed Lissom Prenthwaite, will be our official observer!' I chuckled, gunfire sounds.

Before anybody could draw breath I raced on. 'The possessions of a lady! Removed from the ancient Thornelthwaite Manor! Item One, a display of Eley's sporting ammunition, arranged as a tableau of central fire gastight cartridge cases.'

'Showing here, sir!' a whiffler cried.

'Who'll start me off?' I called, beckoning for a gavel and something to whack it on. Lydia came forward smiling kilowatts of anger, handed me her gavel, and I was away.

Tinker was thunderstruck, because I should be sloping off in his wagon. And two bulky hulks from some black lagoon were darkening the crowded double doors where daylight should have entered. My spirit stalled. One was Derry, Big John Sheehan's ultimate correctional argument. The nickname's not Londonderry, merely short for deranged. I've seen Derry walk up to eight grinning blokes, each armed with crowbars and such, and blam the lot while they flailed away. He hadn't even breathed heavy, just grumbled at the mess the destroyed octet made, bleeding on the warehouse floor, as if they were to blame. As, I'd hastened to agree at the time, they were.

'Come on, friends,' I bleated when the bidding faltered. 'Are you all done?'

'Get on with it, Lovejoy,' some dealer called.

'This is for charity.' What more could I lose? I'd lost everything, even me. Tinker was shaking his head. 'Don't let the ten per cent premium daunt you.'

A growl rose from the dealers, but what the hell. Auctioneers' premiums are nothing but sheer extortion, a robber baron's private tax. If Christies and Sotheby's do it, why shouldn't I?

The dealers lowered their heads like charging bison. The innocent populace looked on, feeling the thrill.

'Nothing in the catalogue about a premium, Lovejoy,' some knowall called.

'Blinking printers,' I said. 'Any more on this item, then?'

Well, I went barmier still. Having got the extra, I did the 'frog', bringing forward a later item, a trick to raise bidding levels.

'I'll advance Item Nineteen,' I chirruped. 'I've been especially asked, by bidders who have to leave early. It *was* a joint prize with the blue lac cabinet, but time was short.'

'Showing here, sir!'

'This Chippendale style cabinet is a beautiful reproduction – Tom Chippendale loved fretted rails, yes, but he always used triple plywood. His fret was never solid heartwood, as on this cabinet. Chippendale's was crisscross ply – the grain goes different ways. And our cabinet here has *one* pane of glass a side, whereas Chippendale's glass doors had several small panes. Notice the drawers, the quarter mouldings so prominent inside? They only became common long after Tom C passed away. Who'll start me off for this repro Chippendale display cabinet? Can I say a thousand?' The dealers' signals started, for the glass panes were multiple, and the fretted rail was old-style ply. Most dealers thought I'd got it wrong, that the fake was genuine.

A Glasgow dealer bought it for a high figure. Within a week he'd have sold it for four times that – to some innocent who'd believe he'd scooped a real Chippendale. Guesswork is the modern fashion.

I surged on, knocking down item after item, while Lydia smiled fury and Tinker all but died from dismay and Derry stood impassive with Bonch his oppo, and Cradhead smiled urbanely, and Mayor Tom beamed at Stella and she smiled back at him.

Best part of three hours, and I was done. There was riotous applause as I handed over the gavel to the announcer man. I grinned and ta'd my way outside, took a mighty swig of the cold moorland air.

Vans were already being loaded up. Successful bidders were paying in to Wanda's team. The town hall's accountants were along, bricks for paperweights on their tables. Wanda'd been right to put it in Bertie's hands. But I was unnerved by the score of policemen who were marshalling motors, checking departing dealers' chits before letting them out. Clever Wanda, using the Plod.

'Lovejoy?' Tinker, stinking of ale, swaying abjectly. 'We in trouble?'

'Not you, Tinker. Me.'

Derry was louring the skies near the chapel. Aureole was beckoning, peering round some van like she was on the run. Nicola headed my way, weeping. Faye, static in the milling crowd, stared at me hard. I honestly didn't need any more vengeance. And Thekla, for heaven's sake, emerged with Rodney in tow, Amy trying to attract her attention, while Roger strolled effetely among the plebeians. He blew Carmel a kiss, cool as you please, as he passed by Amy's massive purple caravan.

'What do I do, Lovejoy? The lorry's ready.'

'Let me think.' I had ten seconds before the sky fell in. 'Did Total do it right?'

'Total did well. Got the antiques – crappy mirrors, them, eh? – loaded in my three-tonner.'

'Any sign of Terence Entwistle?' We were being buffeted by the crowd on its way to the stalls, sideshows, entertainments. Intermission time. Bands were striking up. It was a fairground again.

'No sign. He must just have stashed Mayor Tom's antiques, then scarpered.'

'Mayor Tom knew Stella had nothing but trash, so he donated what antiques he could. He loves Stella, see, Tinker.'

'Oh, aye.'

I might have been talking about the weather.

'Stella's husband Terence decided to scupper her auction. Nicked Mayor Tom's stuff, hid them in the old house. Maybe he was going to return them afterwards!'

'Honest?' Tinker savoured the strange word, brought out a soiled pasty from his greatcoat pocket, picked something off it, offered me a bite. I declined. I like pasties, but there's a limit. 'Nar. He'll be as crooked as the rest of us.'

'As the rest of *them*, Dill,' Cradhead corrected, from among the jostling mob.

'Where'd you spring from, Cradhead?'

'Just passing, Lovejoy. A splendid do, what?'

I shrugged, making it obvious. I didn't want any dealers, or Derry, thinking I was Plod-friendly.

'Where is Tinker's lorryload going, Lovejoy?'

'Eh? Oh, it's Wanda's. Did she say, Tinker?'

'What load's that, son?' Tinker did a coughing fit. Cradhead winced, wrote him off.

'I take it that you will be around for a few days, Lovejoy? Questions I want cleared up.'

'Of course. I've relatives to see.'

Briony Finch came to interrupt, breathless.

'Oh, Lovejoy! You were wonderful!' She looked starry-eyed at Cradhead. 'Wasn't he wonderful?'

'Absolutely, Briony,' Cradhead replied gravely. *Briony*? I didn't even know they'd met.

'I took longer than I expected. Hope I didn't delay the fashion show.'

'They've worked so hard, poor lambs!' from Briony.

I waved to Old Alice. 'Excuse me, please. An old neighbour. Any way I can help, Craddie, just ask.'

He smiled. I hate his smiles. They're horrible, though you'd never know that if you didn't mistrust him.

'Thank you, Lovejoy. You'll keep to our arrangement? I paid up front, remember.'

'Right right.' I watched him go, and was enveloped in Old Alice's crowd of well-wishers. They'd saved some grub for me in a nosh tent.

'Pasties, eccles cakes, chorleys, chips, mushy peas,' Old Alice fluttered. 'Everything you like!'

'Ta, love.' I beckoned Tinker to come along. 'First sense I've heard.'

Staying with this lot, and then going to the fashion show with the crowd, might buy me a few hours before perdition finally struck. With Old Alice's crack geriatric charity team, I was free to think. As we sat and prattled, I set my mind free.

Teachers teach a prevailing opinion that we'd still be back in the Dark Ages were it not for aluminium. It's the chemical-element theory of civilisation. It's rubbish.

France's Napoleon III begged his scientists to discover some way of making the pure metal from bauxite. By 1886 electrolysis had aluminium on the market. Eastman Kodak cameras of 1915, motor car bodies. Then aeroplanes, engines, airships like the R100. That's the theory: no aluminium, no mass travel, no modern civilisation.

It's a naff theory, the goon's guess, and misses the point. Take away people, you've got nothing. Okay, there'd be bricks and mortar left, machinery and other marvellous residues. Things, but no people. No people? It's too high a price to pay. Stuff aluminium.

So with doom approaching, I noshed with Old Alice's cronies the stodge of childhood, and was content. Let it come. I'd stand by folk. Unless I could wriggle out from under.

36

M Y REVERIE ABOUT the good old times – were there ever such? – was doomed as the last frantic TV crews poured in. Keystone Kops, destroying anything. Bongs went, crowds dashed screaming. I recognised the signs. Fashion was going to happen. Hours late, but fashion, like royalty, has that right.

Sadly, I thanked Old Alice. She told me, eyes glistening, to look after myself.

'Are those men chasing you, Lovejoy?' She actually pointed with her arm out.

'No, love. Just old friends.'

Derry and his oppo, Bonch, were standing staring. Another couple of dozen, we could have tableaued a biologic Stonehenge. Cradhead was talking amiably with Mayor Tom. Stella had joined them. I bussed the old lady, beckoned Tinker. He left the ale tent.

'Tinker. That lorry.'

'We going to make the dash, son? I'll decoy, 'f you like.'

Friends weaken selfishness, I find.

'Ta, Tinker, but no. Look. When the modern dresses start, hitch it to yon purple caravan. It should be dusk by then. Everybody'll be gawping at the parading models coming down the covered gangways.'

'Then?' He sounded dubious.

'Somebody's planning to nick the Victorian dresses. We'll do it before they can.'

'Who? How? What for, Lovejoy?'

How much to tell him? 'I'll be at the fashion show. The Victorian frocks parade first. Then they'll go back into Amy's purple trailer. It'll be quiet outside. Inside will be pandemonium.'

'And I make off?'

'Tow Amy's caravan away, with the Victorian dresses in. It'll be easy.' I hesitated. Things never are, around me. 'Well, maybe.'

'What if ... ?'

'Shut it, Tinker.'

Try to do right by everybody, and I get lip from Joe Soap. It's a life and a half, this. They announced the fashion show. I left him and went into the chapel. People made way, friends everywhere, not a killer in sight. My seat was alongside the catwalk. The main stage was a-glitter, the antiques and dealers gone. The unsaleable dross was cleared away.

The place was in hubbub. No Aureole. Roger though, Carmel, Tubb beyond her making mystic signs at the remnants of holiness on the walls. Pews had made a miraculous reappearance, but too few. Folk were sitting in the aisles, already enraptured at the thought of seeing dresses, when clothes are in every shop in every street. It beats me.

Faye was on stage, really bonny. No Nicola. Cradhead was seated almost directly facing. I didn't like that. Derry and Bonch had vanished.

Thekla was also up there. I didn't like that, either. She saw me, swiftly scribbled a note, gave it to a girl I was starting to recognise. Thekla pointed me out, her expression one of concern. I'd seen it on the faces of gunners taking aim. She could keep her neffie old message, whatever it said. Rodney, in a luminous suit, was being admired.

Amy tore through a cluster of people in the wings, trailing material in a panic. Still frantic, when she'd had weeks? The girl with the note slid along the rows.

'Wotcher, Vyna.'

She bent, smiling. 'Love letter from Thekla. With her fondest, Lovejoy.'

'I'll bet.' I put the note away unread. She was miffed.

'It's time we came to an arrangement, Lovejoy. We could sing dollar music.'

'Too late, love. You've missed what chances were going.'

She slid away, prettier still now she was white hot with anger. I resigned my cerebral cortex to oblivion as TV crews rolled cameras about, making everybody shift. They live for disruption, even give each other annual awards for it. Loony. I'd almost nodded off when Nicola whispered into my ear from the row behind. No disturbance. She'd never get a job in television.

'I've come to my senses, Lovejoy. I understand.'

'You do?' I turned to look. She was so bashful, her eyes lowered.

238

'Why?' I thought I'd given up whys. But if she'd worked out why Spoolie got done, I needed to know.

She whispered. 'Sweet, Lovejoy.' True. 'You drove all that way, to rescue me from that dreadful Florsston.'

'Er, look, love ... ' I turned away.

'Don't speak, darling,' she whispered. This in a horde. 'It's dawned on me. My place is with you. I've been blind. I'll make it up to you, Lovejoy.'

Appalled, I listened to her terrifying litany. Apologies, promises, flowed from her lips into my earhole. I thought, no, no, a thousand times no. I wanted to start tunnelling, flee to the fells.

Rodney meanwhile had begun the show up there, to thumping music. Strobe lighting, searchbeams, silvery colours from rolling panels. He strutted, sang. I watched, numb. Screens lowered slowly. Old movie scenes of carriages, seemingly in heavy rain, showed in back projection as that stultifying noise pounded on.

The crowd went wild, stamping feet as Rodney waggled and high-stepped. I wondered why the heck anybody in his right mind would want to do it. TV crews tracked his every wriggle. Monitors glowed, one jauntily suspended from a crucifix that had seen better – though not crazier – days.

He finally froze, staring at the floor, arm raised, legs apart, breathing heavily as if he'd just given his all for art. Maybe he had.

'Luvvers, bruvvers! Achievers, reevers!' He got a roar of approval. Fashion students climbed on tables, pew ends, dangled from walls. 'Can *you* out *there* see *me* in *here*?' he cried. Roars. Was it some code? I was mystified.

People were driving cars up to the chapel's entrances, to provide vantage points.

Rodney posed in camp petulance, fist on hip, and pouted, 'Because if you can't – *the show won't happen, see!*' which got the biggest cheer of all. God knows whose cars they were, but their roofs were getting danced on, the sound of distant impis.

'Now a delectational exquisitorial display that is *theeee* fashion durbar of the entire galactic *yeeeeear!*' I got sick of the howls. Mind you, it's hysteria that caesars and presidents – add fashion – have survived on through centuries.

'We begin with *exquatiously* modelled Belle Époque dresses!' He began a rhythmic swaying, as if suddenly mutated into female, stepping to the crashing music. Couldn't they simply pin the dresses up on a stand without all this?

'And who,' Rodney carolled, trotting and twisting, 'brought *all* the *way* from *Man*chester this *glor-yerss* display, but our – *my* – *your* – very own *Amy!*'

Bedlam. Amy walked on, pretending humility. All phoney. She curtseyed. Manchester was ten miles; he made it sound like Amy'd dragged it from the Yukon by sledge. Her eyes locked mine, moved quickly away to where her fashioneer's heart lay, the mass of admirers. She bowed herself off. It brought the house down. Rodney wept copious tears for a beat.

'Now!' he shrieked, leaving praise to mere mortals. 'For your utteracious delectation, the Grand Parade of Dresses of Centuries A-gone! Your narrator-*ess*,' he squealed, making a joke out of gender, 'is Faye, the Gay Way of To*day!*' He handed over to her. She advanced, taking over the microphone. Rodney couldn't bear to, but went.

Faye began to speak in a neutral tone as the spotlights fixed the catwalk.

'First, a particularly fine long ball dress, severe for modern taste but avant garde before the twentieth century. Modelled by Clementine, it shows … '

The music changed to wrong melodies from the Fifties, Thirties, inappropriate World War Two songs, with 1920 decade numbers. Models danced on, doing the Yam, the Charleston, miming some startlingly ectopic Great War ballads, then WW2 *Lili Marlene.* They even had early Beatles tunes, film scores.

These last had me looking at my knees, but evasion doesn't work. I felt Spoolie's spirit gazing sorrowfully in. He'd want to know what I'd done about him, who was going to pay. Spoolie had been robbed.

The *Casablanca* theme made me feel worse. Cradhead's steady gaze was on me. I glared. He didn't look away, the swine. No chortles.

Meanwhile, the thin girls swaggered down the catwalk, swirling, wrong for the old dresses they wore. When I watch 'period' dramas, the actresses stride, like if they're wearing jeans. You watch, see if I'm not right. Nil out of ten. They ought to take shorter paces, moving within the compass of the hem. Daft, when they could look really authentic. Somebody tell them.

Then my mind registered the dresses' jewellery as two more models frolicked on, followed by a file of six more. Okay, lovely lasses, blonde, raven, brunette, and bonny with it. But the jewellery.

It was so deafening, so blinding, that it all but blanked out the girls themselves as they carried those precious items past and back, glowing with a radiance I could feel. I stared, open-mouthed. I even started counting. One, five, six. Then ten, twelve. I strove to see closer. Were the pinkos in their original settings? You can change diamonds' colour by irradiation – electrons, neutrons, deutrons, alpha particles, protons, the 'heavy' particles from linear accelerators – with or without heat. But you need the naked gem to muck about. And these looked mounted just as they'd been in Victoria's day. I almost fainted from relief.

One dazzled me so I actually moaned aloud. There was (still is) a precious aigrette called the Jika of Nadir Shah. Aigrettes are named from the egret. Think of a small feather made of jewels for ladies' hats. English and French, especially, in and out of fashion these 400 years, they quiver as the ladies wearing them dance in the ballroom. Tremblants are another form, taking off flowers on little springs of silver, set sometimes into slim miniature 'vases' made of precious metal. Semi-precious stones are commoner in aigrettes than diamonds, that El Supremo of gems. Maybe it's because 'hair furniture' – as Amy quaintly introduced the aigrette – was easily stolen by fast-running thieves in the crowded cities of the past?

This was a copy of the famous Jika. Nadir Shah was a great Middle East eighteenth century warrior. Jewellers are raised on historic pieces, like aspiring footballers have footballing heroes. This aigrette has a massive emerald in the middle, and five smaller emeralds, the whole done as a feather. They say it's a hefty 781 carats. It was the fashion in Victoria's day to copy famous jewels in cheap materials – silver-plated steel instead of gold, cheap gemstones instead of rubies. And the once cheapo pink 'fancy rose' diamonds, instead of the priceless colourless 'white' gems.

The girl twirled, flounced, wearing some dress I didn't even see, so seared was I by the rose-pink diamonds in her aigrette. An exact copy of the Jika, but with pinkos substituting for the original's emeralds. Once, the 'taint' of pink colour destroyed a diamond's value, to the Victorians. Yellow diamonds, even blue, were regarded as debris. Once mere curios, they now lurk undetected in cheap discarded Victorian costume jewellery. I've never yet had the luck to find one, though I know a dealer who bought a box of old Edwardian neckties and almost amazed himself into a heart attack by becoming the proud possessor of a pink diamond tiepin. He bought two new cars and a new house. They're out there.

God plays tricks like this. Gifts are sometimes snatched back. As the pounding beat marched the aigrette girl off and brought on another, I remembered a forgery. I must have painted seven, eight, of the famous lost Van Gogh *Vase with Cornflowers and Poppies*, guessing the colours, copying the layout from black-and-white book illustrations. Then calamity struck. Somebody actually found the original, sold it for a fortune in a New York international fair. I'd plunged into poverty that very day, and had to go on the knocker, touting door-to-door.

The fashion show was brilliantly exciting. There were sixteen pieces of pinko jewellery, two yellows, and one, possibly two, with blues I wasn't close enough to see well. I was in a fever. Good old Australia. I realised I worshipped fashion after all.

'And now,' Faye announced as the music sank to a mere million decibels, 'Modern days! The Northern Fashion Durbar is ... *here!*'

Thump, thump, went the drums. Searchlights swung. Dancers emerged, the audience clapped. It was so thrilling that I upped and left, making a plea in mime to Faye that I was thirsty, would be back. I was almost tempted. She wore lemon yellow, a colour I particularly like, very simple, better than the creatures in their big moment.

Outside, I was surprised to see it was dusk. The noise receded as I went to sit on the drystone wall. The fair was packing up. The ice cream vans were gone. The stalls and side shows were already trundling out. A cold wind blew.

In the distance I could see the road's orange neon lights strung seawards, a reflection of the Irish Sea where the Ribble estuary cuts land away. Christ's Croft, these lands were called in the old days, Windmill Land beyond, once crammed with whirling giants. Now, no busy ports were left, the canals silent stretches where anglers counted themselves lucky to bring out a single fish.

'Lovejoy? I'm ready to do it.'

'Wotcher, Tinker. Give them time to get the old dresses back into Amy's purple caravan, then go.'

A fortune here, a fortune there, sooner or later they added up to real money. What could I do?

'Where're the plods, Tinker?' No sign of the police on the dwindling fairground.

'Them?' He spat with scorn. 'They've swarmed inside to see the lassies, randy sods.' He grew censorious. 'Is that why we pay our taxes?'

You have to cut Tinker short when he's indignant, or he goes on all day. 'They're guarding the fashioneers' designs. In case they get stolen, like the Emanuels'.'

I listened. Rodney was compering. Lights flickered from inside the chapel, darkening the night sky further. Faye must be reporting in to her newspapers, Wanda and Bertie totting up. 'Did Manchester send guards of their own?' I didn't want any commissionaires baulking me at the last minute.

'Nary a sign, Lovejoy. I looked.'

'Give that Rodney ten minutes, then do it.'

'Him.' Tinker hawked up more contempt. 'A right screamer. Ought to be locked up.'

'Tinker,' I said wearily. I felt heartbroken at the night-laden countryside, and didn't know why. 'Shut it. Last time of telling. Did you leave the Braithwaite where I said?'

'Aye. On the moorside by the saint's well.'

'Okay. Check you've got the trailer properly hitched when the Victoriana's inside.'

'Awreet, Lovejoy,' he said. 'Keep your hair on.'

Sometimes friends make me sick. As bad as enemies.

'You not coming in the lorry, Lovejoy?' he asked.

'Drive it on your own. Meet me at Brannan Hey.'

Wanda had done well for Briony. She deserved a good slice. It would be enough for Briony to settle her sister's debts and buy her emporium. I sighed. It could have been worse. Soon, Wanda would come demanding my services as her private divvy. At least I'd saved the charity auction from being a penniless fiasco. I would come out of this with Mayor Tom's antiques, that I hadn't yet seen but which were safely sealed in Tinker's lorry. Fair's fair. Charity at last being its own reward.

'Why're you not coming, Lovejoy?' Tinker asked.

'I'll follow in a sec. Go now.'

He went, grumbling. I'd no illusions. If Cradhead's men were watching, they'd arrest Tinker, not me. There was still the threat of Derry and Bonch. Sheehan's malignant troops wouldn't leave with a job half done. When the fashion show ended I'd lose my last chance of escape. This way, with Tinker leaving apparently alone, they'd assume I was hiding in the purple trailer and follow Tinker. Maybe they'd crash Tinker and his lorry over some handy cliff. There were plenty about. It'd be the usual story, drunken old driver mishandles his wagon off some lonely Pennine road.

If all went well, though, I could get to Brannan Hey, thank you very much. Much safer than in Tinker's lorry pulling its gaudy least unnoticeable trailer in the known world. It was the sort of decoy a coward like me wanted. When the going gets tough, this tough gets out.

Whistling noisily, I strolled towards the chapel, now a glittering galaxy of noise and lights. Between motors, I ducked and ran for it.

37

THE WELL, AND the big motor, were a mile up on the moors above the chapel. I sat on a stone in the dark, watching the gleams of the stallholders' departing trucks, the unwieldy carousel lorry manoeuvering on the Blackburn road. The fashion riot was oddly reduced to something warming, beckoning even, instead of maddening. I imagined I could hear Lydia, and pretty Faye boosting the fashion parade. I kept looking about at the black moors.

The moors frightened me. I once got lost in a June snowfall with my cousin Arn, children out marauding. A chance bus came along a chance road. The conductor wouldn't let us on, not enough money. An hour later, same road, an elderly lady demanded explanations. She trudged us through the snow, put us on another bus, had a shrieking war with the conductor. We'd had enough coppers all the time. I've never forgotten the two vital lessons: always remember the possibility of chance malice from a jack-a'back. And, countryside might promise a warm June day, but it's secretly planning a blizzard.

A stone skittered. I froze. Remembering childhood always scares you. Something flew past my face. I hunched, arms wrapped round my head. Something screeched, another creature whimpered. I stifled a moan. Countryside is sheer unprovoked carnage. I was sweating cobs from fear. I'd been forced into this, all for, how had I started the auction, 'The possessions of a lady'. Though all antiques, all mankind, me, are the possessions of some lady somewhere.

Down below the music bumped. I longed to be back there, among enemies. At least foes are human.

'Come on, Tinker, you drunken old sod.'

It was high time he left. I could see light reflected on the roof of the purple caravan – moving! The thicker black rectangle between it and the other vehicles shifted slowly. Tinker was doing it. I couldn't hear the engine. Some show event caused a momentary uproar, obliterating it. Rockets shot skywards of a sudden. I ducked, foolish in the glare. Tinker's lorry stilled. Sensible.

The coloured light dimmed. I heard his engine thrumming. Good old Tinker started up in the explosions. The music resumed. Time to go.

The old motor was on a slope. I could leave the moor along the track, emerge in Rivington. I got the motor going, drove carefully. Nothing for it but to use the headlamps. Who'd notice me, with all the excitement down there?

One faint niggle. Had there been a light inside the purple caravan? I'd thought for one second that maybe ... But there were still some two hundred cars there reflecting gleams. Inevitable, with rockets overhead and sudden strobe lights shafting the darkness. It must have been my inbuilt terror making for panic.

Quarter of an hour later, I put the great car down the metalled road that left the moorland near a small lake. Let night anglers wonder. I rolled serenely towards the town. With growing confidence I turned up the side road to Brannan Hey. There, I'd finally ditch the Braithwaite, whip the pinkos off the Victorian dresses, have a quick shufti at Mayor Tom's antiques in Tinker's lorry – fingers crossed. Undo the purple trailer. Anything else?

'Yes, Lovejoy,' somebody whispered in my ear.

With a sharp howl, I swerved almost into a stone wall, slithered to a halt, stalling the engine. I gibbered, recoiling from the apparition behind me.

'Sorry, darling. Did I startle you?'

'You stupid fucking cow!' I put my face into my hands and gasped, panted, inhaled life back.

'Well you *did* ask, Lovejoy! You've been talking ... '

'I was talking to *myself*, you silly mare!'

Nicola was quite put out. 'There's no need for abuse, Lovejoy. If we're to live together ... '

I leaned back, eyes closed. What the hell was she on about? I hardly knew the bloody woman. She was talking like we'd wed. I groped for lies.

'You're right,' I said. Start with a winner. 'Doowerlink. Will you do something?'

'Of course, darling!' she cried.

'Wait by the farm gate, please. Tinker will be along. We don't want him driving past, do we?'

'His lorry, that big caravan? Have you ever seen such a horrid purple? What is Amy *thinking* about?'

246

'Thanks, doowerlink.' I bussed her. 'He'll see you in his beams. Okay?'

'Very well, sweetheart. Will it be safe?'

'That's a promise,' I lied magnanimously.

'Right, darling. A kiss, please?'

We snogged. Just when you're desperate for something else instead of the one thing that matters, you get the one thing that matters. I ripped my lips away.

'Goodness!' I cried. 'We'll never get away if we keep on!'

The engine started, I bowled into the farmyard, looking for Tinker's lorry. We'd arranged that he'd wait with his lights off.

No Tinker. No lorry. I brought the Braithwaite to a halt. Its engine panted, rocking the chassis. I switched off. Silence. The headlights seemed suddenly too dim. I wanted light, a searchlight tattoo.

The farm buildings felt derelict, empty. Nothing on the exterior staircase that led to the upper floor. No comforting red flicker of a fire sinking to embers.

The grey Pennine stone merged with the darkness. Not even a lantern. Had I told Tinker to leave the outside one lit? If I had, he should have, the drunken sot. If I hadn't, he should have used his hooch-addled brain and left a lamp burning. I get narked at folks' lack of enterprise. And Nicola should have come with me instead of waiting at the gate, selfish cow.

Then I talked myself into sense, sitting in the motor, the wind moaning, rain now tapping the bonnet.

Who saw me leave? I demanded. Nobody. I'd sloped off quietly. Everybody else was at the show hoping to get their faces on telly. Therefore I was safe, because I was here alone.

Maybe I'd actually seen the last of Wanda? I fervently hoped so. Wanda might be so grateful at the profit she'd made, that she'd let me go? If Briony's antiques bought my freedom, it was a small price for her to pay. If Briony didn't agree, she shouldn't be selfish.

My feet plopped on the farmyard mud as I got down. I hesitated. Why not wait until Tinker bowled up? Two's company, one's at risk. It's headachery. But things are predictable. Lonely farms are never haunted. Those squeaks, like one I'd just heard, are always bats. They're famous for squeaking all night long. Nothing in real life is mysterious, either. Every six weeks, sure as eggs, some holy statue'll cry its blood-soaked eyes out, like in Civitavecchia or Eire's Grangecou, or shed blood from its ribs as in Salerno's pottery mural of Padre Pio. Not blasphemous, I persuaded myself, feeling my heart beat a little faster than it had. Real life shirks fable. Aesop of fable fame learned the hard way that real life is different, when a tortoise fell on his head and killed him. It was the only irony he'd never written a fable about. Real life's different, no mystery.

A car swished past on the wet moorland road. It didn't turn in. Where was Tinker? Surely he wouldn't have stopped off at a pub?

No noise. Unless you counted that creak. It was a sort of old floorboard creak, a slow sort of creak. The creak you get in farmhouses.

It came from the barn to my right. Probably a fox. Did I want to go and investigate? Not likely. I stepped across, started up the non-creaking exterior staircase. I could have gone in through the front door, but didn't. This doesn't prove that I was scared, because I don't get spooked. Not even if it's something really scary, like a midnight film. I just carry that sort of fear off light-heartedly, the very idea. I don't watch scary films.

Going slowly up the stairs to the landing where the door was, I forced a grin. Me, worried? The things I've been through?

Tinker would be along any minute. I realised I was getting soaked, standing with my hand on the latch. I must have been there several minutes. Less? I was wet through, rain outside, sweat within.

Creak. Who the hell? I was listening for, and hearing, creaks that weren't even creaking. Honest to God. I mean, working it out, who was possibly against me, now the whole thing was done with? Roadie? I could handle him any day of the week. Or at least I could scarper faster. Derry and Bonch would prove a problem, but Big John Sheehan has a sort of rum fairness, ends up with you in the mire and him righteous at St Cuthbert's at evensong. Skulking isn't his game.

The reason I didn't go straight in was that the door was ajar. I could feel the draught on my face from the slice of deeper black. I shoved it experimentally. Was Briony here? But there'd been no car below. Aureole? No car below for her either. Vyna? Carmel? But n.c.b.

Lydia, come to make up, pulled by my sheer animal magnetism? Hardly. She detested me now. And she must still be at Scout Hey with Wanda going over the auction lists. Thekla? No.

Two choices. One, go inside, believing in the friendly real world. Or stay out here like a lemon, scared by figments, old frights.

The door opened as I shoved. Why didn't it creak, then? I tried to remember if it had creaked before, or if the floorboards had creaked when Wanda and I had made smiles. Couldn't recollect. Step inside, I'd know for sure.

Inside, then. My leg took a lot of persuading to move, my foot to find the floor, my weight to sway forward. I did it, almost sinking with relief. An engine, car approaching. Lights switched across the interior of the great old farmhouse. I saw that nobody was here at all. But the car didn't turn down the track. No Tinker.

The light dowsed, the engine silenced. Might it be Tinker, after all? I stepped forward, confident, felt for the rail. The upstairs was more of a balcony, rather a wide landing, and could be used as an impromptu bedroom for some rustic visitor. It was bounded by a stout wooden railing that became a banister down the interior staircase to the living-room floor.

No flashlight. I fumbled for matches. Had I kept them, when lighting the fire? No. Wanda, selfish bitch, had used her cigarette lighter. I remembered her returning it to her handbag. That's how helpful she is.

The stairs creaked as I went down, a step at a time. Definite, creak, creak. Very like any old wooden staircase would creak, as when a person descended. Or ascended. So as to be behind anybody entering from the exterior staircase, say? Coming in through the door above, at balcony level? I reached the ground floor, relieved and safe.

So as to be behind?

A flashlight snapped on behind me, casting my grotesquely huge shadow onto the chimney breast. I was almost blinded, turned, felt about in front of me, hands spread.

'So you're Lovejoy.'

'Eh?' I screwed my eyes up. 'Who're you?'

I could hardly see against the light, but I was sure I'd never seen the bloke before. He was a small intense man, should be at his books instead of haunting remote farms. Specs, waistcoat shopsoiled. It wasn't his normal condition, I could tell. He held a knobkerrie.

'Terence Entwistle?' I was guessing.

'Lovejoy.' He was interested. 'You're the one who stole the antiques I hid at the mansion. You gave them to Stella's auction.'

'No,' I lied swiftly. 'It wasn't me, Terence. They'll be here any sec. For you. I want to help, see?'

'You made her auction a success, Lovejoy. I planned to make it fail.'

'I didn't!' I cried, gauging the distance to the stairs, any door. But he held the light on me, swung the knobkerrie the way somebody might who knew how to use it. I pressed on, desperate to lie my way out. 'Where you'd hidden them was bound to be discovered, see? So I had them moved. They're in a truck. Tinker my mate's bringing it.'

'Don't try to run, Lovejoy.' He was smiling, really proud of something. 'My friend's at the door.'

'Friend?' I swallowed. 'Two of you?'

'I was sabre finalist, Lovejoy. I know hand weapons. Tell me about Stella and Enderton.'

'Eh? I don't know! Honest! I only just met him.'

'Own up, Lovejoy,' Tubb said from the landing above, leaning nonchalantly on the rail, looking casually down as if at a play. 'Terence was betrayed all along, weren't you, Terence?'

'It's true!' Entwistle's cheeks were a single point of red outrage. 'By that ... *politician!*'

'Tubb?' I said stupidly. Him, and this madman?

'Me, Lovejoy. I'm here to help Terence. He's going to do for you.' Tubb sighed, shook his head. 'Terence's plan would have worked. The auction would have been a failure, Stella would have hated Mayor Tom. Terence wouldn't have lost his wife. But you messed it up.'

Entwistle swung the weapon, rolling it as a drum major does a marcher's mace. I stepped back. He stepped after, shining the torch in my eyes.

'Terence. Please. One more minute!' I begged, hands joined in supplication. This wasn't fair. 'I know you've been wronged. I understand ... '

'Terence,' Tubb said regretfully. 'Are you going to listen to him?'

'No.' Terence swung the implement. Christ, he looked strong. That knobkerrie, perhaps from some old African campaign. 'You must pay, Lovejoy.'

'Please!' I shouted, retreating to the inglenook, but my voice only echoed up the chimney. I was standing in the warm ashes of the peat fire that had burned so welcomingly. 'Please, Terence. I'm your friend!'

Tubb heaved a great sigh, enjoying it. 'Don't believe his crap, Terence. A friend, spoiling your clever plan? Lovejoy and Stella were more than just old friends. He was her boyfriend years ago. That's why I tried to ... '

'Crisp me in the archway!' I yelled. It suddenly dawned. 'Tubb!' I pointed, aghast. 'You! You who did Spoolie! And tried to molotov me.' I'd shrunk to a crouch among the ashes, hoping to avoid the blows that were going to fall. My shoulder caught on the jack spit, its great iron hook.

'Who?' Terence paused. 'Spoolie who?'

'The police are looking for Spoolie's murderer!' I bawled hysterically at Entwistle, pointing with a shaking hand. 'It's him!' I raised my shoulder. The iron hook lifted, fell behind me into the ash.

'Don't try it, Lovejoy.' Tubb lit a cigarette. 'Don't listen, Terence.'

'And that Viktor Vasho bloke! You did him, too?'

Tubb shook his head, as if at a querulous child.

'Viktor Vasho tried to defect from Roger's arrangements, so of course he had to suffer. Viktor reneged on the plan to raid a few fashion houses that Vyna was picking out. You don't understand the forces, Lovejoy. Roger pays well. Him and Carmel are an unstoppable pair, Lovejoy. You had your chance.'

'What *is* this?' Terence's weapon had almost stilled.

'Lovejoy's trying to distract you, Terence.' Tubb blew a smoke ring. He had muscles to spare, the demented workouts he was always doing. I'd thought him a wimp. Now, he seemed to grow before my eyes. 'Does it alter the wrong he's done, Terence?'

'No.' Entwistle said dully. He hefted his weapon, stepped close. 'It's in the Good Book, Lovejoy. An eye for an eye.'

The door behind Tubb suddenly swung inwards. A woman's voice called, 'Lovejoy?'

'Stella!' I screeched.

Entwistle turned, caught himself as he recognised that the voice wasn't Stella's. I grabbed the hook and swung it across in front of me out into the room where Entwistle was standing before the hearth. It met something with a thunk. Wetness spurted onto me, poured down my face. I was blinded.

I rolled, begging and whining, clawed at my eyes, then screamed some more as my face slammed into Entwistle's. He was on the wooden floor, gagging, seeming to be trying to speak. Blood was everywhere.

'No!' I screamed, standing up. He had an iron hook in his throat. Blood spurted out five, six feet, going whirr, whirr. I tried to back away, hearing myself howling, seeing the room in dreadful tableau. 'No! No!' I kept bawling, blotting my eyes.

The torch had fallen against a couch, sending shadows slantwards. Tubb had hold of Nicola, his hand over her mouth. I picked up the knobkerrie. It was slippery. I had the sense to wipe it on my jacket, get a grip. I could hear myself whining, keening.

'Lovejoy!' Nicola cried, struggling. Tubb semi-throttled her to silence.

Entwistle stopped threshing. He lay there, the blood down to a trickle. I judged Tubb. He looked even bigger, Nicola small and terrified. Thinking always comes too late.

'They'll be here soon, Tubb.'

'Who?' He actually seemed to be enjoying himself. He hauled Nicola up, lifted her so she sat on the railing over the drop. 'All your friends?' And he laughed. I'd never seen him laugh before. 'Roadie? He was our informer, Lovejoy. Roger? He pays me. Carmel? She's Roger's partner. Thekla, well, wanted to warn you. Good job you were too stubborn to heed her, eh?'

'Thekla?' A friend? When she'd made me homeless?

'I'm coming for you, Lovejoy.' Tubb set Nicola screaming by pretending to let her drop over. 'It's time.'

I tried not to look. Entwistle had stopped breathing, I think. I pulled the hook from his throat. Like a fool, I said, 'Excuse me, please.' Then, 'Let her go, Tubb.'

'I hate that nickname, Lovejoy.' He sighed, hard-done-by. 'What good do you think that hook's going to do you? And that shillelagh? I pick my teeth with bigger sticks than those. I'll drop the woman.'

'Chuck her, then, Tubb.' I stepped towards the staircase, not rushing because I wouldn't know what to do when I got there. 'She's no good to me.'

'Lovejoy!' Nicola shrieked, struggling. One of her shoes flew off, whizzed by me.

'As long as you know what day it is, Tubb,' I said on the bottom step. I moved to the next. For the first time he looked uncertain.

'Day? What day?'

'Patron saint of farms,' I invented. 'Saint Aloysius. Used to live hereabouts. That old well was his. It starts a stream that flows through this farm.'

'What's that to do with anything?' He licked his lips. I was on the third, fourth step. I might make the door past him, get out.

'Today's his saint's day, Tubb. He's buried by the well. His spirit's supposed to live here.'

'Balls, Lovejoy.' He looked at Nicola, petrified in his grip. Fifth, another, seventh.

'The saint abhorred killing, Tubb. Even animals. This farm never succeeds. Farmers have to kill sheep, see? Bullocks, cows, the lot. It'll grow good barley, but farmers go for animals. Profit. Anybody'll tell you.'

'What happens?' he asked, wary.

'Ask Tinker. I told Entwistle the truth. Tinker'll be here soon, with the dresses you're all after, and the pinkos on them that Vyna must have guessed weren't cheap costume jewellery. This was Tinker's family's farm.'

'Tinker's family's?'

'His parents died. They had their own abattoir across the farmyard, went bankrupt before they died. See? Seventeen generations tried it. Death, Tubb. And you killed poor Entwistle on the saint's holy day.'

'It wasn't me,' Tubb cried, triumphant. 'You did him, Lovejoy.'

'But you topped Spoolie. You and Roger.'

'Not here, we didn't!'

'Where doesn't count. Can't talk yourself out of a killing where a saint's concerned. Top me, you'll die yourself before the day's out.'

I stepped onto the landing. Level. If he chucked Nicola over, I could maybe clout him and flee. Except like an idiot I'd got the jack-spit hook in my right hand and the knobkerrie in my left, and he was facing the wrong way. Could I maybe hook him and then dash for it? The door was ajar. Maybe I could be off before he came blundering after? My heart was whooshing in my ears, deafening. Had I left the keys in the old motor's ignition? And it always took an age before it got going.

It's hopeless trying to look threatening when you can't. I did try, frowning like I'd seen in films. His brow suddenly cleared. I thought, Christ.

'Then I'll take you, Lovejoy. And the bird. Do you somewhere else, after midnight.'

'No!' I said, panicking. 'That won't work. The legend says – *don't*!'

It was a trick. He lobbed Nicola over. I swung the hook round-arm, felt it hit. I clubbed with the knobkerrie left-handed, missed, swiped back-handed and got him on the head. He rolled along the rail. I heard myself yelling, followed and hit, clubbed, swiped. He leant away, vanished over the railing. I stopped, rasping for breath, heard him slam, breaking something. There was blood everywhere, on me, on the landing floor.

Below, I saw in the bizarre slantwise light Nicola weeping and mewling. Her leg was at an angle it shouldn't have been. She was trying to grasp a wooden chair, pull herself away from the ghastliness of the two fallen blood-covered things nearby.

There was no question. I raced out into the cold wet darkness, blundered down the outside stairs to the ground, fell once dashing to the car, fumbled, talking rubbish, blubbering like a frightened child. I slammed into the motor, clambered in, found with a screech that I'd still got the hook and the knobkerrie, dropped them with a cry, managed fiftieth go to get the key into the ignition, fired the engine and the headlights came on.

Cradhead and three uniformed men were standing a yard in front of the car.

'Evening, Lovejoy.' He palmed the air down, but I wasn't going to dowse the lights for anybody. 'You wish to explain?' They walked up, shone torches on me.

'Explain what?'

'That bloody hook. The bloody knobkerrie on the passenger seat. Your blood-soaked appearance.'

'In here, sir,' some Old Bill called. Another talked into some gadget. God, I was sick of gadgets.

'Ambulances,' Cradhead called, not taking his eyes off me. 'Plural. Brewer? Who's your first-aider?'

'Foster, sir. Inside, Foster. See what you can do.'

'Cradhead,' I said feebly. 'I can explain.'

Cradhead said, pleasant, 'I *thought* you'd say that.'

A lorry trundled down the cobbles, its brakes shrill. I got out as Tinker alighted. He swayed, sloshed out of his mind. I looked closer. He *wasn't* drunk. Drunk was normal. This Tinker was cold sober. He hawked, spat, grinned. There was no purple trailer.

'Wotcher, Lovejoy. Awreet?'

'Yes, ta.' I alighted and went to his lorry, flipped open the sagging canvas. Empty. 'Tinker? The antiques.'

'Eh?' He acted horrified. 'Was I suppose to collect some stuff, Lovejoy?' He looked sheepish. 'Only, I didn't feel well, had to stop for an ale.'

'Book him, lads,' Cradhead said. 'Drunken driving.'

'Here, Lovejoy.' Tinker finally noticed I was covered in blood. 'You hurt?'

'Not Lovejoy,' Cradhead said, still affable. 'Just everybody else. You were saying, Lovejoy?'

Lamely, I started stuttering my tale. All I could think was, it hadn't been such an auspicious day for Tubb after all. What had he said? 'Certainty's the best feeling on earth.' Treacherous stuff, certainty.

38

THEY HAD ME dictating, remembering, all night long. Except memory's not much good, is it? It's treacherous, only picks out good bits. Like, everybody remembers Lady Godiva, but who remembers her wicked husband Leofric?

I didn't mind tiredly telling my tale. Nicola, in the Royal Infirmary with her broken leg, dislocated shoulder, minus two teeth, exonerated me. She told them I was a hero, had risked all to save her.

'It seems you're in good,' said a smart, attractive woman who came to drive the final nail in. Her assistant, one Ackers, kept eating toffee, nougat, Pontefract cakes, sucking Uncle Joe's Mint Balls (these last the best sweets ever made) without offering me one, selfish sod.

'Well, I'm a hero.'

'She maintains that you only *pretended* to run for it, Lovejoy.'

Cradhead chortled disbelief. Police have this system, being so short of manpower. One talks, two more sit idle, one runs a tape recorder, another yawns, a sixth brings more toffees, tea, biscuits.

'Listen, missus,' I said to the newcomer.

'Orla M. Featherstonehaugh,' she said. 'We spoke once. I'm the suspicious hoary old cow, you told Viktor Vasho at the hospital.'

I nodded, after a minute, the ball in her court.

'And all the time,' Ackers said, cracking an Uncle Joe's with pot teeth, 'you were fighting for Nicola?'

'I was under threat, sir.' A bit of grovel never does harm. 'And scared.'

'He stole the antiques,' Cradhead said.

'I didn't!' They had me on a chair, facing.

'After he'd told me about poor Spoolie.'

'I've told you all I know, sir.' I tried to remember what I'd said in the babble of the moment. 'Boxgrove and Tubb did Spoolie because he was getting scared. They were all in it. Thekla backed out.'

'We have Napier Montrose Shelvenham, a.k.a. Roger Boxgrove.

And Carmel. And Roadie. You make enemies without even trying, Lovejoy.'

'Why's everything my fault?' I growled, tough. It emerged as a sheep's baa.

'You should have known that Boxgrove was crazy about Vyna.' Orla was so innocent. 'Have you heard of something called a chain-date agency, Lovejoy?'

'No?' I lied politely. 'Why?'

'Boxgrove met Vyna through it. They thought up a scheme to lead you north, to divvy the textile jewellery.'

'No good explaining,' Ackers said, nasty. 'Lovejoy's thick.'

'Thekla tried to warn you, Lovejoy.' Orla read from the note Thekla had got Vyna to slip me. '*Please forgive me, darling. Beware Roger, Carmel and Tubb. Come back. Please? I will tell you everything. I need you to find Galberti Rappada urgently. All my love, darling, Thekla.*'

Galberti who? Then I vaguely remembered making some frock designer up. Was she still believing my lies?

'Are we sure Lovejoy didn't do it?' Ackers asked Cradhead, as if I wasn't there.

'Me? Look, sir. I was nowhere near.'

Orla crossed her legs, got my full attention.

'The problem is,' Ackers went on, ignoring me, 'the Manchester trinkets. You were pinching them, right?'

'Certainly not. I told Tinker to move them to a safe place.'

Cradhead and Ackers looked downcast. My spirits rose. Good news? Ackers spoke, morose.

'The police officer we installed in the purple caravan – a justified trespass – reported that the vehicle was abandoned at the Lostock road.' I'd guessed right, that too-swift light in its window.

'The towing lorry then drove off.' Cradhead sipped his tea. 'To join us when you'd finished killing everybody in the farmhouse.'

'I didn't!' But I did. 'Self defence, sir.'

'The trouble is,' Cradhead said, 'a thousand witnesses saw Thekla write that message.'

Relief came in sweat. 'Can I go, then?' It was four o'clock in the morning. I didn't mind.

'One thing, Lovejoy.' Orla held up some papers. 'Why did Tinker Dill try to steal the few antiques donated by the mayor?'

'I didn't!' I tried it saner. 'He didn't!'

'But he did, Lovejoy,' Orla said, watching me. 'He drove to Mrs Wanda Curthouse, gave them to her.'

'He *what*?' I'd thought at least I'd get away with something. Tinker, betraying me for honesty?

'Mrs Curthouse was only just in time to sell them to the last dealers to leave. High prices, I hear.'

'Wanda sold them?' I couldn't believe it. I wanted them for me. 'Er, good!'

'Wasn't that the arrangement, Lovejoy?' said Cradhead.

I felt bitter. Wanda, typical woman, going honest. Do they never get wrong right? I had a hell of a headache. 'Can I have some tea, please?'

'No,' Ackers said urbanely, sipping his. He brought out an Uncle Joe's, examined it in the light. We used to do that, look for the transfixed bubble. It was supposed to be good luck, though the edge of the bubble cut your tongue.

'Mrs Curthouse and her husband run a very tight ship, antiques wise,' Ackers said. 'Right, Lovejoy?'

'Yes, sir.'

'Accurate accounts. Precision itself.'

Bertie'd been hard at it, then.

'You see our trouble, Lovejoy?' Cradhead took a biscuit, smiling his thanks at a bonny police woman. She smiled fondly. None for me.

'No, sir.' I was under arrest, not them.

'Mrs Finch, Faye, Amy, Wanda, the rest all to exonerate you, Lovejoy. But you have committed some awful crimes. You've stolen a commemorative wedding mug, for example, from a Mrs Mavis Winwick. You've stolen a valuable touring car. And, Lovejoy, killed two people. Nicola implicates you in a disappearance.'

'She what?'

Orla took it up. 'Florsston Valeece. Nicola believes that you competed with him for her, Lovejoy.' Ackers heaved a sigh. I scented the aroma of his toffee.

'That's nonsense, sir.'

'This Valeece,' he said, 'is missing.'

'He's gone to Italy. He told me. He bribed me with a faked blue lacquered cabinet.'

'Bribed?' They cheered up, incrimination at last.

'To take Nicola off his hands.'

They beamed. 'Let me get this straight, Lovejoy,' Ackers said, mirth brimming. 'You seriously expect us to believe that a man in his right mind *gave* you a rare antique as a bribe, to accept the sexual favours of an attractive woman?'

'No,' I stammered. 'Yes. I mean, no.' I added weakly, 'It's fake'. But would Florsston ever admit our deal to the police?

'When did you sleep, cohabit, or otherwise cash in on, this, ah, sordid arrangement, Lovejoy?'

'I didn't. Haven't.'

'Given a gorgeous lady, and *didn't*? You want us to believe that, Lovejoy? And why exactly did you steal that valuable car?'

I licked my lips. 'I can explain.'

'Go on, then, Lovejoy.' Ackers was all heart. They leant back. 'We're waiting.'

They let me go at six that evening, Cradhead watching me from the lobby window. I was knackered. I'd declined to accept messages in posh police envelopes. Tinker was nowhere to be seen. The Braithwaite had been impounded. I was to be charged with something or other on account of it. I'd just had enough. I wanted to sleep on a train going anywhere.

Wanda waved me over. I went to her car.

'Evening, Lovejoy. You took your time. Get in. We've a long way to go.'

I inhaled my first free breath. Or last.

'Thanks for coming, love,' I said. Start as you mean to go on. 'You took everything to the auction, then?'

Wanda smiled. 'Too many Old Bill not to, Lovejoy. I played it straight, collected the mayor's antiques from Tinker's truck. Lydia helped me to sell them, a last-minuter.'

'Trained her myself.' I felt proud, then felt whatever the opposite of proud is. Sad? 'You've made Briony a fortune, eh?'

'Bertie's at the accounts now. Her new chip shop will be among the superleaguers. And the charity is quids in.'

'Great.' Everybody but me.

'Get in. Incidentally, Lovejoy.' She went iron.

'I've settled with Total and his team. And paid off somebody called Maurice for a damned dog.'

'Ta.' I turned aside. 'Have to sign my release form, then I'll be out. Will you wait, doowerlink?' She jerked her head, beckoning me closer, brought her mouth up to mine. She tasted of apple. Every woman tastes different.

'My lawyers said it was all done,' she said, irritated. 'Hurry, Lovejoy. I've waited long enough.'

'Right, love.' I hurried in. Cradhead was still there. 'Craddie. Can I leave the back way?'

'You really want to, Lovejoy? I'd think twice.' He wasn't smiling. 'Your messages.'

The desk man handed me the envelopes. I opened one. Briony wanted me to call urgently. She'd declared me her partner in a fried fish emporium, Streatham Hill. Best offer I'd had lately. Could I be an incognito partner?

Cradhead said, 'Mrs Finch is a determined lady.'

So was Wanda. The second was Nicola's.

'The ward sister had to write it for her, Lovejoy.' Cradhead shrugged. 'Sorry. We had to read it.'

It went:

Darling Lovejoy,
Thank you for saving my life. I shall come to you the minute they let me travel. Please visit when the police finish taking statements.
All my love, darling,
Nicola.

'There's one phone message, Lovejoy. I feel like your secretary. Lissom and Prenthwaite auctioneers want you to be an advisor.' Cradhead almost nearly smiled. 'Lydia is waiting at the Man and Scythe.'

Good old Lydia. 'How's that Viktor Vasho?'

'Brilliant. Some idiot chatted to him when he was moribund. Did wonders. Heard from his woman Faye, a journalist. You met her.' He paused. I said nothing.

'Remember you owe me, Lovejoy.'

'Eh?'

He smiled. 'The Pascal Paradox replica was expensive. And you hardly kept your part of our bargain.' He patted my shoulder. 'Pay it back any time, old chap. Report in, daily.'

'Who to?'

'Orla Featherstonehaugh. She's on secondment from the Antiques Squad, in Mayfair. All for you.' He did that chortle just to madden me. 'You have her number?'

They showed me the way out. I might get to Manchester before Wanda twigged, then it was up to me. I went through the compound where they park their expensive police motors when they're not being used for a sly kip, and stepped out into the bright evening. I hurried across the street, bumped into a bloke coming the other way.

'Sorry, mate,' I said, and halted. I felt myself go pale.

'That's all right, Lovejoy.' Derry, with Bonch.

Quickly I glanced about, relieved to see some late shoppers, but town centres empty fast, and dusk was closing in.

'B.J.S.'s impatient, Lovejoy.' Derry swung his great head from side to side like a bear zooed up in a cage too small for sanity.

'Look, Bonch.' I got into my imploring posture. He raised a hand for silence.

'That wooden thing's yours, Lovejoy. She bought it back. It's bonded with Gumbo, the Antiques Centre.'

'She has?' What was Bonch on about? She who, exactly?

'But she messed John about. It won't do,' he added. Derry growled, did his distressed-bear head swing. I felt my own head begin to move in time, desperate to agree with whatever they were on about.

'No, no,' I said. 'It won't, will it?'

'And you didn't help, racing across the kingdom. Though that mostly wasn't your fault, Lovejoy.'

I rose to mid-grovel. Was there a silver lining to this cloud? I still hadn't a clue, but any approval was better than a bollocking.

'So John's decided that you run the Aureole Halcyonic C-2-D Agency, that chain-dating thing ...'

Aureole! He meant Aureole! I'd forgotten. Big John had refereed the Berkley Horse, and Aureole had defaulted in a temper. I came erect, nodded gravely, a gentleman accepting an honourable settlement.

' ... for six months. Course, you pay Mr Sheehan the profits, keeping a third. She gets no income, delivers that wooden thing to you before Sunday.'

Derry murmured aggression. I agreed, nodding. How the hell did you run a chain-dating agency? But ignorance of Sheehan's wish is no excuse.

'Thank you, lads,' I said fervently. 'Could you please thank Mr Sheehan? I'll do anything he ... '

'He says you'll get his sister's daughter-in-law into a decent firm of auctioneers, to start next June, Lovejoy. He'll send her to you Thursday.' Bonch didn't pause. 'You'll do it free of charge.'

'Right, right, lads. Please say ta ... ' Gone.

'Lovejoy?' Aureole was standing on the corner of the great crescent, 1930s architecture.

'Wotcher, Aureole.' She looked scared. I strolled across. 'It seems we're partners for a while. Me boss, you Jane.'

'Thanks, Lovejoy.' She shivered. 'I'd no idea.'

'Aye, well.' Her only experience of the antiques game had been trinketry in a small East Anglian town. Sheehan's experience was like mine. Let one chink show in armour, arrows and other missiles home in. 'You weren't to know.'

'I've hired a car, Lovejoy, to take you home.'

She sounded so timid. 'Ta, love. I have to call in at the town hospital. A stone's throw. There's a lady I must visit, make a few promises to. There's also a couple of people I'd better avoid as we travel south. Okay?'

'Yes, Lovejoy. I was becoming so frightened.' She held my hand. I felt close. She pressed my hand to her. I felt closer.

We walked to her motor. 'With me, love, you're safe as houses.'

She hugged my arm. It gave me a lovely feeling, one I'd missed for days. I realised how bonny she looked now that relief had cheered her.

'How will we manage the chain-dating agency, sweetheart?' she asked. 'I'll still operate it under the guise of an antiques firm, won't I?'

'We'll head for some motel. I'm starving. I'll explain it all to you over nosh. Er, got any money?'

'Yes,' she said eagerly, delving in her handbag.

'Not in the street, silly cow,' I said. 'Later.'

'Sorry, darling,' she said. We got in. 'I can't tell you how relieved I am, Lovejoy. I was frightened they would ... '

'Not while I'm around.' I made my lips a hero's, tight and grim. She pressed her mouth on mine. I broke away quickly. Wanda was lurking nearby, and where Wanda went her team was never far behind.

If Wanda caught me up in East Anglia, I'd go to earth somewhere. Possibly, I thought, spirits lifting, with Lizbet among her sweetpeas. I had a brief mental image of fields, that beautiful fragrant blossom. I tried to invent a new title for Aureole's re-fashioned agency. *Possessions of a Lady*, maybe?

That was how I'd started Briony's — or was it Amy's, Wanda's, or Thekla's — auction? I had a hunger, thirst, a love-starved headache. 'Get going, love, or we'll be here all night.'

'Sorry, Lovejoy,' she said breathlessly.

A sports car's sudden deep-throated start nearby made me think of possible pursuers as we moved off.

'Head for Rotherham,' I said quickly, looking over my shoulder. 'They've got the world's best collection of Rockingham china. Their museum's security might be naff.' Also, Wanda would assume I'd zoom south.

'You can't mean you're going to *steal*?'

'Me? Course not.' I glanced anxiously back one more time. Not me. But I couldn't help remembering that she was a quick learner.